The Death of Gavroche.

Drawn by P. G. Jeanniot.

JEAN VALJEAN (LES MISÉRABLES, V.).

LES MISÉRABLES.

By VICTOR HUGO.

PART FIFTH.

JEAN VALJEAN.

BOSTON:

LITTLE, BROWN, AND COMPANY.

1907.

THE UNIVERSITY PRESS, CAMBRIDGE, MASS., U. S. A.

TABLE OF CONTENTS.

JEAN VALJEAN.

Book I.

THE WAR WITHIN FOUR WALLS.

Book II.

THE INTESTINE OF LEVIATHAN.

Book III.

MUD, BUT SOUL.

Book IV.

Book V.

GRANDSON AND GRANDFATHER.

Book VI.

THE SLEEPLESS NIGHT.

Book VII.

THE LAST DROP IN THE BITTER CUP.

Book VIII.

TWILIGHT DECLINES.

Book IX.

SUPREME DARKNESS, SUPREME DAWN.

JEAN VALJEAN.

BOOK I.

THE WAR WITHIN FOUR WALLS.

CHAPTER I.

THE CHARYBDIS OF THE FAUBOURG ST. ANTOINE AND THE SCYLLA OF THE FAUBOURG DU TEMPLE.

THE two most memorable barricades which the observer of social diseases can mention do not belong to the period in which the action of this book is laid. These two barricades, both symbols under different aspects of a formidable situation, emerged from the earth during the fatal insurrection of June, 1848, the greatest street-war which history has seen. It happens sometimes that the canaille, that great despairing crowd, contrary to principles, even contrary to liberty, equality, and fraternity, even contrary to the universal vote, the government of all by all, protests, in the depths of its agony, its discouragement, its destitution, its fevers, its distresses, its miasmas, its ignorance, and its darkness, and the populace offers battle to the people. The beggars attack the common right, the ochlocracy rises in insurrection against the demos. Those are mournful days ; for there is always a certain amount of right even in this mania, there is suicide in this duel, and these words, intended to be insults, such as beggars, canaille, ochlocracy, and populace, prove, alas! rather the fault of those who reign than the fault of those who suffer ; rather the fault of the privileged than the fault of the disinherited. For our part, we never pronounce these words without grief and respect, for when philosophy probes the facts with which they correspond it often finds much grandeur by the side of misery. Athens was an ochlocracy ; the beggars produced Holland ; the populace more than once saved Rome ; and the canaille followed the Saviour. There is no thinker who has not at times contemplated the magnificence below. Saint Jerome doubtless thought of this canaille, of all these poor people, all these vagabonds, and all the wretches whence the apostles and martyrs issued, when he uttered the mysterious words, — "Fex urbis, lux orbis."

The exasperations of this mob, which suffers and which bleeds, its unwilling violence against the principles which are its life, its assaults upon the right, are popular coups d'état, and must be repressed. The just man devotes himself, and through love for this very mob, combats it. But how excusable he finds it while resisting it ; how he venerates it, even while opposing it ! It is one of those rare moments in which a man while doing his duty feels something that disconcerts him, and almost dissuades him from going further ; he persists, and must do so, but the satisfied conscience is sad, and the accomplishment of the duty is complicated by a contraction of the heart. June, 1848, was, let us hasten to say, a separate fact, and almost impossible to classify in the philosophy of history. All the words we have uttered must be laid aside when we have to deal with this extraordinary riot, in which the holy anxiety of labor claiming its right was felt. It must be combated, and it was a duty to do so, for it attacked the Republic; but, in reality, what was June, 1848? A revolt of the people against itself. When the subject is not left out of sight there is no digression, and hence we may be permitted to concentrate the reader's attention momentarily upon the two absolutely unique barricades to which we have alluded, and which characterized this insurrection. The one blocked up the entrance to the Faubourg St. Antoine, the other defended the approaches to the Faubourg du Temple; those before whom these two frightful masterpieces of civil war were raised in the dazzling June sun will never forget them.

The St. Antoine barricade was monstrous; it was three stories high and seven hundred feet in width. It barred from one corner to the other the vast mouth of the faubourg, that is to say, three streets; ravined, slashed, serrated, surmounted by an immense jagged line, supported by masses which were themselves bastions, pushing out capes here and there, and powerfully reinforced by the two great promontories of the houses of the faubourg, it rose like a Cyclopean wall at the back of the formidable square which had seen July 14. There were nine-

teen barricades erected in the streets behind the
mother barricade ; but, on seeing it, you felt in the
faubourg the immense agonizing suffering which had
reached that extreme stage in which misery desires
to come to a catastrophe. Of what was this barricade made ? Of the tumbling in of three six-storied
houses demolished on purpose, say some ; of the
prodigy of all the passions, say others. It possessed
the lamentable aspect of all the buildings of hatred,
ruin. You might ask who built this, and you
might also ask who destroyed this. It was the
improvisation of the ebullition. Here with that door,
that grating, that awning, that chimney, that broken
stove, that cracked stewpan ! Give us anything !
Throw everything in ! Push, roll, pick, dismantle,
overthrow, and pull down everything ! It was a
collaboration of the pavement-stones, beams, iron
bars, planks, broken windows, unseated chairs, cab-
bage-stalks, rags, tatters, and curses. It was great
and it was little ; it was the abyss parodied on the
square by the hurly-burly. It was the mass side by
side with the atom, a pulled-down wall and a broken
pipkin, a menacing fraternization of all fragments,
into which Sisyphus had cast his rock and Job his
potsherds. Altogether it was terrible, — it was the
acropolis of the barefooted. Overturned carts studded
the slope ; an immense wagon spread out across it,
with its wheels to the sky, and looked like a scar
on this tumultuous façade ; an omnibus gayly hoisted
by strength of arm to the very top of the pile, as
if the architects of this savage edifice had wished
to add mockery to the horror, offered its bare pole

to the horses of the air. This gigantic mound, the alluvium of the riot, represented to the mind an Ossa upon Pelion of all revolutions, — '93 upon '89, the 9th Thermidor upon the 10th August, the 18th Brumaire upon January 21st, Vendémiaire upon Prairial, 1848 upon 1830. The place was worth the trouble, and this barricade was worthy of appearing upon the very spot whence the Bastille had disappeared. If the ocean made dykes it would build them in this way, and the fury of the tide was stamped on this shapeless encumbrance. What tide? The multitude. You fancied that you saw a petrified riot, and heard the enormous dark bees of violent progress humming about this barricade as if they had their hive there. Was it a thicket? Was it a Bacchanalian feast? Was it a fortress? Vertigo seemed to have built it with the flapping of its wings. There was a sewer in this redoubt, and something Olympian in this mass. You saw there in a confused heap, full of desperation, gables of roofs, pieces of garrets with their painted paper, window-frames with all their panes planted in the rubbish and awaiting the cannon, pulled-down mantel-pieces, chests of drawers, tables, benches, a howling topsy-turvy, and those thousand wretched things cast away even by a beggar which contain at once fury and nothingness. It may be said that it was the rags of a people, rags of wood, of iron, of bronze, of stone; that the Faubourg St. Antoine had swept them to their door with a gigantic broom, and made a barricade of their misery. Logs resembling executioners' blocks, disjointed chains, anvil-frames of the shape of gallows, horizontal wheels emerging from the heap, produced on this edifice of anarchy the representation of the old punishment suffered by the people. The St. Antoine barricade made a weapon of everything. All that civil war can throw at the head of society came from it; it was not a fight but a paroxysm : the muskets which defended this redoubt, among which were several blunder-busses, discharged stones, bones, coat-buttons, and even the casters of night-commodes, very dangerous owing to the copper. This barricade was furious ; it hurled an indescribable clamor into the clouds ; at certain moments when challenging the army it was covered with a crowd and a tempest; it had a prickly crest of guns, sabres, sticks, axes, pikes, and bayonets ; a mighty red flag fluttered upon it in the breeze, and the cries of command, the songs of attack, the rolling of the drum, the sobs of women, and the sardonic laughter of men dying of starvation could be heard there. It was immeasurable and living, and a flash of lightning issued from it as from the back of an electric animal. The spirit of revolution covered with its cloud this summit, where that voice of the people which resembles the voice of God was growling, and a strange majesty was disengaged from this Titanic mass of stones. It was a dungheap, and it was Sinai.

As we said above, it attacked in the name of the revolution — what? The revolution. It, this barri-cade, an accident, a disorder, a misunderstanding, an unknown thing, had, facing it, the constituent assem-bly, the sovereignty of the people, universal suffrage, the nation, the republic : and it was the Carmagnole defying the Marseillaise. A mad defiance, but heroic, for this old faubourg is a hero. The faubourg and its redoubt supported each other ; the faubourg rested on the redoubt, and the redoubt backed against the faubourg. The vast barricade was like a cliff against which the strategy of the African generals was broken. Its caverns, its excrescences, its warts, its humps, made grimaces, if we may employ the expression, and grinned behind the smoke. The grape-shot vanished in the shapeless heap; shells buried themselves in it and were swallowed up; cannon-balls only succeeded in forming holes, for of what use is it bombarding chaos? And the regiments, accustomed to the sternest visions of war, gazed with anxious eye at this species of wild-beast redoubt, which was a boar through its bristling and a mountain through its enormity.

A quarter of a league farther on, at the corner of the Rue du Temple, which debouches on the boulevard near the Château d'Eau, if you boldly advanced your head beyond the point formed by the projection of the magazine Dallemagne, you could see in the distance across the canal, and at the highest point of the ascent to Belleville, a strange wall rising to the second floor and forming a sort of connecting link between the houses on the right and those on the left, as if the street had folded back its highest wall in order to close itself up. This was built of paving-stones; it was tall, straight, correct, cold, perpendicular, and levelled with the plumb-line and the square; of course there was no cement, but,

as in some Roman walls, this in no way disturbed its
rigid architecture.   From its height, its thickness
could be guessed, for the entablature was mathemati-
cally parallel to the basement.   At regular distances
almost invisible loopholes, resembling black threads,
could be distinguished in the gray wall, separated
from each other by equal intervals.   This street was
deserted throughout its length, and all the windows
and doors were closed.   In the background rose this
bar, which converted the street into a blind alley; it
was a motionless and tranquil wall; no one was seen,
nothing was heard, not a cry, nor a sound, nor a
breath.   It was a sepulchre.   The dazzling June sun
inundated this terrible thing with light, — it was the
barricade of the Faubourg du Temple.   So soon as
you reached the ground and perceived it, it was impossible even for the boldest not to become pensive
in the presence of this mysterious apparition.   It
was adjusted, clamped, imbricated, rectilinear, sym-
metrical, and funereal; science and darkness were
there.   You felt that the chief of this barricade was
a geometrician or a spectre, and as you gazed you
spoke in a whisper.   From time to time if any one —
private, officer, or representative of the people — ventured to cross the solitary road, a shrill faint whistling was heard, and the passer-by fell wounded or
dead; or, if he escaped, a bullet could be seen to
bury itself in some shutter, or the stucco of the wall.
Sometimes it was a grape-shot, for the man of the
barricade had made out of gas-pipes, stopped up
at one end with tow and clay, two small cannon.
There was no useless expenditure of gunpowder, and

nearly every shot told. There were a few corpses here and there, and patches of blood on the pavement. I remember a white butterfly that fluttered up and down the street; summer does not abdicate. All the gateways in the vicinity were crowded with corpses, and you felt in this street that you were covered by some one you could not see, and that the whole street was under the marksman's aim.

The soldiers of the attacking column, massed behind the species of ridge which the canal bridge forms at the entrance of the Faubourg du Temple, watched gravely and thoughtfully this mournful redoubt, this immobility, this impassiveness, from which death issued. Some crawled on their stomachs to the top of the pitch of the bridge, while careful not to let their shakos pass beyond it. Brave Colonel Monteynard admired this barricade with a tremor. "How it is built," he said to a representative; "not a single paving-stone projects beyond the other. It is made of porcelain." At this moment a bullet smashed the cross on his chest and he fell. "The cowards!" the troops shouted, "Why do they not show themselves? They dare not! They hide!" The barricade of the Faubourg du Temple, defended by eighty men and attacked by ten thousand, held out for three days, and on the fourth day the troops acted as they had done at Zaatcha and Constantine, —they broke through houses, passed along roofs, and the barricade was taken. Not one of the eighty cowards dreamed of flying; all were killed with the exception of Barthélemy, the chief, to whom we shall allude directly. The barricade of St. Antoine was the tumult of the thunder; the barricade of the Temple was the silence. There was between the two barricades the same difference as exists between the formidable and the sinister. The one seemed a throat, the other a mask. Admitting that the gigantic and dark insurrection of June was composed of a fury and an enigma, the dragon was seen in the first barricade and the sphinx behind the second.

These two fortresses were built by two men, Cournet and Barthélemy: Cournet made the St. Antoine barricade, Barthélemy the Temple barricade, and each of them was the image of the man who built it. Cournet was a man of tall stature; he had wide shoulders, a red face, a smashing fist, a brave heart, a loyal soul, a sincere and terrible eye. He was intrepid, energetic, irascible, and stormy; the most cordial of men, and the most formidable of combatants. War, contest, medley were the air he breathed, and put him in good temper. He had been an officer in the navy, and from his gestures and his voice it could be divined that he issued from the ocean and came from the tempest; he continued the hurricane in battle. Omitting the genius, there was in Cournet something of Danton, as, omitting the divinity, there was in Danton something of Hercules. Barthélemy, thin, weak, pale, and taciturn, was a species of tragical gamin, who, having been struck by a policeman, watched for him, waited for him, and killed him, and at the age of seventeen was sent to the galleys. He came out and built this barricade. At a later date, when both were exiles in London, Barthélemy killed Cournet: it was a melancholy duel.   Some time after that, Barthélemy, caught in the cog-wheels of one of those mysterious adventures in which passion is mingled, catastrophes in which French justice sees extenuating circumstances and English justice only sees death, was hanged.   The gloomy social edifice is so built that, owing to maternal denudation and moral darkness, this wretched being, who had had an intellect, certainly firm and possibly great, began with the galleys in France and ended with the gibbet in England. Barthélemy only hoisted one flag, — it was the black one.

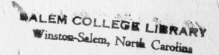

CHAPTER II.

NOTHING TO DO IN THE ABYSS BUT TALK.

SIXTEEN years count in the subterranean education of revolt, and June, 1848, knew a great deal more than June, 1832. Hence the barricade in the Rue de la Chanvrerie was only a sketch and an embryo when compared with the two colossal barricades which we have just described; but for the period it was formidable. The insurgents, under the eye of Enjolras,—for Marius no longer looked at anything, — had turned the night to good account : the barricade had not only been repaired but increased. It had been raised two feet, and iron bars planted in the paving-stones resembled lances in rest. All sorts of rubbish, added and brought from all sides, complicated the external confusion, and the redoubt had been cleverly converted into a wall inside and a thicket outside. The staircase of paving-stones, which allowed the top of the barricade to be reached, was restored, the ground-floor of the room of the inn was cleared out, the kitchen converted into an infirmary, the wounds were dressed, the powder scattered about the tables and floor was collected, bullets were cast, cartridges manufactured, lint plucked, the fallen arms distributed ; the dead were carried off and laid in a heap in the Mondétour Lane, of which they were still masters. The pavement remained for a long time red at that spot. Among the dead were four suburban National Guards, and Enjolras ordered their uniforms to be laid on one side. Enjolras had advised two hours' sleep, and his advice was an order; still, only three or four took advantage of it, and Feuilly employed the two hours in engraving this inscription on the wall facing the wine-shop, —

"LONG LIVE THE PEOPLES."

These four words, carved in the stone with a nail, could still be read on this wall in 1848. The three women took advantage of the respite to disappear entirely, which allowed the insurgents to breathe more at their ease ; and they contrived to find refuge in some neighboring house. Most of the wounded could and would still fight. There were, on a pile of mattresses and trusses of straw laid in the kitchen converted into an infirmary, five men seriously wounded, of whom two were Municipal Guards ; the wounds of the latter were dressed first. No one remained in the ground-floor room save Mabœuf under his black cere-cloth, and Javert fastened to the post.

"This is the charnel-house," said Enjolras.

In the interior of this room, which was scarce lighted by a solitary candle, the mortuary table at the end being behind the post like a horizontal bar, a sort of large vague cross resulted from Javert standing and Mabœuf lying down. Although the pole of the omnibus was mutilated by the bullets, sufficient remained for a flag to be attached to it. Enjolras, who possessed that quality of a chief of always doing what he said, fastened to it the bullet-pierced and blood-stained coat of the killed old man. No meal was possible, for there was neither bread nor meat. The fifty men during the sixteen hours they had stood at the barricade speedily exhausted the scanty provisions of the inn. At a given moment every barricade that holds out becomes the raft of the *Méduse*, and the combatants must resign themselves to hunger. They had reached the early hours of that Spartan day, June 6, when at the barricade of St. Merry, Jeanne, surrounded by insurgents who cried for bread, answered, "What for? It is three o'clock; at four we shall be dead." As they could no longer eat, Enjolras prohibited drinking; he put the wine under an interdict, and served out the spirits. Some fifteen full bottles, hermetically sealed, were found in the cellar, which Enjolras and Combeferre examined. Combeferre on coming up again said, "It belongs to Father Hucheloup's stock at the time when he was a grocer." "It must be real wine," Bossuet observed; "it is lucky that Grantaire is asleep, for if he were up, we should have a difficulty in saving those bottles." Enjolras, in spite of the murmurs, put his veto on the fifteen bottles, and in order that no one might touch them, and that they should be to some extent sacred, he had placed them under the table on which Father Mabœuf lay.

At about two in the morning they counted their strength; there were still thirty-seven. Day was beginning to appear, and the torch, which had been returned to its stone lantern, was extinguished. The interior of the barricade, that species of small yard taken from the street, was bathed in darkness, and resembled, through the vague twilight horror, the deck of a dismasted ship. The combatants moved about like black forms. Above this frightful nest of gloom the floors of the silent houses stood out lividly, and above them again the chimney-pots were assuming a roseate hue. The sky had that charming tint which may be white and may be blue, and the birds flew about in it with twitterings of joy. The tall house which formed the background of the barricade looked to the east, and had a pink reflection on its roof. At the third-floor window the morning breeze blew about the gray hair on the head of the dead man.

"I am delighted that the torch is put out," Courfeyrac said to Feuilly. "That flame flickering in the breeze annoyed me, for it seemed to be frightened. The light of torches resembles the wisdom of cowards; it illumines badly because it trembles."

The dawn arouses minds like birds, and all were talking. Joly, seeing a cat stalking along a gutter, extracted this philosophy from the fact.

"What is the cat?" he exclaimed. "It is a correction. *Le bon Dieu* having made a mouse, said to himself, 'Hilloh! I have done a foolish trick,' and he made the cat, which is the erratum of the mouse. The mouse plus the cat is the revised and corrected proof of creation."

Combeferre, surrounded by students and workmen, was talking of the dead, of Jean Prouvaire, of Bahorel, of Mabœuf, and even of Cabuc, and the stern sorrow of Enjolras. He said, —

"Harmodius and Aristogiton, Brutus, Chereas, Stephanus, Cromwell, Charlotte Corday, Sand, all had their moment of agony after the blow was struck. Our heart is so quivering, and human life such a mystery, that even in a civic murder, even in a liberating murder, if there be such a thing, the remorse at having struck a man exceeds the joy of having benefited the human race."

And, such are the meanderings of interchanged words, a moment later, by a transition which came from Jean Prouvaire's verses, Combeferre was comparing together the translators of the Georgics, Raux with Cournand, Cournand with Delille, and pointing out the few passages translated by Malfilâtre, especially the wonders of the death of Cæsar, and at that name the conversation reverted to Brutus.

"Cæsar," said Combeferre, "fell justly. Cicero was severe to Cæsar, and was in the right, for such severity is not a diatribe. When Zoïlus insults Homer, when Mævius insults Virgil, when Visé insults Molière, when Pope insults Shakspeare, when Fréron insults Voltaire, it is an old law of envy and hatred being carried out; for genius attracts insult, and great men are all barked at more or less. But Zoïlus and Cicero are different. Cicero is a justiciary with thought in the same way as Brutus is a justiciary with the sword. For my part, I blame that last justice, the glaive; antiquity allowed it. Cæsar, the violator of the Rubicon, conferring, as if coming from him, dignities that came from the people, and not rising on the entrance of the senate, behaved, as Eutropius said, like a king, and almost like a tyrant,

regiâ ac pene tyrannica.   He was a great man; all
the worse or all the better, the lesson is the more
elevated.   His three-and-twenty wounds affect me
less than the spitting on the brow of Christ.   Cæsar
is stabbed by the senators, Christ is buffeted by soldiers.   God is felt in the greater outrage."

Bossuet, standing on a pile of stones, and com-
manding the speaker, exclaimed, gun in hand, —

" O Cydathenæum !   O Myrrhinus !   O Probalyn-
thus !   O graces of Æanthus !   Oh, who will inspire
me to pronounce the verses of Homer like a Greek
of Laureum or Edapteon ! "

CHAPTER III.

ENJOLRAS had gone out to reconnoitre, and had left by the Mondétour Lane, keeping in the shadow of the houses. The insurgents, we must state, were full of hope : the way in which they had repulsed the night attack almost made them disdain before-hand the attack at daybreak. They waited for it and smiled at it, and no more doubted of their success than of their cause ; moreover, help was evidently going to reach them, and they reckoned on it. With that facility of triumphant prophecy which is a part of the strength of the French fighter, they divided into three certain phases the opening day, — at six in the morning a regiment, which had been worked upon, would turn ; at mid-day insurrection all over Paris ; at sunset the revolution. The tocsin of St. Merry, which had not ceased once since the previous evening, could be heard, and this was a proof that the other barricade, the great one, Jeanne's, still held out. All these hopes were interchanged by the groups with a species of gay and formidable buzzing which resemble the war-hum of a swarm of bees. Enjolras reappeared returning from his gloomy walk in the external darkness. He listened for a moment to all this joy with his arms folded, and then said, fresh and rosy in the growing light of dawn, —

"The whole army of Paris is out, and one third of that army is preparing to attack the barricade behind which you now are. There is, too, the National Guard. I distinguished the shakos of the fifth line regiment and the colors of the sixth legion. You will be attacked in an hour ; as for the people, they were in a state of ferment yesterday, but this morning do not stir. There is nothing to wait for, nothing to hope ; no more a faubourg than a regiment. You are abandoned."

These words fell on the buzzing groups, and produced the same effect as the first drops of a storm do on a swarm. All remained dumb, and there was a moment of inexpressible silence, in which death might have been heard flying past. This moment was short, and a voice shouted to Enjolras from the thickest of the crowd, —

"Be it so. Let us raise the barricade to a height of twenty feet, and all fall upon it. Citizens, let us offer the protest of corpses, and show that if the people abandon the republicans, the republicans do not abandon the people."

These words disengaged the thoughts of all from the painful cloud of individual anxieties, and an enthusiastic shout greeted them. The name of the man who spoke thus was never known ; he was some unknown blouse-wearer, an unknown man, a forgotten man, a passing hero, that great anonymous always mixed up in human crises and social

Geneses, who at the given moment utters the decisive word in a supreme fashion, and who fades away
into darkness after having represented for a minute,
in the light of a flash, the people and God. This
inexorable resolution was so strongly in the air of
June 6, 1832, that almost at the same hour the insurgents of the St. Merry barricade uttered this cry,
which became historical, — " Whether they come to
our help, or whether they do not, what matter !
Let us all fall here, to the last man ! " As we see,
the two barricades, though materially isolated, communicated.

CHAPTER IV.

FIVE LESS AND ONE MORE.

AFTER the man, whoever he might be, who decreed the "protest of corpses," had spoken, and given the formula of the common soul, a strangely satisfied and terrible cry issued from every mouth, funereal in its meaning and triumphal in its accent.

"Long live death! Let us all remain here."

"Why all?" Enjolras asked.

"All, all!"

Enjolras continued, —

"The position is good and the barricade fine. Thirty men are sufficient, then why sacrifice forty?"

They replied, —

"Because not one of us will go away."

"Citizens," Enjolras cried, and there was in his voice an almost irritated vibration, "the republic is not rich enough in men to make an unnecessary outlay. If it be the duty of some to go away, that duty must be performed like any other."

Enjolras, the man-principle, had over his co-religionists that kind of omnipotence which is evolved from the absolute. Still, however great that omnipotence might be, they murmured. A chief to the tips of his fingers, Enjolras, on seeing that they murmured, insisted. He continued haughtily, —

"Let those who are afraid to be only thirty say so."

The murmurs were redoubled.

"Besides," a voice in the throng remarked, ".it is easy to say, 'Go away,' but the barricade is surrounded."

"Not on the side of the markets," said Enjolras. "The Rue Mondétour is free, and the Marché des Innocents can be reached by the Rue des Prêcheurs."

"And then," another voice in the group remarked, "we should be caught by falling in with some grand rounds of the line or the National Guard. They will see a man passing in blouse and cap : 'Where do you come from ? Don't you belong to the barricade ?' and they will look at your hands ; you smell of powder, and will be shot."

Enjolras, without answering, touched Combeferre's shoulder, and both entered the ground-floor room. They came out again a moment after, Enjolras holding in his outstretched hands the four uniforms which he had laid on one side, and Combeferre followed him carrying the cross-belts and shakos.

"In this uniform," Enjolras said, "it is easy to enter the ranks and escape. Here are four at any rate."

And he threw the four uniforms on the unpaved ground ; but as no one moved in the stoical audience, Combeferre resolved to make an appeal.

"Come," he said, "you must show a little pity. Do you know what the question is here ? It is

about women. Look you, are there wives, — yes or
no ? Are there children, — yes or no ? Are these
nothing, who rock a cradle with their foot, and have
a heap of children around them ? Let him among
you who has never seen a nurse's breast hold up his
hand. Ah! you wish to be killed. I wish it too,
I who am addressing you ; but I do not wish to feel
the ghosts of women twining their arms around me.
Die, — very good ; but do not cause people to die.
Suicides like the one which is about to take place
here are sublime ; but suicide is restricted, and does
not allow of extension, and so soon as it affects your
relations, suicide is called murder. Think of the
little fair heads, and think too of the white hair.
Listen to me ! Enjolras tells me that just now he
saw at the corner of the Rue du Cygne a candle
at a poor window on the fifth floor, and on the panes
the shaking shadow of an old woman who appeared
to have spent the night in watching at the window ;
she is perhaps the mother of one of you. Well,
let that man go, and hasten to say to his mother,
' Mother, here I am !' Let him be easy in his mind,
for the work will be done here all the same. When
a man supports his relatives by his toil, he has no
longer any right to sacrifice himself, for that is de-
serting his family. And then, too, those who have
daughters, and those who have sisters ! Only think
of them. You let yourselves be killed, you are dead,
very good ; and to-morrow ? It is terrible when
girls have no bread, for man begs, but woman sells.
Oh, those charming, graceful, and gentle creatures
with flowers in their caps, who fill the house with

chastity, who sing, who prattle, who are like a living
perfume, who prove the existence of angels in heaven
by the purity of virgins on earth ; that Jeanne, that
Lise, that Mimi, those adorable and honest creatures,
who are your blessing and your pride, — ah, my God !
they will starve.   What would you have me say to
you ?   There is a human flesh-market, and you will
not prevent them entering it with your shadowy
hands trembling around them.   Think of the street ;
think of the pavement covered with strollers ; think
of the shops before which women in low-necked
dresses come and go in the mud.   Those women,
too, were pure.   Think of your sisters, you who
have any ; misery, prostitution, the police.   St.
Lazare, that is what these delicate maidens, these
fragile marvels of chastity, modesty, and beauty,
fresher than the lilies in May, will fall to.   Ah, you
have let yourselves be killed !   Ah, you are no longer
there !   That is, — very good, — you have wished to
withdraw the people from royalty, and you give your
daughters to the police.   My friends, take care and
have compassion ; we are not wont to think much
about women, hapless women ; we trust to the fact
that women have not received the education of men.
They are prevented reading, thinking, or occupying
themselves with politics ; but will you prevent them
going to-night to the Morgue and recognizing your
corpses ?   Come, those who have families must be
good fellows, and shake our hand and go away,
leaving us to do the job here all alone.   I am well
aware that courage is needed to go away, and that
it is difficult ; but the more difficult the more meri-

torious it is. You say, 'I have a gun and am at the barricade; all the worse, I remain.' 'All the worse' is easily said. My friends, there is a morrow, and that morrow you will not see; but your families will see it. And what sufferings! Stay; do you know what becomes of a healthy child with cheeks like an apple, who chatters, prattles, laughs, and smiles as fresh as a kiss, when he is abandoned? I saw one, quite little, about so high; his father was dead, and poor people had taken him in through charity; but they had not bread for themselves. The child was always hungry; it was winter-time, but though he was always hungry he did not cry. He was seen to go close to the stove, whose pipe was covered with yellow earth. The boy detached with his fingers a piece of this earth and ate it; his breathing was hoarse, his face livid, his legs soft, and his stomach swollen. He said nothing, and when spoken to made no answer. He is dead, and was brought to die at the Necker Hospital, where I saw him, for I was a student there. Now, if there be any fathers among you, fathers who delight in taking a walk on Sunday, holding in their powerful hand a child's small fingers, let each of these fathers fancy this lad his own. The poor brat I can remember perfectly; I fancy I see him now, and when he lay on the dissecting table, his bones stood out under his skin like the tombs under the grass of a cemetery. We found a sort of mud in his stomach, and he had ashes between his teeth. Come, let us examine our conscience and take the advice of our heart; statistics prove that the mortality

among deserted children is fifty-five per cent. I
repeat, it is a question of wives, of mothers, of
daughters, and babes. Am I saying anything about
you? I know very well what you are. I know that
you are all brave. I know that you have all in your
hearts the joy and glory of laying down your lives
for the great cause. I know very well that you feel
yourselves chosen to die usefully and magnificently,
and that each of you clings to his share of the
triumph. Very good. But you are not alone in
this world, and there are other beings of whom you
must think ; you should not be selfish."

All hung their heads with a gloomy air. Strange
contradictions of the human heart in the sublimest
moments ! Combeferre, who spoke thus, was not an
orphan ; he remembered the mothers of others and
forgot his own ; he was going to let himself be killed,
and was "selfish." Marius, fasting and feverish, who
had successively given up all hope, cast ashore on
grief, the most mournful of shipwrecks, saturated
with violent emotions, and feeling the end coming,
had buried himself deeper and deeper in that visionary stupor which ever precedes the fatal and voluntarily accepted hour. A physiologist might have
studied in him the growing symptoms of that febrile
absorption which is known and classified by science,
and which is to suffering what voluptuousness is to
pleasure, for despair also has its ecstasy. Marius
had attained that stage ; as we have said, things
which occurred before him appeared to him remote,
he distinguished the ensemble, but did not perceive
the details. He saw people coming and going before

him in a flash, and he heard voices speaking as if
from the bottom of an abyss. Still this affected
him, for there was in this scene a point which
pierced to him and aroused him. He had but
one idea, to die, and he did not wish to avert his
attention from it; but he thought in his gloomy
somnambulism that in destroying himself he was
not prohibited from saving somebody. He raised
his voice, —

"Enjolras and Combeferre are right," he said; "let
us have no useless sacrifice. I join them, and we
must make haste. Combeferre has told you decisive
things: there are men among you who have families,
mothers, sisters, wives, and children. Such must
leave the ranks."

Not a soul stirred.

"Married men and supporters of families will
leave the ranks," Marius repeated.

His authority was great, for though Enjolras was
really the chief of the barricade, Marius was its
savior.

"I order it," Enjolras cried.

"I implore it," Marius said.

Then these heroic men, stirred up by Combeferre's
speech, shaken by Enjolras's order, and moved by
Marius's entreaty, began denouncing one another.
"It is true," a young man said to a grown-up man,
"you are a father of a family; begone!" "No!
you ought to do so rather," the man replied, "for
you have two sisters to support;" and an extraordinary contest broke out, in which each struggled not
to be thrust out of the tomb.

"Make haste," said Combeferre; "in a quarter of an hour there will no longer be time."

"Citizens," Enjolras added, "we have a republic here, and universal suffrage reigns. Point out yourselves the men who are to leave us."

They obeyed, and at the end of a few minutes five were unanimously pointed out and left the ranks.

"There are five of them!" Marius exclaimed.

There were only four uniforms.

"Well," the five replied, "one will have to remain behind."

And then came who should remain, and who should find reasons for others not to remain. The generous quarrel began again.

"You have a wife who loves you. — You have your old mother. — You have neither father nor mother; what will become of your three little brothers? — You are the father of five children. — You have a right to live, for you are only seventeen, and it is too early to die."

These great revolutionary barricades were meeting-places of heroisms. The improbable was simple there, and these men did not astonish one another.

"Make haste," Courfeyrac repeated.

Cries to Marius came from the groups.

"You must point out the one who is to remain."

"Yes," the five said; "do you choose, and we will obey you."

Marius did not believe himself capable of any emotion; still, at this idea of choosing a man for death all the blood flowed back to his heart, and he would have turned pale could he have grown paler. He walked up to the five, who smiled upon him, and each, with his eye full of that great flame which gleams through history on Thermopylæ, cried to him, —

"I! I! I!"

And Marius stupidly counted them. There were still five! Then his eyes settled on the four uniforms. All at once a fifth uniform fell, as if from heaven, on the other four; the fifth man was saved. Marius raised his eyes, and recognized M. Fauchelevent.

Jean Valjean had just entered the barricade; either through information he had obtained, through instinct, or through accident, he arrived by the Mondétour Lane, and, thanks to his National Guard uniform, passed without difficulty. The vedette stationed by the insurgents in the Rue Mondétour had no cause to give the alarm-signal for a single National Guard, and had let him enter the street, saying to himself, "He is probably a reinforcement, or at the worst a prisoner." The moment was too serious for a sentry to turn away from his duty or his post of observation. At the moment when Jean Valjean entered the redoubt, no one noticed him, for all eyes were fixed on the five chosen men and the four uniforms. Jean Valjean, however, had seen and heard, and silently took off his coat and threw it on the pile formed by the other coats. The emotion was indescribable.

"Who is this man?" Bossuet asked.

"He is a man," Combeferre replied, "who saves his fellow-man."

Marius added in a grave voice, —

" I know him."

This bail was sufficient for all, and Enjolras turned to Jean Valjean.

" Citizen, you are welcome."

And he added, —

" You are aware that you will die."

Jean Valjean, without answering, helped the man he was saving to put on his uniform.

CHAPTER V.

THE situation of the whole party in this fatal hour, and at this inexorable spot, had as result and pinnacle the supreme melancholy of Enjolras. Enjolras had within him the plenitude of the revolution; he was imperfect, however, so far as the absolute can be so, — he had too much of St. Just and not enough of Anacharsis Clootz; still his mind in the society of the Friends of the A. B. C. had eventually received a certain magnetism of Combeferre's ideas. For some time past he had been gradually emerging from the narrow form of dogmatism and yielding to the expansion of progress, and in the end he had accepted, as the definitive and magnificent evolution, the transformation of the great French republic into the immense human republic. As for the immediate means, a violent situation being given, he was willing to be violent; in that he did not vary, and he still belonged to that epic and formidable school which is resumed in the words "'93." Enjolras was standing on the paving-stone steps, with one of his elbows on the muzzle of his gun. He was thinking; he trembled, as men do when a blast passes, for spots where death lurks produce this tripod effect. A sort of stifled fire

issued from beneath his eyelashes, which were full of
the internal glance.   All at once he raised his head,
his light hair fell back like that of the angel on the
dark quadriga composed of stars, and he cried : —

"Citizens, do you represent the future to yourselves?
The streets of towns inundated with light, green
branches on the thresholds, nations sisters, men just,
old men blessing children, the past loving the present, men thinking at perfect liberty, believers enjoying perfect equality, for religion the heaven, God,
the direct priest, the human conscience converted
into an altar, no more hatred, the fraternity of the
workshop and the school, notoriety the sole punishment and reward, work for all, right for all, peace
for all, no more bloodshed, no more wars, and happy
mothers ! To subdue the matter is the first step, to
realize the ideal is the second.   Reflect on what progress has already done ; formerly the first human
races saw with terror the hydra that breathed upon
the waters, the dragon that vomited fire, the griffin
which was the monster of the air, and which flew
with the wings of an eagle and the claws of a tiger,
pass before their eyes, — frightful beasts which were
below man.   Man, however, set his snares, the
sacred snares of intellect, and ended by catching the
monsters in them.   We have subdued the hydra, and
it is called the steamer ; we have tamed the dragon,
and it is called the locomotive ; we are on the point
of taming the griffin, we hold it already, and it is
called the balloon.   The day on which that Prome-
thean task is terminated and man has definitively
attached to his will the triple antique chimera, the

dragon, the hydra, and the griffin, he will be master of
water, fire, and air, and he will be to the rest of ani-
mated creation what the ancient gods were formerly
to him. Courage, and forward! Citizens, whither
are we going? To science made government, to the
strength of things converted into the sole public
strength, to the natural law having its sanction and
penalty in itself and promulgating itself by evidence, and to a dawn of truth corresponding with
the dawn of day. We are proceeding to a union
of the peoples; we are proceeding to a unity of
man. No more fictions, no more parasites. The
real governed by the true is our object. Civilization
will hold its assize on the summit of Europe, and
eventually in the centre of the continent, in a great
Parliament of intellect. Something like this has
been seen already; the Amphictyons held two ses-
sions a year, one at Delphi, the place of the gods,
the other at Thermopylæ, the place of heroes.
Europe will have her Amphictyons, the globe will
have its Amphictyons, France bears the sublime
future within her, and this is the gestation of
the 19th century. What Greece sketched out is
worthy of being finished by France. Hearken to
me, Feuilly, valiant workman, man of the people,
man of the people. I venerate thee; yes, thou seest
clearly future times; yes, thou art right. Thou hast
neither father nor mother, Feuilly, and thou hast
adopted humanity as thy mother and right as thy
father. Thou art about to die here, that is to say,
to triumph. Citizens, whatever may happen to-day,
we are about to make a revolution, by our defeat as

well as by our victory. In the same way as fires
light up a whole city, revolutions light up the whole
human race. And what a revolution shall we make?
I have just told you, the revolution of the True.
From the political point of view, there is but one
principle, the sovereignty of man over himself. This
sovereignty of me over me is called liberty, and
where two or three of these liberties are associated
the State begins. But in this association there is
no abdication, and each sovereignty concedes a certain amount of itself to form the common right. This
quality is the same for all, and this identity of concession which each makes to all is called Equality.
The common right is nought but the protection of
all radiating over the right of each. This protection
of all over each is termed Fraternity. The point
of intersection of all aggregated societies is called
Society, and this intersection being a junction, the
point is a knot. Hence comes what is called the
social tie; some say the social contract, which is
the same thing, as the word contract is etymologi-
cally formed with the idea of a tie. Let us come
to an understanding about equality; for if liberty be
the summit, equality is the base. Equality, citizens,
is not all vegetation on a level, a society of tall
blades of grass and small oaks, or a neighbor-
hood of entangled jealousies; it is, civilly, every
aptitude having the same opening, politically, all
votes having the same weight, and religiously, all
consciences having the same right. Equality has an
organ in gratuitous and compulsory education, and
it should begin with the right to the alphabet. The

primary school imposed on all, the secondary school offered to all, such is the law, and from the identical school issues equal instruction.   Yes, instruction ! Light, light!   Everything comes from light and everything returns to it.   Citizens, the 19th century is great, but the 20th century will be happy.   Then there will be nothing left resembling ancient history, there will be no cause to fear, as at the present day a conquest, an invasion, usurpation, an armed rivalry of nations, an interruption of civilization depending on a marriage of kings, a birth in hereditary tyrannies, a division of peoples by Congress, a dismemberment by the collapse of dynasties, a combat of two religions, clashing, like two goats of the darkness, on the bridge of infinity ; there will be no cause longer to fear famine, exhaustion, prostitution through destiny, misery through stoppage of work, and the scaffold, and the sword, and battles, and all the brigandage of accident in the forest of events ; we might almost say there will be no more events, we shall be happy ; the human race will accomplish its law as the terrestrial globe does its law ; harmony will be restored between the soul and the planet, and the soul will gravitate round the truth as the planet does round light.   Friends, the hour we are now standing in is a gloomy hour, but there are such terrible purchases of the future.   Oh, the human race will be delivered, relieved, and consoled !   We affirm it on this barricade, and where should the cry of love be raised if not on the summit of the sacrifice ?   Oh, my brothers, this is the point of junction between those who think and those who suffer.   This

barricade is not made of paving-stones, beams, and
iron bars; it is made of two masses, — a mass of
ideas and a mass of sorrows. Misery meets then the
ideal ; day embraces the night there, and says to it,
'I am about to die with thee, and thou wilt be born
again with me.' Faith springs from the embrace
of all the desolations ; sufferings bring hither their
agony, and ideas their immortality. This agony and
this immortality are about to be mingled and com-
pose one death. Brothers, the man who dies here
dies in the radiance of the future, and we shall enter
a tomb all filled with dawn."

Enjolras interrupted himself rather than was silent; his lips moved silently as if he were talking to
himself, which attracted attention, and in order still
to try to hear him they held their tongues. There
was no applause, but they whispered together for a
long time. Language being breath, the rustling of
intellects resembles the rustling of leaves.

CHAPTER VI.

MARIUS HAGGARD, JAVERT LACONIC.

LET us describe what was going on in Marius's thoughts. Our readers will remember his state of mind, for, as we just now said, everything was only a vision to him. His appreciation was troubled, for he was (we urge the fact) beneath the shadow of the great gloomy wings opened above the dying. He felt that he had entered the tomb, he fancied that he was already on the other side of the wall, and he only saw the faces of the living with the eyes of a dead man. How was M. Fauchelevent present? Why was he here, and what did he come to do? Marius did not ask himself all these questions. Moreover, as our despair has the peculiar thing about it that it envelops others as it does ourselves, it appeared to him logical that everybody should die. Still he thought of Cosette with a contraction of the heart. However, M. Fauchelevent did not speak to him, did not look at him, and did not even seem to hear Marius when he raised his voice, saying, "I know him." As for Marius, this attitude of M. Fauchelevent relieved him, and if such a word were permissible for such impressions, we might say that it pleased him. He had ever felt an absolute impossibility in addressing this enigmatical man, who was at once equivocal and imposing to him. It was a very long time too since he had seen him ; and this augumented the impossibility for a timid and reserved nature like Marius's.

The five men selected left the barricade by the Mondétour Lane, perfectly resembling National Guards. One of them wept as he went away, and before doing so they embraced those who remained. When the five men sent back to life had left, Enjolras thought of the one condemned to death. He went to the ground-floor room, where Javert, tied to the post, was reflecting.

" Do you want anything ? " Enjolras asked him.

Javert answered, —

" When will you kill me ? "

" Wait. We require all our cartridges at this moment."

" In that case, give me some drink," Javert said.

Enjolras himself held out to him a glass of water, and, as Javert was bound, helped him to drink.

" Is that all ? " Enjolras resumed.

" I feel uncomfortable at this post," Javert replied ; " you did not act kindly in leaving me fastened to it the whole night. Bind me as you please, but you might surely lay me on a table, like the other man."

And with a nod of the head he pointed to M. Mabœuf's corpse. It will be remembered that there was at the end of the room a long, wide table on which bullets had been run and cartridges made. All the cartridges being made, and all the powder expended, this table was free. By Enjolras's order, four insurgents unfastened Javert from the post, and while they did so a fifth held a bayonet to his chest. His hands remained fastened behind his back, a thin strong cord was attached to his feet, which enabled him to step fifteen inches, like those who are going to ascend the scaffold, and he was forced to walk to the table at the end of the room, on which they laid him, securely fastened round the waist. For greater security, a system of knotting was employed by means of a cord fastened to the neck, which rendered any escape impossible ; it was the sort of fastening called in prisons a martingale, which starts from the nape of the neck, is crossed on the stomach, and is turned round the hands after passing between the legs. While Javert was being bound, a man standing in the doorway regarded him with singular attention, and the shadow this man cast caused Javert to turn his head. He raised his eyes and recognized Jean Valjean, but he did not even start ; he merely looked down haughtily, and restricted himself to saying, " It is all plain."

CHAPTER VII.

DAY grew rapidly, but not a window opened, not
a door was ajar; it was the dawn, not an awaking.
The end of the Rue de la Chanvrerie opposed to the
barricade had been evacuated by the troops, as we
stated; it appeared to be free and open for passers-
by with sinister tranquillity. The Rue St. Denis was
dumb as the Avenue of the Sphinxes at Thebes;
there was not a living being on the square, which a
sunbeam whitened. Nothing is so melancholy as this
brightness of deserted streets; nothing could be seen,
but something could be heard, and there was a mysterious movement at a certain distance off. It was
evident that the critical moment was arriving, and, as
on the previous evening, the vedettes fell back, but
this time all of them did so. The barricade was
stronger than at the prior attack, for since the departure of the five it had been heightened. By the advice of the vedette who had been watching the region
of the Halles, Enjolras, through fear of a surprise in
the rear, formed a serious resolution. He barricaded
the small passage of the Mondétour Lane, which had
hitherto remained free, and for this purpose a further
portion of the street was unpaved. In this way the

barricade, walled in on three sides, — in front by the
Rue de la Chanvrerie, on the left by the Rue du
Cygne, and on the right by the Rue Mondétour, —
was truly almost impregnable, but it is true that they
were fatally enclosed within it.   It had three fronts
but no issue, it was a fortress but a mouse-trap, as
Courfeyrac said with a smile.   Enjolras had some
thirty paving-stones piled up by the door of the
inn.   "They dug up more than enough," said
Bossuet.   The silence was now so profound in the
direction whence the attack must come, that Enjolras
ordered all his men to return to their fighting-posts,
and a ration of brandy was distributed to each
man.

Nothing is more curious than a barricade preparing for an assault; every man chooses his place, as at
the theatre.   They crowd, elbow, and shoulder one
another, and some make stalls of paving-stones.
Here an angle of the wall is in the way, and it is
avoided; there is a redan which may offer protection,
and they seek shelter in it.   Left-handed men are
precious, for they take places inconvenient for others.
Many arrange so as to fight seated, for they wish to
be at their ease to kill, and comfortable in dying.
In the fatal war of June, 1848, an insurgent, who
was a wonderful marksman, and who fought from a
terraced roof, had a Voltaire easy-chair carried there,
and was knocked over in it by a volley of grape-shot.
So soon as the chief has given the signal for action
all disorderly movements cease; there is no longer
any sharp-shooting, any conversations or asides: all
that minds contain converges, and is changed into

the expectation of the assailant. A barricade before danger is a chaos, in danger discipline, for peril produces order. So soon as Enjolras had taken his double-barrelled gun, and placed himself at a species of parapet which he reserved for himself, all were silent; a quick, sharp crackling ran confusedly along the wall of paving-stones; it was the muskets being cocked. However, the attitudes were haughtier and more confident than ever, for an excess of sacrifice is a consolidation, and though they no longer had hope, they had despair, — despair, that last weapon, which at times gives victory, as Virgil tells us. Supreme resources issue from extreme resolutions. To embark on death is at times the means of escaping the shipwreck, and the cover of the coffin becomes a plank of salvation. As on the previous evening, all their attention was turned upon the end of the street, which was now lighted up and visible. They had not long to wait ere the movement began again, distinctly in the direction of St. Leu, but it did not resemble the sound of the first attack. A rattling of chains, the alarming rolling of a heavy weight, a clang of bronze leaping on the pavement, and a species of solemn noise, announced that a sinister engine was approaching; there was a tremor in the entrails of these old peaceful streets, pierced and built for the fruitful circulation of interests and ideas, and which are not made for the monstrous rolling of the wheels of war. The fixity of the eyes turned toward the end of the street became stern, as a cannon appeared. The gunners pushed the gun on; the limber was detached, and two men supported the carriage, while four were at the wheels; others followed with the tumbril, and the lighted match could be seen smoking.

"Fire!" shouted Enjolras.

The whole barricade burst into a flame, and the detonation was frightful; an avalanche of smoke covered and concealed the gun and the men. A few seconds after the cloud was dispersed, and the gun and the men reappeared; the gunners were bringing it up to the front of the barricade, slowly, correctly, and without hurry; not one had been wounded. Then the captain of the gun, hanging with his whole weight on the breech to elevate the muzzle, began pointing the gun with the gravity of an astronomer setting a telescope.

"Bravo for the artillery!" cried Bossuet.

And all the men at the barricade clapped their hands. A moment after the gun, standing in the very centre of the street across the gutter, was in position, and a formidable mouth yawned at the barricade.

"Come, we are going to be gay," said Courfeyrac. "Here is the brutality; after the fillip the blow with the fist. The army is extending its heavy paw toward us, and the barricade is going to be seriously shaken. The musketry-fire feels, and the cannon takes."

"It is an eight-pounder of the new pattern in bronze," Combeferre added. "Those guns, if the proportion of ten parts of tin to one hundred of copper is exceeded, are liable to burst, for the excess of tin renders them too soft. It thus happens that they have holes and cavities in the vent, and in order to obviate this danger and be able to load, it would perhaps be advisable to revert to the process of the 14th century, circling and reinforcing the gun with a series of steel rings, without any welding from the breech to the trunnions. In the mean while they remedy the defect as well as they can, and they manage to discover where the holes are in the vent of the gun by means of a searcher; but there is a better method in Gribeauval's movable star."

" In the 16th century," Bossuet observed, "guns were rifled."

" Yes," Combeferre replied; "that augments the ballistic force, but lessens the correctness of aim. At short distances the trajectory has not all the desirable rigidness, the parabola is exaggerated, the path of the projectile is not sufficiently rectilinear for it to hit intermediate objects, though that is a condition of fighting whose importance grows with the proximity of the enemy and the precipitation of the firing. This defective tension of the curve of the projectile in rifled cannon of the 16th century emanated from the weakness of the charge; weak charges for such engines are imposed by the ballistic necessities, such, for instance, as the preservation of the carriage. After all, the cannon, that despot, cannot do all that it wishes, and strength is a great weakness. A cannon-ball goes only six hundred leagues an hour, while light covers seventy thousand leagues per second. This is the superiority of Jesus Christ over Napoleon."

" Reload your guns," said Enjolras.

In what manner would the revetment of the bar-

ricade behave against a cannon-ball ? Would a breach
be formed ? That was the question. While the insurgents were reloading their guns the artillerymen
loaded the cannon. The anxiety within the redoubt
was profound ; the shot was fired, and the detonation burst forth.

"Present !" a joyous voice cried.

And at the same time as the cannon-ball struck
the barricade, Gavroche bounded inside it. He
came from the direction of the Rue du Cygne,
and actively clambered over the accessory barricade
which fronted the labyrinth of the Little Truanderie.
Gavroche produced greater effect at the barricade
than the cannon-ball did ; for the latter was lost in
the heap of rubbish. It had broken a wheel of the
omnibus, and finished the old truck, on seeing which
the insurgents burst into a laugh.

"Persevere !" cried Bossuet to the gunners.

CHAPTER VIII.

THE ARTILLERY SETS TO WORK IN EARNEST.

GAVROCHE was surrounded, but he had no time to report anything, as Marius, shuddering, drew him on one side.

" What have you come to do here ? "

" What a question ? " the boy said ; " and you, pray ? "

And he gazed fixedly at Marius with his epic effrontery : his eyes were dilated by the proud brightness which they contained. It was with a stern accent that Marius continued, —

" Who told you to return ? I only trust that you have delivered my letter at its address."

Gavroche felt some degree of remorse in the matter of the letter ; for, in his hurry to return to the barricade, he had got rid of it rather than delivered it. He was forced to confess to himself that he had confided somewhat too lightly in this stranger, whose face he had not even been able to distinguish. It is true that this man was bareheaded, but that was not enough. In short, he reproached himself quietly for his conduct, and feared Marius's reproaches. He took the simplest process to get out of the scrape, — he told an abominable falsehood.

"Citizen, I delivered the letter to the porter. The lady was asleep, and she will have the letter when she wakes."

Marius had two objects in sending the letter, — to bid Cosette farewell and save Gavroche. He was obliged to satisfy himself with one half of what he wanted. The connection between the sending of the letter and M. Fauchelevent's presence at the barricade occurred to his mind, and he pointed him out to Gavroche.

"Do you know that man?"

"No," said Gavroche.

Gavroche, in truth, as we know, had only seen Jean Valjean by night. The troubled and sickly conjectures formed in Marius's mind were dissipated. Did he know M. Fauchelevent's opinions? Perhaps he was a republican; hence his presence in the action would be perfectly simple. In the mean while Gavroche had run to the other end of the barricade, crying, "My gun!" and Courfeyrac ordered it to be given to him. Gavroche warned "his comrades," as he called them, that the barricade was invested, and he had found great difficulty in reaching it. A battalion of the line, with their arms piled in the Little Truanderie, was observing on the side of the Rue du Petit Cygne; on the opposite side the Municipal Guard occupied the Rue des Prêcheurs; while in front of them they had the main body of the army. This information given, Gavroche added, —

"I authorize you to give them a famous pill."

Enjolras was in the mean while watching at his loop-hole with open ears; for the assailants, doubtless little satisfied with the gun-shot, had not repeated it. A company of line infantry had come up to occupy the extremity of the street behind the gun. The soldiers unpaved the street, and erected with the stones a small low wall, a species of epaulement, only eighteen inches high, and facing the barricade. At the left-hand angle of this work could be seen the head of a suburban column, massed in the Rue St. Denis. Enjolras, from his post, fancied he could hear the peculiar sound produced by canister when taken out of its box, and he saw the captain of the gun change his aim and turn the gun's muzzle slightly to the left. Then the gunners began loading, and the captain of the gun himself took the port-fire and walked up to the vent.

"Fall on your knees all along the barricade," Enjolras shouted.

The insurgents, scattered in front of the wine-shop, and who had left their posts on Gavroche's arrival, rushed pell-mell toward the barricade; but ere Enjolras's order was executed, the discharge took place with the frightful rattle of a round of grape-shot; it was one, in fact. The shot was aimed at the opening in the redoubt, and ricochetted against the wall, killing two men and wounding three. If this continued, the barricade would be no longer tenable, for the grape-shot entered it. There was a murmur of consternation.

"Let us stop a second round," Enjolras said: and levelling his carbine he aimed at the captain of the gun, who was leaning over the breech and rectifying the aim. He was a handsome young sergeant of artillery, fair, gentle-faced, and having the intelligent look peculiar to that predestined and formidable arm which, owing to its constant improvement, must end by killing war. Combeferre, who was standing by Enjolras's side, gazed at this young man.

"What a pity!" said Combeferre. "What a hideous thing such butchery is! Well, when there are no kings left there will be no war. Enjolras, you aim at that sergeant, but do not notice him. Just reflect that he is a handsome young man; he is intrepid. You can see that he is a thinker, and these young artillerymen are well educated; he has a father, mother, and family; he is probably in love; he is but twenty-five years of age at the most, and might be your brother."

"He is so," said Enjolras.

"Yes," Combeferre added, "and mine too. Do not kill him."

"Let me alone. It must be."

And a tear slowly coursed down Enjolras's marble cheek. At the same time he pulled the trigger and the fire flashed forth. The artilleryman turned twice on his heel, with his arms stretched out before him, and his head raised as if to breathe the air, and then fell across the cannon motionless. His back could be seen, from the middle of which a jet of blood gushed forth; the bullet had gone right through his chest, and he was dead. It was necessary to bear him away and fill up his place, and thus a few minutes were gained.

CHAPTER IX.

OPINIONS varied in the barricade, for the firing of the piece was going to begin again, and the barricade could not hold out for a quarter of an hour under the grape-shot; it was absolutely necessary to abate the firing. Enjolras gave the command.

" We must have a mattress here."

" We have none," said Combeferre; "the wounded are lying on them."

Jean Valjean, seated apart on a bench, near the corner of the wine-shop, with his gun between his legs, had not up to the present taken any part in what was going on. He did not seem to hear the combatants saying around him, " There is a gun that does nothing." On hearing the order given by En-jolras, he rose. It will be remembered that on the arrival of the insurgents in the Rue de la Chanvrerie, an old woman, in her terror of the bullets, placed her mattress in front of her window. This window, a garret window, was on the roof of a six-storied house, a little beyond the barricade. The mattress, placed across it, leaning at the bottom upon two clothes-props, was held above by two ropes, which, at a distance, seemed two pieces of pack-thread, and were fastened to nails driven into the frames of the roof. These cords could be distinctly seen on the sky, like hairs.

" Can any one lend me a double-barrelled gun ? " Jean Valjean asked.

Enjolras, who had just reloaded his, handed it to him. Jean Valjean aimed at the garret window and fired ; one of the two cords of the mattress was cut asunder, and it hung by only one thread. Jean Valjean fired the second shot, and the second cord lashed the garret window ; the mattress glided between the two poles and fell into the street. The insurgents applauded, and every voice cried, —

" There is a mattress."

" Yes," said Combeferre, " but who will go and fetch it ? "

The mattress, in truth, had fallen outside the barricade, between the besiegers and besieged. Now, as the death of the sergeant of artillery had exasperated the troops, for some time past they had been lying flat behind the pile of paving-stones which they had raised ; and in order to make up for the enforced silence of the gun, they had opened fire on the barricade. The insurgents, wishing to save their ammunition, did not return this musketry : the fusillade broke against the barricade, but the street which it filled with bullets was terrible. Jean Valjean stepped out of the gap, entered the street, traversed the hail of bullets, went to the mattress, picked it up, placed it on his back, and re-entering the barricade, himself placed the mattress in the gap, and fixed it against the wall, so that the gunners should not see it. This done, they waited for the next round, which was soon fired. The gun belched forth its canister with a hoarse roar, but there was no ricochet, and the grape-shot was checked by the mattress. The expected result was obtained, and the barricade saved.

"Citizen," Enjolras said to Jean Valjean, "the republic thanks you."

Bossuet admired, and laughingly said, —

"It is immoral for a mattress to have so much power: it is the triumph of that which yields over that which thunders. But no matter, glory to the mattress that annuls a cannon!"

CHAPTER X.

DAWN.

At this moment Cosette awoke: her bed-room was narrow, clean, circumspect, with a long window on the east side looking out into the court-yard of the house. Cosette knew nothing of what was going on in Paris, for she had returned to her bed-room at the time when Toussaint said, "There is a row." Cosette had slept but a few hours, though well. She had had sweet dreams, which resulted perhaps from the fact that her small bed was very white. Somebody, who was Marius, appeared to her in light; and she rose with the sun in her eyes, which at first produced the effect of a continuation of her dream upon her. Her first thought on coming out of the dream was of a smiling nature, and she felt quite reassured. Like Jean Valjean a few hours before, she was passing through that reaction of the soul which absolutely desires no misfortune. She began hoping with all her strength, without knowing why, and then suffered from a contraction of the heart. She had not seen Marius for three days; but she said to herself that he must have received her letter, that he knew where she was, that he was clever and would find means to get to her, — certainly to-day, and perhaps that very morning. It was bright day, but the sunbeam was nearly horizontal, and so she thought that it must be early, but that she ought to rise in order to receive Marius. She felt that she could not live without Marius, and that consequently was sufficient, and Marius would come. No objection was admissible; all this was certain. It was monstrous enough to have suffered for three days: Marius absent for three days, that was horrible on the part of le bon Dieu. Now this cruel suspense sent from on high was a trial passed through; Marius was about to come and bring good news. Thus is youth constituted: it wipes away its tears quickly, and finding sorrow useless, does not accept it. Youth is the smile of the future of an unknown thing, which is itself: it is natural for it to be happy, and it seems as if its breath were made of hope.

However, Cosette could not succeed in recalling to mind what Marius had said to her on the subject of this absence, which was only to last one day, and what explanation he had given her about it. Every one will have noticed with what skill a coin let fall on the ground runs to hide itself, and what art it has in rendering itself invisible. There are thoughts which play us the same trick; they conceal themselves in a corner of our brain: it is all over, they are lost, and it is impossible to recall them to memory. Cosette felt somewhat vexed at the little useless effort her memory made, and said to herself that it was very wrong and culpable of her to forget words pronounced by Marius. She left her bed, and performed the two ablutions of the soul and the body, her prayers and her toilette.

We may, if absolutely required, introduce a reader into a nuptial chamber, but not into a virgin's room. Verse could hardly venture it, prose ought not. It is the interior of a still closed flower, a whiteness in the gloaming, the inner cell of a closed lily, which must not be gazed at by man till it has been gazed at by the sun. Woman in the bud is sacred: this innocent bud which discovers itself, this adorable semi-nudity which is afraid of itself, this white foot which takes refuge in a slipper, this throat which veils itself before a mirror as if the mirror were an eye, this chemise which hurriedly rises and covers the shoulder at the sound of a piece of furniture creaking or a passing vehicle, these knotted strings, this stay-lace, this tremor, this shudder of cold and shame, this exquisite shyness in every movement, this almost winged anxiety when there is nothing to fear, the successive phases of the apparel, which are as charming as the clouds of dawn, — it is not befitting that all this should be described, and it is too much to have merely indicated it. The eye of man must be even more religious before the rising of a maiden than before the rising of a star. The possibility of attaining ought to be turned into augmented respect. The down of the peach, the first bloom of the plum, the crystal radiate of the snow, the butterfly's wing powdered with feathers, are but coarse things by the side of this chastity, which does not know itself that it is chaste. The maiden is only the flash of the dream, and is not yet a statue; her alcove is con-

cealed in the dim part of the ideal, and the indiscreet
touch of the eye brutalizes this vague twilight.   In
this case contemplation is profanation.   We will
therefore say nothing about the sweet awaking and
rising of Cosette.   An Eastern fable tells us that
the rose was made white by God, but that Adam
having looked at it for a moment when it opened,
it felt ashamed, and turned pink.   We are of those
who feel themselves abashed in the presence of
maidens and flowers, for we find them worthy of
veneration.

Cosette dressed herself very rapidly, and combed
and dressed her hair, which was very simple at that
day, when women did not swell their ringlets and
plaits with cushions and pads, and placed no crino-
line in their hair.   Then she opened the window and
looked all around, hoping to discern a little of the
street, an angle of the house, or a corner of the pavement, to watch for Marius.   But nothing could be
seen of the outside : the court-yard was surrounded
by rather lofty walls, and was bounded by other gardens.   Cosette declared these gardens hideous, and
for the first time in her life considered flowers ugly.
The paltriest street gutter would have suited her purpose better ; and she resolved to look up to heaven,
as if she thought that Marius might possibly come
thence.   Suddenly she burst into tears, not through
any fickleness of temperament, but her situation consisted of hopes dashed with despondency.   She confusedly felt something horrible ; that it was really in
the air.   She said to herself that she was sure of
nothing, that letting herself out of sight was losing

herself; and the idea that Marius might return to
her from heaven appeared to her no longer charming but lugubrious. Then — for such these clouds
are — calmness returned, and hope, and a species
of smile, unconscious, but trusting in God.

Everybody was still asleep in the house, and a
provincial silence prevailed. No shutter was opened,
and the porter's lodge was still closed. Toussaint
was not up, and Cosette naturally thought that her
father was asleep. She must have suffered greatly,
and must still be suffering, for she said to herself
that her father had been unkind, but she reckoned
on Marius. The eclipse of such a light was decidedly
impossible. At moments she heard some distance
off a sort of heavy shock, and thought how singular
it was that gates were opened and shut at so early
an hour; it was the sound of the cannon-balls batter-
ing the barricade. There was a martin's nest a few
feet below Cosette's window in the old smoke-
blackened cornice, and the mouth of the nest pro-
jected a little beyond the cornice, so that the interior
of this little Paradise could be seen from above. The
mother was there expanding her wings like a fan
over her brood; the male bird fluttered round, went
away, and then returned, bringing in his bill food
and kisses. The rising day gilded this happy thing;
the great law, increase and multiply, was there smiling and august; and the sweet mystery was unfolded
in the glory of the morn. Cosette, with her hair in
the sunshine, her soul in flames, enlightened by love
within and the dawn without, bent forward as if
mechanically, and, almost without daring to confess

to herself that she was thinking at the same time of
Marius, she began looking at these birds, this family,
this male and female, this mother and her little ones,
with all the profound agitation which the sight of a
nest occasions a virgin.

CHAPTER XI.

THE SHOT WHICH DOES NOT MISS AND WHICH KILLS NOBODY.

THE fire of the assailants continued, and the musketry and grape-shot alternated, though without producing much mischief. The upper part of Corinth alone suffered, and the first-floor and garret windows, pierced by slugs and bullets, gradually lost their shape. The combatants posted there were compelled to withdraw ; but, in fact, such are the tactics of an attack on a barricade, — to skirmish for a long time and exhaust the ammunition of the insurgents, if they commit the error of returning the fire. When it is discovered by the slackening of their fire that they have no powder or ball left, the assault is made. Enjolras had not fallen into this trap, and the barricade did not reply. At each platoon fire Gavroche thrust his tongue into his cheek, a sign of supreme disdain.

" That's good," he said ; " tear up the linen, for we require lint."

Courfeyrac addressed the grape-shot on its want of effect, and said to the cannon, —

" You are becoming diffuse, my good fellow."

In battle, intrigues take place as at a ball ; and it is probable that the silence of the redoubt was

beginning to render the assailants anxious, and make
them fear lest some unexpected incident had occurred.
They felt a need of seeing clearly through this pile of
paving-stones, and what was going on behind this
impassive wall, which received shots without answering them.   The insurgents suddenly perceived
a helmet glistening in the sun upon an adjoining
roof : a sapper was leaning against a tall chimney-
pot and apparently a sentry there.   He looked down
into the barricade.

"That's a troublesome spy," said Enjolras.

Jean had returned Enjolras his fowling-piece, but
still had his own musket.   Without saying a word
he aimed at the sapper, and a second later the helmet, struck by a bullet, fell noisily into the street.
The soldier disappeared with all possible haste.   A
second watchman took his place, and it was an
officer.   Jean Valjean, who had reloaded his musket,
aimed at the new-comer, and sent the officer's helmet
to join the private's.   The officer was not obstinate,
but withdrew very quickly.   This time the hint was
understood, and no one again appeared on the roof.

"Why did you not kill the man?" Bossuet asked
Jean Valjean, who, however, made no reply.

CHAPTER XII.

BOSSUET muttered in Combeferre's ear, —
" He has not answered my question."
" He is a man who does kind actions with musket-shots," said Combeferre.

Those who have any recollection of this now distant epoch know that the suburban National Guards were valiant against the insurrection, and they were peculiarly brave and obstinate in the days of June, 1832. Any worthy landlord, whose establishment the insurrection injured, became leonine on seeing his dancing-room deserted, and let himself be killed in order to save order represented by the suburban public-house. At this time, which was at once heroic and bourgeois, in the presence of ideas which had their knights, interests had their Paladins, and the prosaic nature of the motive took away none of the bravery of the movement. The decrease of a pile of crowns made bankers sing the Marseillaise, men lyrically shed their blood for the till, and defended with Lacedæmonian enthusiasm the shop, that immense diminutive of the country. Altogether there was a good deal that was very serious in all this; social interests were entering into a contest, while awaiting the day when they would enter a state of equilibrium. Another sign of this time was the anarchy mingled with the governmentalism (a barbarous name of the correct party), and men were for order without discipline. The drums played unexpectedly fancy calls, at the command of some colonel of the National Guard : one captain went under fire through inspiration, while some National Guards fought " for the idea," and on their own account. In critical moments during the riots men followed the advice of their chiefs less than their own instincts, and there were in the army of order real Guerilleros, some of the sword like Fannicot, and others of the pen like Henry Fonfrède. Civilization, unhappily represented at this period more by an aggregation of interests than by a group of principles, was, or believed itself to be, in danger ; it uttered the alarm cry, and every man, constituting himself a centre, defended, succored, and protected it in his own way, and the first comer took on himself to save society.

Zeal sometimes went as far as extermination ; a platoon of National Guards constituted themselves of their own authority a council of war, and tried and executed in five minutes an insurgent prisoner. It was an improvisation of this nature which killed Jean Prouvaire. It is that ferocious Lynch law with which no party has the right to reproach another, for it is applied by the Republic in America as by monarchy in Europe. This Lynch law was complicated by mistakes. On a day of riot a young poet of the name of Paul Aimé Garnier was pursued on the Place Royale at the bayonet's point, and only escaped by taking shelter under the gateway at No. 6. "There's another of those Saint Simonians," they shouted, and wished to kill him. Now, he had under his arm a volume of the Memoirs of the Duc de Saint Simon; a National Guard read on the back the words "Saint Simon," and shouted, "Death to him!" On June 6, 1832, a company of suburban National Guards, commanded by Captain Fannicot, to whom we have already referred, decimated the Rue de la Chanvrerie for his own good pleasure, and on his own authority. This fact, singular though it is, was proved by the judicial report drawn up in consequence of the insurrection of 1832. Captain Fannicot, an impatient and bold bourgeois, a species of condottiere of order, and a fanatical and insubmissive governmentalist, could not resist the attraction of firing prematurely, and taking the barricade all by himself, that is to say, with his company. Exasperated at the successive apparition of the red flag and the old coat, which he took for the black flag, he loudly blamed the generals and commanders of corps, who were holding councils, as they did not think the decisive moment for assault had arrived, but were "letting the insurrection stew in its own gravy," according to a celebrated expression of one of them. As for him, he thought the barricade ripe, and as everything that is ripe is bound to fall, he made the attempt.

He commanded men as resolute as himself. "Madmen," a witness called them. His company, the same which had shot Jean Prouvaire, was the first of the battalion posted at the street corner. At the moment when it was least expected the captain dashed his men at the barricade; but this movement, executed with more good-will than strategy, cost Fannicot's company dearly. Before it had covered two thirds of the street a general discharge from the barricade greeted it; four, the boldest men of all, running at the head, were shot down in pointblank range at the very foot of the barricade, and this courageous mob of National Guards, very brave men, but not possessing the military tenacity, was compelled to fall back after a few moments, leaving fifteen corpses in the street. The momentary hesitation gave the insurgents time to reload, and a second and most deadly discharge assailed the company before the men were able to regain their shelter at the corner of the street. In a moment they were caught between two fires, and received the volley from the cannon, which, having no orders to the contrary, did not cease firing. The intrepid and imprudent Fannicot was one of those killed by this round of grape-shot; he was laid low by the cannon. This attack, which was more furious than serious, irritated Enjolras.

"The asses!" he said, "they have their men killed and expend our ammunition for nothing."

Enjolras spoke like the true general of the riot that he was: insurrection and repression do not fight with equal arms; for the insurrection, which can be soon exhausted, has only a certain number of rounds to fire and of combatants to expend. An expended cartouche-box and a killed man cannot have their place filled up. Repression, on the other hand, having the army, does not count men, and having Vincennes, does not count rounds. Repression has as many regiments as the barricade has men, and as many arsenals as the barricade has cartouche-boxes. Hence these are always contests of one man against a hundred, which ever end by the destruction of the barricade, unless revolution, suddenly dashing up, casts into the balance its flashing archangel's glaive. Such things happen, and then everything rises, paving-stones get into a state of ebullition, and popular redoubts swarm. Paris has a sovereign tremor, the *quid divinum* is evolved; there is an August 10 or a July 29 in the air, a prodigious light appears, the yawning throat of force recoils, and the army, that lion, sees before it, standing erect and tranquil, that prophet, France.

CHAPTER XIII.

GLEAMS WHICH FADE.

In the chaos of feelings and passions which defend a barricade there is everything, — bravery, youth, the point of honor, enthusiasm, the ideal, conviction, the obstinacy of the gambler, and above all intermitting gleams of hope. One of these intermittences, one of these vague quiverings of hope, suddenly ran along the Chanvrerie barricade at the most unexpected moment.

"Listen," Enjolras, who was ever on the watch, exclaimed. "I fancy that Paris is waking up."

It is certain that on the morning of June 6 the insurrection had for an hour or two a certain re-animation. The obstinacy of the tocsin of St. Merry aroused a few slight desires, and barricades were begun in the Rue du Poirier and in the Rue des Gravilliers. In front of the Porte St. Martin, a young man armed with a gun attacked a squadron of cavalry alone, unprotected, and on the open boulevard he knelt down, raised his gun, fired and killed the Major, and then turned away, saying, "There's another who will do us no more mischief." He was cut down. In the Rue St. Denis a woman fired at the National Guard from behind a Venetian shutter, and the wooden laths could be seen to tremble every moment. A boy of fourteen was arrested in the Rue de la Cossonnerie with his pockets full of cartridges, and several guard-houses were attacked. At the entrance of the Rue Bertin Poirée a very sharp and quite unexpected fusillade greeted a regiment of cuirassiers, at the head of which rode General Cavaignac de Barague. In the Rue Planche Mibray old crockery and household utensils were thrown from the roofs down on the troops; this was a bad sign, and when Marshal Soult was informed of the fact, Napoleon's old lieutenant became pensive, for he remembered Suchet's remark at Saragossa : " We are lost when old women empty their pots de chambre on our heads." These general symptoms manifested at a moment when the riots were supposed to be localized, this fever of anger which regained the upper hand, these will-o'-the-wisps flying here and there over the profound masses of combustible matter which are called the faubourgs of Paris, and all the accompanying facts, rendered the chiefs anxious, and they hastened to extinguish the beginnings of the conflagration. Until these sparks were quenched, the attacks on the barricades Maubuée, de la Chanvrerie, and St. Merry were deferred, so that all might be finished at one blow. Columns of troops were sent through the streets in a state of fermentation, clearing the large streets and searching the smaller ones, on the right and on the left, at one moment slowly and cautiously, at another at quick march. The troops broke open the doors of the houses whence firing was heard, and at the same time cavalry manœuvres dispersed the groups on the boulevards. This repression was not effected without turmoil, and that tumultuous noise peculiar to collisions between the army and the people, and it was this that had attracted Enjolras's attention in the intervals between the cannonading and the platoon fire. Moreover, he had seen wounded men carried along the end of the street on litters, and said to Courfeyrac, "Those wounded are not our handiwork."

The hope lasted but a short time, and the gleam was quickly eclipsed. In less than half an hour what there was in the air vanished; it was like a flash of lightning without thunder, and the insurgents felt that leaden pall, which the indifference of the people casts upon abandoned obstinate men, fall upon them again. The general movement, which seemed to have been obscurely designed, failed, and the attention of the Minister of War and the strategy of the generals could now be concentrated on the three or four barricades that remained standing. The sun rose on the horizon, and an insurgent addressed Enjolras, —

"We are hungry here. Are we really going to die like this, without eating?"

Enjolras, still leaning at his parapet, made a nod of affirmation, without taking his eyes off the end of the street.

CHAPTER XIV.

IN WHICH WE READ THE NAME OF THE MIS-
TRESS OF ENJOLRAS.

COURFEYRAC, seated on a stone by the side of
Enjolras, continued to insult the cannon, and each
time that the gloomy shower of projectiles which is
called a grape-shot passed with its monstrous noise
he greeted it with an ironical remark.

"You are wasting your breath, my poor old brute,
and I feel sorry for you, as your row is thrown away.
That is not thunder, but a cough."

And those around him laughed. Courfeyrac and
Bossuet, whose valiant good-humor increased with
danger, made up for the want of food, like Madame
Scarron, by jests, and as wine was short, poured out
gayety for all.

"I admire Enjolras," said Bossuet. "His temerity
astonishes me. He lives alone, which, perhaps, renders him a little sad; and Enjolras is to be pitied
for his greatness, which attaches him to widowhood.
We fellows have all, more or less, mistresses, who
make us mad, that is to say brave, and when a man
is as full of love as a tiger the least he can do is to
fight like a lion. That is a way of avenging ourselves for the tricks which our grisettes play us.
Roland lets himself be killed to vex Angelique, and

all our heroism comes from our women. A man
without a woman is like a pistol without a hammer,
and it is the woman who makes the man go off.
Well, Enjolras has no woman, he is not in love, and
finds means to be intrepid. It is extraordinary that
a man can be cold as ice and daring as fire."

Enjolras did not appear to listen; but any one who
had been near him might have heard him murmur,
in a low voice, *Patria*. Bossuet laughed again, when
Courfeyrac shouted, " Here 's something fresh."

And assuming the voice of a groom of the cham-
bers who announces a visitor, he added, — " Mr.
Eight-Pounder."

In fact, a new character had come on the stage ;
it was a second piece of artillery. The gunners
rapidly got it into position by the side of the first
one, and this was the beginning of the end. A few
minutes later both guns, being actively served, were
at work against the barricade, and the platoon fire of
the line and the suburban National Guards supported
the artillery. Another cannonade was audible some
distance off. At the same time that the two guns
were furiously assaulting the redoubt in the Rue de la
Chanvrerie, two other pieces placed in position, one
in the Rue St. Denis, the other in the Rue Aubry
le Boucher, were pounding the St. Merry barricade.
The four guns formed a lugubrious echo to one
another, the barks of the grim dogs of war answered one another. Of the two guns now opened
on the barricade of the Rue de la Chanvrerie, one
fired shell, the other solid shot. The gun which fired
the latter was pointed at a slight elevation, and the

firing was so calculated that the ball struck the extreme edge of the crest of the barricades, and hurled the broken paving-stones on the heads of the insurgents. This mode of fire was intended to drive the combatants from the top of the redoubt, and compel them to close up in the interior; that is to say, it announced the assault. Once the combatants were driven from the top of the barricade by the cannon, and from the windows of the public-house by the canister, the columns of attack could venture into the street without being aimed at, perhaps without even being seen, suddenly escalade the barricade, as on the previous evening, and take it by surprise.

" The annoyance of these guns must be reduced," said Enjolras; and he shouted, " Fire at the artillery-men ! "

All were ready: the barricade, which had so long been silent, was belted with flame; seven or eight rounds succeeded one another with a sort of rage and joy; the street was filled with a blinding smoke, and at the expiration of a few minutes there might be confusedly seen through the mist, all striped with flame, two thirds of the artillerymen lying under the gun-wheels. Those who remained standing continued to serve the guns with a stern tranquillity, but the fire was reduced.

" Things are going well," said Bossuet to Enjolras; " that is a success."

Enjolras shook his head, and replied, —

" Another quarter of an hour of that success, and there will not be ten cartridges left in the barricade."

It appears that Gavroche heard the remark.

CHAPTER XV.

COURFEYRAC all at once perceived somebody in the street, at the foot of the barricade, amid the shower of bullets. Gavroche had fetched a hamper from the pot-house, passed through the gap, and was quickly engaged in emptying into it the full cartouche-boxes of the National Guards killed on the slope of the barricade.

"What are you doing there?" Courfeyrac said.

Gavroche looked up.

"Citizen, I am filling my hamper."

"Do you not see the grape-shot?"

Gavroche replied,—

"Well, it is raining; what then?"

Courfeyrac cried, "Come in."

"Directly," said Gavroche.

And with one bound he reached the street. It will be borne in mind that Fannicot's company, in retiring, left behind it a number of corpses; some twenty dead lay here and there all along the pavement of the street. That made twenty cartouche-boxes for Gavroche, and a stock of cartridges for the barricade. The smoke lay in the street like a fog; any one who has seen a cloud in a mountain gorge, between two precipitous escarpments, can form an idea of this smoke, contracted, and as it were rendered denser, by the two dark lines of tall houses. It rose slowly, and was incessantly renewed ; whence came a gradual obscurity, which dulled even the bright daylight. The combatants could scarce see one another from either end of the street, which was, however, very short. This darkness, probably desired and calculated on by the chiefs who were about to direct the assault on the barricade, was useful for Gavroche. Under the cloak of this smoke, and thanks to his shortness, he was enabled to advance a considerable distance along the street unnoticed, and he plundered the first seven or eight cartouche-boxes without any great danger. He crawled on his stomach, galloped on all fours, took his hamper in his teeth, writhed, glided, undulated, wound from one corpse to another, and emptied the cartouche-box as a monkey opens a nut. They did not cry to him from the barricade, to which he was still rather close, to return, for fear of attracting attention to him. On one corpse, which was a corporal's, he found a powder-flask.

"For thirst," he said, as he put it in his pocket.

While moving forward, he at length reached the point where the fog of the fire became transparent, so that the sharp-shooters of the line, drawn up behind their parapet of paving-stones, and the National Guard at the corner of the street, all at once pointed out to one another something stirring in the street. At the moment when Gavroche was taking the cartridges from a sergeant lying near a post, a bullet struck the corpse.

"Oh, for shame!" said Gavroche; "they are killing my dead for me."

A second bullet caused the stones to strike fire close to him, while a third upset his hamper. Gavroche looked and saw that it came from the National Guards. He stood upright, with his hair floating in the breeze, his hands on his hips, and his eyes fixed on the National Guards who were firing, and he sang, —

> " On est laid à Nanterre,
>   C'est la faute à Voltaire,
>   Et bête à Palaiseau,
>   C'est la faute à Rousseau."

Then he picked up his hamper, put into it the cartridges scattered around without missing one, and walked toward the firing party, to despoil another cartouche-box. Then a fourth bullet missed him. Gavroche sang, —

> " Je ne suis pas notaire,
>   C'est la faute à Voltaire;
>   Je suis petit oiseau,
>   C'est la faute à Rousseau."

A fifth bullet only succeeded so far as to draw a third couplet from him, —

> " Joie est mon caractère,
>   C'est la faute à Voltaire;
>   Misère est mon trousseau,
>   C'est la faute à Rousseau."

They went on for some time longer, and the sight was at once terrific and charming; Gavroche, while fired at, ridiculed the firing, and appeared to be greatly amused. He was like a sparrow deriding the sportsmen, and answered each discharge by a verse. The troops aimed at him incessantly, and constantly missed him, and the National Guards and the soldiers laughed while covering him. He lay down, then rose again, hid himself in a doorway, then bounded, disappeared, reappeared, ran off, came back, replied to the grape-shot by putting his fingers to his nose, and all the while plundered cartridges, emptied boxes, and filled his hamper. The insurgents watched him, as they panted with anxiety, but while the barricade trembled he sang. He was not a child, he was not a man, he was a strange goblin gamin, and he resembled the invulnerable dwarf of the combat. The bullets ran after him, but he was more active than they ; he played a frightful game of hide-and-seek with death : and each time that the snub-nosed face of the spectre approached the gamin gave it a fillip. One bullet, however, better aimed or more treacherous than the rest, at length struck the will-o'-the-wisp lad ; Gavroche was seen to totter and then sink. The whole barricade uttered a cry, but there was an Antæus in this pygmy : for a gamin to touch the pavement is like the giant touching the earth ; and Gavroche had only fallen to rise again. He remained in a sitting posture, a long jet of blood ran down his face, he raised both arms in the air, looked in the direction whence the shot had come, and began singing, —

" Je suis tombé par terre,
   C'est la faute à Voltaire ;
   Le nez dans le ruisseau,
   C'est la faute à — "

He did not finish, for a second shot from the same marksman stopped him short. This time he lay with his face on the pavement, and did not stir again. This little great soul had flown away.

CHAPTER XVI.

HOW A BROTHER BECOMES A FATHER.

THERE were at this very moment in the Luxembourg garden — for the eye of the drama must be everywhere present — two lads holding each other's hand. One might be seven, the other five, years of age. As they were wet through with the rain they walked along sunshiny paths; the elder led the younger, both were in rags and pale, and they looked like wild birds. The younger said, "I am very hungry." The elder, who had already a protecting air, led his brother with the left hand, and had a switch in his right. They were alone in the garden, which was deserted, as the gates were closed by police order on account of the insurrection. The troops who had bivouacked there had issued forth for the exigences of the combat. How were these children here? Perhaps they had escaped from some guard-room where the door was left ajar; perhaps in the vicinity, at the Barrière d'Enfer, on the esplanade of the Observatory, or in the neighboring square overshadowed by the cornice, on which may be read, *Invenerunt parvulum pannis involutum*, there was some mountebank's booth from which they had fled; perhaps they had on the previous evening kept out of sight of the garden inspectors at the hour of closing, and had spent the night in one of those summer-houses in which people read the papers : the fact is, that they were wandering about, and seemed to be free. To be a wanderer, and to appear free, is to be lost, and these poor little creatures were really lost. The two lads were the same about whom Gavroche had been in trouble, and whom the reader will remember, sons of Thénardier, let out to Magnon, attributed to M. Gillenormand, and now leaves fallen from all these rootless branches, and rolled along the ground by the wind.

Their clothes, clean in the time of Magnon, and which served her as a prospectus to M. Gillenormand, had become rags ; and these beings henceforth belonged to the statistics of "deserted children," whom the police pick up, lose, and find again on the pavement of Paris. It needed the confusion of such a day as this for these two poor little wretches to be in this garden. If the inspectors had noticed these rags they would have expelled them, for poor little lads do not enter public gardens, and yet it ought to be remembered that as children they have a right to flowers. They were here, thanks to the locked gates, and were committing an offence; they had stepped into the garden and remained there. Though locked gates do not give a holiday to the keepers, and their surveillance is supposed to continue, it grows weaker and rests ; and the inspectors, also affected by the public affairs, and more busied about the outside than the inside, did not look at the garden, and had not seen the two delinquents. It had rained on the previous evening, and even slightly on this morning, but in June, showers are of no great consequence. People hardly perceive, an hour after a storm, that this fair beauteous day has wept, for the earth dries up as rapidly as a child's cheek. At this moment of the solstice the midday light is, so to speak, poignant, and it seizes everything. It clings to and spreads itself over the earth with a sort of suction, and we might say that the sun is thirsty. A shower is a glass of water, and rain is at once drunk up. In the morning everything glistens, in the afternoon everything is dusty. Nothing is so admirable as verdure cleansed by the rain and dried by the sun ; it is warm freshness. Gardens and fields, having water in their roots and sunshine in their flowers, become censers of incense, and smoke with all their perfumes at once. Everything laughs, sings, and offers itself, and we feel softly intoxicated : summer is a temporary Paradise, and the sun helps man to be patient.

There are beings who ask no more,—living creatures who, having the azure of heaven, say it is enough ; dreamers absorbed in the prodigy, drawing from the idolatry of nature indifference to good and evil ; contemplators of the Cosmos, radiantly distracted from man, who do not understand how people can trouble themselves about the hunger of one person, the thirst of another, the nudity of the poor man in winter, the lymphatic curvature of a small backbone, the truck-bed, the garret, the cell, and the rags of young shivering girls, when they can dream under the trees : they are peaceful and terrible minds, pitilessly satisfied, and, strange to say, infinitude suffices them. They ignore that great want of man, the finite which admits of an embrace, and do not dream of the finite which admits of progress, that sublime toil. The indefinite, which springs from the divine and human combination of the infinite and the finite, escapes them, and provided that they can be face to face with immensity, they smile. They never feel joy, but always ecstasy, and their life is one of abstraction. The history of humanity is to them but a grand detail : the All is not in it, the All remains outside of it. Of what use is it to trouble one's self about that item, man? Man suffers, it is possible, but just look at Aldebaran rising! The mother has no milk left, the new-born babe is dying. I know nothing of all that, but just look at the marvellous rose made by a sprig of hawthorn when looked at through a microscope ; just compare the finest Mechlin lace with that! These thinkers forget to love, and the zodiac has such an attraction over them that it prevents them seeing the weeping child. God eclipses their soul, and they are a family of minds at once great and little. Homer belonged to it ; so did Goethe, and possibly Lafontaine, magnificent egotists of the infinite, calm spectators of sorrow, who do not see Nero if the weather be fine ; from whom the sun hides the pyre ; who would look at a guillotining to seek a light effect in it ; who hear neither cries nor sobs, nor the death-rattle nor the tocsin ; for whom everything is good, since there is the month of May ; who so long as they have clouds of purple and gold above their heads declare themselves satisfied ; and who are determined to be happy until the radiance of the stars and the song of birds are exhausted.

These are darkly radiant, and they do not suspect that they are to be pitied. But they are certainly so, for the man who does not weep does not see. We must admire and pity them, as we would pity and admire a being at once night and day, who had no eyes under his brows, but a star in the centre of his forehead. The indifference of these thinkers is, according to some, a grand philosophy. Be it so ; but in this superiority there is infirmity. A man may be immortal and limp, as witness Vulcan, and he may be more than man and less than man ; there is immense incompleteness in nature, and who knows whether the sun be not blind ? But in that case, whom to trust ? *Solem quis dicere falsum audeat?* Hence, certain geniuses, certain human deities, star-men, might be mistaken ? What is above at the summit, at the zenith, which pours so much light on the earth, might see little, see badly, not see at all ? Is not that desperate ? No : but what is there above the sun ? God.

On June 6, 1832, at about eleven in the forenoon, the Luxembourg, solitary and depopulated, was delicious. The quincunxes and flower-beds sent balm and dazzlement into the light, and the branches, wild in the brilliancy of midday, seemed trying to embrace one another. There was in the sycamores a twittering of linnets, the sparrows were triumphal, and the woodpeckers crept along the chestnut, gently tapping holes in the bark. The beds accepted the legitimate royalty of the lilies, for the most august of

perfumes is that which issues from whiteness. The
sharp odor of the carnations was inhaled, and the old
rooks of Marie de Medicis made love on the lofty
trees. The sun gilded, purpled, and illumined the
tulips, which are nothing but all the varieties of
flame made into flowers. All around the tulip-beds
hummed the bees, the flashes of these fire-flowers.
All was grace and gayety, even the coming shower,
for that relapse by which the lilies of the valley and
honeysuckles would profit had nothing alarming about
it, and the swallows made the delicious menace of
flying low. What was there inhaled happiness: life
smelt pleasantly, and all this nature exhaled candor,
help, assistance, paternity, caresses, and dawn. The
thoughts that fell from heaven were as soft as a babe's
little hand that we kiss. The statues under the trees,
nude and white, were robed in dresses of shadow
shot with light; these goddesses were all ragged
with sunshine, and beams hung from them on all
sides. Around the great basin the earth was already
so dry as to be parched, and there was a breeze suffi-
ciently strong to create here and there small riots of
dust. A few yellow leaves remaining from the last
autumn joyously pursued one another, and seemed to
be sporting.

The abundance of light had something strangely
reassuring about it; life, sap, heat, and exhalations
overflowed, and the greatness of the source could be
felt beneath creation. In all these blasts penetrated
with love, in this movement of reflections and gleams,
in this prodigious expenditure of beams, and in this
indefinite outpouring of fluid gold, the prodigality of

the inexhaustible could be felt ; and behind this splendor, as behind a curtain of flames, glimpses of God, that
millionnaire of the stars, could be caught.   Thanks
to the sand, there was not a speck of mud ; and,
thanks to the rain, there was not a grain of dust.
The bouquets had just performed their ablutions, and
all the velvets, all the satins, all the varnish, and all
the gold which issue from the earth in the shape of
flowers, were irreproachable.   This magnificence was
clean, and the grand silence of happy nature filled
the garden, — a heavenly silence, compatible with a
thousand strains of music, the fondling tones from
the nests, the buzzing of the swarms, and the pal-
pitations of the wind.   All the harmony of the
season was blended into a graceful whole, the entrances and exits of spring took place in the desired
order, the lilacs were finishing, and the jessamine
beginning, a few flowers were behindhand, a few
insects before their time, and the vanguard of the
red butterflies of June fraternized with the rearguard
of the white butterflies of May.   The plane-trees
were putting on a fresh skin, and the breeze formed
undulations in the magnificent enormity of the chest-
nut-trees.   It was splendid.   A veteran from the
adjoining barracks who was looking through the
railings said, " Spring presents arms in full dress."

All nature was breakfasting ; the creation was at
table ; it was the hour : the great blue cloth was laid
in heaven, and the great green one on earth, while
the sun gave an *à giorno* illumination.   God was
serving His universal meal, and each being had its
pasture or its pasty.   The wood-pigeon found hemp-

seed, the chaffinch found millet, the goldfinch found chickweed, the redbreast found worms, the bee found flowers, the fly found infusoria, and the greenfinch found flies. They certainly devoured one another to some extent, which is the mystery of evil mingled with good, but not a single animal had an empty stomach. The two poor abandoned boys had got near the great basin, and somewhat confused by all this light, tried to hide themselves, which is the instinct of the poor and the weak in the presence of magnificence, even when it is impersonal, and they kept behind the swan's house. Now and then, at intervals when the wind blew, confused shouts, a rumbling, a sort of tumultuous death-rattle which was musketry, and dull blows which were cannon-shots, could be heard. There was smoke above the roofs in the direction of the markets, and a bell which seemed to be summoning sounded in the distance. The children did not seem to notice the noises, and the younger lad repeated every now and then in a low voice, " I am hungry."

Almost simultaneously with the two boys another couple approached the basin, consisting of a man of about fifty, leading by the hand a boy of six years of age. It was doubtless a father with his son. The younger of the two had a cake in his hand. At this period certain contiguous houses in the Rue Madame and the Rue d'Enfer had keys to the Luxembourg, by which the lodgers could let themselves in when the gates were locked ; but this permission has since been withdrawn. This father and son evidently came from one of these houses. The two poor little creatures saw "this gentleman" coming, and hid themselves a little more. He was a citizen, and perhaps the same whom Marius during his love-fever had one day heard near the same great basin counselling his son "to avoid excesses." He had an affable and haughty look, and a mouth which, as it did not close, always smiled. This mechanical smile, produced by too much jaw and too little skin, shows the teeth rather than the soul. The boy with the bitten cake which he had not finished, seemed glutted; the boy was dressed in a National Guard's uniform, on account of the riots, and the father remained in civilian garb for the sake of prudence. Father and son had halted near the great basin, in which the two swans were disporting. This bourgeois appeared to have a special admiration for the swans, and resembled them in the sense that he walked like them. At this moment the swans were swimming, which is their principal talent, and were superb. Had the two little fellows listened, and been of an age to comprehend, they might have overheard the remarks of a serious man; the father was saying to his son, —

"The sage lives contented with little; look at me, my son, I do not care for luxury. You never see me in a coat glistening with gold and precious stones; I leave that false lustre to badly-organized minds."

Here the deep shouts which came from the direction of the Halles broke out, with a redoublement of bells and noise.

"What is that?" the lad asked.

The father replied, —

"That is the saturnalia."

All at once he perceived the two little ragged boys standing motionless behind the swan's green house.

"Here is the beginning," he said.

And after a silence he added, —

"Anarchy enters this garden."

In the mean while the boy bit the cake, spat it out again, and suddenly began crying.

"Why are you crying?" the father asked.

"I am no longer hungry," said the boy.

The father's smile became more marked than ever.

"You need not be hungry to eat a cake."

"I am tired of cake; it is so filling."

"Don't you want any more?"

"No."

The father showed him the swans.

"Throw it to those palmipeds."

The boy hesitated, for if he did not want any more cake that was no reason to give it away.

The father continued, —

"Be humane : you ought to have pity on animals."

And, taking the cake from his son, he threw it into the basin, where it fell rather near the bank. The swans were some distance off, near the centre of the basin, and engaged with some prey : they had seen neither the citizen nor the cake. The citizen, feeling that the cake ran a risk of being lost, and affected by this useless shipwreck, began a telegraphic agitation which eventually attracted the attention of the swans. They noticed something floating on the surface, tacked, like the vessels they are, and came towards the cake slowly, with the majesty that befits white beasts.

"Swans understand signs," said the bourgeois, pleased at his own cleverness.

At this moment the distant tumult of the city was suddenly swollen. This time it was sinister, and there are some puffs of wind which speak more distinctly than others. The one which blew at this moment distinctly brought up the rolling of drums, shouts, platoon fires, and the mournful replies of the tocsin, and the cannon. This coincided with a black cloud which suddenly veiled the sky. The swans had not yet reached the cake.

"Let us go home," the father said; "they are attacking the Tuileries."

He seized his son's hand again, and then continued, —

"From the Tuileries to the Luxembourg there is only the distance which separates the royalty from the peerage; and that is not far. It is going to rain musketry."

He looked at the cloud, —

"And perhaps we shall have rain of the other sort too; heaven is interfering: the younger branch is condemned. Let us make haste home."

"I should like to see the swans eat the cake," said the boy.

"It would be imprudent," the father answered; and he led away his little bourgeois. The son, regretting the swans, turned his head toward the basin, until a bend in the quincunxes concealed it from him. The two little vagabonds had in the mean

while approached the cake simultaneously with the
swans. It was floating on the water; the smaller
boy looked at the cake; the other looked at the
citizen, who was going off. Father and son entered
the labyrinth of trees that runs to the grand staircase of the clump of trees in the direction of the
Rue Madame. When they were no longer in sight,
the elder hurriedly lay down full length on the
rounded bank of the basin, and holding by his left
hand, while bending over the water, till he all but
fell in, he stretched out his switch toward the cake
with the other. The swans, seeing the enemy, hastened up, and in hastening their breasts produced an
effect useful to the little fisher: the water flowed
back in front of the swans, and one of the gentle,
concentric undulations slightly impelled the cake
toward the boy's switch. When the swans came up,
the stick was touching the cake; the lad gave a
quick blow, startled the swans, seized the cake, and
arose. The cake was soaking, but they were hungry
and thirsty. The elder boy divided the cake into
two parts, a large one and a small one, kept the
small one for himself, and gave the larger piece to
his brother, saying, —

"Shove that into your gun."

CHAPTER XVII.

MORTUUS PATER FILIUM MORITURUM EXPECTAT.

MARIUS rushed out of the barricade, and Combeferre followed him; but it was too late, and Gavroche was dead. Combeferre brought in the hamper of cartridges, and Marius the boy. Alas! he thought he was requiting the son for what the father had done, for his father; but Thénardier had brought in his father alive, while he brought in the lad dead. When Marius re-entered the barricade with Gavroche in his arms, his face was deluged with blood, like the boy's; for at the very instant when he stooped to pick up Gavroche, a bullet had grazed his skull, but he had not noticed it. Courfeyrac took off his neckcloth and bound Marius's forehead; Gavroche was deposited on the same table with Mabœuf, and the black shawl was spread over both bodies; it was large enough for the old man and the child. Combeferre distributed the cartridges which he had brought in, and they gave each man fifteen rounds to fire. Jean Valjean was still at the same spot, motionless on his bench. When Combeferre offered him his fifteen cartridges he shook his head.

"That is a strange eccentric," Combeferre said in a whisper to Enjolras. "He manages not to fight inside this barricade."

"Which does not prevent him from defending it," Enjolras answered.

"Heroism has its original characters," Combeferre resumed.

And Courfeyrac, who overheard him,, said, —

"He is a different sort from Father Mabœuf."

It is a thing worth mentioning, that the fire which struck the barricade scarce disturbed the interior. Those who have never passed the tornado of a warfare of this nature cannot form any idea of the singular moments of calmness mingled with these convulsions. Men come and go, they talk, they jest, they idle. A friend of ours heard a combatant say to him, in the midst of the grape-shot, "It is like being at a bachelor's breakfast here." The redoubt in the Rue de la Chanvrerie, we repeat, appeared internally most calm; and all the incidents and phases were, or would shortly be, exhausted. The position had become from critical menacing, and from menacing was probably about to become desperate. In proportion as the situation grew darker an heroic gleam more and more purpled the barricade. Enjolras commanded it in the attitude of a young Spartan, devoting his bare sword to the gloomy genius, Epidotas. Combeferre, with an apron tied round him, was dressing the wounded. Bossuet and Feuilly were making cartridges with the powder-flask found by Gavroche on the dead corporal, and Bossuet was saying to Feuilly, "We are soon going to take the diligence for another planet." Courfeyrac, seated on the few paving-stones which he had set aside near Enjolras, was preparing and arranging an entire arsenal — his sword-cane, his gun, two hostler-pistols, and a club — with the ease of a girl setting a small what-not in order. Jean Valjean was silently looking at the wall facing him, and a workman was fastening on his head, with a piece of string, a broad-brimmed straw bonnet of Mother Hucheloup's, "for fear of sunstrokes," as he said. The young men of the Aix Cougourde were gayly chatting together, as if desirous to talk patois for the last time. Joly, who had taken down Widow Hucheloup's mirror, was examining his tongue in it; while a few combatants, who had discovered some nearly mouldering crusts of bread in a drawer, were eating them greedily. Marius was anxious about what his father would say to him.

CHAPTER XVIII.

THE VULTURE BECOMES PREY.

WE must lay a stress upon a psychological fact peculiar to barricades, for nothing which characterizes this surprising war of streets ought to be omitted. Whatever the internal tranquillity to which we have just referred may be, the barricade does not the less remain a vision for those who are inside it. There is an apocalypse in a civil war, all the darkness of the unknown world is mingled with these stern flashes, revolutions are sphinxes, and any one who has stood behind a barricade believes that he has gone through a dream. What is felt at these spots, as we have shown in the matter of Marius, and whose consequences we shall see, is more and less than life. On leaving a barricade, a man no longer knows what he has seen; he may have been terrible, but he is ignorant of the fact. He has been surrounded there by combating ideas which possessed human faces, and had his head in the light of futurity. There were corpses laid low and phantoms standing upright; and the hours were colossal, and seemed hours of eternity. A man has lived in death, and shadows have passed. What was it? He has seen hands on which was blood; it was a deafening din, but at the same time a startling silence: there were open mouths that cried, and other open mouths which were silent, and men were in smoke, perhaps in night. A man fancies he has touched the sinister dripping of unknown depths, and he looks at something red which he has in his nails, but he no longer recollects anything.

Let us return to the Rue de la Chanvrerie. Suddenly, between two discharges, the distant sound of a clock striking was heard.

"It is midday," said Combeferre.

The twelve strokes had not died out ere Enjolras drew himself up to his full height and hurled the loud cry from the top of the barricade, —

"Take up the paving-stones into the house, and line the windows with them. One half of you to the stones, the other half to the muskets. There is not a moment to lose."

A party of sappers, with their axes on their shoulders, had just appeared in battle-array at the end of the street. This could only be the head of a column; and of what column? Evidently the column of attack; for the sappers ordered to demolish the barricade always precede the troops appointed to escalade it. It was plain that the moment was at hand which M. Clermont Tonnerre called in 1822 "a strong pull."

Enjolras's order was carried out with that correct speed peculiar to ships and barricades, the only two battle-fields whence escape is impossible. In less than a minute two thirds of the paving-stones which Enjolras had ordered to be piled up against the door of Corinth were carried to the first-floor and attic, and before a second minute had passed these paving-stones, artistically laid on one another, walled up one half of the window. A few spaces carefully arranged by Feuilly, the chief constructor, allowed the gun-barrels to pass through. This armament of the windows was the more easily effected because the grape-shot had ceased. The two cannon were now firing solid shot at the centre of the barricade, in order to make a hole, and if possible a breach, for the assault. When the stones intended for the final assault were in their places, Enjolras carried to the first-floor the bottles he had placed under the table on which Mabœuf lay.

" Who will drink that ? " Bossuet asked him.

" They will," Enjolras answered.

Then the ground-floor window was also barricaded, and the iron bars which closed the door at night were held in readiness. The fortress was complete ; the barricade was the rampart, and the wine-shop the keep. With the paving-stones left over the gap was stopped up. As the defenders of a barricade are always obliged to save their ammunition, and the besiegers are aware of the fact, the latter combine their arrangements with a sort of irritating leisure, expose themselves before the time to the fire, though more apparently than in reality, and take their ease. The preparations for the attack are always made with a certain methodical slowness, and after that comes the thunder. This slowness enabled Enjolras to revise and render everything perfect. He felt that since such men were about to die, their death must be a masterpiece. He said to Marius, —

"We are the two chiefs. I am going to give the final orders inside, while you remain outside and watch."

Marius posted himself in observation on the crest of the barricade, while Enjolras had the door of the kitchen, which it will be remembered served as ambulance, nailed up.

"No splashing on the wounded," he said.

He gave his final instructions in the ground-floor room in a sharp but wonderfully calm voice, and Feuilly listened and answered in the name of all.

"At the first-floor hold axes ready to cut down the stairs. Have you them?"

"Yes," Feuilly answered.

"How many?"

"Two axes and a crowbar."

"Very good. In all, twenty-six fighting men left. How many guns are there?"

"Thirty-four."

"Eight too many. Keep those guns loaded like the others, and within reach. Place your sabres and pistols in your belts. Twenty men to the barricade. Six will ambush themselves in the garret and at the first-floor window, to fire on the assailants through the loop-holes in the paving-stones. There must not be an idle workman here. Presently, when the drummer sounds the charge, the twenty men below will rush to the barricade, and the first to arrive will be the best placed."

These arrangements made, he turned to Javert, and said to him, —

"I have not forgotten you."

And laying a pistol on the table he added, —

"The last man to leave here will blow out this spy's brains."

"Here?" a voice answered.

"No, let us not have this corpse near ours. It is easy to stride over the small barricade in Mondétour Lane, as it is only four feet high. This man is securely bound, so lead him there and execute him."

Some one was at this moment even more stoical than Enjolras; it was Javert. Here Jean Valjean appeared; he was mixed up with the group of insurgents, but stepped forward and said to Enjolras, —

"Are you the commander?"

"Yes."

"You thanked me just now."

"In the name of the Republic. The barricade has two saviors, — Marius Pontmercy and yourself."

"Do you think that I deserve a reward?"

"Certainly."

"Well, then, I ask one."

"What is it?"

"To let me blow out that man's brains myself."

Javert raised his head, saw Jean Valjean, gave an imperceptible start, and said, "It is fair."

As for Enjolras, he was reloading his gun. He looked around him.

"Is there no objection?"

And he turned to Jean Valjean.

"Take the spy."

Jean Valjean took possession of Javert by seating himself on the end of the table. He seized the pistol, and a faint clink showed that he had cocked it. Almost at the same moment the bugle-call was heard.

" Mind yourselves! " Marius shouted from the top of the barricade.

Javert began laughing that noiseless laugh peculiar to him, and, looking intently at the insurgents, said to them, —

" You are no healthier than I am."

" All outside," Enjolras cried.

The insurgents rushed tumultuously forth, and as they passed, Javert smote them on the back, so to speak, with the expression, " We shall meet again soon."

CHAPTER XIX.

JEAN VALJEAN REVENGES HIMSELF.

So soon as Jean Valjean was alone with Javert he undid the rope which fastened the prisoner round the waist, the knot of which was under the table. After this, he made him a signal to rise. Javert obeyed with that indefinable smile in which the supremacy of enchained authority is condensed. Jean Valjean seized Javert by the martingale, as he would have taken an ox by its halter, and dragging him after him, quitted the wine-shop slowly, for Javert, having his feet hobbled, could only take very short steps. Jean Valjean held the pistol in his hand, and they thus crossed the inner trapeze of the barricade; the insurgents, prepared for the imminent attack, turned their backs.

Marius alone, placed at the left extremity of the barricade, saw them pass. This group of the victim and the executioner was illumined by the sepulchral gleams which he had in his soul. Jean Valjean forced Javert to climb over the barricade with some difficulty, but did not loosen the cord. When they had crossed the bar, they found themselves alone in the lane, and no one could now see them, for the elbow formed by the houses hid them from the insurgents. The corpses removed from the barricade formed a horrible pile a few paces from them. Among the dead could be distinguished a livid face, dishevelled hair, a pierced hand, and a half-naked female bosom ; it was Éponine. Javert looked askance at this dead girl, and said with profound calmness, —

" It seems to me I know that girl."

Then he turned to Jean Valjean, who placed the pistol under his arm, and fixed on Javert a glance which had no need of words to say, " Javert, it is I."

Javert answered, " Take your revenge."

Jean Valjean took a knife from his pocket and opened it.

" A clasp-knife," Javert exclaimed. " You are right, that suits you better."

Jean Valjean cut the martingale which Javert had round his neck, then he cut the ropes on his wrists, and stooping down, those on his feet ; then rising again, he said, " You are free."

It was not easy to astonish Javert, still, master though he was of himself, he could not suppress his emotion ; he stood gaping and motionless, while Jean Valjean continued, —

" I do not believe that I shall leave this place. Still, if by accident I do, I live under the name of Fauchelevent, at No. 7, Rue de l'Homme Armé."

Javert gave a tigerish frown, which opened a corner of his mouth, and muttered between his teeth, —

" Take care ! "

" Begone ! " said Jean Valjean.

Javert added, —

"You said Fauchelevent, Rue de l'Homme Armé?"
"No. 7."

Javert repeated in a low voice, — "No. 7."

He rebuttoned his frock-coat, restored his military stiffness between his shoulders, made a half turn, crossed his arms while supporting his chin with one of his hands, and walked off in the direction of the markets. Jean Valjean looked after him. After going a few yards Javert turned and said, —

"You annoy me. I would sooner be killed by you."

Javert did not even notice that he no longer addressed Jean Valjean with familiarity.

"Begone!" said Jean Valjean.

Javert retired slowly, and a moment after turned the corner of the Rue des Prêcheurs. When Javert had disappeared, Jean Valjean discharged the pistol in the air, and then returned to the barricade, saying, —

"It is all over."

This is what had taken place in the mean while. Marius, more occupied with the outside than the inside, had not hitherto attentively regarded the spy fastened up at the darkened end of the ground-floor room. When he saw him in the open daylight bestriding the barricade, he recognized him, and a sudden hope entered his mind. He remembered the inspector of the Rue de Pontoise, and the two pistols he had given him, which he, Marius, had employed at this very barricade, and he not only remembered his face but his name.

This recollection, however, was foggy and dis-

turbed, like all his ideas.   It was not an affirmation
he made so much as a question which he asked himself.   "Is that not the Police Inspector, who told
me that his name was Javert?"   Marius shouted to
Enjolras, who had just stationed himself at the other
end of the barricade, —

"Enjolras?"

"Well?" ·

"What is that man's name?"

"Which man?"

"The police agent.   Do you know his name?"

"Of course I do, for he told it to us."

"What is it?"

"Javert."

Marius started, but at this moment a pistol-shot
was heard, and Jean Valjean reappeared, saying,
"It is all over."   A dark chill crossed Marius's
heart.

CHAPTER XX.

THE DEAD ARE RIGHT AND THE LIVING ARE NOT WRONG.

THE death-struggles of the barricade were about to begin, and everything added to the tragical majesty of this supreme moment, — a thousand mysterious sounds in the air, the breathing of armed masses set in motion in streets which could not be seen, the intermittent gallop of cavalry, the heavy rumor of artillery, the platoon firing and the cannonade crossing each other in the labyrinth of Paris, the smoke of the battle rising all golden above the roofs, distant and vaguely terrible cries, flashes of menace everywhere, the tocsin of St. Merry, which now had the sound of a sob, the mildness of the season, the splendor of the sky full of sunshine and clouds, the beauty of the day, and the fearful silence of the houses. For since the previous evening the two rows of houses in the Rue de la Chanvrerie had become two walls, — ferocious walls with closed doors, closed windows, and closed shutters.

At that day, so different from the present time, when the hour arrived in which the people wished to be done with a situation which had lasted too long, with a conceded charter or a restricted suffrage, when the universal wrath was diffused in the atmosphere, when the city consented to an upheaving of paving-stones, when the insurrection made the bourgeoisie smile by whispering its watchword in their ear, then the inhabitant, impregnated with riot, so to speak, was the auxiliary of the combatant, and the house fraternized with the improvised fortress which it supported. When the situation was not ripe, when the insurrection was not decidedly accepted, when the masses disavowed the movement, it was all over with the combatants, the town was changed into a desert round the revolt, minds were chilled, the asylums were walled up, and the street became converted into a defile to help the army in taking the barricade. A people cannot be forced to move faster than it wishes by a surprise, and woe to the man who tries to compel it ; a people will not put up with it, and then it abandons the insurrection to itself. The insurgents become lepers ; a house is an escarpment, a door is a refusal, and a façade is a wall. This wall sees, hears, and will not ; it might open and save you, but no, the wall is a judge, and it looks at you and condemns you. What gloomy things are these closed houses ! They seem dead though they are alive, and life, which is, as it were, suspended, clings to them. No one has come out for the last four-and-twenty hours, but no one is absent. In the interior of this rock people come and go, retire to bed and rise again ; they are in the bosom of their family, they eat and drink, and are afraid, terrible to say. Fear excuses this formidable inhospitality, and the alarm offers extenuating circumstances. At times even, and this has been wit-

nessed, the fear becomes a passion, and terror may
be changed into fury, and prudence into rage; hence
the profound remark, " The enraged moderates."
There are flashes of supreme terror, from which
passion issues like a mournful smoke. " What do
these people want ? They are never satisfied; they
compromise peaceable men. As if we had not had
revolutions of that nature ! What have they come to
do here ? Let them get out of it as they can. All
the worse for them, it is their fault, and they have
only what they deserve. That does not concern us.
Look at our poor street torn to pieces by cannon:
they are a heap of scamps; above all do not open
the door." And the house assumes the aspect of a
tomb: the insurgent dies a lingering death before
their door; he sees the grape-shot and naked sabres
arrive; if he cries out, he knows there are people
who hear him but will not help him; there are
walls which might protect him, and men who might
save him, and these walls have ears of flesh, and
these men have entrails of stone.

Whom should we accuse ? Nobody and everybody, — the imperfect times in which we live. It
is always at its own risk and peril that the Utopia
converts itself into an insurrection, and becomes an
armed protest instead of a philosophic protest, — a
Pallas and no longer a Minerva. The Utopia which
grows impatient and becomes a riot knows what
awaits it, and it nearly always arrives too soon. In
that case it resigns itself, and stoically accepts the
catastrophe in lieu of a triumph. It serves, without
complaining, and almost exculpating them, those who

deny it, and its magnanimity is to consent to aban-
donment. It is indomitable against obstacles, and
gentle toward ingratitude. Is it ingratitude after
all? Yes, from the human point of view; no, from
the individual point of view. Progress is the fashion
of man; the general life of the human race is called
progress; and the collective step of the human race
is also called progress. Progress marches; it makes
the great human and earthly journey toward the
celestial and divine; it has its halts where it rallies
the straying flock; it has its stations where it medi-
tates, in the presence of some splendid Canaan suddenly unveiling its horizon; it has its nights when
it sleeps; and it is one of the poignant anxieties
of the thinker to see the shadow on the human
soul, and to feel in the darkness sleeping progress,
without being able to awaken it.

"God is perhaps dead," Gérard de Nerval said
one day to the writer of these lines, confounding
progress with God, and taking the interruption of
the movement for the death of the Being. The man
who despairs is wrong: progress infallibly reawakens,
and we might say that it moves even when sleeping,
for it has grown. When we see it upright again
we find that it is taller. To be ever peaceful depends no more on progress than on the river; do
not raise a bar, or throw in a rock, for the obstacle
makes the water foam, and humanity boil. Hence
come troubles; but after these troubles we notice
that way has been made. Until order, which is
nought else than universal peace, is established, until
harmony and unity reign, progress will have revo-

lutions for its halting-places. What, then, is progress? We have just said, the permanent life of the peoples. Now, it happens at times that the momentary life of individuals offers a resistance to the eternal life of the human race.

Let us avow without bitterness that the individual has his distinct interest, and can without felony stipulate for that interest and defend it ; the present has its excusable amount of egotism, momentary right has its claims, and cannot be expected to sacrifice itself incessantly to the future. The generation which at the present moment is passing over the earth is not forced to abridge it for the generations, its equals, after all, whose turn will come at a later date. "I exist," murmurs that some one, who is everybody. "I am young and in love, I am old and wish to rest, I am father of a family, I work, I prosper, I do a good business, I have houses to let, I have money in the funds, I am happy, I have wife and children, I like all that, I wish to live, and so leave us at peace." Hence at certain hours a profound coldness falls on the magnanimous vanguard of the human race. Utopia, moreover, we confess it, emerges from its radiant sphere in waging war. It, the truth of to-morrow, borrows its process, battle, from the falsehood of yesterday. It, the future, acts like the past ; it, the pure idea, becomes an assault. It complicates its heroism with a violence for which it is but fair that it should answer, — a violence of opportunity and expediency, contrary to principles, and for which it is fatally punished. The Utopia, when in a state of insurrection, combats with the old military code in its hand ; it shoots spies, executes traitors, suppresses living beings and hurls them into unknown darkness. It makes use of death, a serious thing. It seems that the Utopia no longer puts faith in the radiance, which is its irresistible and incorruptible strength. It strikes with the sword, but no sword is simple ; every sword has two edges, and the man who wounds with one wounds himself with the other.

This reservation made, and made with all severity, it is impossible for us not to admire, whether they succeed or no, the glorious combatants of the future, the confessors of the Utopia. Even when they fail they are venerable, and it is perhaps in ill-success that they possess most majesty. Victory, when in accordance with progress, deserves the applause of the peoples, but an heroic defeat merits their tenderness. The one is magnificent, the other sublime. With us who prefer martyrdom to success, John Brown is greater than Washington, and Pisacane greater than Garibaldi. There should be somebody to take the part of the conquered, and people are unjust to these great assayers of the future when they fail. Revolutionists are accused of sowing terror, and every barricade appears an attack. Their theory is incriminated, their object is suspected, their after-thought is apprehended, and their conscience is denounced. They are reproached with elevating and erecting against the reigning social fact a pile of miseries, griefs, iniquities, and despair, and with pulling down in order to barricade themselves behind the ruins and combat. People shout to them, " You are

unpaving hell!" And they might answer, "That is
the reason why our barricade is made of good intentions." The best thing is certainly the pacific solution; after all, let us allow, when people see the
pavement, they think of the bear, and it is a good
will by which society is alarmed. But it depends on
society to save itself, and we appeal to its own good-
will. No violent remedy is necessary : study the evil
amicably, and then cure it, — that is all we desire.

However this may be, those men, even when they
have fallen, and especially then, are august, who at
all points of the universe, with their eyes fixed on
France, are struggling for the great work with the
inflexible logic of the ideal ; they give their life as a
pure gift for progress, they accomplish the will of
Providence, and perform a religious act. At the appointed hour, with as much disinterestedness as an
actor who takes up his cue, they enter the tomb in
obedience to the divine scenario, and they accept this
hopeless combat and this stoical disappearance in
order to lead to its splendid and superior universal
consequences. The magnificent human movement
irresistibly began on July 14. These soldiers are
priests, and the French revolution is a gesture of God.
Moreover, there are — and it is proper to add this
distinction to the distinctions already indicated in
another chapter, — there are accepted insurrections
which are called revolutions ; and there are rejected
revolutions which are called riots. An insurrection
which breaks out is an idea which passes its examination in the presence of the people. If the people drops its blackball, the idea is dry fruit, and the

insurrection is a street-riot. Waging war at every appeal and each time that the Utopia desires it is not the fact of the peoples; for nations have not always, and at all hours, the temperament of heroes and martyrs. They are positive; *a priori* insurrection is repulsive to them, in the first place, because it frequently has a catastrophe for result, and, secondly, because it always has an abstraction as its starting-point.

For, and this is a grand fact, those who devote themselves do so for the ideal, and the ideal alone. An insurrection is an enthusiasm, and enthusiasm may become a fury, whence comes an upraising of muskets. But every insurrection which aims at a government or a régime aims higher. Hence, for instance, we will dwell on the fact that what the chiefs of the insurrection of 1832, and especially the young enthusiasts of the Rue de la Chanvrerie, combated was not precisely Louis Philippe. The majority, speaking candidly, did justice to the qualities of this king who stood between monarchy and revolution, and not one of them hated him. But they attacked the younger branch of the right divine in Louis Philippe, as they had attacked the elder branch in Charles X., and what they wished to overthrow in overthrowing the Monarchy in France was, as we have explained, the usurpation of man over man, and the privilege opposing right throughout the universe. Paris without a king has as its counterstroke the world without despots. They reasoned in this way. Their object was far off without doubt, vague perhaps, and retreating before the effort, but grand.

So it is. And men sacrifice themselves for these visions, which are for the sacrificed nearly always illusions, but illusions with which the whole of human certainty is mingled. The insurgent poetizes and gilds the insurrection, and men hurl themselves into these tragical things, intoxicating themselves upon what they are about to do. Who knows? Perhaps they will succeed; they are the minority; they have against them an entire army; but they are defending the right, natural law, the sovereignty of each over himself, which allows of no possible abdication, justice, and truth, and, if necessary, they die like the three hundred Spartans. They do not think of Don Quixote, but of Leonidas, and they go onward, and once the battle has begun they do not recoil, but dash forward head downwards, having for hope an extraordinary victory, the revolution completed, progress restored to liberty, the aggrandizement of the human race, universal deliverance, and at the worst a Thermopylæ. These combats for progress frequently fail, and we have explained the cause. The mob is restive against the impulse of the Paladins ; the heavy masses, the multitudes, fragile on account of their very heaviness, fear adventures, and there is adventure in the ideal. Moreover, it must not be forgotten that these are interests which are no great friends of the ideal and the sentimental. Sometimes the stomach paralyzes the heart. The greatness and beauty of France are, that she does not grow so stout as other nations, and knots the rope round her hips with greater facility. She is the first to wake and the last to fall asleep; she goes onward. She is seeking.

The reason of this is because she is artistic. The ideal is nought else than the culminating point of logic, in the same way as the beautiful is only the summit of the true. Artistic peoples are also consistent peoples; loving beauty is to see light. The result of this is, that the torch of Europe, that is to say of civilization, was first borne by Greece, who passed it to Italy, who passed it to France. Divine enlightening nations! *Vitæ lampada tradunt.* It is an admirable thing that the poetry of a people is the element of its progress, and the amount of civilization is measured by the amount of imagination. Still, a civilizing people must remain masculine; Corinth yes, but Sybaris no, for the man who grows effeminate is bastardized. A man must be neither dilettante nor virtuoso, but he should be artistic. In the matter of civilization, there must not be refinement, but sublimation, and on that condition the pattern of the ideal is given to the human race. The modern ideal has its type in art and its means in science. It is by science that the august vision of the poet, the social beauty, will be realized, and Eden will be remade by A + B. At the point which civilization has reached exactitude is a necessary element of the splendid, and the artistic feeling is not only served but completed by the scientific organ; the dream must calculate. Art, which is the conqueror, ought to have science, which is the mover, as its base. The strength of the steed is an important factor, and the modern mind is the genius of

Greece, having for vehicle the genius of India, —
Alexander mounted on an elephant. Races petrified
in dogma or demoralized by time are unsuited to
act as guides to civilization. Genuflection before
the idol or the crown-piece ruins the muscle which
moves and the will that goes. Hieratic or mercan-
tile absorption reduces the radiance of a people,
lowers its horizon by lowering its level, and with-
draws from it that both human and divine intel-
ligence of the universal object which renders
nations missionaries. Babylon has no ideal, nor
has Carthage while Athens and Rome have, and
retain, even through all the nocturnal density of
ages, a halo of civilization.

France is of the same quality, as a people, as
Greece and Rome; she is Athenian through the
beautiful, and Roman through her grandeur. Besides, she is good, and is more often than other
nations in the humor for devotion and sacrifice.
Still, this humor takes her and leaves her; and this is
the great danger for those who run when she merely
wishes to walk, or who walk when she wishes to
halt. France has her relapses into materialism, and
at seasons the ideas which obstruct this sublime
brain have nothing that recalls French grandeur, and
are of the dimensions of a Missouri or a South
Carolina. What is to be done? The giantess plays
the dwarf, and immense France feels a fancy for
littleness. That is all. To this nothing can be said,
for peoples like planets have the right to be eclipsed.
And that is well, provided that light return and the
eclipse does not degenerate into night. Dawn and

resurrection are synonymous, and the reappearance of light is synonymous with the existence of the Ego. Let us state these facts calmly. Death on a barricade, or a tomb in exile, is an acceptable occasion for devotion, for the real name of devotion is disinterestedness. Let the abandoned be abandoned, let the exiles be exiled, and let us confine ourselves to imploring great nations not to recoil too far when they do recoil. Under the pretext of returning to reason, it is not necessary to go too far down the incline. Matter exists, the moment exists, interests exist, the stomach exists, but the stomach must not be the sole wisdom. Momentary life has its rights, we admit, but permanent life has them also. Alas! To have mounted does not prevent falling, and we see this in history more frequently than we wish; a nation is illustrious, it tastes of the ideal, then it bites into the mud and finds it good, and when we ask it why it abandons Socrates for Falstaff, it replies, " Because I like statesmen."

One word before returning to the barricade. A battle like the one which we are describing at this moment is only a convulsion toward the ideal. Impeded progress is sickly, and has such tragic attacks of epilepsy. This malady of progress, civil war, we have met as we passed along, and it is one of the social phases, at once an act and an interlude of that drama whose pivot is a social condemnation, and whose veritable title is " Progress." Progress! This cry, which we raise so frequently, is our entire thought, and at the point of our drama which we have reached, as the idea which it contains has still more than one trial to undergo, we may be permitted, even if we do not raise the veil, to let its gleams pierce through clearly. The book which the reader has before him at this moment is, from one end to the other, in its entirety and its details, whatever the intermittences, exceptions, and short-comings may be, the progress from evil to good, from injustice to justice, from falsehood to truth, from night to day, from appetite to conscience, from corruption to life, from bestiality to duty, from hell to heaven, and from nothingness to God. The starting-point is matter, the terminus the soul ; the hydra at the commencement, the angel at the end.

CHAPTER XXI.

THE HEROES.

SUDDENLY the drum beat the charge, and the attack was a hurricane. On the previous evening the barricade had been silently approached in the darkness as by a boa; but at present, in broad daylight, within this gutted street, surprise was impossible; besides, the armed force was unmasked, the cannon had begun the roaring, and the troops rushed upon the barricade. Fury was now skill. A powerful column of line infantry, intersected at regular intervals by National Guards and dismounted Municipal Guards, and supported by heavy masses that could be heard if not seen, debouched into the street at a running step, with drums beating, bugles braying, bayonets levelled, and sappers in front, and imperturbable under the shower of projectiles dashed straight at the barricade with all the weight of a bronze battering-ram. But the wall held out firmly, and the insurgents fired impetuously; the escaladed barricade displayed a flashing mane. The attack was so violent that it was in a moment inundated by assailants; but it shook off the soldiers as the lion does the dogs, and it was only covered with besiegers as the cliff is with foam, to reappear a minute later scarped, black, and formidable.

The columns, compelled to fall back, remained massed in the street, exposed but terrible, and answered the redoubt by a tremendous musketry-fire. Any one who has seen fireworks will remember the piece composed of a cross-fire of lightnings, which is called a bouquet. Imagine this bouquet, no longer vertical but horizontal, and bearing at the end of each jet a bullet, slugs, or iron balls, and scattering death. The barricade was beneath it. On either side was equal resolution. The bravery was almost barbarous, and was complicated by a species of heroic ferocity which began with self-sacrifice. It was the epoch when a National Guard fought like a Zouave. The troops desired an end, and the insurrection wished to wrestle. The acceptance of death in the height of youth and health converts intrepidity into a frenzy, and each man in this action had the grandeur of the last hour. The street was covered with corpses. The barricade had Marius at one of its ends and Enjolras at the other. Enjolras, who carried the whole barricade in his head, reserved and concealed himself. Three soldiers fell under his loop-hole without even seeing him, while Marius displayed himself openly, and made himself a mark. More than once half his body rose above the barricade. There is no more violent prodigal than a miser who takes the bit between his teeth, and no man more startling in action than a dreamer. Marius was formidable and pensive, and in the battle was like a dream. He looked like a ghost firing. The cartridges of the besieged were exhausted, but not their sarcasms; and they laughed in the tornado of the tomb in which they stood. Courfeyrac was bareheaded.

"What have you done with your hat?" Bossuet asked him; and Courfeyrac answered, —

"They carried it away at last with cannon-balls."

Or else they made haughty remarks.

"Can you understand," Feuilly exclaimed bitterly, "those men," — and he mentioned names, well-known and even celebrated names that belonged to the old army, — "who promised to join us and pledged their honor to aid us, and who are generals, and abandon us?"

And Combeferre restricted himself to replying with a grave smile, —

"They are people who observe the rules of honor as they do the stars, — a long distance off."

The interior of the barricade was so sown with torn cartridges that it seemed as if there had been a snow-storm. The assailants had the numbers and the insurgents the position. They were behind a wall, and crushed at point-blank range the soldiers who were stumbling over the dead and wounded. This barricade, built as it was, and admirably strengthened, was really one of those situations in which a handful of men holds a legion in check. Still, constantly recruited and growing beneath the shower of bullets, the column of attack inexorably approached, and little by little, step by step, but with certainty, the army squeezed the barricade as the screw does the press.

The assaults succeeded each other, and the horror became constantly greater. Then there broke out on

this pile of paving-stones, in this Rue de la Chanvrerie, a struggle worthy of the wall of Troy. These
sallow, ragged, and exhausted men, who had not
eaten for four-and-twenty hours, who had not slept,
who had only a few rounds more to fire, who felt
their empty pockets for cartridges, — these men, nearly
all wounded, with head or arm bound round with a
blood-stained blackish rag, having holes in their coat
from which the blood flowed, scarce armed with bad
guns and old rusty sabres, became Titans. The barricade was ten times approached, assaulted, escaladed,
and never captured. To form an idea of the contest
it would be necessary to imagine a heap of terrible
courages set on fire, and that you are watching the
flames. It was not a combat, but the interior of a
furnace ; mouths breathed flames there, and the faces
were extraordinary. The human form seemed impossible there, the combatants flashed, and it was a
formidable sight to see these salamanders of the
mêlée flitting about in this red smoke. The successive and simultaneous scenes of this butchery are beyond our power to depict, for the epic alone has the
right to fill twelve thousand verses with a battle.
It might have been called that Inferno of Brahmin-
ism, the most formidable of the seventeen abysses,
which the Veda calls the Forest of Swords. They
fought foot to foot, body to body, with pistol-shots,
sabre-cuts, and fists, close by, at a distance, above,
below, on all sides, from the roof of the house, from
the wine-shop, and even from the traps of the cellars
into which some had slipped. The odds were sixty
to one, and the frontage of Corinth half demolished

was hideous. The window, pock-marked with grape-shot, had lost glass and frame, and was only a shape-less hole tumultuously stopped up with paving-stones. Bossuet was killed, Feuilly was killed, Courfeyrac was killed, Joly was killed. Combeferre, traversed by three bayonet stabs in the breast at the moment when he was raising a wounded soldier, had only time to look up to heaven, and expired. Marius, still fighting, had received so many wounds, especially in the head, that his face disappeared in blood and looked as if it were covered by a red handkerchief. Enjolras alone was not wounded ; when he had no weapon he held out his arm to the right or left, and an insurgent placed some instrument in his hand. He had only four broken sword-blades left, — one more than Francis I. had at Marignano.

Homer says : " Diomed slew Axylus, the son of Teuthras, who dwelt in well-built Arisba ; Euryalus, son of Mecisteus, slew Dresus and Opheltius, Æsepus and Pedasus, whom the Naiad Abarbarea brought forth to blameless Bucolion ; Ulysses killed Percosian Pidytes ; Antilochus, Ablerus ; Polypœtes, Astyalus ; Polydamas, Otus of Cyllene ; and Teucer, Aretaus. Meganthius fell by the spear of Euripilus ; Agamem-non, king of heroes, struck down Elatus, born in the lofty walled town which the sounding river Satniois washes."

In our old poems of the Gesta, Esplandian attacks with a flaming falchion Swantibore, the giant mar-quis, who defends himself by storming the knight with towers which he uproots. Our old mural fres-cos show us the two Dukes of Brittany and Bourbon armed for war and mounted, and approaching each other, axe in hand, masked with steel, shod with steel, gloved with steel, one caparisoned with ermine and the other draped in azure; Brittany with his lion between the two horns of his crown, and Bourbon with an enormous *fleur-de-lys* at his visor. But in order to be superb it is not necessary to wear, like Yvon, the ducal morion, or to have in one hand a living flame like Esplandian; it is sufficient to lay down one's life for a conviction or a loyal deed. This little simple soldier, yesterday a peasant of Bearne or the Limousin, who prowls about, cabbage-cutter by his side, round the nursemaids in the Luxembourg, this young, pale student bowed over an anatomical study or book, a fair-haired boy who shaves himself with a pair of scissors, — take them both, breathe duty into them, put them face to face in the Carrefour Boucherat or the Planche Mibray blind alley, and let one fight for his flag and the other combat for his ideal, and let them both imagine that they are contending for their country, and the struggle will be colossal; and the shadow cast by these two contending lads on the great epic field where humanity is struggling will be equal to that thrown by Megarion, King of Lycia, abounding in tigers, as he wrestles with the immense Ajax, the equal of the gods.

CHAPTER XXII.

STEP BY STEP.

WHEN there were no chiefs left but Enjolras and
Marius at the two ends of the barricade, the centre,
which had so long been supported by Courfeyrac,
Bossuet, Joly, Feuilly, and Combeferre, yielded.
The cannon, without making a practicable breach,
had severely injured the centre of the redoubt, then
the crest of the wall had disappeared under the balls
and fallen down, and the fragments which had collected both inside and out had in the end formed two
slopes, the outer one of which offered an inclined
plane by which to attack. A final assault was attempted thus, and this assault was successful; the
bristling mass of bayonets, hurled forward at a run,
came up irresistibly, and the dense line of the attacking column appeared in the smoke on the top of the
scarp. This time it was all over, and the band of
insurgents defending the centre recoiled pell-mell.

Then the gloomy love of life was rekindled in
some; covered by this forest of muskets, several did
not wish to die. It is the moment when the spirit of
self-preservation utters yells, and when the beast
reappears in man. They were drawn up against the
six-storied house at the back of the barricade, and

this house might be their salvation. This house was barricaded, as it were walled up from top to bottom, but before the troops reached the interior of the redoubt, a door would have time to open and shut, and it would be life for these desperate men; for at the back of this house were streets, possible flight, and space. They began kicking and knocking at the door, while calling, crying, imploring, and clasping their hands. But no one opened. The dead head looked down on them from the third-floor window. But Marius and Enjolras, and seven or eight men who rallied round them, had rushed forward to protect them. Enjolras shouted to the soldiers, " Do not advance," and as an officer declined to obey he killed the officer. He was in the inner yard of the redoubt, close to Corinth, with his sword in one hand and carbine in the other, holding open the door of the wine-shop, which he barred against the assailants. He shouted to the desperate men, " There is only one door open, and it is this one; " and covering them with his person, and alone facing a battalion, he made them pass behind him. All rushed in, and Enjolras, whirling his musket round his head, drove back the bayonets and entered the last, and there was a frightful moment, during which the troops tried to enter and the insurgents to bar the door. The latter was closed with such violence that the five fingers of a soldier who had caught hold of a doorpost were cut off clean, and remained in the crevice. Marius remained outside; a bullet broke his collar-bone, and he felt himself fainting and falling. At this moment, when his eyes were already closed, he felt the shock of a powerful hand seizing him, and his fainting-fit scarce left him time for this thought, blended with the supreme recollection of Cosette, " I am made prisoner and shall be shot."

Enjolras, not seeing Marius among those who had sought shelter in the house, had the same idea, but they had reached that moment when each could only think of his own death. Enjolras put the bar on the door, bolted and locked it, while the soldiers beat it with musket-butts, and the sappers attacked it with their axes outside. The assailants were grouped round this door, and the siege of the wine-shop now began. The soldiers, let us add, were full of fury ; the death of the sergeant of artillery had irritated them, and then, more mournful still, during the few hours that preceded the attack a whisper ran along the ranks that the insurgents were mutilating their prisoners, and that there was the headless body of a soldier in the cellar. This species of fatal rumor is the general accompaniment of civil wars, and it was a false report of the same nature which at a later date produced the catastrophe of the Rue Trans-nonain. When the door was secured, Enjolras said to the others, —

" Let us sell our lives dearly."

Then he went up to the table on which Mabœuf and Gavroche were lying ; under the black cloth two forms could be seen straight and livid, one tall, the other short, and the two faces were vaguely designed under the cold folds of the winding-sheet. A hand emerged from under it, and hung toward the ground ; it was that of the old man. Enjolras bent down and kissed this venerable hand, in the same way as he had done the forehead on the previous evening. They were the only two kisses he had ever given in his life.

Let us abridge. The barricade had resisted like a gate of Thebes, and the wine-shop resisted like a house of Saragossa. Such resistances are violent, and there is no quarter, and a flag of truce is impossible ; people are willing to die provided that they can kill. When Suchet says "capitulate," Palafox answers, "After the war with cannon, the war with the knife." Nothing was wanting in the attack on the Hucheloup wine-shop : neither paving-stone showering from the window and roof on the assailants, and exasperating the troops by the frightful damage they committed, nor shots from the attics and cellar, nor the fury of the attack, nor the rage of the defence, nor, finally, when the door gave way, the frenzied mania of extermination. When the assailants rushed into the wine-shop, their feet entangled in the panels of the broken door which lay on the ground, they did not find a single combatant. The winding staircase, cut away with axes, lay in the middle of the ground-floor room, a few wounded men were on the point of dying, all who were not killed were on the first-floor, and a terrific fire was discharged thence through the hole in the ceiling which had been the entrance to the restaurant. These were the last cartridges, and when they were expended and nobody had any powder or balls left, each man took up two of the bottles reserved by Enjolras, and defended the stairs with these frightfully fragile weapons. They were bottles of aquafortis. We describe the gloomy things of carnage exactly as they are : the besieged, alas ! makes a weapon of everything. Greek fire did not dishonor Archimedes, boiling pitch did not dishonor Bayard ; every war is a horror, and there is no choice. The musketry-fire of the assailants, though impeded and discharged from below, was murderous ; and the brink of the hole was soon lined with dead heads, whence dripped long red and steaming jets. The noise was indescribable, and a compressed burning smoke almost threw night over the combat. Words fail to describe horror when it has reached this stage. There were no longer men in this now infernal struggle, no longer giants contending against Titans. It resembled Milton and Dante more than Homer, for demons attacked and spectres resisted. It was a monster heroism.

CHAPTER XXIII.

ORESTES SOBER AND PYLADES DRUNK.

At length, by employing the skeleton of the stair-case, by climbing up the walls, clinging to the ceiling, and killing on the very edge of the trap the last who resisted, some twenty assailants, soldiers, National and Municipal Guards, mostly disfigured by wounds in the face received in this formidable ascent, blinded by blood, furious and savage, burst into the first-floor room. There was only one man standing there, — Enjolras; without cartridges or sword, he only held in his hand the barrel of his carbine, whose butt he had broken on the heads of those who entered. He had placed the billiard-table between himself and his assailants, he had fallen back to the end of the room, and there, with flashing eye and head erect, holding the piece of a weapon in his hand, he was still suffi-ciently alarming for a space to be formed round him. A cry was raised, —

"It is the chief; it was he who killed the artillery-man; as he has placed himself there, we will let him remain there. Shoot him on the spot!"

"Shoot me!" Enjolras said.

And throwing away his weapon and folding his arms, he offered his chest. The boldness of dying bravely always moves men. So soon as Enjolras folded his arms, accepting the end, the din of the struggle ceased in the room, and the chaos was suddenly appeased in a species of sepulchral solemnity. It seemed as if the menacing majesty of Enjolras, disarmed and motionless, produced an effect on the tumult, and that merely by the authority of his tranquil glance, this young man, who alone was unwounded, superb, blood-stained, charming, and indifferent like one invulnerable, constrained this sinister mob to kill him respectfully. His beauty, heightened at this moment by his haughtiness, was dazzling, and as if he could be no more fatigued than wounded after the frightful four-and-twenty hours which had elapsed, he was fresh and rosy. It was to him that the witness referred when he said at a later date before the court-martial, "There was an insurgent whom I heard called Apollo." A National Guard who aimed at Enjolras lowered his musket, saying, "I feel as if I were going to kill a flower." Twelve men formed into a platoon in the corner opposite to the one in which Enjolras stood, and got their muskets ready in silence. Then a sergeant shouted, "Present!"

An officer interposed.

"Wait a minute."

And, addressing Enjolras, —

"Do you wish to have your eyes bandaged?"

"No."

"It was really you who killed the sergeant of artillery?"

"Yes."

Grantaire had been awake for some minutes past. Grantaire, it will be remembered, had been sleeping since the past evening in the upper room, with his head lying on a table. He realized in all its energy the old metaphor, dead drunk. The hideous philter of absinthe, stout, and alcohol, had thrown him into a lethargic state, and, as his table was small, and of no use at the barricade, they had left it him. He was still in the same posture, with his chest upon the table, his head reeling on his arms, and surrounded by glasses and bottles. He was sleeping the deadly sleep of the hibernating bear or the filled leech. Nothing had roused him, — neither the platoon fire, nor the cannon-balls, nor the canister which penetrated through the window into the room where he was, nor the prodigious noise of the assault. Still, he at times responded to the cannon by a snore. He seemed to be waiting for a bullet to save him the trouble of waking; several corpses lay around him, and at the first glance nothing distinguished him from these deep sleepers of death.

Noise does not wake a drunkard, but silence arouses him, and this peculiarity has been more than once observed. The fall of anything near him increased Grantaire's lethargy, and noise lulled him. The species of halt which the tumult made before Enjolras was a shock for this heavy sleep. It is the effect of a galloping coach which stops short. Grantaire started up, stretched out his arms, rubbed his eyes, looked, yawned, and understood. Intoxication wearing off resembles a curtain that is rent, and a man sees at once, and at a single glance, all that it concealed. Everything presents itself suddenly to the memory, and the drunkard, who knows nothing of what has happened during the last twenty-four hours, has scarce opened his eyes ere he understands it all. Ideas return with a sudden lucidity ; the species of suds that blinded the brain is dispersed, and makes way for a clear and distinctive apprehension of the reality.

Concealed, as he was, in a corner, and sheltered, so to speak, by the billiard-table, the soldiers, who had their eyes fixed on Enjolras, had not even perceived Grantaire, and the sergeant was preparing to repeat the order to fire, when all at once they heard a powerful voice crying at their side, —

"Long live the Republic ! I belong to it."

Grantaire had risen ; and the immense gleam of all the combat which he had missed appeared in the flashing glance of the transfigured drunkard. He repeated, "Long live the Republic !" crossed the room with a firm step, and placed himself before the muskets by Enjolras's side.

"Kill us both at once," he said.

And turning gently to Enjolras, he asked him, —

"Do you permit it ? "

Enjolras pressed his hand with a smile, and this smile had not passed away ere the detonation took place. Enjolras, pierced by eight bullets, remained leaning against the wall as if nailed to it ; he merely hung his head. Grantaire was lying stark dead at his feet. A few minutes later the soldiers dislodged the last insurgents who had taken refuge at the top of the house, and were firing through a partition

in the garret. They fought desperately, and threw
bodies out of windows, some still alive. Two vol-
tigeurs, who were trying to raise the smashed omnibus, were killed by two shots from the attics; a
man in a blouse rushed out of them, with a bayonet
thrust in his stomach, and lay on the ground expiring.
A private and insurgent slipped together down the
tiles of the roof, and as they would not loosen their
hold fell into the street, holding each other in a
ferocious embrace. There was a similar struggle in
the cellar, — cries, shots, and a fierce clashing, — then
a silence. The barricade was captured, and the
soldiers began searching the adjacent houses and
pursuing the fugitives.

CHAPTER XXIV.

PRISONER !

MARIUS was really a prisoner; — prisoner to Jean Valjean.

The hand which had clutched him behind at the moment when he was falling, and of which he felt the pressure as he lost his senses, was that of Jean Valjean.

Jean Valjean had taken no other part in the struggle than that of exposing himself. Had it not been for him, in the supreme moment of agony no one would have thought of the wounded. Thanks to him, who was everywhere present in the carnage like a Providence, those who fell were picked up, carried to the ground-floor room, and had their wounds dressed, and in the intervals he repaired the barricade. But nothing that could resemble a blow, an attack, or even personal defence, could be seen with him, and he kept quiet and succored. However, he had only a few scratches, and the bullets had no billet for him. If suicide formed part of what he dreamed of when he came to this sepulchre, he had not been successful ; but we doubt whether he thought of suicide, which is an irreligious act. Jean Valjean did not appear to see Marius in the thick of the combat; but in truth he did not take his eyes off him. When a bullet laid Marius low, Jean Valjean leaped upon him with the agility of a tiger, dashed upon him as on a prey, and carried him off.

The whirlwind of the attack was at this moment so violently concentrated on Enjolras and the door of the wine-shop, that no one saw Jean Valjean, supporting the fainting Marius in his arms, cross the unpaved ground of the barricade and disappear round the corner of Corinth. Our readers will remember this corner, which formed a sort of cape in the street, and protected a few square feet of ground from bullets and grape-shot, and from glances as well. There is thus at times in fires a room which does not burn, and in the most raging seas, beyond a promontory, or at the end of a reef, a little quiet nook. It was in this corner of the inner trapeze of the barricade that Éponine drew her last breath. Here Jean Valjean stopped, let Marius slip to the ground, leaned against a wall, and looked around him.

The situation was frightful; for the instant, for two or three minutes perhaps, this piece of wall was a shelter, but how to get out of this massacre? He recalled the agony he had felt in the Rue Polonceau, eight years previously, and in what way he had succeeded in escaping; it was difficult then, but now it was impossible. He had in front of him that implacable and silent six-storied house, which only seemed inhabited by the dead man leaning out of his window; he had on his right the low barricade which closed the Petite Truanderie; to climb over this obstacle appeared easy, but a row of bayonet-points could be seen over the crest of the barricade ; they were line troops posted beyond the barricade and on the watch. It was evident that crossing the barricade was seeking a platoon fire, and that any head which appeared above the wall of paving-stones would serve as a mark for sixty muskets. He had on his left the battle-field, and death was behind the corner of the wall.

What was he to do ? A bird alone could have escaped from this place. And he must decide at once, find an expedient, and make up his mind. They were fighting a few paces from him, but fortunately all were obstinately engaged at one point, the wine-shop door ; but if a single soldier had the idea of turning the house or attacking it on the flank all would be over. Jean Valjean looked at the house opposite to him, he looked at the barricade by his side, and then looked on the ground, with the violence of supreme extremity, wildly, and as if he would have liked to dig a hole with his eyes. By much looking, something vaguely discernible in such an agony became perceptible, and assumed a shape at his feet, as if the eyes had the power to produce the thing demanded. He perceived a few paces from him, at the foot of the small barricade so pitilessly guarded and watched from without, and beneath a pile of paving-stones which almost concealed it, an iron grating, laid flat and flush with the ground. This grating made of strong cross-bars was about two feet square, and the framework of paving-stones which supported it had been torn out, and it was as it were dismounted. Through the bars a glimpse could be caught of an obscure opening, something like a chimney-pot or the cylinder of a cistern. Jean Valjean dashed up, and his old skill in escapes rose to his brain like a beam of light. To remove the paving-stones, tear up the grating, take Marius, who was inert as a dead body, on his shoulders, descend with this burden on his loins, helping himself with his elbows and knees, into this sort of well which was fortunately of no great depth, to let the grating fall again over his head, to set foot on a paved surface, about ten feet below the earth, — all this was executed like something done in delirium, with a giant's strength and the rapidity of an eagle : this occupied but a few minutes. Jean Valjean found himself with the still fainting Marius in a sort of long subterranean corridor, where there was profound peace, absolute silence, and night. The impression which he had formerly felt in falling out of the street into the convent recurred to him ; still, what he now carried was not Cosette, but Marius.

He had scarce heard above his head like a vague murmur the formidable tumult of the wine-shop being taken by assault.

BOOK II.

THE INTESTINE OF LEVIATHAN.

CHAPTER I.

THE EARTH IMPOVERISHED BY THE SEA.

PARIS casts twenty-five millions of francs annually into the sea; and we assert this without any metaphor. How so, and in what way? By day and night. For what object? For no object. With what thought? Without thinking. What to do? Nothing. By means of what organ? Its intestines. What are its intestines? Its sewers. Twenty-five millions are the most moderate of the approximative amounts given by the estimates of modern science. Science, after groping for a long time, knows now that the most fertilizing and effective of manures is human manure. The Chinese, let us say it to our shame, knew this before we did; not a Chinese peasant — it is Eckeberg who states the fact — who goes to the city, but brings at either end of his bamboo a bucket full of what we call filth. Thanks to the human manure, the soil in China is still as youthful as in the days of Abraham, and Chinese wheat yields just one hundred and twenty fold the sowing. There is no guano comparable in fertility to the detritus of a capital, and a large city is the strongest of stercoraries. To employ the town in manuring the plain would be certain success; for if gold be dung, on the other hand our dung is gold.

What is done with this golden dung? It is swept into the gulf. We send at a great expense fleets of ships to collect at the southern pole the guano of petrels and penguins, and cast into the sea the incalculable element of wealth which we have under our hand. All the human and animal manure which the world loses, if returned to the land instead of being thrown into the sea, would suffice to nourish the world. Do you know what those piles of ordure are, collected at the corners of streets, those carts of mud carried off at night from the streets, the frightful barrels of the night-man, and the fetid streams of subterranean mud which the pavement conceals from you? All this is a flowering field, it is green grass, it is mint and thyme and sage, it is game, it is cattle, it is the satisfied lowing of heavy kine at night, it is perfumed hay, it is gilded wheat, it is bread on your table, it is warm blood in your veins, it is health, it is joy, it is life. So desires that mysterious creation, which is transformation on earth and transfiguration in heaven; restore this to the great crucible, and your abundance will issue from it, for the nutrition of the plains produces the nourishment of men. You are at liberty to lose this wealth and consider me ridiculous into the bargain; it would be the masterpiece of your ignorance. Statistics have calculated that France alone pours every year into the Atlantic a sum of half a milliard. Note this; with these five hundred millions one quarter of the expenses of the budget would be paid. The cleverness of man is so great that he prefers to get rid of these five hundred millions in the gutter. The very substance of the people is borne away, here drop by drop, and there in streams, by the wretched vomiting of our sewers into the rivers, and the gigantic vomiting of our rivers into the ocean. Each eructation of our cloacas costs us one thousand francs, and this has two results, — the earth impoverished and the water poisoned; hunger issuing from the furrow and illness from the river. It is notorious that at this very hour the Thames poisons London; and as regards Paris, it has been found necessary to remove most of the mouths of the sewers down the river below the last bridge.

A double tubular apparatus supplied with valves and flood-gates, a system of elementary drainage as simple as the human lungs, and which is already in full work in several English parishes, would suffice to bring into our towns the pure water of the fields and send to the fields the rich water of the towns; and this easy ebb and flow, the most simple in the world, would retain among us the five hundred millions thrown away. But people are thinking of other things. The present process does mischief while meaning well. The intention is good, but the result is sorrowful; they believe they are draining the city, while they are destroying the population. A sewer is a misunderstanding; and when drainage, with its double functions, restoring what it takes, is

everywhere substituted for the sewer, that simple
and impoverishing washing, and is also combined
with the data of a new social economy, the produce
of the soil will be increased tenfold, and the problem of misery will be singularly attenuated. Add
the suppression of parasitisms, and it will be solved.
In the mean while the public wealth goes to the
river, and a sinking takes place, — sinking is the
right word, for Europe is being ruined in this way
by exhaustion. As for France, we have mentioned
the figures. Now, as Paris contains one twenty-
fifth of the whole French population, and the Parisian guano is the richest of all, we are beneath the
truth when we estimate at twenty-five millions the
share of Paris in the half-milliard which France
annually refuses. These twenty-five millions, employed in assistance and enjoyment, would double
the splendor of Paris, and the city expends them in
sewers. So that we may say, the great prodigality
of Paris, its marvellous fête, its Folie Beaujon, its
orgie, its lavishing of gold, its luxury, splendor, and
magnificence, is its sewerage. It is in this way that
in the blindness of a bad political economy people
allow the comfort of all to be drowned and wasted
in the water ; there ought to be St. Cloud nets to
catch the public fortunes.

Economically regarded, the fact may be thus sum-
marized : Paris is a regular spendthrift. Paris, that
model city, that pattern of well-conducted capitals,
of which every people strives to have a copy, that
metropolis of the ideal, that august home of initia-
tive, impulse, and experiment, that centre and gath-

ering-place of minds, that nation city, that beehive of the future, that marvellous composite of Babylon and Corinth, would make a peasant of Fo-Kian shrug his shoulders, from our present point of view. Imitate Paris, and you will ruin yourself; moreover, Paris imitates itself particularly in this immemorial and insensate squandering. These surprising follies are not new; it is no youthful nonsense. The ancients acted like the moderns. "The cloacas of Rome," says Liebig, "absorbed the entire welfare of the Roman peasant." When the Campagna of Rome was ruined by the Roman sewer, Rome exhausted Italy; and when it had placed Italy in its cloaca, it poured into it Sicily, and then Sardinia, and then Africa. The sewer of Rome swallowed up the world. This cloaca offered its tunnels to the city and to the world. *Urbi et orbi.* Eternal city and unfathomable drain.

For these things, as for others, Rome gives the example, and this example Paris follows with all the folly peculiar to witty cities. For the requirements of the operation which we have been explaining, Paris has beneath it another Paris, a Paris of sewers, which has its streets, squares, lanes, arteries, and circulation, which is mud, with the human forces at least. For nothing must be flattered, not even a great people. Where there is everything, there is ignominy by the side of sublimity; and if Paris contain Athens the city of light, Tyre the city of power, Sparta the city of virtue, Nineveh the city of prodigies, it also contains Lutetia the city of mud. Moreover, the stamp of its power is there too, and the Titanic sewer of Paris realizes among monuments the strange ideal realized in humanity by a few men like Machiavelli, Bacon, and Mirabeau, — the grand abject. The subsoil of Paris, if the eye could pierce the surface, would offer the aspect of a gigantic madrepore; a sponge has not more passages and holes than the piece of ground, six leagues in circumference, upon which the old great city rests. Without alluding to the catacombs, which are a separate cellar, without speaking of the inextricable net of gas-pipes, without referring to the vast tubular system for the distribution of running water, the drains alone form on either bank of the river a prodigious dark ramification, a labyrinth which has its incline for its clew. In the damp mist of this labyrinth is seen the rat, which seems the produce of the accouchement of Paris.

CHAPTER II.

IF we imagine Paris removed like a cover, the subterranean network of sewers, regarded from a birds'-eye view, would represent on either bank a sort of large branch grafted upon the river. On the right bank the encircling sewer will be the trunk of this branch, the secondary tubes the branches, and the blind alleys the twigs. This figure is only summary and half correct, as the right angle, which is the usual angle in subterranean ramifications of this nature, is very rare in vegetation. Our readers will form a better likeness of this strange geometric plan by supposing that they see lying on a bed of darkness some strange Oriental alphabet as confused as a thicket, and whose shapeless letters are welded to each other in an apparent confusion, and as if accidentally, here by their angles and there by their ends. The sewers and drains played a great part in the Middle Ages, under the Lower Empire and in the old East. Plague sprang from them and despots died of it. The multitudes regarded almost with a religious awe these beds of corruption, these monstrous cradles of death. The vermin-ditch at Benares is not more fearful than the Lion's den at Babylon. Tiglath-Pileser, according to the rabbinical books, swore by the sink of Nineveh. It was from the drain of Munster that John of Leyden produced his false moon, and it was from the cesspool-well of Kekhscheb that his Oriental menæchmus, Mokanna, the veiled prophet of Khorassan, brought his false sun.

The history of men is reflected in the history of the sewers, and the Gemoniæ narrated the story of Rome. The sewer of Paris is an old formidable thing, it has been a sepulchre, and it has been an asylum. Crime, intellect, the social protest, liberty of conscience, thought, robbery, all that human laws pursue or have pursued, have concealed themselves in this den, — the Maillotins in the fourteenth century, the cloak-stealers in the fifteenth, the Huguenots in the sixteenth, the illuminés of Morin in the seventeenth, and the Chauffeurs in the eighteenth. One hundred years ago the nocturnal dagger issued from it, and the rogue in danger glided into it; the wood had the cave and Paris had the drain. The Truanderie, that Gallic *picareria*, accepted the drain as an annex of the Court of Miracles, and at night, cunning and ferocious, entered beneath the Maubuée vomitory as into an alcove. It was very simple that those who had for their place of daily toil the Vide-Gousset lane, or the Rue Coupe-Gorge, should have for their nightly abode the ponceau of the Chemin-Vert or the Hurepoix cagnard. Hence comes a swarm of recollections, all sorts of phantoms haunt these long solitary corridors, on all sides are putridity and miasma, and here and there is a trap through which Villon inside converses with Rabelais outside.

The sewer in old Paris is the meeting-place of all exhaustions and of all experiments; political economy sees there a detritus, and social philosophy a residuum. The sewer is the conscience of the city, and everything converges and is confronted there. In this livid spot there is darkness, but there are no secrets. Each thing has its true form, or at least its definitive form. The pile of ordure has this in its favor, that it tells no falsehood, and simplicity has taken refuge there. Basile's mask is found there, but you see the pasteboard, the threads, the inside and out, and it is marked with honest filth. Scapin's false nose is lying close by. All the uncleanlinesses of civilization, where no longer of service, fall into this pit of truth; they are swallowed up, but display themselves in it. This pell-mell is a confession : there no false appearance nor any plastering is possible, order takes off its shirt, there is an absolute nudity, a rout of illusions and mirage, and there nothing but what is assuming the gloomy face of what is finishing. Reality and disappearance. There a bottle-heel confesses intoxication, and a basket-handle talks about domesticity; there, the apple-core which has had literary opinions becomes once again the apple-core, the effigy on the double sou grows frankly vert-de-grised, the saliva of Caiaphas meets the vomit of Falstaff, the louis-d'or which comes from the gambling-hell dashes against the nail whence hangs the end of the suicide's rope, a livid fœtus rolls along wrapped in spangles, which danced last Shrove Tuesday at the opera, a wig which has judged men wallows by the side of a rottenness which was

Margotton's petticoat: it is more than fraternity, it
is the extremest familiarity. All that painted itself
is bedaubed, and the last veil is torn away. The
sewer is a cynic and says everything. This sincerity
of uncleanliness pleases us and reposes the mind.
When a man has spent his time upon the earth in
enduring the great airs assumed by state reasons, the
oath, political wisdom, human justice, professional
probity, the austerities of the situation, and incorruptible robes, it relieves him to enter a sewer and
see there the mire which suits it.

It is instructive at the same time, for, as we said
just now, history passes through the sewer. St.
Bartholomew filters there drop by drop through the
paving-stones, and great public assassinations, political
and religious butcheries, traverse this subterranean
way of civilization, and thrust their corpses into it.
For the eye of the dreamer all historical murderers
are there, in the hideous gloom, on their knees, with
a bit of their winding-sheet for an apron, and mournfully sponging their task. Louis XI. is there with
Tristan, Francis I. is there with Duprat, Charles IX.
is there with his mother, Richelieu is there with
Louis XIII., Louvois is there, Letellier is there,
Hébert and Maillard are there, scratching the stones,
and trying to efface the trace of their deeds. The
brooms of these spectres can be heard under these
vaults, and the enormous fetidness of social catastrophes is breathed there. You see in corners red
flashes, and a terrible water flows there in which
blood-stained hands have been washed.

The social observer should enter these shadows,

for they form part of his laboratory.   Philosophy is
the microscope of thought ; everything strives to fly
from it, but nothing escapes it.   Tergiversation is
useless, for what side of himself does a man show
in tergiversating ?   His ashamed side.   Philosophy
pursues evil with its upright glance, and does not
allow it to escape into nothingness.   It recognizes
everything in the effacement of disappearing things,
and in the diminution of vanishing things.   It re-
constructs the purple after the rags, and the woman
after the tatters.   With the sewer it re-makes the
town ; with the mud it re-makes manners.   It judges
from the potsherds whether it were an amphora or
an earthenware jar.   It recognizes by a nail-mark
on a parchment the difference which separates the
Jewry of the Juden-gasse from the Jewry of the
Ghetto.   It finds again in what is left what has been,
— the good, the bad, the false, the true, the patch of
blood in the palace, the ink-stain of the cavern, the
tallow-drop of the brothel, trials undergone, tempta-
tions welcome, orgies vomited up, the wrinkle which
characters have formed in abasing themselves, the
traces of prostitution in the souls whose coarseness
rendered them capable of it, and on the jacket of
the street-porters of Rome the mark of the nudge
of Messalina.

CHAPTER III.

THE sewer of Paris in the Middle Ages was legendary. In the sixteenth century Henry II. attempted soundings which failed, and not a hundred years ago, as Mercier testifies, the cloaca was abandoned to itself, and became what it could. Such was that ancient Paris, handed over to quarrels, indecisions, and groping. It was for a long time thus stupid, and a later period, '89, showed how cities acquire sense. But in the good old times the capital had but little head; it did not know how to transact its business either morally or materially, and could no more sweep away its ordure than its abuses. Everything was an obstacle, everything raised a question. The sewer, for instance, was refractory to any itinerary, and people could no more get on under the city than they did in it; above, everything was unintelligible; below, inextricable; beneath the confusion of tongues was the confusion of cellars, and Dædalus duplicated Babel. At times the sewer of Paris thought proper to overflow, as if this misunderstood Nile had suddenly fallen into a passion. There were, infamous to relate, inundations of the sewer. At moments this stomach of civilization digested badly, the sewer flowed back into the throat of the city, and Paris had the after-taste of its ordure. These resemblances of the drain to remorse had some good about them, for they were warnings, very badly taken however; for the city was indignant that its mud should have so much boldness, and did not admit that the ordure should return. Discharge it better.

The inundation of 1802 is in the memory of Parisians of eighty years of age. The mud spread across the Place des Victoires, on which is the statue of Louis XIV.; it entered Rue St. Honoré by the two mouths of the sewer of the Champs Élysées, Rue St. Florentin by the St. Florentin sewer, Rue Pierre à Poisson by the sewer of the Sonnerie, Rue Popincourt by the Chemin-Vert sewer, and Rue de la Roquette by the Rue de Lappe sewer; it covered the level of the Rue des Champs Élysées to a height of fourteen inches, and in the south, owing to the vomitory of the Seine performing its duties contrariwise, it entered Rue Mazarine, Rue de l'Échaudé, and Rue des Marais, where it stopped after running on a hundred and twenty yards, just a few yards from the house which Racine had inhabited, respecting, in the seventeenth century, the poet more than the king. It reached its maximum depth in the Rue St. Pierre, where it rose three feet above the gutter, and its maximum extent in the Rue St. Sabin, where it extended over a length of two hundred and fifty yards.

At the beginning of the present century the sewer of Paris was still a mysterious spot. Mud can never

be well famed, but here the ill reputation extended
almost to terror.   Paris knew confusedly that it had
beneath it a grewsome cave; people talked about it
as of that monstrous mud-bed of Thebes, in which
centipedes fifteen feet in length swarmed, and which
could have served as a bathing-place for Behemoth.
The great boots of the sewers-men never ventured
beyond certain known points.   It was still very close
to the time when the scavengers' carts, from the top
of which St. Foix fraternized with the Marquis de
Créqui, were simply unloaded into the sewer.   As
for the cleansing, the duty was intrusted to the
showers, which choked up rather than swept away.
Rome allowed some poetry to her cloaca, and called
it the Gemoniæ, but Paris insulted its own, and
called it the stench-hole.   Science and superstition
were agreed as to the horror, and the stench-hole
was quite as repugnant to hygiene as to the
legend.   The goblin was hatched under the fetid
arches of the Mouffetard sewer : the corpses of
the Marmousets were thrown into the Barillerie
sewer : Fagot attributed the malignant fever of
1685 to the great opening of the Marais sewer,
which remained yawning until 1833 in the Rue
St. Louis, nearly opposite the sign of the Messager
Galant.   The mouth of the sewer in the Rue de
la Mortellerie was celebrated for the pestilences
which issued from it ; with its iron-pointed grating
that resembled a row of teeth it yawned in this
fatal street like the throat of a dragon breathing
hell on mankind.   The popular imagination sea-
soned the gloomy Parisian sewer with some hideous

mixture of infinitude : the sewer was bottomless, the sewer was a Barathrum, and the idea of exploring these leprous regions never even occurred to the police. Who would have dared to cast a sound into this darkness, and go on a journey of discovery in this abyss ? It was frightful, and yet some one presented himself at last. The cloaca had its Christopher Columbus.

One day in 1805, during one of the rare apparitions which the Emperor made in Paris, the Minister of the Interior attended at his master's *petit lever*. In the court-yard could be heard the clanging sabres of all the extraordinary soldiers of the great Republic and the great Empire ; there was a swarm of heroes at Napoleon's gates ; men of the Rhine, the Schelde, the Adage, and the Nile ; comrades of Joubert, of Desaix, of Marceau, Hoche, and Kléber, aeronauts of Fleurus, grenadiers of Mayence, pontooners of Genoa, hussars whom the Pyramids had gazed at, artillerymen who had bespattered Junot's cannon-balls, cuirassiers who had taken by assault the fleet anchored in the Zuyderzee ; some had followed Bonaparte upon the bridge of Lodi, others had accompanied Murat to the trenches of Mantua, while others had outstripped Lannes in the hollow way of Montebello. The whole army of that day was in the court of the Tuileries, represented by a squadron or a company, and guarding Napoleon, then resting ; and it was the splendid period when the great army had Marengo behind it and Austerlitz before it. "Sire," said the Minister of the Interior to Napoleon, "I have seen to-day the

most intrepid man of your Empire." "Who is
the man?" the Emperor asked sharply, "and what
has he done?" "He wishes to do something,
Sire." "What is it?" "To visit the sewers of
Paris." This man existed, and his name was
Bruneseau.

CHAPTER IV.

CONCEALED DETAILS.

THE visit took place, and was a formidable campaign, — a nocturnal battle against asphyxia and plague. It was at the same time a voyage of discovery, and one of the survivors of the exploration, an intelligent workman, very young at that time, used to recount a few years ago the curious details which Bruneseau thought it right to omit in his report to the Prefect of Police, as unworthy of the administrative style. Disinfecting processes were very rudimentary at that day, and Bruneseau had scarce passed the first articulations of the subterranean network ere eight workmen out of twenty refused to go farther. The operation was complicated, for the visit entailed cleansing : it was, therefore, requisite to cleanse and at the same time take measurements ; note the water entrances, count the traps and mouths, detail the branches, indicate the currents, recognize the respective dimensions of the different basins, sound the small sewers grafted on the main, measure the height under the key-stone of each passage, and the width both at the bottom and the top, in order to determine the ordinates for levelling at the right of each entrance of water. They advanced with difficulty, and it was not rare for the ladders to sink into three feet of mud. The lanterns would scarce burn in the mephitic atmosphere, and from time to time a sewer-man was carried away in a fainting state. At certain spots there was a precipice; the soil had given way, the stones were swallowed up, and the drain was converted into a lost well; nothing solid could be found, and they had great difficulty in dragging out a man who suddenly disappeared. By the advice of Fourcroy large cages filled with tow saturated with resin were set fire to at regular distances. The wall was covered in spots with shapeless fungi, which might have been called tumors, and the stone itself seemed diseased in this unbreathable medium.

Bruneseau, in his exploration, proceeded down-hill. At the point where the two water-pipes of the Grand Hurleur separate he deciphered on a projecting stone the date 1550; this stone indicated the limit where Philibert Delorme, instructed by Henri II. to inspect the subways of Paris, stopped. This stone was the mark of the sixteenth century in the drain, and Bruneseau found the handiwork of the seventeenth in the Ponceau conduit and that of the Rue Vieille du Temple, which were arched between 1600 and 1650, and the mark of the eighteenth in the west section of the collecting canal, enclosed and arched in 1740. These two arches, especially the younger one, that of 1740, were more decrepit and cracked than the masonry of the begirding drain, which dated from 1412, the period when the Menilmontant stream of running water was raised to the dignity of the

Great Sewer of Paris, a promotion analogous to that of a peasant who became first valet to the king; something like Gros Jean transformed into Lébel.

They fancied they recognized here and there, especially under the Palais du Justice, the form of old dungeons formed in the sewer itself, hideous *in pace*. An iron collar hung in one of these cells, and they were all bricked up. A few of the things found were peculiar; among others the skeleton of an ourang-outang, which disappeared from the Jardin des Plantes in 1800, a disappearance probably connected with the famous and incontestable apparition of the devil in the Rue des Bernardins in the last year of the eighteenth century. The poor animal eventually drowned itself in the sewer. Under the long vaulted passage leading to the Arche Marion a rag-picker's *hotte* in a perfect state of preservation caused the admiration of connoisseurs. Everywhere the mud, which the sewer-men had come to handle intrepidly, abounded in precious objects; gold and silver, jewelry, precious stones, and coin. A giant who had filtered this cloaca would have found in his sieve the wealth of centuries. At the point where the two branches of the Rue du Temple and the Rue Sainte Avoye divide, a singular copper Huguenot medal was picked up, bearing on one side a pig wearing a cardinal's hat, and on the other a wolf with the tiara on its head.

The most surprising discovery was at the entrance of the Great Sewer. This entrance had been formerly closed by a gate, of which only the hinges now

remained. From one of these hinges hung a filthy
shapeless rag, which doubtless caught there as it
passed, floated in the shadow, and was gradually
mouldering away. Bruneseau raised his lantern
and examined this fragment; it was of very fine
linen, and at one of the corners less gnawed
than the rest could be distinguished an heraldic
crown embroidered above these seven letters,
LAVBESP. The crown was a Marquis's crown,
and the seven letters signified *Laubespine.* What
they had under their eyes was no less than a
piece of Marat's winding-sheet. Marat, in his
youth, had had amours, at the time when he was
attached to the household of the Comte d'Artois
in the capacity of physician to the stables. Of
these amours with a great lady, which are histori-
cally notorious, this sheet had remained to him as
a waif or a souvenir ; on his death, as it was the
only fine linen at his lodgings, he was buried in it.
Old women wrapped up the tragic friend of the people for the tomb in this sheet which had known
voluptuousness. Bruneseau passed on ; the strip
was left where it was. Was it through contempt or
respect? Marat deserved both. And then destiny
was so impressed on it that a hesitation was felt
about touching it. Moreover, things of the sepulchre should be left at the place which they select.
Altogether the relic was a strange one : a Marquise
had slept in it, Marat had rotted in it ; and it had
passed through the Pantheon to reach the sewer-
rats. This rag from an alcove, every crease in
which Watteau in former days would joyously have

painted, ended by becoming worthy of the intent glance of Dante.

The visit to the subways of Paris lasted for seven years, — from 1805 to 1812. While going along, Bruneseau designed, directed, and carried out considerable operations. In 1808 he lowered the Ponceau sewer, and everywhere pushing out new lines, carried the sewer in 1809 under the Rue St. Denis to the Fountain of the Innocents ; in 1810 under the Rue Froidmanteau and the Salpêtrière ; in 1811 under the Rue Neuve des Petits Pères, under the Rue du Mail, the Rue de l'Écharpe and the Place Royal ; in 1812 under the Rue de la Paix and the Chaussée d'Antin. At the same time he disinfected and cleansed the entire network, and in the second year called his son-in-law Nargaud to his assistance. It is thus that at the beginning of this century the old society flushed its subway and performed the toilette of its sewer. It was so much cleaned at any rate. Winding, cracked, unpaved, full of pits, broken by strange elbows, ascending and descending illogically, fetid, savage, ferocious, submerged in darkness, with cicatrices on its stones and scars on its walls, and grewsome, — such was the old sewer of Paris, retrospectively regarded. Ramifications in all directions, crossings of trenches, branches, dials and stars as in saps, blind guts and alleys, arches covered with saltpetre, infected pits, scabby exudations on the walls, drops falling from the roof, and darkness, nothing equalled the horror of this old excremental crypt, — the digestive apparatus of Babylon, a den, a trench, a gulf pierced with streets, a Titanic mole-hill, in which the mind fancies that it sees crawling through the shadow, amid the ordure which had been splendor, that enormous blind mole, the Past.

Such, we repeat, was the sewer of the olden time.

CHAPTER V.

AT the present day the sewer is clean, cold, straight, and correct, and almost realizes the ideal of what is understood in England by the word "respectable." It is neat and gray, built with the plumb-line, — we might almost say coquettishly. It resembles a contractor who has become a Councillor of State. You almost see clearly in it, and the mud behaves itself decently. At the first glance you might be inclined to take it for one of those subterranean passages so common formerly, and so useful for the flights of monarchs and princes in the good old times "when the people loved its kings." The present sewer is a handsome sewer; the pure style prevails there, — the classic rectilinear Alexandrine, which, expelled from poetry, appears to have taken refuge in architecture, seems blended with all the stones of this long, dark, and white vault; each vomitory is an arcade, and the Rue de Rivoli sets the fashion even in the cloaca. However, if the geometric line be anywhere in its place, it is assuredly so in the stercoraceous trench of a great city, where everything must be subordinated to the shortest road. The sewer has at the present day assumed a certain official aspect, and the police reports of which it is sometimes the object are no longer deficient in respect to it. The words which characterize it in the administrative language are lofty and dignified; what used to be called a gut is now called a gallery, and what used to be a hole is now a " look." Villon would no longer recognize the ancient lodgings he used for emergencies. This network of cellars still has its population of rodents, pullulating more than ever; from time to time a rat, an old veteran, ventures his head at the window of the drain and examines the Parisians; but even these vermin are growing tame, as they are satisfied with their subterranean palace. The cloaca no longer retains its primitive ferocity, and the rain which sullied the sewer of olden times, washes that of the present day. Still, do not trust to it too entirely, for miasmas yet inhabit it, and it is rather hypocritical than irreproachable. In spite of all the préfecture of police and the Board of Health have done, it exhales a vague suspicious odor, like Tartuffe after confession. Still, we must allow that, take it all together, sweeping is an homage which the sewer pays to civilization, and as from this point of view Tartuffe's conscience is a progress upon the Augean stable, it is certain that the sewer of Paris has been improved. It is more than a progress, it is a transmutation; between the old and the present sewer there is a revolution. Who effected this revolution? The man whom every one forgets, and whom we have named, — Bruneseau.

CHAPTER VI.

FUTURE PROGRESS.

DIGGING the sewerage of Paris was no small task. The last ten centuries have toiled at it without being able to finish, any more than they could finish Paris. The sewer, in fact, receives all the counterstrokes of the growth of Paris. It is in the ground a species of dark polypus with a thousand antennæ, which grows below, equally with the city above. Each time that the city forms a street, the sewer stretches out an arm. The old monarchy only constructed twenty-three thousand three hundred metres of sewers, and Paris had reached that point on Jan. 1, 1806. From this period, to which we shall presently revert, the work has been usefully and energetically taken up and continued. Napoleon built — and the figures are curious — four thousand eight hundred and four metres; Charles X., ten thousand eight hundred and thirty-six; Louis Philippe, eighty-nine thousand and twenty; the Republic of 1848, twenty-three thousand three hundred and eighty-one; the present government, seventy thousand five hundred : all together two hundred and twenty-six thousand six hundred metres, or sixty leagues, of sewer, — the enormous entrails of Paris, — an obscure ramification constantly at work, an unknown and immense construction. As we see, the subterranean labyrinth of Paris is, at the present day, more than tenfold what it was at the beginning of the century. It would be difficult to imagine all the perseverance and efforts required to raise this cloaca to the point of relative perfection at which it now is. It was with great trouble that the old monarchical Provostry, and in the last ten years of the eighteenth century the revolutionary Mayoralty, succeeded in boring the five leagues of sewers which existed prior to 1806. All sorts of obstacles impeded this operation; some peculiar to the nature of the soil, others inherent in the prejudices of the working population of Paris. Paris is built on a stratum strangely rebellious to the pick, the spade, the borer, and human manipulation. Nothing is more difficult to pierce and penetrate than this geological formation on which the marvellous historical formation called Paris is superposed. So soon as labor in any shape ventures into this layer of alluvium, subterranean resistances abound. They are liquid clay, running springs, hard rocks, and that soft and deep mud which the special science calls " mustard." The pick advances laboriously in the calcareous layers alternating with very thin veins of clay and schistose strata incrusted with oyster-shells, which are contemporaries of the Pre-Adamite oceans. At times a stream suddenly bursts into a tunnel just commenced, and inundates the workmen, or a slip of chalk takes place and rushes forward with the fury of a cataract, breaking like glass the largest supporting shores. Very recently at La Villette, when it was found necessary to carry

the collecting sewer under the St. Martin canal without stopping the navigation or letting off the water,
a fissure formed in the bed of the canal, and the water
poured into the tunnel deriding the efforts of the
draining-pumps. It was found necessary to employ a
diver to seek for the fissure which was in the mouth
of the great basin, and it was only stopped up with
great difficulty. Elsewhere, near the Seine, and even
at some distance from the river, as, for instance, at
Belleville, Grande Rue, and Passage Lunière, bottomless sands are found, in which men have been swallowed up. Add asphyxia by miasmas, interment by
slips and sudden breaking in of the soil; add typhus,
too, with which the workmen are slowly impregnated.
In our days, after having hollowed the gallery of
Clichy with a *banquette* to convey the mainwater
conduit of the Ourque, a work performed by trenches
ten metres in depth; after having arched the Bièvre
from the Boulevard de l'Hôpital to the Seine, in the
midst of earth-slips and by the help of trenching often
through putrid matter, and of shores; after having,
in order to deliver Paris from the torrent-like waters
of the Montmartre, and give an outlet to the fluvi-
atic pond of twenty-three acres which stagnated near
the Barrière des Martyrs; after having, we say, constructed the line of sewers from the Barrière Blanche
to the Aubervilliers road, in four months, by working
day and night at a depth of eleven metres; after
having — a thing unknown before — executed subterraneously a sewer in the Rue Barre du Bec, without
trench, at a depth of six metres, the surveyor
Monnot died. After arching three thousand metres

of sewer in all parts of the city, from the Rue Traver-
sière St. Antoine to the Rue de l'Ourcine; after
having, by the Arbalète branch, freed the Censier-
Mouffetard square from pluvial inundations; after
having constructed the St. George sewer through
liquid sand upon rubble and béton, and after having
lowered the formidable pitch of the Nôtre Dame de
Nazareth branch, the engineer Duleau died. There
are no bulletins for such acts of bravery, which are
more useful, however, than the brutal butchery of
battle-fields.

The sewers of Paris were in 1832 far from being
what they are now. Bruneseau gave the impulse,
but it required the cholera to determine the vast
reconstruction which has taken place since. It is
surprising to say, for instance, that in 1821 a portion
of the begirding sewer, called the Grand Canal, as
at Venice, still stagnated in the open air, in the Rue
des Gourdes. It was not till 1823 that the city of
Paris found in its pocket the twenty-six thousand
six hundred and eighty francs, six centimes, needed
for covering this turpitude. The three absorbing
wells of the Combat, la Cunette, and St. Mandè,
with their disgorging apparatus, draining-wells, and
deodorizing branches, merely date from 1836. The
intestine canal of Paris has been re-made, and, as
we said, augmented more than tenfold during the
last quarter of a century. Thirty years ago, at the
period of the insurrection of June 5 and 6, it was
still in many parts almost the old sewer. A great
number of streets, now convex, were at that time
broken causeways. There could be frequently seen

at the bottom of the water-sheds of streets and squares, large square gratings, whose iron glistened from the constant passage of the crowd, dangerous and slippery for vehicles, and throwing horses down. The official language of the department of the roads and bridges gave these gratings the expressive name of *Cassis.* In 1832 in a number of streets, — Rue de l'Étoile, Rue St. Louis, Rue du Temple, Rue Vieille du Temple, Rue Nôtre Dame de Nazareth, Rue Folie Méricourt, Quai aux Fleurs, Rue du Petit Musc, Rue de Normandie, Rue Pont aux Biches, Rue des Marais, Faubourg St. Martin, Rue Nôtre Dame des Victoires, Faubourg Montmartre, Rue Grange Batelière, at the Champs Élysées, the Rue Jacob, and the Rue de Tournon, the old Gothic cloaca still cynically displayed its throats. They were enormous stone orifices, sometimes surrounded with posts, with a monumental effrontery. Paris in 1806 was much in the same state as regards sewers as in May, 1663, — five thousand three hundred and twenty-eight toises. After Bruneseau, on Jan. 1, 1832, there were forty thousand three hundred metres. From 1806 to 1831 seven hundred and fifty metres were on the average constructed annually; since then eight and even ten thousand metres have been made every year in brick-work, with a coating of concrete on a foundation of béton. At two hundred francs the metre, the sixty leagues of drainage in the Paris of to-day represent forty-eight million francs.

In addition to the economic progress to which we alluded at the outset, serious considerations as to the public health are attached to this immense question, — the drainage of Paris. Paris is situated between two sheets, — a sheet of water and a sheet of air. The sheet of water, lying at a very great depth, but already tapped by two borings, is supplied by the stratum of green sandstone situated between the chalk and the Jurassic limestone; this stratum may be represented by a disc with a radius of twenty-five leagues; a multitude of rivers and streams drip into it, and the Seine, the Marne, the Yonne, the Oisin, the Aisne, the Cher, the Vienne, and the Loire are drunk in a glass of water from the Grenelle well. The sheet of water is salubrious, for it comes from the sky first, and then from the earth; but the sheet of air is unhealthy, for it comes from the sewer. All the miasmas of the cloaca are mingled with the breathing of the city; hence this bad breath. The atmosphere taken from above a dung-heap, it has been proved scientifically, is purer than the atmosphere taken from over Paris. Within a given time, by the aid of progress, improvements in machinery, and enlightenment, the sheet of water will be employed to purify the sheet of air, that is to say, to wash the sewer. It is known that by washing the sewer we mean restoring the ordure to the earth by sending dung to the arable lands and manure to the grass lands. Through this simple fact there will be for the whole social community a diminution of wretchedness and an augmentation of health. At the present hour the radiation of the diseases of Paris extends for fifty leagues round the Louvre, taken as the axle of this pestilential wheel.

We might say that for the last ten centuries the cloaca has been the misery of Paris, and the sewer is the viciousness which the city has in its blood. The popular instinct has never been deceived, and the trade of the sewer-man was formerly almost as dangerous and almost as repulsive to the people as that of the horse-slaughterer, which so long was regarded with horror and left to the hangman. Great wages were required to induce a bricklayer to disappear in this fetid sap; the ladder of the well-digger hesitated to plunge into it. It was said proverbially, " Going into the sewer is entering the tomb ; " and all sorts of hideous legends, as we said, covered this colossal cesspool with terrors. It is a formidable fosse which bears traces of the revolutions of the globe as well as the revolutions of men ; and vestiges may be found there of every cataclysm from the shells of the Deluge to the ragged sheet of Marat.

BOOK III.

MUD, BUT SOUL.

CHAPTER I.

THE CLOACA AND ITS SURPRISES.

IT was in the sewer of Paris that Jean Valjean
found himself. This is a further resemblance of
Paris with the sea, as in the ocean the diver can
disappear there. It was an extraordinary transition,
in the very heart of the city. Jean Valjean had left
the city, and in a twinkling, the time required to
lift a trap and let it fall again, he had passed from
broad daylight to complete darkness, from midday
to midnight, from noise to silence, from the uproar
of thunder to the stagnation of the tomb, and, by
an incident far more prodigious even than that of
the Rue Polonceau, from the extremest peril to the
most absolute security. A sudden fall into a cellar,
disappearance in the oubliette of Paris, leaving this
street where death was all around for this species of
sepulchre in which was life, — it was a strange moment. He stood for some minutes as if stunned,
listening and amazed. The trap-door of safety had
suddenly opened beneath him, and the Celestial Good-

ness had to some extent taken him by treachery.
Admirable ambuscades of Providence! Still, the
wounded man did not stir, and Jean Valjean did not
know whether what he was carrying in this pit were
alive or dead.

His first sensation was blindness, for he all at once
could see nothing. He felt too that in a moment he
had become deaf, for he could hear nothing more.
The frenzied storm of murder maintained a few yards
above him only reached him confusedly and indis-
tinctly, and like a noise from a depth. He felt that
he had something solid under his feet, but that was
all; still, it was sufficient. He stretched out one
arm, then the other; he touched the wall on both
sides and understood that the passage was narrow;
his foot slipped, and he understood that the pavement was damp. He advanced one foot cautiously,
fearing a hole, a cesspool, or some gulf, and satisfied
himself that the pavement went onwards. A fetid
gust warned him of the spot where he was. At the
expiration of a few minutes he was no longer blind,
a little light fell through the trap by which he descended, and his eye grew used to this vault. He
began to distinguish something. The passage in
which he had run to earth — no other word expresses
the situation better — was walled up behind him;
it was one of those blind alleys called in the professional language branches. Before him he had
another wall, — a wall of night. The light of the trap
expired ten or twelve feet from the spot where Jean
Valjean was, and scarce produced a livid whiteness
on a few yards of the damp wall of the sewer. Be-

yond that the opaqueness was massive; to pierce it
appeared horrible, and to enter it seemed like being
swallowed up. Yet it was possible to bury one's self
in this wall of fog, and it must be done; and must
even be done quickly. Jean Valjean thought that
the grating which he had noticed in the street might
also be noticed by the troops, and that all depended
on chance. They might also come down into the
well and search, so he had not a minute to lose. He
had laid Marius on the ground and now picked him
up, — that is again the right expression, — took him
on his shoulders, and set out. He resolutely entered
the darkness.

The truth is, that they were less saved than
Jean Valjean believed; perils of another nature, but
equally great, awaited them. After the flashing
whirlwind of the combat came the cavern of miasmas
and snares; after the chaos, the cloaca. Jean Valjean had passed from one circle of the Inferno into
another. When he had gone fifty yards he was
obliged to stop, for a question occurred to him; the
passage ran into another, which it intersected, and
two roads offered themselves. Which should he
take? Ought he to turn to the left, or right? How
was he to find his way in this black labyrinth? This
labyrinth, we have said, has a clew in its slope, and
following the slope leads to the river. Jean Valjean understood this immediately; he said to himself
that he was probably in the sewer of the markets;
that if he turned to the left and followed the incline
he would arrive in a quarter of an hour at some
opening on the Seine between the Pont au Change

and the Pont Neuf, that is to say, appear in broad
daylight in the busiest part of Paris. Perhaps he
might come out at some street opening, and passers-
by would be stupefied at seeing two blood-stained
men emerge from the ground at their feet. The
police would come up and they would be carried
off to the nearest guard-room; they would be prisoners before they had come out. It would be
better, therefore, to bury himself in the labyrinth,
confide in the darkness, and leave the issue to
Providence.

He went up the incline and turned to the right;
when he had gone round the corner of the gallery
the distant light from the trap disappeared, the
curtain of darkness fell on him again, and he became blind once more. For all that he advanced as
rapidly as he could; Marius's arms were passed
round his neck, and his feet hung down behind.
He held the two arms with one hand and felt the
wall with the other. Marius's cheek touched his
and was glued to it, as it was bloody, and he felt
a warm stream which came from Marius drip on
him and penetrate his clothing. Still, a warm breath
in his ear, which touched the wounded man's mouth,
indicated respiration, and consequently life. The
passage in which Jean Valjean was now walking
was not so narrow as the former, and he advanced
with some difficulty. The rain of the previous night
had not yet passed off, and formed a small torrent
in the centre, and he was forced to hug the wall
in order not to lave his feet in the water. He went
on thus darkly, like a creature of the night groping

in the invisible, and subterraneously lost in the veins of gloom. Still, by degrees, either that a distant grating sent a little floating light into this opaque mist, or that his eyes grew accustomed to the obscurity, he regained some vague vision, and began to notice confusedly, at one moment the wall he was touching, at another the vault under which he was passing. The pupil is dilated at night and eventually finds daylight in it, in the same way as the soul is dilated in misfortune and eventually finds God in it.

To direct himself was difficult, for the sewers represent, so to speak, the outline of the streets standing over them. There were in the Paris of that day two thousand two hundred streets, and imagine beneath them that forest of dark branches called the sewer. The system of sewers existing at that day, if placed end on end, would have given a length of eleven leagues. We have already said that the present network, owing to the special activity of the last thirty years, is no less than sixty leagues. Jean Valjean began by deceiving himself; he fancied that he was under the Rue St. Denis, and it was unlucky that he was not so. There is under that street an old stone drain, dating from Louis XIII., which runs straight to the collecting sewer, called the Great Sewer, with only one turn on the right, by the old Cour des Miracles, and a single branch, the St. Martin sewer, whose four arms cut each other at right angles. But the passage of the Little Truanderie, whose entrance was near the Corinth wine-shop, never communicated with the sewer of the Rue St. Denis ; it falls into the Montmartre sewer, and that is where Jean Valjean now was. There opportunities for losing himself were abundant, for the Montmartre drain is one of the most labyrinthian of the old network. Luckily Jean Valjean had left behind him the sewer of the markets, whose geometrical plan represents a number of entangled top-gallant-masts ; but he had before him more than one embarrassing encounter, and more than one street corner — for they are streets — offering itself in the obscurity as a note of interrogation. In the first place on his left, the vast Plâtrière sewer, a sort of Chinese puzzle, thrusting forth and intermingling its chaos of T and Z under the Post Office, and the rotunda of the grain-markets, as far as the Seine, where it terminates in Y ; secondly, on his right the curved passage of the Rue du Cadran, with its three teeth, which are so many blind alleys ; thirdly, on his left the Mail branch, complicated almost at the entrance by a species of fork, and running with repeated zigzags to the great cesspool of the Louvre, which ramifies in every direction ; and lastly, on his right the blind alley of the Rue des Jeûneurs, without counting other pitfalls, ere he reached the engirdling sewer, which alone could lead him to some issue sufficiently distant to be safe.

Had Jean Valjean had any notion of all we have just stated he would have quickly perceived, merely by feeling the wall, that he was not in the subterranean gallery of the Rue St. Denis. Instead of the old freestone, instead of the old architecture, haughty and royal even in the sewer, with its arches

and continuous courses of granite, which cost eight
hundred livres the fathom, he would feel under his
hand modern cheapness, the economic expedient,
brick-work supported on a layer of béton, which
costs two hundred francs the metre, — that bourgeois
masonry known as *à petits materiaux ;* but he knew
nothing of all this. / He advanced anxiously but
calmly, seeing nothing, hearing nothing, plunged into
chance, that is to say, swallowed up in Providence.
By degrees, however, we are bound to state that
a certain amount of horror beset him, and the shadow
which enveloped him entered his mind. He was
walking in an enigma. This aqueduct of the cloaca
is formidable, for it intersects itself in a vertiginous
manner, and it is a mournful thing to be caught in
this Paris of darkness. Jean Valjean was obliged
to find, and almost invent, his road without seeing
it. In this unknown region each step that he ventured might be his last. How was he to get out
of it ? Would he find an issue ? Would he find
it in time ? Could he pierce and penetrate this
colossal subterranean sponge with its passages of
stone ? Would he meet there some unexpected
knot of darkness ? Would he arrive at something
inextricable and impassable ? Would Marius die
of hemorrhage, and himself of hunger ? Would
they both end by being lost there, and form two
skeletons in a corner of this night ? He did not
know ; he asked himself all this and could not find
an answer. The intestines of Paris are a precipice, and like the prophet he was in the monster's
belly.

He suddenly had a surprise; at the most unexpected moment, and without ceasing to walk in a
straight line, he perceived that he was no longer ascending; the water of the gutter plashed against his
heels instead of coming to his toes. The sewer was
now descending; why? Was he about to reach the
Seine suddenly? That danger was great, but the
peril of turning back was greater still, and he continued to advance. He was not proceeding toward
the Seine; the shelving ridge which the soil of Paris
makes on the right bank empties one of its water-
sheds into the Seine and the other into the Great
Sewer. The crest of this ridge, which determines
the division of the waters, designs a most capricious
line; the highest point is in the Sainte Avoye sewer,
beyond the Rue Michel-le-comte, in the Louvre sewer,
near the boulevards, and in the Montmartre drain,
near the markets. This highest point Jean Valjean
had reached, and he was proceeding toward the engirdling sewer, or in the right direction, but he knew
it not. Each time that he reached a branch he felt
the corners, and if he found the opening narrower
than the passage in which he was he did not enter,
but continued his march, correctly judging that any
narrower way must end in a blind alley, and could
only take him from his object, that is to say, an outlet. He thus avoided the fourfold snare laid for him
in the darkness by the four labyrinths which we have
enumerated. At a certain moment he recognized that
he was getting from under that part of Paris petrified
by the riot, where the barricades had suppressed circulation, and returning under living and normal

Paris. He suddenly heard above his head a sound like thunder, distant but continuous; it was the rolling of vehicles.

He had been walking about half an hour, at least that was the calculation he made, and had not thought of resting; he had merely changed the hand which held Marius up. The darkness was more profound than ever, but this darkness reassured him. All at once he saw his shadow before him; it stood out upon a faint and almost indistinct redness, which vaguely impurpled the roadway at his feet and the vault above his head, and glided along the greasy walls of the passage. Stupefied, he turned around.

Behind him, in the part of the passage he had come from, at a distance which appeared immense, shone a sort of horrible star, obliterating the dark density, which seemed to be looking at him. It was the gloomy police star rising in the sewer. Behind this star there moved confusedly nine or ten black, upright, indistinct, and terrible forms.

CHAPTER II.

EXPLANATION.

On the day of June 6 a battue of the sewers was ordered, for it was feared lest the conquered should fly to them as a refuge, and Prefect Gisquet ordered occult Paris to be searched, while General Bugeaud swept public Paris, — a double connected operation, which required a double strategy of the public force, represented above by the army and beneath by the police. Three squads of agents and sewer-men explored the subway of Paris, — the first the right bank, the second the left bank, and the third the Cité. The agents were armed with carbines, bludgeons, swords, and daggers, and what was at this moment pointed at Jean Valjean was the lantern of the round of the right bank. This round had just inspected the winding gallery and three blind alleys which are under the Rue du Cadran. While the lantern was moved about at the bottom of these blind alleys, Jean Valjean in his progress came to the entrance of the gallery, found it narrower than the main gallery, and had not entered it. The police, on coming out of the Cadran gallery, fancied that they could hear the sound of footsteps in the direction of the engirdling sewer, and they were really Jean Valjean's footsteps. The head sergeant of the round

raised his lantern, and the squad began peering into
the mist in the direction whence the noise had come.

It was an indescribable moment for Jean Valjean ;
luckily, if he saw the lantern well the lantern saw
him badly, for it was the light and he was the darkness. He was too far off, and blended with the
blackness of the spot, so he drew himself up against
the wall and stopped. However, he did not explain
to himself what was moving behind him, want of
sleep and food and emotion having made him pass into
a visionary state. He saw a flash, and round this flash,
spectres. What was it ? He did not understand.
When Jean Valjean stopped the noise ceased ; the
police listened and heard nothing, they looked and saw
nothing, and hence consulted together. There was
at that period at that point in the Montmartre sewer
a sort of square called *de service*, which has since
been done away with, owing to the small internal
lake which the torrents of rain formed there, and the
squad assembled on this square. Jean Valjean saw
them make a sort of circle, and then bull-dog heads
came together and whispered. The result of this
council held by the watch-dogs was that they were
mistaken, that there had been no noise, that there
was nobody there, that it was useless to enter the
surrounding sewer, that it would be time wasted, but
that they must hasten to the St. Merry drain ; for if
there were anything to be done and any " boussingot "
to track, it would be there. From time to time
parties new-sole their old insults. In 1832 the
word " boussingot " formed the transition between the
word " jacobin," no longer current, and the word

"demagogue," at that time almost unused, and which has since done such excellent service. The sergeant gave orders to left-wheel toward the watershed of the Seine. Had they thought of dividing into two squads and going in both directions, Jean Valjean would have been caught. It is probable that the instructions of the Préfecture, fearing the chance of a fight with a large body of insurgents, forbade the round from dividing. The squad set out again, leaving Jean Valjean behind; and in all this movement he perceived nothing except the eclipse of the lantern, which was suddenly turned away.

Before starting, the sergeant, to satisfy his police conscience, discharged his carbine in the direction where Jean Valjean was. The detonation rolled echoing along the crypt, like the rumbling of these Titanic bowels. A piece of plaster which fell into the gutter and plashed up the water a few yards from Jean Valjean warned him that the bullet had struck the vault above his head. Measured and slow steps echoed for some time along the wooden causeway, growing more and more deadened by the growing distance; the group of black forms disappeared; a light oscillated and floated, forming on the vault a ruddy circle, which decreased and disappeared; the silence again became profound, the obscurity again became complete, and blindness and deafness again took possession of the gloom; Jean Valjean, not daring yet to stir, remained leaning for a long time against the wall, with outstretched ear and dilated eyeballs, watching the vanishing of this patrol of phantoms.

CHAPTER III.

THE TRACKED MAN.

WE must do the police of that day the justice of saying that even in the gravest public conjunctures they imperturbably accomplished their duties of watching the highways and of inspectorship. A riot was not in their eyes a pretext to leave the bridle to malefactors, and to neglect society for the reason that the Government was in danger. The ordinary duties were performed correctly in addition to the extraordinary duties, and were in no way disturbed. In the midst of an incalculable political event, under the pressure of a possible revolution, an agent, not allowing himself to be affected by the insurrection and the barricade, would track a robber. Something very like this occurred on the afternoon of June 6, on the right bank of the Seine, a little beyond the Pont des Invalides. There is no bank there at the present day, and the appearance of the spot has been altered. On this slope two men, a certain distance apart, were observing each other; the one in front seemed to be trying to get away, while the one behind wanted to catch him up. It was like a game of chess played at a distance and silently; neither of them seemed to be in a hurry, and both walked slowly, as if they

were afraid that increased speed on the part of one
would be imitated by the other. It might have been
called an appetite following a prey, without appearing to do so purposely; the prey was crafty, and
kept on guard.

The proportions required between the tracked mar-
ten and the tracking dog were observed. The one
trying to escape was thin and mean looking; the one
trying to capture was a tall determined fellow, of rug-
ged aspect, and a rough one to meet. The first, feeling himself the weaker, avoided the second, but did
so in a deeply furious way; any one who could have
observed him would have seen in his eyes the gloomy
hostility of flight, and all the threat which there is in
fear; the slope was deserted, there were no passers-
by, not even a boatman or raftsman in the boats
moored here and there. They could only be noticed
easily from the opposite quay, and any one who had
watched them at that distance would have seen that
the man in front appeared a bristling, ragged, and
shambling fellow, anxious and shivering under a torn
blouse, while the other was a classic and official personage, wearing the frock-coat of authority buttoned
up to the chin. The reader would probably recognize
these two men, were he to see them more closely.
What was the object of the last one? Probably he
wished to clothe the other man more warmly. When
a man dressed by the State pursues a man in rags, it
is in order to make him also a man dressed by the
State. The difference of color is the sole question;
to be dressed in blue is glorious, to be dressed in red
is disagreeable, for there is a purple of the lower

classes. It was probably some disagreeable thing, and some purple of this sort, which the first man desired to avoid.

If the other allowed him to go on ahead, and did not yet arrest him, it was, in all appearance, in the hope of seeing him arrive at some significative rendezvous and some group worth capturing. This delicate operation is called tracking. What renders this conjecture highly probable, is the fact that the buttoned-up man, perceiving from the slope an empty fiacre passing, made a sign to the driver; the driver understood, evidently perceived with whom he had to deal, turned round, and began following the two men along the quay. This was not perceived by the ragged, shambling fellow in front. The hackney coach rolled along under the trees of the Champs Élysées, and over the parapet could be seen the bust of the driver, whip in hand. One of the secret instructions of the police to the agents is, "Always have a hackney coach at hand in case of need." While each of these men manœuvred with irreproachable strategy, they approached an incline in the quay, which allowed drivers coming from Passy to water their horses in the river. This incline has since been suppressed for the sake of symmetry, — horses die of thirst, but the eye is gratified. It was probable that the man in the blouse would ascend by this incline in order to try to escape in the Champs Élysées, a place adorned with trees, but, in return, much frequented by police agents, where the other could easily procure assisttance. This point of the quay is a very little distance from the house brought from Moret to Paris in 1824

by Colonel Brack, and called the house of Francis I.
A guard is at hand there. To the great surprise of
his watcher, the tracked man did not turn up the
road to the watering-place, but continued to advance
along the bank parallel with the quay. His position
was evidently becoming critical, for unless he threw
himself into the Seine, what could he do?

There were no means now left him of returning to
the quay, no incline and no steps, and they were close
to the spot marked by the turn in the Seine, near the
Pont de Jena, where the bank, gradually contracting,
ended in a narrow strip, and was lost in the water.
There he must inevitably find himself blockaded between the tall wall on his right, the river on his left
and facing him, and authority at his heels. It is
true that this termination of the bank was masked
from sight by a pile of rubbish seven feet high, the
result of some demolition. But did this man hope
to conceal himself profitably behind this heap? The
expedient would have been puerile. He evidently
did not dream of that, for the innocence of robbers
does not go so far. The pile of rubbish formed on
the water-side a sort of eminence extending in a promontory to the quay wall; the pursued man reached
this small mound and went round it, so that he was
no longer seen by the other. The latter, not seeing,
was not seen, and he took advantage of this to give
up all dissimulation and walk very fast. In a few
minutes he reached the heap and turned it, but there
stood stupefied. The man he was pursuing was not
there; it was a total eclipse of the man in the blouse.
The bank did not run more than thirty yards beyond

the heap, and then plunged under the water which washed the quay wall. The fugitive could not have thrown himself into the Seine, or have climbed up the quay wall, without being seen by his pursuer. What had become of him?

The man in the buttoned-up coat walked to the end of the bank and stood there for a moment, thoughtfully, with clenched fists and scowling eye. All at once he smote his forehead; he had just perceived, at the point where the ground ended and the water began, a wide, low, arched iron grating, provided with a heavy lock and three massive hinges. This grating, a sort of gate pierced at the bottom of the quay, opened on the river as much as on the bank, and a black stream poured from under it into the Seine. Beyond the heavy rusty bars could be distinguished a sort of arched and dark passage. The man folded his arms and looked at the grating reproachfully, and this look not being sufficient, he tried to push it open, he shook it, but it offered a sturdy resistance. It was probable that it had just been opened, although no sound had been heard,— a singular thing with so rusty a gate, — but it was certain that it had been closed again. This indicated that the man who had opened the gate had not a pick-lock but a key. This evidence at once burst on the mind of the man who was trying to open the grating, and drew from him this indignant apostrophe, —

"That is strong! A government key!"

Then calming himself immediately, he expressed a whole internal world of ideas by this outburst

of monosyllables, marked by an almost ironical
accent, —

"Well! Well! Well! Well!"

This said, hoping we know not what, either to see
the man come out or others enter, he posted himself
on the watch behind the heap of rubbish, with the
patient rage of a yard-mastiff. On its side, the hackney coach, which regulated itself by all his movements, stopped above him near the parapet. The
driver, foreseeing a long halt, put on his horses the
nose-bag full of damp oats so well known to the Parisians, upon whom the Government, we may remark
parenthetically, sometimes puts it. The few passers
over the Pont de Jena, before going on, turned their
heads to look for a moment at these motionless objects, — the man on the bank and the hackney coach
on the quay.

CHAPTER IV.

HE TOO BEARS HIS CROSS.

JEAN VALJEAN had resumed his march, and had not stopped again. This march grew more and more laborious, for the level of these passages varies; the average height is about five feet six inches, and was calculated for a man's stature. Jean Valjean was compelled to stoop so as not to dash Marius against the roof, and was forced at each moment to bend down, then draw himself up and incessantly feel the wall. The dampness of the stones and of the flooring rendered them bad supports, either for the hand or the foot, and he tottered in the hideous dungheap of the city. The intermittent flashes of the street gratings only appeared at lengthened intervals, and were so faint that the bright sunshine seemed to be moonlight; all the rest was fog, miasma, opaqueness, and blackness. Jean Valjean was hungry and thirsty, the latter most, and it was like the sea; there was " water, water everywhere, but not a drop to drink." His strength, which, as we know, was prodigious, and but slightly diminished by age, owing to his chaste and sober life, was, however, beginning to give way; fatigue assailed him, and his decreasing strength increased the weight of his burden. Marius, who was perhaps dead, was heavy, like all inert bodies ; but Jean Valjean held him so that his chest was not affected, and he could breathe as easily as possible. He felt between his legs the rapid gliding of rats, and one was so startled as to bite him. From time to time a gush of fresh air came through the gratings, which revived him.

It might be about 3 P. M. when he reached the engirdling sewer, and he was at first amazed by the sudden widening. He unexpectedly found himself in a gallery whose two walls his outstretched arms did not reach, and under an arch which his head did not touch. The Great Sewer, in fact, is eight feet in width by seven high. At the point where the Montmartre drain joins the Great Sewer two other subterranean galleries, that of the Rue de Provence and that of the Abattoir, form cross-roads. Between these four ways a less sagacious man would have been undecided ; but Jean Valjean selected the widest, that is to say, the engirdling sewer. But here the question came back again, "Should he ascend or descend?" He thought that the situation was pressing, and that he must at all risks now reach the Seine, in other words, descend, so he turned to the left. It was fortunate that he did so, for it would be an error to suppose that the engirdling sewer has two issues, one toward Bercy, the other toward Passy, and that it is, as its name indicates, the subterranean belt of Paris on the right bank. The Great Sewer, which is nought else, it must be borne in mind, than the old Menilmontant stream, leads, if you ascend it, to a blind alley, that is to say, to its old starting-point, a spring at the foot of the Menilmontant mound. It has no direct communication with the branch which collects the waters of Paris after leaving the Popincourt quarter, and which falls into the Seine by the Amelot sewer above the old isle of Louviers. This branch, which completes the collecting sewer, is separated from it under the Rue Menilmontant by masonry-work, which marks the point of the division of the waters into up-stream and down-stream. If Jean Valjean had remounted the gallery he would have arrived, exhausted by fatigue and dying, at a wall; he would have been lost.

Strictly speaking, by going back a little way, entering the passage of the Filles du Calvaire, on condition that he did not hesitate at the subterranean point of junction of the Boucherat cross-roads, by taking the St. Louis passage, then on the left the St. Gilles trench, then by turning to the right and avoiding the St. Sebastian gallery, Jean Valjean might have reached the Amelot sewer; and then if he did not lose his way in the species of F which is under the Bastille, he would have reached the outlet on the Seine near the Arsenal. But for that he must have thoroughly known, in all its ramifications and piercings, the enormous madrepore of the sewer. Now, we dwell on the fact that he knew nothing of this frightful labyrinth in which he was marching, and had he been asked where he was he would have replied, " In night." His instinct served him well; going down, in fact, was the only salvation possible. He left on his right the two passages which ramify in the shape of a claw under the Rues Laffitte and St. Georges, and the long bifurcate corridor of the Chaussée d'Antin. A little beyond an affluent, which was likely the Madeleine branch, he stopped, for he was very weary. A large grating, probably the one in the Rue d'Anjou, produced an almost bright light. Jean Valjean, with the gentle movements which a brother would bestow on a wounded brother, laid Marius on the banquette of the sewer, and his white face gleamed under the white light of the air-hole as from the bottom of a tomb. His eyes were closed, his hair stuck to his forehead like paint-brushes on which the red paint had dried, his hands were hanging and dead, his limbs cold, and blood was clotted at the corner of his lips. Coagulated blood had collected in his cravat knot, his shirt entered the wounds, and the cloth of his coat rubbed the gaping edges of the quivering flesh. Jean Valjean, removing the clothes with the tips of his fingers, laid his hand on his chest; the heart still beat. Jean Valjean tore up his shirt, bandaged the wounds as well as he could, and stopped the blood that was flowing; then, stooping down in this half daylight over Marius, who was still unconscious and almost breathless, he looked at him with indescribable hatred.

In moving Marius's clothes he had found in his pockets two things, — the loaf, which he had forgotten the previous evening, and his pocket-book. He ate the bread and opened the pocket-book. On the first page he read the lines written by Marius, as will be remembered, —

" My name is Marius Pontmercy. Carry my body to my grandfather, M. Gillenormand, No. 6, Rue des Filles du Calvaire, in the Marais."

Jean Valjean read by the light of the grating these lines, and remained for a time as it were absorbed in himself, and repeating in a low voice, M. Gillenormand, No. 6, Rue des Filles du Calvaire. He returned the portfolio to Marius's pocket; he had eaten, and his strength had come back to him. He raised Marius again, carefully laid his head on his right shoulder, and began descending the sewer. The Great Sewer, running along the roadway of the valley of Menilmontant, is nearly two leagues in length, and is paved for a considerable portion of the distance. This torch of names of Paris streets, with which we enlighten for the reader Jean Valjean's subterranean march, he did not possess. Nothing informed him what zone of the city he was traversing, nor what distance he had gone; still, the growing paleness of the flakes of light which he met from time to time indicated to him that the sun was retiring from the pavement, and that day would be soon ended, and the rolling of vehicles over his head, which had become intermittent instead of continuous, and then almost ceased, proved to him that he was no longer under central Paris, and was approaching some solitary region, near the external boulevards or most distant quays, where there are fewer houses and streets, and the drain has fewer gratings. The obscurity thickened around Jean Valjean; still he continued to advance, groping his way in the shadow.

This shadow suddenly became terrible.

CHAPTER V.

SAND, LIKE WOMAN, HAS A FINENESS THAT IS
PERFIDIOUS.

HE felt that he was entering water, and that he
had under his feet no longer stone but mud. It often
happens on certain coasts of Brittany or Scotland that
a man, whether traveller or fisherman, walking at low
tide on the sand, some distance from the shore, suddenly perceives that during the last few minutes he has
found some difficulty in walking. The shore beneath
his feet is like pitch, his heels are attached to it, it is
no longer sand but bird-lime ; the sand is perfectly dry,
but at every step taken, so soon as the foot is raised
the imprint it leaves fills with water. The eye, however, has perceived no change, the immense expanse
is smooth and calm, all the sand seems alike, nothing
distinguishes the soil which is solid from that which
is no longer so, and the little merry swarm of water-
fleas continue to leap tumultuously round the feet of
the wayfarer. The man follows his road, turns toward
the land, and tries to approach the coast, not that he
is alarmed ; alarmed at what ? Still, he feels as if the
heaviness of his feet increased at every step that he
takes ; all at once he sinks in, sinks in two or three
inches. He is decidedly not on the right road, and
stops to look about him. Suddenly he looks at his

feet, but they have disappeared, the sand covers them. He draws his feet out of the sand and tries to turn back, but he sinks in deeper still. The sand comes up to his ankle; he pulls it out and turns to his left, when the sand comes to his knee; he turns to the right, and the sand comes up to his thigh; then he recognizes with indescribable terror that he is caught in a quicksand, and has under him the frightful medium in which a man can no more walk than a fish can swim. He throws away his load, if he have one, and lightens himself like a ship in distress; but it is too late, for the sand is already above his knees. He calls out, waves his hat or handkerchief, but the sand gains on him more and more. If the shore is deserted, if land is too distant, if the sand-bank is too ill-famed, if there is no hero in the vicinity, it is all over with him, and he is condemned to be swallowed by the quicksands. He is doomed to that long, awful, implacable interment, impossible to delay or hasten, which lasts hours; which never ends; which seizes you when erect, free, and in perfect health; which drags you by the feet; which, at every effort you attempt, every cry you utter, drags you a little deeper; which seems to punish you for your resistance by a redoubled clutch; which makes a man slowly enter the ground while allowing him ample time to regard the houses, the trees, the green fields, the smoke from the villages on the plain, the sails of the vessels on the sea, the birds that fly and sing, the sun, and the sky. A quicksand is a sepulchre that converts itself into a tide, and ascends from the bottom of the earth toward a living man. Each moment inexorably wraps

grave-clothes about him. The wretch tries to sit, to
lie down, to walk, to crawl; all the movements that
he makes bury him; he draws himself up, and only
sinks deeper; he feels himself being swallowed up;
he yells, implores, cries to the clouds, writhes his
arms, and grows desperate. Then he is in the sand
up to his waist; the sand reaches his chest, he is but
a bust. He raises his hands, utters furious groans,
digs his nails into the sand, tries to hold by this dust,
raises himself on his elbows to tear himself from this
soft sheath, and sobs frenziedly. The sand mounts,
the sand reaches his shoulders, the sand reaches his
neck, the face alone is visible now. The mouth cries,
the sand fills it; silence. The eyes still look, the
sand closes them; night. Then the forehead sinks,
and a little hair waves above the sand; a hand
emerges, digs up the sand, is waved, and disappears,
— a sinister effacement of a man.

At times the rider is swallowed up with his horse,
at times the carter with his cart. It is a shipwreck
otherwhere than in the water; it is the land drowning
man. The land penetrated by the ocean becomes a
snare; it offers itself as a plain, and opens like a
wave. The abyss has its acts of treachery.

Such a mournful adventure, always possible on
some seashore, was also possible some thirty years
ago in the sewer of Paris. Before the important
works began in 1833 the subway of Paris was subject to sudden breakings-in. The water filtered
through a subjacent and peculiarly friable soil; and
the roadway, if made of paving-stones, as in the old
drains, or of concrete upon béton, as in the new

galleries, having no support, bent. A bend in a planking of this nature is a crevice, and a crevice is a bursting-in. The roadway broke away for a certain length, and such a gap, a gulf of mud, was called in professional language *fontis*. What is a fontis? It is the quicksand of the seashore suddenly met with underground; it is the strand of Mont St. Michel in a sewer. The moistened soil is in a state of fusion, all its particles are held in suspense in a shifting medium; it is not land and it is not water. The depth is at times very great. Nothing can be more formidable than meeting with such a thing; if water predominate death is quick, for a man is drowned; if earth predominate death is slow, for he is sucked down.

Can our readers imagine such a death? If it be frightful to sink in the sea-strand, what is it in a cloaca? Instead of fresh air, daylight, a clear horizon, vast sounds, the free clouds from which life rains, the barque perceived in the distance, that hope under every form, of possible passers-by, of possible help up to the last minute,— instead of all this, deafness, blindness, a black archway, the interior of a tomb already made, death in the mud under a tombstone! Slow asphyxia by uncleanliness, a sarcophagus where asphyxia opens its claws in the filth and clutches you by the throat; fetidness mingled with the death-rattle, mud instead of the sand, sulphuretted hydrogen in lieu of the hurricane, ordure instead of the ocean! And to call and gnash the teeth, and writhe and struggle and expire, with this enormous city which knows nothing of it above one's head.

Inexpressible the horror of dying thus! Death sometimes expiates its atrocity by a certain terrible dignity. On the pyre, in shipwreck, a man may be great; in the flames, as in the foam, a superb attitude is possible, and a man transfigures himself. But in this case it is not so, for the death is unclean. It is humiliating to expire in such a way, and the last floating visions are abject. Mud is the synonym of shame, and is little, ugly, and infamous. To die in a butt of Malmsey like Clarence, — very well; but in a sewer like d'Escoubleau is horrible. To struggle in it is hideous, for at the same time as a man is dying, he is dabbling. There is enough darkness for it to be Hell, and enough mud for it to be merely a slough, and the dying man does not know whether he is about to become a spectre or a frog. Everywhere else the sepulchre is sinister, but here it is deformed.

The depth of the fontis varied, as did the length and density, according to the nature of the subsoil. At times a fontis was three or four feet deep, at times eight or ten, and sometimes it was bottomless. In one the mud was almost solid, in another nearly liquid. In the Lunière fontis, a man would have taken a day in disappearing, while he would have been devoured in five minutes by the Phélippeaux slough. The mud bears more or less well according to its degree of density, and a lad escapes where a man is lost. The first law of safety is to throw away every sort of loading, and every sewer-man who felt the ground giving way under him began by getting rid of his basket of tools. The fontis had various causes,— friability of soil, some convulsion at a depth beyond a man's reach, violent summer showers, the incessant winter rain, and long drizzling rains. At times the weight of the surrounding houses upon a marshy or sandy soil broke the roofs of the subterranean galleries and made them shrink, or else it happened that the roadway broke and slit up under the terrific pressure. The pile of the Panthéon destroyed in this way about a century ago a portion of the cellars in Mont Sainte Geneviève. When a sewer gave way under the weight of the houses, the disorder was expressed above in the street by a sort of saw-toothed parting between the paving-stones. This rent was developed in a serpentine line, along the whole length of the cracked vault, and in such a case, the evil being visible, the remedy might be prompt. It often happened also that the internal ravage was not revealed by any scar outside, and in that case, woe to the sewer-men. Entering the injured drain incautiously, they might be lost in it. The old registers mention several night-men buried in this manner in the fontis. They mention several names, among others that of the sewer-man swallowed up in a slough under the opening on the Rue Carême Prenant, of the name of Blaise Poutrain ; this Blaise was brother of Nicholas Poutrain, who was the last sexton of the cemetery called the Charnier des Innocents in 1785, when that cemetery expired. There was also the young and charming Vicomte d'Escoubleau, to whom we have alluded, one of the heroes of the siege of Lerida, where the assault was made in silk stockings and with violins at their head. D'Escoubleau, surprised one night with his cousin,

the Duchesse de Sourdis, drowned himself in a cesspool of the Beautreillis sewer, where he had taken
refuge to escape the Duc. Madame de Sourdis,
when told the story of this death, asked for her
smelling-bottle, and forgot to weep through inhal-
ing her salts. In such a case there is no love that
holds out; the cloaca extinguishes it. Hero refuses
to wash the corpse of Leander. Thisbe holds her
nose in the presence of Pyramus, and says, Pah!

CHAPTER VI.

THE FONTIS.

JEAN VALJEAN found himself in presence of a fontis: this sort of breaking-in was frequent at that day in the subsoil of the Champs Élysées, which was difficult to manage in hydraulic works, and not preservative of subterranean constructions, owing to its extreme fluidity. This fluidity exceeds even the inconsistency of the sands of the Quartier St. Georges, which could only be overcome by laying rubble on béton, and of the gas-infected clay strata in the Quartier des Martyrs, which are so liquid that a passage could be effected under the gallery only by means of an iron tube. When in 1836 the authorities demolished and rebuilt under the Faubourg St. Honoré the old stone sewer in which Jean Valjean is now engaged, the shifting sand which is the subsoil of the Champs Élysées as far as the Seine offered such an obstacle that the operation lasted six months, to the great annoyance of those living on the waterside, especially such as had mansions and coaches. The works were more than difficult, they were dangerous; but we must allow that it rained for four and a half months, and the Seine overflowed thrice. The fontis which Jean Valjean came across was occasioned by the shower of the previous evening. A giving way of the pavement, which was badly supported by the subjacent sand, had produced a deposit of rain-water, and when the filtering had taken place the ground broke in, and the roadway, being dislocated, fell into the mud. How far? It was impossible to say, for the darkness was denser there than anywhere else; it was a slough of mud in a cavern of night. Jean Valjean felt the pavement depart from under him as he entered the slough; there was water at top and mud underneath. He must pass it, for it was impossible to turn back; Marius was dying, and Jean Valjean worn out. Where else could he go? Jean Valjean advanced; the slough appeared but of slight depth at the first few steps, but as he advanced his legs sank in. He soon had mud up to the middle of the leg, and water up to the middle of the knee. He walked along, raising Marius with both arms as high as he could above the surface of the water; the mud now came up to his knees and the water to his waist. He could no longer draw back, and he sank in deeper and deeper. This mud, dense enough for the weight of one man, could not evidently bear two; Marius and Jean Valjean might have had a chance of getting out separately; but, for all that, Jean Valjean continued to advance, bearing the dying man, who was perhaps a corpse. The water came up to his armpits, and he felt himself drowning; he could scarce move in the depth of mud in which he was standing, for the density which was the support was also the obstacle. He still kept Marius up, and advanced with an ex-

traordinary expenditure of strength, but he was sinking. He had only his head out of water and his two
arms sustaining Marius. In the old paintings of the
Deluge there is a mother holding her child in the
same way. As he still sank he threw back his face
to escape the water and be able to breathe; any one
who saw him in this darkness would have fancied
he saw a mask floating on the gloomy waters; he
vaguely perceived above him Marius's hanging head
and livid face; he made a desperate effort and advanced his foot, which struck against something
solid, — a resting-place. It was high time.

He drew himself up, and writhed and rooted himself with a species of fury upon this support. It produced on him the effect of the first step of a staircase
reascending to life. This support, met with in the
mud at the supreme moment, was the beginning of
the other side of the roadway, which had fallen in
without breaking, and bent under the water like a
plank in a single piece. A well-constructed pavement forms a curve, and possesses such firmness.
This fragment of roadway, partly submerged, but
solid, was a real incline, and once upon it they were
saved. Jean Valjean ascended it, and attained the
other side of the slough. On leaving the water his
foot caught against a stone and he fell on his knees.
He found that this was just, and remained on them
for some time, with his soul absorbed in words
addressed to God.

He rose, shivering, chilled, polluted, bent beneath
the dying man he carried, all dripping with filth, but
with his soul full of a strange brightness.

CHAPTER VII.

SOMETIMES ONE IS STRANDED WHERE HE THINKS TO LAND.

He set out once again; still, if he had not left his life in the fontis, he seemed to have left his strength there. This supreme effort had exhausted him, and his fatigue was now so great that he was obliged to rest every three or four paces to take breath, and leaned against the wall. Once he was obliged to sit down on the banquette in order to alter Marius's position, and believed that he should remain there. But if his vigor were dead his energy was not so, and he rose again. He walked desperately, almost quickly, went thus one hundred yards without raising his head, almost without breathing, and all at once ran against the wall. He had reached an elbow of the drain, and on arriving head down at the turning, came against the wall. He raised his eyes, and at the end of the passage down there, far, very far away, perceived a light. But this time it was no terrible light, but white, fair light. It was daylight. Jean Valjean saw the outlet. A condemned soul that suddenly saw from the middle of the furnace the issue from Gehenna would feel what Jean Valjean felt. It would fly wildly with the stumps of its burnt wings toward the radiant gate. Jean Valjean

no longer felt fatigue, he no longer felt Marius's
weight, he found again his muscles of steel, and ran
rather than walked. As he drew nearer, the outlet
became more distinctly designed; it was an arch,
not so tall as the roof, which gradually contracted,
and not so wide as the gallery, which grew narrower
at the same time as the roof became lowered. The
tunnel finished inside in the shape of a funnel, — a
faulty reduction, imitated from the wickets of houses
of correction, logical in a prison, but illogical in a
drain, and which has since been corrected.

Jean Valjean reached the issue and then stopped;
it was certainly the outlet, but they could not get
out. The arch was closed by a strong grating, and
this grating, which apparently rarely turned on its
oxidized hinges, was fastened to the stone wall by a
heavy lock, which, red with rust, seemed an enormous brick. The key-hole was visible, as well as
the bolt deeply plunged into its iron box. It was
one of those Bastille locks of which ancient Paris
was so prodigal. Beyond the grating were the open
air, the river, daylight, the bank, — very narrow but
sufficient to depart, — the distant quays, Paris, — that
gulf in which a man hides himself so easily, — the
wide horizon, and liberty. On the right could be
distinguished, down the river, the Pont de Jéna, and
at the left, up stream, the Pont des Invalides; the
spot would have been a favorable one to await night
and escape. It was one of the most solitary points
in Paris, the bank facing the Gros-Caillou. The flies
went in and out through the grating bars. It might
be about half-past eight in the evening, and day was

drawing in: Jean Valjean laid Marius along the wall on the dry part of the way, then walked up to the grating and seized the bars with both hands; the shock was frenzied, but the effect *nil*. The grating did not stir. Jean Valjean seized the bars one after the other, hoping he might be able to break out the least substantial one and employ it as a lever to lift the gate off the hinges or break the lock, but not a bar stirred. A tiger's teeth are not more solidly set in their sockets. Without a lever it was impossible to open the grating, and the obstacle was invincible.

Must he finish, then, there? What should he do? What would become of him? He had not the strength to turn back and recommence the frightful journey which he had already made. Moreover, how was he to cross again that slough from which he had only escaped by a miracle? And after the slough, was there not the police squad, which he assuredly would not escape twice; and then where should he go, and what direction take? Following the slope would not lead to his object, for if he reached another outlet he would find it obstructed by an iron plate or a grating. All the issues were indubitably closed in that way; accident had left the grating by which they entered open, but it was plain that all the other mouths of the sewer were closed. They had only succeeded in escaping into a prison.

It was all over, and all that Jean Valjean had done was useless: God opposed it. They were both caught in the dark and immense web of death, and Jean Valjean felt the fearful spider already running along the black threads in the darkness. He turned his back to the grating and fell on the pavement near Marius, who was still motionless, and whose head had fallen between his knees. There was no outlet; that was the last drop of agony. Of whom did he think in this profound despondency? Neither of himself nor of Marius! He thought of Cosette.

CHAPTER VIII.

THE TORN COAT-SKIRT.

In the midst of his annihilation a hand was laid on his shoulder, and a low voice said, —

"Half shares."

Some one in this shadow? As nothing so resembles a dream as despair, Jean Valjean fancied that he was dreaming. He had not heard a footstep. Was it possible? He raised his eyes, and a man was standing before him. This man was dressed in a blouse, his feet were naked, and he held his shoes in his hand; he had evidently taken them off in order to be able to reach Jean Valjean without letting his footsteps be heard. Jean Valjean had not a moment's hesitation : however unexpected the meeting might be, the man was known to him: it was Thénardier. Although, so to speak, aroused with a start, Jean Valjean, accustomed to alarms and to unexpected blows which it is necessary to parry quickly, at once regained possession of all his presence of mind. Besides, the situation could not be worse ; a certain degree of distress is not capable of any crescendo, and Thénardier himself could not add any blackness to this night. There was a moment's expectation. Thénardier, raising his right hand to the level of his forehead, made a screen of it; then he drew his eyebrows together with a wink, which, with a slight pinching of the lips, characterizes the sagacious attention of a man who is striving to recognize another. He did not succeed. Jean Valjean, as we said, was turning his back to the light, and was besides so disfigured, so filthy, and blood-stained that he could not have been recognized in broad daylight. On the other hand, Thénardier, with his face lit up by the light from the grating, — a cellar brightness, it is true, — livid but precise in his lividness, leaped at once into Jean Valjean's eyes, to employ the energetic popular metaphor. This inequality of conditions sufficed to insure some advantage to Jean Valjean in the mysterious duel which was about to begin between the two situations and the two men. The meeting took place between Jean Valjean masked and Thénardier unmasked. Jean Valjean at once perceived that Thénardier did not recognize him; and they looked at each other silently in this gloom, as if taking each other's measure. Thénardier was the first to break the silence.

"How do you mean to get out?"

Jean Valjean not replying, Thénardier continued:

"It is impossible to pick the lock: and yet you must get out of here."

"That is true," said Jean Valjean.

"Well, then, half shares."

"What do you mean?"

"You have killed the man; very good, and I have the key."

Thénardier pointed to Marius, and continued, —

" I do not know you, but you must be a friend, and I wish to help you."

Jean Valjean began to understand. Thénardier took him for an assassin. The latter continued, —

" Listen, mate ; you did not kill this man without looking to see what he had in his pockets. Give me my half and I open the gate."

And half drawing a heavy key from under his ragged blouse, he added, —

" Would you like to see how the key to liberty is made ? Look here."

Jean Valjean was so dazed that he doubted whether what he saw was real. It was Providence appearing in a horrible form, and the good angel issuing from the ground in the shape of Thénardier. The latter thrust his hand into a wide pocket hidden under his blouse, drew out a rope, and handed it to Jean Valjean.

" There," he said, " I give you the rope into the bargain."

" What am I to do with the rope ? "

" You also want a stone, but you will find that outside, as there is a heap of them."

" What am I to do with a stone ? "

" Why, you ass, as you are going to throw the stiff into the river, you want a rope and a stone, or else the body will float on the water."

Jean Valjean took the rope mechanically, and Thénardier snapped his fingers as if a sudden idea had occurred to him.

" Hilloh, mate ! how did you manage to get

through that slough? I did not dare venture into it.
Peuh! you do not smell pleasant."

After a pause he added, —

"I ask you questions, but you are right not to
answer : it is an apprenticeship for the examining
magistrate's ugly quarter of an hour. And then, by
not speaking at all a man runs no risk of speaking
too loud. No matter, though I cannot see your face
and do not know your name, you would do wrong in
supposing that I do not know who you are and what
you want. I know all about it : you have rather
split this gentleman, and now want to get rid of
him somewhere. You prefer the river, that great
nonsense-hider, and I will help you out of the hob-
ble. It is my delight to aid a good fellow when
in trouble."

While commending Jean Valjean for his silence
it was plain that he was trying to make him speak.
He pushed his shoulder, so as to be able to see his
profile, and exclaimed, though without raising the
pitch of his voice, —

"Talking of the slough, you are a precious ass.
Why did you not throw the man into it?"

Jean Valjean preserved silence. Thénardier continued, raising his rag of a cravat to the Adam's
apple, — a gesture which completes the capable air
of a serious man.

"Really, you may have acted sensibly, for the
workmen who will come to-morrow to stop up the
hole would certainly have found the swell, and your
trail would be followed up. Some one has passed
through the sewer. Who? How did he get out?

Was he seen to do so? The police are full of sense; the drain is a traitor, and denounces you. Such a find is a rarity; it attracts attention; for few people employ the sewer for their little business, while the river belongs to everybody, and is the real grave. At the end of a month your man is fished up at the nets of St. Cloud. Well, who troubles himself about that? It's carrion, that's all. Who killed the man? Paris. And justice makes no inquiries. You acted wisely."

The more loquacious Thénardier became, the more silent Jean Valjean was. Thénardier shook his shoulder again.

"And now, let's settle our business. You have seen my key, so show me your money."

Thénardier was haggard, firm, slightly menacing, but remarkably friendly. There was one strange fact: Thénardier's manner was not simple; he did not appear entirely at his ease. While not affecting any mysterious air, he spoke in a low voice. From time to time he laid his finger on his lip, and muttered "Chut!" It was difficult to guess why, for there were only themselves present. Jean Valjean thought that other bandits were probably hidden in some corner no great distance off, and that Thénardier was not anxious to share with them. The latter continued, —

"Now for a finish. How much had the swell about him?"

Jean Valjean felt in his pockets. It was, as will be remembered, always his rule to have money about him, for the gloomy life of expedients to which he was condemned rendered it a law for him. This time, however, he was unprovided. In putting on upon the previous evening his National Guard uniform, he forgot, mournfully absorbed as he was, to take out his pocket-book, and he had only some change in his waistcoat-pocket. He turned out his pocket, which was saturated with slime, and laid on the banquette a louis d'or, two five-franc pieces, and five or six double sous. Thénardier thrust out his lower lip with a significant twist of the neck.

" You did not kill him for much," he said.

He began most familiarly feeling in Jean Valjean and Marius's pockets, and Jean Valjean, who was most anxious to keep his back to the light, allowed him to do so. While feeling in Marius's coat, Thénardier, with the dexterity of a conjurer, managed to tear off, without Jean Valjean perceiving the fact, a strip, which he concealed under his blouse ; probably thinking that this piece of cloth might help him to recognize hereafter the assassinated man and the assassin. However, he found no more than the thirty francs.

" It is true," he said ; " one with the other, you have no more than that."

And forgetting his phrase, half-shares, he took all. He hesitated a little at the double sous, but on reflection he took them too, while grumbling, " I don't care, it is killing people too cheaply."

This done, he again took the key from under his blouse.

" Now, my friend, you must be off. It is here

as at the fairs ; you pay when you go out. You
have paid, so you can go."

And he began laughing. We may be permitted
to doubt whether he had the pure and disinterested
intention of saving an assassin, when he gave a
stranger the help of this key, and allowed any one
but himself to pass through this gate. Thénardier
helped Jean Valjean to replace Marius on his back,
and then proceeded to the grating on the tips of
his naked feet. After making Jean Valjean a sign
to follow him, he placed his finger on his lip, and
remained for some seconds as if in suspense ; but
when the inspection was over he put the key in
the lock. The bolt slid, and the gate turned on
its hinges without either grinding or creaking. It
was plain that this grating and these hinges, carefully oiled, opened more frequently than might be
supposed. This smoothness was ill-omened ; it spoke
of furtive comings and goings, of the mysterious entrances and exits of night-men, and the crafty foot-
fall of crime. The sewer was evidently an accomplice
of some dark band, and this taciturn grating was a
receiver. Thénardier held the door ajar, left just
room for Jean Valjean to pass, relocked the gate,
and plunged back into the darkness, making no more
noise than a breath ; he seemed to walk with the
velvety pads of a tiger. A moment later this hideous
providence had disappeared, and Jean Valjean was
outside.

CHAPTER IX.

MARIUS APPEARS DEAD TO A CONNOISSEUR.

HE let Marius slip down on to the bank. They were outside : the miasmas, the darkness, the horror, were behind him ; the healthy, pure, living, joyous, freely respirable air inundated him. All around him was silence, but it was the charming silence of the sun setting in the full azure. Twilight was passing, and night, the great liberator, the friend of all those who need a cloak of darkness to escape from an agony, was at hand. The sky presented itself on all sides like an enormous calm, and the river rippled up to his feet with the sound of a kiss. The aerial dialogue of the nests bidding each other good-night in the elms of the Champs Élysées was audible. A few stars, faintly studding the pale blue of the zenith, formed in the immensity little imperceptible flashes. Night unfolded over Jean Valjean's head all the sweetness of infinitude. It was the undecided and exquisite hour which says neither yes nor no. There was already sufficient night for a man to lose himself in it a short distance off, and yet sufficient daylight to recognize any one close by. Jean Valjean was for a few seconds irresistibly overcome by all this august and caressing serenity. There are minutes of obliv-

ion in which suffering gives up harassing the wretch;
all is eclipsed in the thought; peace covers the
dreamer like night, and under the gleaming twilight
the soul is lit with stars in imitation of the sky which
is becoming illumined. Jean Valjean could not refrain from contemplating the vast clear night above
him, and pensively took a bath of ecstasy and prayer
in the majestic silence of the eternal heavens. Then,
as if the feeling of duty returned to him, he eagerly
bent down over Marius, and lifting some water in
the hollow of his hand, softly threw a few drops into
his face. Marius's eyelids did not move, but he still
breathed through his parted lips. Jean Valjean was
again about to plunge his hand into the river, when
he suddenly felt an indescribable uneasiness, as when
we feel there is some one behind us without seeing
him. He turned round, and there was really some
one behind him, as there had been just before.

A man of tall stature, dressed in a long coat, with
folded arms, and carrying in his right hand a "life-
preserver," whose leaden knob could be seen, was
standing a few paces behind Jean Valjean, who was
leaning over Marius. It was with the help of the
darkness a species of apparition; a simple man would
have been frightened at it owing to the twilight, and
a thoughtful one on account of the bludgeon. Jean
Valjean recognized Javert. The reader has doubtless
guessed that the tracker of Thénardier was no other
than Javert. Javert, after his unhoped-for escape
from the barricade, went to the Prefecture of Police,
made a verbal report to the prefect in person in a
short audience, and then immediately returned to

duty, which implied — the note found on him will be remembered — a certain surveillance of the right bank of the river at the Champs Élysées, which had for some time past attracted the attention of the police. There he perceived Thénardier and followed him. The rest is known.

It will be also understood that the grating so obligingly opened for Jean Valjean was a clever trick on the part of Thénardier. He felt that Javert was still there, — the watched man has a scent which never deceives him, — and it was necessary to throw a bone to this greyhound. An asssasin, — what a chance ! he could not let it slip. Thénardier, on putting Jean Valjean outside in his place, offered a prey to the policeman, made him loose his hold, caused himself to be forgotten in a greater adventure, recompensed Javert for his loss of time, — which always flatters a spy, — gained thirty francs, and fully intended for his own part to escape by the help of this diversion.

Jean Valjean had passed from one reef to another.

These two meetings one upon the other, falling from Thénardier on Javert, were rude. Javert did not recognize Jean Valjean, who, as we have said, no longer resembled himself. He did not unfold his arms, but made sure his "life-preserver" by an imperceptible movement, and said, in a sharp, calm voice, —

"Who are you ? "

"Myself."

"What do you mean ? "

"I am Jean Valjean."

Javert placed his life-preserver between his teeth, bent his knees, bowed his back, laid his two powerful hands on Jean Valjean's shoulders, which they held as in two vises, examined and recognized him. Their faces almost touched, and Javert's glance was terrific. Jean Valjean remained inert under Javert's gripe, like a lion enduring the claw of a lynx.

" Inspector Javert," he said, " you have me. Besides, since this morning I have considered myself your prisoner. I did not give you my address in order to try to escape you. Take me, but grant me one thing."

Javert did not seem to hear, but kept his eyeballs fixed on Jean Valjean. His wrinkled chin thrust up his lips toward his nose, a sign of stern reverie. At length he loosed his hold of Jean Valjean, drew himself up, clutched his cudgel, and, as if in a dream, muttered rather than asked this question, —

" What are you doing here, and who is that man ? "

Jean Valjean replied, and the sound of his voice seemed to awaken Javert, —

" It is of him that I wished to speak. Do with me as you please, but help me first to carry him home. I only ask this of you."

Javert's face was contracted in the same way as it always was when any one believed him capable of a concession ; still he did not say no. He stopped again, took from his pocket a handkerchief, which he dipped in the water, and wiped Marius's ensanguined forehead.

" This man was at the barricade," he said in a

low voice, and as if speaking to himself; "he was the one whom they called Marius."

He was a first-class spy, who had observed everything, listened to everything, heard everything, and picked up everything, when he believed himself a dead man; who spied even in his death agony, and, standing on the first step of the sepulchre, took notes. He seized Marius's hand, and felt his pulse.

"He is wounded," said Jean Valjean.

"He is a dead man," said Javert.

Jean Valjean replied, —

"No; not yet."

"Then you brought him from the barricade here?" Javert observed.

His preoccupation must have been great for him not to dwell on this alarming escape through the sewers, and not even remark Jean Valjean's silence after his question. Jean Valjean, on his side, seemed to have a sole thought; he continued, —

"He lives in the Marais, in the Rue des Filles du Calvaire, with his grandfather. I do not know his name."

Jean Valjean felt in Marius's pocket, took out the portfolio, opened it at the page on which Marius had written in pencil, and offered it to Javert. There was still sufficient floating light in the air to be able to read, and Javert, besides, had in his eyes the feline phosphorescence of night-birds. He deciphered the few lines written by Marius, and growled, "Gillenormand, No. 6, Rue des Filles du Calvaire." Then he cried, "Driver!"

Our readers will remember the coachman waiting

above in case of need.   A moment after the hackney,
which came down the incline leading to the watering-
place, was on the bank.   Marius was deposited on
the back seat, and Javert sat down by Jean Valjean's
side on the front one.   When the door was closed
the fiacre started off rapidly along the quays in the
direction of the Bastille.   They quitted the quay
and turned into the streets ; and the driver, a black
outline on his seat, lashed his lean horses.   There
was an icy silence in the hackney coach ; Marius
motionless, with his body reclining in one corner,
his head on his chest, his arms pendent, and his legs
stiff, appeared to be only waiting for a coffin.   Jean
Valjean seemed made of gloom, and Javert of stone ;
and in this fiacre full of night, whose interior, each
time that it passed a lamp, seemed to be lividly lit
up as if by an intermittent flash, accident united and
appeared to confront the three immobilities of tragedy,
— the corpse, the spectre, and the statue.

CHAPTER X.

RETURN OF THE SON PRODIGAL OF HIS LIFE.

At each jolt over the pavement a drop of blood fell from Marius's hair. It was quite night when the hackney coach reached No. 6, Rue des Filles du Calvaire. Javert got out first, examined at a glance the number over the gateway, and raising the heavy knocker of hammered steel, embellished in the old style with a goat and a satyr contending, gave a violent knock. The folding-door opened slightly, and Javert pushed it open. The porter half showed himself, yawning, and scarce awake, candle in hand. All were asleep in the house, for people go to bed early at the Marais, especially on days of rioting. This good old district, terrified by the revolution, takes refuge in sleep, like children who, when they hear " old Bogey coming," quickly hide their heads under the counterpane. In the mean while Jean Valjean and the driver removed Marius from the hackney coach, Valjean holding him under the armpits and the coachman under the knees. While carrying Marius in this way Jean Valjean passed his hands under his clothes, which were terribly torn, felt his chest, and assured himself that his heart still beat. It even beat a little less feebly, as if the motion of the vehicle had produced a certain renewal of vitality. Javert addressed the porter in the tone which becomes the government in the presence of the porter of a factionist.

" Any one live here of the name of Gillenormand? "

" It is here. What do you want with him? "

" We bring him his son."

" His son ? " the porter asked in amazement.

" He is dead."

Jean Valjean, who came up ragged and filthy behind Javert, and whom the porter regarded with some horror, made him a sign that it was not so. The porter seemed neither to understand Javert's re-mark nor Jean Valjean's sign. Javert continued, —

" He has been to the barricade, and here he is."

" To the barricade ! " the porter exclaimed.

" He has been killed. Go and wake his father."

The porter did not stir.

" Be off ! " Javert continued ; and added, " There will be a funeral here to-morrow."

For Javert, the ordinary incidents of the streets were classified categorically, which is the commence-ment of foresight and surveillance, and each eventu-ality had its compartment ; the possible facts were to some extent kept in drawers, whence they issued on occasions, in variable quantities ; there were in the streets, disturbance, riot, carnival, and interments.

The porter limited himself to awaking Basque ; Basque awoke Nicolette ; Nicolette awoke Aunt Gillenormand. As for the grandfather, he was left to sleep, as it was thought that he would know the affair quite soon enough as it was. Marius was carried to the first-floor, no one being acquainted with the fact in the rest of the house, and he was laid on an old sofa in M. Gillenormand's ante-room, and while Basque went to fetch a physician and Nicolette opened the linen-presses, Jean Valjean felt Javert touch his shoulder. He understood, and went down, Javert following close at his heels. The porter saw them depart, as he had seen them arrive, with a startled sleepiness. They got into the hackney coach, and the driver on his box.

"Inspector Javert," Jean Valjean said, "grant me one thing more."

"What is it?" Javert answered roughly.

"Let me go home for a moment, and you can then do with me what you please."

Javert remained silent for a few moments with his chin thrust into the collar of his great-coat, and then let down the front window.

"Driver," he said, "No. 7, Rue de l'Homme Armé."

CHAPTER XI.

THEY did not speak during the entire ride. What did Jean Valjean want ? To finish what he had begun ; to warn Cosette, tell her where Marius was, give her perhaps some other useful information, and make, if he could, certain final arrangements. For his own part, as regarded what concerned him personally, it was all over ; he had been arrested by Javert, and did not resist. Any other than he, in such a situation, would perhaps have thought vaguely of the rope which Thénardier had given him, and the bars of the first cell he entered ; but since his meeting with the Bishop, Jean Valjean had within him a profound religious hesitation against every assault, even on himself. Suicide, that mysterious attack on the unknown, which may contain to a certain extent the death of the soul, was impossible to Jean Valjean.

On entering the Rue de l'Homme Armé the coach stopped, as the street was too narrow for vehicles to pass along it. Jean Valjean and Javert got out. The driver humbly represented to " Mr. Inspector " that the Utrecht velvet of his coach was quite spoiled by the blood of the assassinated man and the filth of the assassin, — that is how he understood the affair, — and he added that an indemnity was due to him. At the same time taking his license-book from his pocket, he begged Mr. Inspector to have the kindness to write him a little bit of a certificate. Javert thrust back the book which the driver offered him and said, —

"How much do you want, including the time you waited and the journey?"

"It's seven hours and a quarter," the driver answered, "and my velvet was brand new. Eighty francs, Mr. Inspector."

Javert took from his pocket four Napoleons, and dismissed the hackney coach. Jean Valjean thought that it was Javert's intention to take him on foot to the Blancs Manteaux post, or that of the Archives, which were close by. They entered the street, which was as usual deserted. Javert followed Jean Valjean, and, on reaching No. 7, the latter rapped, and the gate opened.

"Very good," said Javert; "go up."

He added, with a strange expression, and as if making an effort to speak in this way, —

"I will wait for you here."

Jean Valjean looked at Javert, for this style of conduct was not at all a habit of Javert's. Still, it could not surprise him greatly that Javert should now place in him a sort of haughty confidence, — the confidence of the cat which grants the mouse liberty to the length of its claw, determined as Jean Valjean was to give himself up and make an end of it. He thrust open the gate, entered the house, shouted to the porter, who was lying down and had pulled the string from his bed, " It is I," and mounted the staircase.   On reaching the first story he paused, for every Via Dolorosa has its stations.   The window at the head of the stairs, a sash-window, was open. As is the case in many old houses, the staircase obtained light from, and looked out on, the street.   The street lantern, situated precisely opposite, threw some little light on the stairs, which caused a saving of a lamp.   Jean Valjean, either to breathe or mechanically, thrust his head out of this window and looked down into the street.   It is short, and the lamp lit it from one end to the other.   Jean Valjean had a bedazzlement of stupor : there was no one in it.

Javert had gone away.

CHAPTER XII.

THE GRANDFATHER.

Basque and the porter had carried Marius, who was still lying motionless on the sofa on which he had been laid on arriving, into the drawing-room. The physician, who had been sent for, hurried in, and Aunt Gillenormand had risen. Aunt Gillenormand came and went, horrified, clasping her hands, and incapable of doing anything but saying, "Can it be possible?" She added at intervals, "Everything will be stained with blood." When the first horror had passed away a certain philosophy of the situation appeared even in her mind, and was translated by the exclamation, "It must end in that way." She did not go so far, though, as "Did I not say so?" which is usual on occasions of this nature.

By the surgeon's orders a folding-bed was put up near the sofa. He examined Marius, and after satisfying himself that the pulse still beat, that the patient had no penetrating wound in the chest, and that the blood at the corners of the lips came from the nostrils, he had him laid flat on the bed, without a pillow, the head level with the body, and even a little lower, the chest bare, in order to facilitate the breathing. Mademoiselle Gillenormand, seeing that Marius was

being undressed, withdrew, and told her beads in her
bed-room.   The body had received no internal injury ;
a ball, deadened by the pocket-book, had deviated,
and passed round the ribs with a frightful gash, but
as it was not deep, it was therefore not dangerous.
The long subterranean march had completed the dis-
location of the collar-bone, and there were serious
injuries there.   The arms were covered with sabre-
cuts ; no scar disfigured the face, but the head was
cut all over with gashes.   What would be the state
of these wounds on the head, — did they stop at the
scalp, or did they reach the brain ?   It was impossible to say yet.   It was a serious symptom that they
had caused the faintness.   And men do not always
awake from such fainting-fits ; the hemorrhage, moreover, had exhausted the wounded man.   From the
waist downward the lower part of the body had been
protected by the barricade.

Basque and Nicolette tore up linen and prepared
bandages : Nicolette sewed them and Basque rolled
them.   As they had no lint, the physician had temporarily checked the effusion of blood with cakes of
wadding.   By the side of the bed three candles burned
on the table on which the surgeon's pocket-book lay
open.   He washed Marius's face and hair with cold
water, and a bucketful was red in an instant.   The
porter, candle in hand, lighted him.   The surgeon
seemed to be thinking sadly : from time to time he
gave a negative shake of the head, as if answering
some question which he mentally addressed to himself.
Such mysterious dialogues of the physician with himself are a bad sign for the patient.   At the moment

when the surgeon was wiping the face and gently touching with his finger the still closed eyelids, a door opened at the end of the room, and a tall, pale figure appeared: it was the grandfather. The riot during the last two days had greatly agitated, offended, and occupied M. Gillenormand; he had not been able to sleep on the previous night, and he had been feverish all day. At night he went to bed at a very early hour, bidding his people bar up the house, and had fallen asleep through weariness.

Old men have a fragile sleep. M. Gillenormand's bed-room joined the drawing-room, and whatever precautions had been taken, the noise awoke him. Surprised by the crack of light which he saw in his door, he had got out of bed and groped his way to the door. He was standing on the threshold, with one hand on the door-handle, his head slightly bent forward and shaking, his body enfolded in a white dressing-gown as straight and creaseless as a winding-sheet: he was surprised, and looked like a ghost peering into a tomb. He noticed the bed, and on the mattress this young bleeding man, of the whiteness of wax, with closed eyes, open mouth, livid cheeks, naked to the waist, marked all over with vermilion, wounded, motionless, and brightly illumined.

The grandfather had from head to foot that shudder which ossified limbs can have. His eyes, whose cornea was yellow owing to their great age, were veiled by a sort of glassy stare; his entire face assumed in an instant the earthly angles of a skeleton's head; his arms fell pendent as if a spring had been

broken in them, and his stupor was displayed by the
outspreading of all the fingers of his two old trembling hands. His knees formed a salient angle, displaying through the opening of his dressing-gown
his poor naked legs bristling with white hairs, and
he murmured, —

" Marius ! "

" He has just been brought here, sir," said Basque;
" he went to the barricade, and — "

" He is dead," the old gentleman exclaimed in a
te rible voice. " Oh, the brigand ! "

Then a sort of sepulchral transfiguration drew up
this centenarian as straight as a young man.

" You are the surgeon, sir," he said; " begin by
telling me one thing. He is dead, is he not ? "

The surgeon, who was frightfully anxious, maintained silence, and M. Gillenormand wrung his hands
with a burst of terrifying laughter.

" He is dead, he is dead ! He has let himself be
killed at the barricade through hatred of me ; it was
against me that he did it ! Ah, the blood-drinker,
that is the way in which he returns to me ! Woe of
my life, he is dead ! "

He went to a window, opened it quite wide, as if
he were stifling, and standing there began speaking
to the night in the street.

"Stabbed, sabred, massacred, exterminated, slashed,
cut to pieces ! Do you see that, the beggar ! He
knew very well that I expected him, and that I had his
room ready, and that I had placed at my bed-head
his portrait when he was a child ! He knew very
well that he need only return, and that for years I

had been recalling him, and that I sat at night by
my fire-side with my hands on my knees, not knowing what to do, and that I was crazy about him!
You knew that very well; you had only to return
and say, 'It is I,' and you would be the master of
the house, and I would obey you, and you could do
anything you liked with your old ass of a grandfather! You knew it very well, and said, 'No, he
is a royalist, I will not go!' and you went to the
barricades, and have let yourself be killed out of
spite, in order to revenge yourself for what I said
on the subject of Monsieur le Duc de Berry! Is not
that infamous! Go to bed and sleep quietly, for he
is dead. This is my awaking."

The surgeon, who was beginning to be anxious for
both, left Marius, and going up to M. Gillenormand,
took his arm. The grandfather turned, looked at
him with eyes that seemed dilated and bloodshot,
and said calmly, —

"I thank you sir, I am calm. I am a man. I
saw the death of Louis XVI., and can endure events.
There is one thing that is terrible, — it is the thought
that it is your newspapers which do all the mischief.
You have scribblers, speakers, lawyers, orators, tri-
bunes, discussions, progress, lights, rights of man,
liberty of the press, and that is the way in which
your children are brought back to your houses. Oh,
Marius, it is abominable! Killed! dead before me!
a barricade! Oh, the bandit! Doctor, you live in
the quarter, I believe? Oh yes, I know you well.
I have seen your cab pass from my window. Well,
I will tell you. You are wrong if you think that I

am in a passion, for people do not get in a passion with a dead man, it would be stupid. That is a boy I brought up; I was old when he was still quite little. He played in the Tuileries with his little spade and his little chair, and, in order that the inspectors should not scold, I used to fill up with my cane the holes which he made with his spade. One day he cried, ' Down with Louis XVIII. !' and went off. It is not my fault. He was all pink and white, and his mother is dead : have you noticed that all little children are light-haired? He is a son of one of those brigands of the Loire, but children are innocent of their fathers' crimes. I remember him when he was so high, and he could never manage to pronounce a *d.* He spoke so sweetly and incomprehensibly that you might have fancied him a bird. I remember one day that a circle was formed in front of the Farnese Hercules to admire that child, he was so lovely. He had a head such as you see in pictures. I used to speak loud to him, and threaten him with my cane ; but he knew very well that it was a joke. In the morning, when he entered my room, I scolded; but it produced the effect of sunshine upon me. It is not possible to defend yourself against these brats, for they take you, and hold you, and do not let you go again. It is the fact that there never was a Cupid like that child. And now what do you say of your Lafayette, your Benjamin Constant, and your Tirecuir de Corcelles, who kill him for me ? Oh, it cannot pass away like that ! "

He went up to Marius, who was still livid and motionless, and began wringing his hands again. The old gentleman's white lips moved as it were mechanically, and allowed indistinct sentences to pass, which were scarce audible. "Ah, heartless! ah, clubbist! ah, scoundrel! ah, Septembrizer!"—reproaches uttered in a low voice by a dying man to a corpse. By degrees, as such internal eruptions must always burst forth, the flood of words returned; but the grandfather seemed no longer to have the strength to utter them; his voice was so hollow and choked that it seemed to come from the other brink of an abyss.

"I do not care a bit; I will die too. And then to think there is not a wench in Paris who would not be happy to produce the happiness of that scoundrel,—a scamp, who, instead of amusing himself and enjoying life, went to fight, and let himself be shot like a brute! And for whom, and for what? For the republic, instead of going to dance at the Chaumière, as is the duty of young men! It is really worth while being twenty years of age. The republic,—a fine absurdity! Poor mothers bring pretty boys into the world for that! Well, he is dead; that will make two hearses under the gateway. So you have got yourself served in that way for love of General Lamarque! What did General Lamarque do for you? A sabrer! a chatterer! to get one's self killed for a dead man! Is it not enough to drive one mad? Can you understand that? At twenty! and without turning his head to see whether he left anything behind him! Now, see the poor old fellows who are obliged to die all alone. Rot in your corner, owl! Well, after all, that is what I hoped for, and is for the best, as it will kill me right off.

I am too old ; I am one hundred ; I am a hundred thousand, and I had a right to be dead long ago. Well, this blow settles it. It is all over. What happiness ! What is the use of making him inhale ammonia and all that pile of drugs ? You ass of a doctor, you are wasting your time. There, he 's dead, quite dead ! I know it, for I am dead too. He did not do the thing by halves. Yes, the present age is infamous, infamous, infamous ! And that is what I think of you, your ideas, your systems, your masters, your oracles, your doctors, your scamps of writers, your rogues of philosophers, and all the revolutions which have startled the Tuileries ravens during the last sixty years. And since you were pitiless in letting yourself be killed so, I will not even feel sorry at your death. Do your hear, assassin ? "

At this moment Marius slowly opened his eyes, and his glance, still veiled by lethargic surprise, settled on M. Gillenormand.

" Marius ! " the old man cried ; " Marius, my little Marius ! My child ! My beloved son ! You open your eyes ! You look at me ! You are alive ! Thanks ! "

And he fell down in a fainting fit.

BOOK IV.

JAVERT DERAILED.

JAVERT retired slowly from the Rue de l'Homme Armé. He walked with drooping head for the first time in his life, and equally for the first time in his life with his hands behind his back. Up to that day Javert had only assumed, of Napoleon's two attitudes, the one which expresses resolution, the arms folded on the chest; the one indicating uncertainty, the arms behind the back, was unknown to him. Now a change had taken place, and his whole person, slow and sombre, was stamped with anxiety. He buried himself in the silent streets, but followed a certain direction. He went by the shortest road to the Seine, reached the Quai des Ormes, walked along it, passed the Grêve, and stopped, a little distance from the Place du Châtelet, at the corner of the Pont Nôtre Dame. The Seine makes there, between that bridge and the Pont au Change on one side, and the Quai de la Mégisserie and the Quai aux Fleurs on the other, a species of square lake traversed by a rapid. This point of the Seine is feared by sailors; nothing can be more dangerous than this rapid, at that period contracted and irritated by the piles of the mill bridge, since demolished. The two bridges, so close to each other, heighten the danger, for the water hurries formidably through the arches. It rolls in broad, terrible waves, it increases, and is heaped up; the flood strives to root out the piles of the bridge with thick liquid cords. Men who fall in there do not reappear, and the best swimmers are drowned.

Javert leaned his elbows on the parapet, his chin on his hand, and while his hands mechanically closed on his thick whiskers, he reflected. A novelty, a revolution, a catastrophe had just taken place within him, and he must examine into it. Javert was suffering horribly, and for some hours past Javert had ceased to be simple. He was troubled; this brain, so limpid in its blindness, had lost its transparency, and there was a cloud in this crystal. Javert felt in his conscience duty doubled, and he could not hide the fact from himself. When he met Jean Valjean so unexpectedly on the Seine bank, he had something within him of the wolf that recaptures its prey and the dog that finds its master again. He saw before him two roads, both equally straight; but he saw two of them, and this terrified him, as he had never known in his life but one straight line. And, poignant agony! these two roads were contrary, and one of these right lines excluded the other. Which of the two was the true one? His situation was indescribable: to owe his life to a malefactor, to accept this debt and repay him; to be, in spite of himself, on the same footing with an escaped convict, and requite one service with another service; to let it be said to him, " Be off! " and to say in his turn, " Be free ! " to sacrifice to personal motives duty, that general obligation, and to feel in these personal motives something general too, and perhaps superior; to betray society in order to remain faithful to his conscience, — that all these absurdities should be realized, and accumulated upon him, was what startled him. One thing had astonished him, — that Jean Valjean had shown him mercy; and one thing had petrified him, — that he, Javert, had shown mercy to Jean Valjean.

Where was he? He sought and no longer found himself. What was he to do now? To give up Jean Valjean was bad, to leave Jean Valjean at liberty was bad. In the former case, the man of authority fell lower than the man of the galleys; in the second, a convict rose higher than the law, and set his foot upon it. In either case, dishonor for him, Javert. Whatever resolution he might form, there was a fall, for destiny has certain extremities projecting over the impossible, beyond which life is only a precipice. Javert had reached one of these extremities: one of his anxieties was to be constrained to think, and the very violence of all these contradictory emotions compelled him to do so. Now, thought was an unusual thing for him, and singularly painful. There is always in thought a certain amount of internal rebellion, and he was irritated at having that within him. Thought, no matter on what subject beyond the narrow circle of his destiny, would have been to him in any case useless and wearisome; but thinking about the day which had just passed was a torture. And yet he must after such shocks look into his conscience, and give himself an account of himself. What he had done caused him to shudder; he, Javert, had thought fit to decide — against all police regulations, against all social and judicial organization, and against the entire codes — a discharge: that had suited him. He had substituted his own affairs for public affairs; was not that unjustifiable? Each time that he stood facing the nameless action which he had committed, he trembled from head to foot. What should he resolve on? Only one resource was left him, — to return at full speed to the Rue de l'Homme Armé and lock up Jean Valjean. It was clear that this was what he ought to do, but he could not do it. Something barred the way on that side. What! is there anything in the world besides sentences, the police, and the authorities? Javert was overwhelmed.

A sacred galley-slave! a convict impregnable by justice, and that through the deed of Javert! Was it not frightful that Javert and Jean Valjean, the man made to punish and the man made to endure, — that these two men, who were both the property of the law, should have reached the point of placing themselves both above the law? What! such enormities could happen and no one be punished? Jean Valjean, stronger than the whole social order, would be free, and he, Javert, would continue to eat the bread of the Government! His reverie gradually became terrible: he might through this reverie have reproached himself slightly on the subject of the insurgent carried home to the Rue des Filles du Cal-

vaire, but he did not think of it. The slighter fault
was lost in the greater ; and besides, this insurgent
was evidently a dead man, and, legally, death checks
persecution. Jean Valjean, — that was the weight
which he had on his mind. Jean Valjean disconcerted
him. All the axioms which had been the support of
his whole life crumbled away before this man, and
the generosity of Jean Valjean to him, Javert, overwhelmed him. Other facts which he remembered, and
which he had formerly treated as falsehoods and folly,
now returned to his mind as realities. M. Madeleine
reappeared behind Jean Valjean, and the two figures
were blended into one, which was venerable. Javert
felt that something horrible, admiration for a convict,
was entering his soul. Respect for a galley-slave,
is it possible ? He shuddered at it, and could not escape from it, although he struggled. He was reduced
to confess in his soul the sublimity of this villain, and
this was odious. A benevolent malefactor, a com-
passionate, gentle, helping, and merciful convict, —
repaying good for evil, pardon for hatred, preferring
pity to vengeance, ready to destroy himself sooner
than his enemy, saving the man who had struck him,
kneeling on the pinnacle of virtue, and nearer to the
angels than to man. Javert was constrained to confess to himself that such a monster existed.

This could not last. Assuredly — and we lay
stress on the fact — he had not yielded without resistance to this monster, to this infamous angel, to
this hideous hero, at whom he felt almost as indignant as stupefied. Twenty times while in that hackney coach face to face with Jean Valjean the legal

tiger had roared within him. Twenty times he had felt tempted to hurl himself on Jean Valjean, to seize and devour him, — that is to say, arrest him. What more simple, in fact, — shout to the nearest post before which he passed, "Here is a convict who has broken his ban!" and then go away, leave the condemned man there, be ignorant of the rest, and interfere no further? This man is eternally the prisoner of the law, and the law will do what it pleases with him. What was fairer? Javert had said all this to himself; he had wished to go further, — to act, apprehend the man, — and then, as now, had been unable; and each time that his hand was convulsively raised to Jean Valjean's collar, it fell back as if under an enormous weight, and he heard in the bottom of his heart a voice, a strange voice, crying to him, "That is well. Give up your saviour, then send for Pontius Pilate's basin, and wash your hands in it!"

Then his thoughts reverted to himself, and by the side of Jean Valjean aggrandized he saw himself degraded. A convict was his benefactor, but why had he allowed that man to let him live? He had the right of being killed at that barricade, and should have employed that right. It would have been better to call the other insurgents to his aid against Jean Valjean, and have himself shot by force. His supreme agony was the disappearance of certainty, and he felt himself uprooted. The code was now only a stump in his hand, and he had to deal with scruples of an unknown species. There was within him a sentimental revelation entirely distinct from the legal affirmation, his sole measure hitherto, and it was not sufficient to remain in his old honesty. A whole order of unexpected facts arose and subjugated him, an entire new world appeared to his soul; benefits accepted and returned, devotion, mercy, indulgence, violence done by pity to austerity, no more definitive condemnation, no more damnation, the possibility of a tear in the eye of the law, and perhaps some justice according to God acting in an inverse ratio to justice according to man. He perceived in the darkness the rising of an unknown moral sun, and he was horrified and dazzled. He was an owl forced to look like the eagle.

He said to himself that it was true, then, that there were exceptions, that authority might be disconcerted, that the rule might fall short in the presence of a fact, that everything was not contained in the text of a code, that the unforeseen made itself obeyed, that the virtue of a convict might set a snare for the virtue of a functionary, that the monstrous might be divine, that destiny had such ambuscades; and he thought with despair that he had himself not been protected from a surprise. He was compelled to recognize that goodness existed; this galley-slave had been good, and he, extraordinary to say, had been good also. Hence he was becoming depraved. He felt that he was a coward, and it horrified him. The ideal for Javert was not to be human, grand, or sublime; it was to be irreproachable, — and now he had broken down. How had he reached this stage? How had all this happened? He could not have told himself. He took his head between his hands; but whatever he might do, he could not succeed in explaining it. He certainly had had the intention of delivering Jean Valjean over to the law, of which Jean Valjean was the captive and of which he was the slave. He had not confessed to himself for a single instant, while he held him, that he had a thought of letting him go; it was to some extent unconsciously that his hand had opened and allowed him to escape.

All sorts of enigmatic novelties passed before his eyes. He asked himself questions and gave himself answers, and his answers terrified him. He asked himself, "What has this convict, this desperate man, whom I followed to persecution, and who had me under his heel, and could have avenged himself, and ought to have acted so, both for his rancor and his security, done in leaving me my life and showing me mercy, — his duty? No, something more. And what have I done in showing him mercy in my turn, — my duty? No, something more. Is there, then, something more than duty?" Here he was terrified, he was thrown off his balance, — one of the scales fell into the abyss, the other ascended to heaven; and Javert felt no less horror at the one above than at the one below. Without being the least in the world what is termed a Voltairian, or philosopher, or incredulous man, respectful, on the contrary, instinctively to the Established Church, he only knew it as an august fragment of the social *ensemble;* order was his dogma, and sufficient for him. Since he had attained man's age and office, he had set nearly all his religion in the police, being, — and we employ the words without the slightest irony, and in their most serious acceptation, — being, as we have said, a spy, as another man is a priest. He had a superior, M. Gisquet; but he had never thought up to this day of that other superior, God. He felt the presence of this new Chief unexpectedly, and was troubled by Him. He was thrown out of gear by this person; he knew not what to do with this Superior, for he was not ignorant that the subordinate is bound always to bow the head, that he must neither disobey, nor blame, nor discuss, and that when facing a superior who astonishes him too much, the inferior has no other resource but his resignation. But how could he manage to give in his resignation to God?

However this might be, one fact to which he constantly returned, and which ruled everything else, was that he had just committed a frightful infraction of the law. He had closed his eyes to a relapsed convict who had broken his ban; he had set a galley-slave at liberty. He had stolen from the laws a man who belonged to them. He had done this, and no longer understood himself. He was not certain of being himself. The very reasons of his deed escaped him, and he only felt the dizziness it produced. He had lived up to this moment in that blind faith which engenders a dark probity; and this faith was leaving him, this probity had failed him. All that he had believed was dissipated, and truths which he did not desire inexorably besieged him. He must henceforth be another man, and he suffered the strange pain of a conscience suddenly operated on for cataract. He saw what it was repulsive to him to see, and felt himself spent, useless, dislocated from his past life, discharged and dissolved. Authority was dead within him, and he no longer had a reason for living. Terrible situation! to be moved. To be made of granite, and doubt! To be the statue of punishment cast all of one piece in the mould of the law, and suddenly to perceive that you have under your bronze bosom something absurd and disobedient, which almost resembles a heart! To have requited good for good, though you have said to yourself up to this day that such good is evil! To be the watch-dog, and fawn! To be ice, and melt! To be a pair of pincers, and become a hand! suddenly to feel your fingers opening! To lose your hold. Oh, what a frightful thing! The man projectile, no longer knowing his road, and recoiling! To be obliged to confess this: infallibility is not infallible; there may be an error in the dogma; all is not said when a code has spoken, society is not perfect, authority is complicated with vacillation, a crack in the immutable is possible, judges are men, the law may be deceived, the courts may make a mistake! To see a flaw in the immense blue window-glass of the firmament.

What was taking place in Javert was the Fampoux of a rectilinear conscience, the overthrow of a mind, the crushing of a probity irresistibly hurled in a straight line and breaking itself against God. It was certainly strange that the fireman of order, the engineer of authority, mounted on the blind iron horse, could be unsaddled by a beam of light! That the incommutable, the direct, the correct, the geo-

metrical, the passive, the perfect, could bend; that
there should be for the locomotive a road to Damas-
cus! God, ever within man, and Himself the true
conscience, refractory to the false conscience; the
spark forbidden to expire, the ray ordered to remember the sun, the mind enjoined to recognize the
true absolute when it confronts itself with the ficti-
tious absolute, a humanity that cannot be lost; the
human heart inadmissible, — did Javert comprehend
this splendid phenomenon, the most glorious, perhaps, of our internal prodigies? Did he penetrate
it? Did he explain it to himself? Evidently no.
But under the pressure of this incomprehensible in-
contestability he felt his brain cracking. He was
less transfigured than the victim of this prodigy: he
endured it with exasperation, and only saw in all
this an immense difficulty of living. It seemed to
him as if henceforth his breathing was eternally impeded. He was not accustomed to have anything
unknown over his head; hitherto everything he had
above him had been to his eye a clear, simple, limpid
surface; there was nothing unknown or obscure,
— nothing but what was definite, co-ordinated, enchained, precise, exact, circumscribed, limited, and
closed. Everything foreseen, authority was a flat surface; there was no fall in it or dizziness before it.
Javert had never seen anything unknown except below him. Irregularity, unexpected things, the disorderly opening of the chaos, and a possible fall over
a precipice, — all this was the doing of the lower
regions, of the rebels, the wicked and the wretched.
How Javert threw himself back, and was suddenly

startled by this extraordinary apparition, — a gulf above him!

What then! the world was dismantled from top to bottom and absolutely disconcerted! In what could men trust, when what they felt convinced of was crumbling away! What! the flaw in the cuirass of society could be formed by a magnanimous scoundrel! What! an honest servant of the law could find himself caught between two crimes, — the crime of letting a man escape and the crime of arresting him! All was not certain, then, in the orders given by the State to the official! There could be blind alleys in duty! What then? all this was real! Was it true that an ex-bandit, bowed under condemnations, could draw himself up, and end by being in the right? Was this credible? Were there, then, cases in which the law must retire before transfigured crime, and stammer its apologies? Yes, it was so! and Javert saw it, and Javert touched it! And not only could he not deny it, but he had a share in it. These were realities, and it was abominable that real facts could attain such a deformity. If facts did their duty they would restrict themselves to bring proofs of the law, for facts are sent by God. Was, then, anarchy about to descend from on high? Thus, both in the exaggeration of agony and the optical illusion of consternation, everything which might have restricted and corrected his impression faded away, and society, the human race, and the universe henceforth were contained for his eyes in a simple and hideous outline. Punishment, the thing tried, the strength due to the legislature, the decrees of

sovereign courts, the magistracy, the government,
prevention and repression, official wisdom, legal infallibility, the principle of authority, all the dogmas
on which political and civil security, the sovereignty,
justice, logic flowing from the code and public truth,
were a heap of ruins, chaos. He himself, Javert, the
watcher of order, incorruptibility in the service of
the police, the trusty mastiff of society, conquered
and hurled to the ground ; and on the summit of all
this ruin stood a man in a green cap, and with a
glory round his brow, — such was the state of overthrow he had reached, such the frightful vision which
he had in his mind. Was this endurable ? No, it
was a violent state, were there ever one, and there
were only two ways of escaping from it : one was to
go resolutely to Jean Valjean and restore to the
dungeon the man of the galleys ; the other —

Javert left the parapet, and with head erect this
time walked firmly toward the guard-room indicated
by a lantern at one of the corners of the Place du
Chatelet. On reaching it he saw through the window
a policeman, and went in. The police recognize each
other merely by the way in which they push open
the door of a guard-room. Javert mentioned his
name, showed his card to the sergeant, and sat down
at the table on which a candle was burning. There
were also on the table a pen, a leaden inkstand, and
paper, ready for contingent reports and the records
of the night patrols. This table, always completed
by a straw chair, is an institution ; it exists in all
police offices ; it is always adorned with a boxwood
saucer full of sawdust, and a box of red wafers, and

it is the lower stage of the official style. It is here that the State literature commences. Javert took the pen and a sheet of paper and began writing. This is what he wrote : —

"A FEW REMARKS FOR THE GOOD OF THE SERVICE.

" 1. I beg M. le Préfet to cast his eyes on this.

" 2. Prisoners when they return from examination at the magistrate's office take off their shoes and remain barefoot on the slabs while they are being searched. Some cough on re-entering prison. This entails infirmary expenses.

" 3. Tracking is good, with relays of agents at regular distances ; but on important occasions two agents at the least should not let each other out of sight, because if for any reason one agent were to fail in his duty, the other would watch him and take his place.

" 4. There is no explanation why the special rules of the prison of the Madelonnettes prohibit a prisoner from having a chair, even if he pay for it.

" 5. At the Madelonnettes there are only two gratings to the canteen, which allows the canteen woman to let the prisoners touch her hand.

" 6. The prisoners called ' barkers,' who call the other prisoners to the visitors' room, demand two sous from each prisoner for crying his name distinctly. This is a robbery.

" 7. Ten sous are kept back from the pay of a prisoner working in the weaving room for a running thread : this is an abuse on the part of the manager, as the cloth is not the less good.

" 8. It is annoying that visitors to La Force are obliged to pass through the boys' court in proceeding to the speaking-room of Sainte Marie l'Égyptienne.

" 9. It is certain that gendarmes are daily heard repeating, in the court-yard of the Préfecture, the examination of prisoners by the magistrates. For a gendarme, who ought to be consecrated, to repeat what he has heard in the examination room is a serious breach of duty.

" 10. Madame Henry is an honest woman, her canteen is very clean ; but it is wrong for a woman to hold the key of the secret cells. This is not worthy of the Conciergerie of a great civilization."

Javert wrote these lines in his calmest and most correct handwriting, not omitting to cross a *t*, and making the paper creak firmly beneath his pen. Under the last line he signed, —

" JAVERT, *Inspector of the first class.*
" At the post of the Place du Chatelet,
about one in the morning, June 7, 1832."

Javert dried the ink on the paper, folded it like a letter, sealed it, wrote on the back, " Note for the Administration," left it on the table, and quitted the guard-room. The glass door fell back after him. He again diagonally crossed the Place du Chatelet, reached the quay again, and went back with automatic precision to the same spot which he had left a quarter of an hour previously ; he bent down and found himself again in the same attitude on the same parapet slab ; it seemed as if he had not stirred. The darkness was complete, for it was the sepulchral moment which follows midnight; a ceiling of clouds hid the stars; the houses in the Cité did not display a single light, no one passed, all the streets and quays that could be seen were deserted, and Nôtre Dame and the towers of the Palace of Justice appeared lineaments of the night. A lamp reddened the edge of the quay, and the shadows of the bridges looked ghostly one behind the other. Rains had swelled the river. The spot where Javert was leaning was, it will be remembered, precisely above the rapids of the Seine and that formidable whirlpool which unrolls itself and rolls itself up again like an endless screw. Javert stooped down and looked; all was dark, and nothing could be distinguished. A sound of spray was audible, but the river was invisible. At moments in this dizzy depth a flash appeared and undulated, for water has the power, even on the darkest night, of obtaining light, no one knows whence, and chang-ing itself into a lizard. The glimmer vanished and all became indistinct again. Immensity seemed open there, and what was beneath was not water, but the gulf. The quay-wall, abrupt, confused, mingled with the vapor, hidden immediately, produced the effect of a precipice of infinitude.

Nothing could be seen but the hostile coldness of the water, and the sickly smell of the damp stones could be felt. A ferocious breath rose from this abyss; and the swelling of the river, divined rather than perceived, the tragic muttering of the water, the mournful immensity of the bridge arches, a pos-sible fall into this gloomy vacuum, — all this shadow was full of horror. Javert remained for some moments motionless, gazing at this opening of the darkness, and considered the invisible with an intentness which resembled attention. All at once he took off his hat and placed it on the brink of the quay. A moment after a tall black figure, which any belated passer-by might have taken at a distance for a ghost, appeared standing on the parapet, stooped toward the Seine, then drew itself up, and fell straight into the darkness. There was a dull plash, and the shadows alone were in the secret of this obscure form which had disappeared beneath the waters.

BOOK V.

GRANDSON AND GRANDFATHER.

CHAPTER I.

WHERE WE AGAIN MEET THE TREE WITH THE ZINC PATCH.

SOME time after the events which we have just recorded, the Sieur Boulatruelle had a lively emotion. The Sieur Boulatruelle is the road-mender of Montfermeil of whom we have already caught a glimpse in the dark portions of this book. Boulatruelle, it will possibly be remembered, was a man occupied with troubled and various things. He broke stones and plundered travellers on the highway. Road-mender and robber, he had a dream : he believed in the treasures buried in the forest of Montfermeil. He hoped some day to find money in the ground at the foot of a tree, and in the mean while willingly fished for it in the pockets of passers-by. Still, for the present he was prudent, for he had just had a narrow escape. He was, as we know, picked up with the other ruffians in Jondrette's garret. There is some usefulness in a vice, for his drunkenness saved him, and it never could be cleared up whether he were there as a robber or as a robbed man. He was set at liberty on account of his proved intoxication on the night of the attack, and returned to the woods. He went back to his road from Gagny to Lagny, to break stones for the State, under surveillance, with hanging head and very thoughtful, slightly chilled by the robbery which had almost ruined him, but turning with all the more tenderness to the wine which had saved him.

As for the lively emotion which he had a short time after his return beneath the turf-roof of his road-mender's cabin, it was this: One morning Boulatruelle, while going as usual to work and to his lurking-place, possibly a little before daybreak, perceived among the branches a man whose back he could alone see, but whose shape, so he fancied, through the mist and darkness, was not entirely unknown to him. Boulatruelle, though a drunkard, had a correct and lucid memory, an indispensable defensive weapon for any man who is at all on bad terms with legal order.

" Where the devil have I seen some one like that man ? " he asked.

But he could give himself no reply, save that he resembled somebody. of whom he had a confused recollection. Boulatruelle, however, made his comparisons and calculations, though he was unable to settle the identity. This man did not belong to those parts, and had come there evidently afoot, as no public vehicle passed through Montfermeil at that hour. He must have been walking all night. Where did he come from ? No great distance, for he had neither haversack nor bundle. Doubtless

from Paris. Why was he in this wood? Why was
he there at such an hour? What did he want there?
Boulatruelle thought of the treasure. By dint of
racking his memory he vaguely remembered having
had, several years previously, a similar alarm on the
subject of a man who might very well be this man.
While meditating he had, under the very weight
of his meditation, hung his head, a natural but not
clever thing. When he raised it again the man had
disappeared in the forest and the mist.

"By the deuce!" said Boulatruelle, "I will find
him again, and discover to what parish that parish-
ioner belongs. This walker of Patron-Minette has a
motive, and I will know it. No one must have
a secret in my forest without my being mixed up
in it."

He took up his pick, which was very sharp.
"Here's something," he growled, "to search the
ground and a man."

And as one thread is attached to another thread,
covering the steps as well as he could in the direction
which the man must have pursued, he began marching through the coppice. When he had gone about
a hundred yards, day, which was beginning to break,
aided him. Footsteps on the sand here and there,
trampled grass, broken heather, young branches bent
into the shrubs and rising with a graceful slowness,
like the arms of a pretty woman who stretches herself on waking, gave him a species of trail. He followed it and then lost it, and time slipped away; he
got deeper into the wood and reached a species of
eminence. An early sportsman passing at a distance

along a path, and whistling the air of Guillery, gave
him the idea of climbing up a tree, and though old,
he was active. There was on the mound a very large
beech, worthy of Tityrus and Boulatruelle, and he
climbed up the tree as high as he could. The idea
was a good one; for while exploring the solitude on
the side where the wood is most entangled, Boulatruelle suddenly perceived the man, but had no
sooner seen him than he lost him out of sight again.
The man entered, or rather glided, into a rather
distant clearing, masked by large trees, but which
Boulatruelle knew very well, because he had noticed
near a large heap of stones a sick chestnut-tree bandaged with a zinc plate nailed upon it. This clearing is what was formerly called the Blaru-bottom,
and the pile of stones, intended no one knows for
what purpose, which could be seen there thirty years
ago, is doubtless there still. Nothing equals the
longevity of a heap of stones, except that of a plank
paling. It is there temporarily; what a reason for
lasting!

Boulatruelle, with the rapidity of joy, tumbled off
the tree rather than came down it. The lair was
found, and now he had only to seize the animal.
The famous treasure he had dreamed of was probably
there. It was no small undertaking to reach the
clearing by beaten paths which make a thousand
annoying windings; it would take a good quarter of
an hour. In a straight line through the wood, which
is at that spot singularly dense, very thorny, and
most aggressive, it would take half an hour at least.
This is what Boulatruelle was wrong in not under-

standing; he believed in the straight line, — a respectable optical illusion which has ruined many men. The wood, bristling though it was, appeared to him the right road.

"Let us go by the Rue de Rivoli of the wolves," he said.

Boulatruelle, accustomed to crooked paths, this time committed the error of going straight, and resolutely cast himself among the shrubs. He had to contend with holly, nettles, hawthorns, eglantines, thistles, and most irascible roots, and was fearfully scratched. At the bottom of the ravine he came to a stream which he was obliged to cross, and at last reached the Blaru clearing after forty minutes, perspiring, wet through, blowing, and ferocious. There was no one in the clearing. Boulatruelle hurried to the heap of stones; it was still in its place, and had not been carried off. As for the man, he had vanished in the forest. He had escaped. Where? In which direction? Into which clump of trees? It were impossible to guess. And, most crushing thing of all, there was behind the heap of stones and in front of the zinc-banded tree a pick, forgotten or abandoned, and a hole; but the hole was empty.

"Robber!" Boulatruelle cried, shaking his fists at heaven.

CHAPTER II.

MARIUS LEAVING CIVIL WAR PREPARES FOR A
DOMESTIC WAR.

MARIUS was for a long time neither dead nor
alive. He had for several weeks a fever accompanied
by delirium, and very serious brain symptoms caused
by the shocks of the wounds in the head rather than
the wounds themselves. He repeated Cosette's name
for whole nights with the lugubrious loquacity of
fever and the gloomy obstinacy of agony. The width
of certain wounds was a serious danger, for the sup-
puration of wide wounds may always be absorbed
into the system, and consequently kill the patient
under certain atmospheric influences ; and at each
change in the weather, at the slightest storm, the
physician became anxious. "Mind that the patient
suffers from no emotion," he repeated. The dressings
were complicated and difficult, for the fixing of bandages and lint by the sparadrap had not been imagined at that period. Nicolette expended in lint a
sheet "as large as a ceiling," she said ; and it was
not without difficulty that the chloruretted lotions
and nitrate of silver reached the end of the gangrene.
So long as there was danger, M. Gillenormand,
broken-hearted by the bedside of his grandson, was
like Marius, neither dead nor alive.

Every day, and sometimes twice a day, a white-haired and well-dressed gentleman, — such was the description given by the porter, — came to inquire after the wounded man, and left a large parcel of lint for the dressings. At length, on September 7th, four months, day by day, from the painful night on which he had been brought home dying to his grandfather, the physician declared that he could answer for him, and that convalescence was setting in. Marius, however, would be obliged to lie for two months longer on a couch, owing to the accidents produced by the fracture of the collar-bone. There is always a last wound like that which will not close, and eternizes the dressings, to the great annoyance of the patient. This long illness and lengthened convalescence, however, saved him from prosecution: in France there is no anger, even public, which six months do not extinguish. Riots, in the present state of society, are so much everybody's fault, that they are followed by a certain necessity of closing the eyes. Let us add that Gisquet's unjustifiable decree which ordered physicians to denounce their patients having outraged opinion, and not merely opinion, but the king first of all, the wounded were covered and protected by this indignation, and, with the exception of those taken prisoners in the act of fighting, the courts-martial did not dare to molest any one. Hence Marius was left undisturbed.

M. Gillenormand first passed through every form of agony, and then through every form of ecstasy. Much difficulty was found in keeping him from passing the whole night by Marius's side; he had his

large easy-chair brought to the bed, and he insisted
on his daughter taking the finest linen in the house
to make compresses and bandages. Mademoiselle
Gillenormand, as a sensible and elderly lady, managed to save the fine linen, while making her father
believe that he was obeyed. M. Gillenormand would
not listen to any explanation, that for the purpose of
making lint fine linen is not so good as coarse, or
new so good as worn. He was present at all the
dressings, from which Mademoiselle Gillenormand
modestly absented herself. When the dead flesh
was cut away with scissors he said, "Aïe, aïe!"
Nothing was so touching as to see him hand the
wounded man a cup of broth with his gentle senile
trembling. He overwhelmed the surgeon with questions, and did not perceive that he constantly repeated the same. On the day when the physician
informed him that Marius was out of danger he
was beside himself. He gave his porter three
louis d'or, and at night, when he went to his bed-
room, danced a gavotte, making castagnettes of his
thumb and forefinger, and sang a song something
like this : —

> " Jeanne est née à Fougère,
> 　Vrai nid d'une bergère ;
> 　J'adore son jupon
> 　　Fripon.

> " Amour, tu vis en elle ;
> 　Car c'est dans sa prunelle
> 　Que tu mets ton carquois,
> 　　Narquois !

> " Moi, je la chante, et j'aime,
> Plus que Diane même,
> Jeanne et ses durs tetons
> Bretons."

Then he knelt on a chair, and Basque, who was watching him through the crack of the door, felt certain that he was praying. Up to that day he had never believed in God. At each new phase in the improvement of the patient, which went on steadily, the grandfather was extravagant. He performed a multitude of mechanical actions full of delight : he went up and down stairs without knowing why. A neighbor's wife, who was very pretty, by the way, was stupefied at receiving one morning a large bouquet : it was M. Gillenormand who sent it to her, and her husband got up a jealous scene. M. Gillenormand tried to draw Nicolette on his knees : he called Marius Monsieur le Baron, and shouted, " Long live the Republic ! " Every moment he asked the medical man, " There is no danger now, is there ? " He looked at Marius with a grandmother's eyes, and gloated over him when he slept. He no longer knew himself, no longer took himself into account. Marius was the master of the house ; there was abdication in his joy, and he was the grandson of his grandson. In his present state of merriment he was the most venerable of children : through fear of wearying or annoying the convalescent he would place himself behind him in order to smile upon him. He was satisfied, joyous, ravished, charming and young, and his white hair added a gentle majesty to the gay light which he had on his face. When

grace is mingled with wrinkles it is adorable; and
there is a peculiar dawn in expansive old age.

As for Marius, while letting himself be nursed and
petted, he had one fixed idea, — Cosette. Since the
fever and delirium had left him he no longer pronounced this name, and it might be supposed that he
had forgotten it; but he was silent precisely because
his soul was there. He knew not what had become
of Cosette: the whole affair of the Rue de la Chanvrerie was like a cloud in his memory; shadows
almost indistinct floated through his spirit. Éponine,
Gavroche, Mabœuf, the Thénardiers, and all his
friends mournfully mingled with the smoke of the
barricade; the strange passage of M. Fauchelevent
through that blood-stained adventure produced upon
him the effect of an enigma in a tempest: he understood nothing of his own life, he knew not how or
by whom he had been saved, and no one about
knew it either: all they were able to tell him was
that he had been brought there at night in a hackney
coach. Past, present, future,— all this was to him like
the mist of a vague idea; but there was in this mist
one immovable point, a clear and precise lineament,
something made of granite, a resolution, a will, — to
find Cosette again. For him the idea of life was not
distinct from the idea of Cosette: he had decreed in
his heart that he would not receive one without the
other, and he unalterably determined to demand of
his grandfather, of destiny, of fate, of Hades itself,
the restitution of his lost Eden.

He did not conceal the obstacles from himself.
Here let us underline one fact: he was not won or

greatly affected by all the anxiety and all the tenderness of his grandfather. In the first place he was not in the secret of them all, and next, in his sick man's reveries, which were perhaps still feverish, he distrusted this gentleness as a strange and new thing intended to subdue him. He remained cold to it, and the poor grandfather lavished his smiles in pure loss. Marius said to himself that it was all very well so long as he did not speak and let matters rest; but when he came to Cosette, he should find another face, and his grandfather's real attitude would be unmasked. Then he would be rough; a warming up of family questions, a comparison of positions, every possible sarcasm and objection at once. Fauchelevent, Coupelevent, fortune, poverty, wretchedness, the stone on the neck, the future a violent resistance, and the conclusion — a refusal. Marius stiffened himself against it beforehand. And then, in proportion as he regained life, his old wrongs reappeared, the old ulcers of his memory reopened, he thought again of the past. Colonel Pontmercy placed himself once more between M. Gillenormand and him, Marius, and he said to himself that he had no real kindness to hope for from a man who had been so unjust and harsh to his father. And with health came back a sort of bitterness against his grandfather, from which the old man gently suffered. M. Gillenormand, without letting it be seen, noticed that Marius, since he had been brought home and regained consciousness, had never once called him father. He did not say Sir, it is true, but he managed to say neither one nor the other, by a certain way of turning his sentences.

17

A crisis was evidently approaching, and, as nearly always happens in such cases, Marius, in order to try himself, skirmished before offering battle; this is called feeling the ground. One morning it happened that M. Gillenormand, alluding to a newspaper which he had come across, spoke lightly of the Convention, and darted a Royalist epigram at Danton, St. Just, and Robespierre. "The men of '93 were giants," Marius said sternly; the old man was silent, and did not utter another syllable all the day. Marius, who had the inflexible grandfather of his early years ever present to his mind, saw in this silence a profound concentration of anger, augured from it an obstinate struggle, and augmented his preparations for the contest in the most hidden corners of his mind. He determined that in case of refusal he would tear off his bandages, dislocate his collar-bone, expose all the wounds still unhealed, and refuse all food. His wounds were his ammunition; he must have Cosette or die. He awaited the favorable moment with the crafty patience of sick persons, and the moment arrived.

CHAPTER III.

MARIUS ATTACKS.

ONE day M. Gillenormand, while his daughter was arranging the phials and cups on the marble slab of the sideboard, leaned over Marius, and said in his most tender accent, —

"Look you, my little Marius, in your place I would rather eat meat than fish ; a fried sole is excellent at the beginning of a convalescence ; but a good cutlet is necessary to put the patient on his legs."

Marius, whose strength had nearly quite returned, sat up, rested his two clenched fists on his sheet, looked his grandfather in the face, assumed a terrible air, and said, —

"That induces me to say one thing to you."

"What is it ? "

"That I wish to marry."

"Foreseen," said the grandfather, bursting into a laugh.

"How foreseen ? "

"Yes, foreseen. You shall have your little maid."

Marius, stupefied and dazzled, trembled in all his limbs, and M. Gillenormand continued, —

"Yes, you shall have the pretty little dear. She comes every day in the form of an old gentleman to ask after you. Ever since you have been wounded she has spent her time in crying and making lint. I made inquiries ; she lives at No. 7, Rue de l'Homme Armé. Ah, there we are ! Ah, you want her, do you ? Well, you shall have her. You're tricked this time ; you had made your little plot, and had said to yourself, ' I will tell it point-blank to that grandfather, that mummy of the Regency and the Directory, that old beau, that Dorante who has become Géronte ; he has had his frolics too, and his amourettes, and his grisettes, and his Cosettes ; he has had his fling, he has had his wings, and he has eaten the bread of spring ; he must surely remember it, we shall see. Battle !' Ah, you take the cock-chafer by the horns ; very good. I offer you a cutlet, and you answer me, ' By the bye, I wish to marry.' By Jupiter ! Here's a transition ! Ah, you made up your mind for a quarrel, but you did not know that I was an old coward. What do you say to that ? You are done ; you did not expect to find your grandfather more stupid than yourself. You have lost the speech you intended to make me, master lawyer, and that is annoying. Well, all the worse, rage away ; I do what you want, and that stops you, stupid ! Listen ! I have made my in-quiries, for I too am cunning ; she is charming, she is virtuous ; the Lancer does not speak the truth, she made heaps of lint. She is a jewel ; she adores you ; if you had died there would have been three of us, and her coffin would have accompanied mine. I had the idea as soon as you were better of planting her there by your bedside ; but it is only in romances that girls are introduced to the beds of handsome young wounded men in whom they take an interest. That would not do, for what would your aunt say? You were quite naked three parts of the time, sir; ask Nicolette, who never left you for a moment, whether it were possible for a female to be here? And then, what would the doctor have said? for a pretty girl does not cure a fever. Well, say no more about it; it is settled and done; take her. Such is my fury. Look you, I saw that you did not love me, and I said, 'What can I do to make that animal love me?' I said, 'Stay, I have my little Cosette ready to hand. I will give her to him, and then he must love me a little, or tell me the reason why.' Ah! you believed that the old man would storm, talk big, cry no, and lift his cane against all this dawn. Not at all. Cosette, very good; love, very good. I ask for nothing better; take the trouble, sir, to marry; be happy, my beloved child!"

After saying this the old man burst into sobs. He took Marius's head and pressed it to his old bosom, and both began weeping. That is one of the forms of supreme happiness.

" My father!" Marius exclaimed.

" Ah, you love me, then!" the old man said.

There was an ineffable moment; they were choking and could not speak. At length the old man stammered, —

" Come! the stopper is taken out of him; he called me father."

Marius disengaged his head from his grandfather's arms, and said gently, —

" Now that I am better, father, I fancy I could see her."

" Foreseen, too ; you will see her to-morrow."

" Father ? "

" Well, what ? "

" Why not to-day ? "

" Well, to-day ; done for to-day. You have called me father thrice, and it's worth that. I will see about it, and she shall be brought here. Foreseen, I tell you. That has already been put in verse, and it is the dénouement of André Chénier's elegy, the 'Jeune Malade,'—André Chénier, who was butchered by the scound— by the giants of '93."

M. Gillenormand fancied he could see a slight frown on Marius's face, though, truth to tell, he was not listening, as he had flown away into ecstasy, and was thinking much more of Cosette than of 1793. The grandfather, trembling at having intro-duced André Chénier so inopportunely, hurriedly continued, —

" Butchered is not the word. The fact is that the great revolutionary geniuses who were not wicked, that is incontestable, who were heroes, Pardi, found that André Chénier was slightly in their way, and they had him guillo— that is to say, these great men on the 7th Thermidor, in the interest of the public safety, begged André Chénier to be kind enough to go — "

M. Gillenormand, garroted by his own sentence, could not continue. Unable to terminate it or retract it, the old man rushed, with all the speed which his age allowed, out of the bed-room, shut the door after him, and purple, choking, and foaming, with his eyes out of his head, found himself nose to nose with honest Basque, who was cleaning boots in the ante-room. He seized Basque by the collar and furiously shouted into his face, " By the hundred thousand Javottes of the devil, those brigands assassinated him ! "

" Whom, sir ? "

" André Chénier."

" Yes, sir," said the horrified Basque.

CHAPTER IV.

MLLE. GILLENORMAND HAS NO OBJECTIONS TO THE MATCH.

COSETTE and Marius saw each other again. We will not attempt to describe the interview, for there are things which we must not attempt to paint : the sun is of the number. The whole family, Basque and Nicolette included, were assembled in Marius's chamber at the moment when Cosette entered. She appeared in the doorway, and seemed to be surrounded by a halo : precisely at this moment the grandfather was going to blow his nose, but he stopped short, holding his nose in his handkerchief and looking over it.

" Adorable ! " he cried.

And then he blew a sonorous blast. Cosette was intoxicated, ravished, startled, in heaven. She was as timid as a person can be through happiness ; she stammered, turned pale and then pink, and wished to throw herself into Marius's arms, but dared not. She was ashamed of loving before so many people ; for the world is merciless to happy lovers, and always remains at the very moment when they most long to be alone. And yet they do not want these people at all. With Cosette, and behind her, had entered a white-haired man, serious, but still smiling, though the smile was wandering and poignant. It was "Monsieur Fauchelevent," — it was Jean Valjean. He was *well-dressed*, as the porter had said, in a new black suit and a white cravat. The porter was a thousand leagues from recognizing in this correct citizen, this probable notary, the frightful corpse-bearer who had arrived at the gate on the night of June 7, ragged, filthy, hideous, and haggard, with a mask of blood and mud on his face, supporting in his arms the unconscious Marius; still his porter's instincts were aroused. When M. Fauchelevent arrived with Cosette, the porter could not refrain from confiding this aside to his wife, " I don't know why, but I fancy that I have seen that face before." M. Fauchelevent remained standing by the door of Marius's room, as if afraid; he held under his arm a packet rather like an octavo volume wrapped in paper. The paper was green, apparently from mildew.

" Has this gentleman always got books under his arm like that?" Mademoiselle Gillenormand, who was not fond of books, asked Nicolette in a whisper.

"Well," M. Gillenormand, who had heard her, answered in the same key, " he is a savant; is that his fault? Monsieur Boulard, whom I knew, never went out without a book either, and like him had always had an old book near his heart."

Then bowing, he said in a loud voice, —

" M. Tranchelevent."

Father Gillenormand did not do it purposely, but an inattention to proper names was an aristocratic way of his.

"Monsieur Tranchelevent, I have the honor of requesting this lady's hand for my grandson, M. le Baron Marius Pontmercy."

Monsieur "Tranchelevent" bowed.

" All right," the grandfather said.

And turning to Marius and Cosette, with both arms extended in benediction, he cried, —

" You have leave to adore each other."

They did not let it be said twice, and the prattling began. They talked in a whisper, Marius reclining on his couch and Cosette standing by his side. " Oh, Heaven ! " Cosette murmured, " I see you again : it is you. To go and fight like that ! But why ? It is horrible. For four months I have been dead. Oh, how wicked it was of you to have been at that battle ! What had I done to you ? I forgive you, but you will not do it again. Just now, when they came to tell me to come to you, I thought again that I was going to die, but it was of joy. I was so sad ! I did not take the time to dress myself, and I must look frightful ; what will your relation say at seeing me in a tumbled collar ? But speak ! you let me speak all alone. We are still in the Rue de l'Homme Armé. It seems that your shoulder was terrible, and I was told that I could have put my hand in it, and that your flesh was as if it had been cut with scissors. How frightful that is ! I wept so that I have no eyes left. It is strange that a person can suffer like that. Your grandfather has a very kind look. Do not disturb yourself, do not rest on your elbow like that, or you will hurt yourself. Oh, how happy I am ! So our misfortunes are all ended ! I am quite foolish.

There were things I wanted to say to you which I have quite forgotten. Do you love me still? We live in the Rue de l'Homme Armé. There is no garden there. I made lint the whole time ; look here, sir, it is your fault, my fingers are quite rough."

"Angel!" said Marius.

Angel is the only word in the language which cannot be worn out; no other word would resist the pitiless use which lovers make of it. Then, as there was company present, they broke off, and did not say a word more, contenting themselves with softly clasping hands. M. Gillenormand turned to all the rest in the room, and cried, —

"Speak loudly, good people ; make a noise, will you? Come, a little row, hang it all! so that these children may prattle at their ease."

And going up to Marius and Cosette, he whispered to them, —

"Go on ; don't put yourselves out of the way."

Aunt Gillenormand witnessed with stupor this irruption of light into her antiquated house. This stupor had nothing aggressive about it ; it was not at all the scandalized and envious glance cast by an owl at two ring-doves : it was the stupid eye of a poor innocent of the age of fifty-seven ; it was a spoiled life looking at that triumph, love.

"Mademoiselle Gillenormand the elder," her father said to her, "I told you that this would happen."

He remained silent for a moment, and added, —

"Look at the happiness of others."

Then he turned to Cosette.

"How pretty she is! how pretty she is! she is a Greuze! So you are going to have all that for yourself, scamp? Ah, my boy, you have had a lucky escape from me; for if I were not fifteen years too old we would fight with swords and see who should have her. There, I am in love with you, Mademoiselle; but it is very natural, it is your right. What a famous, charming little wedding we will have! St. Denis du Saint-Sacrament is our parish; but I will procure a dispensation, so that you may be married at St. Paul, for the church is better. It was built for the Jesuits, and more coquettish. It is opposite Cardinal Birague's fountain. The masterpiece of Jesuit architecture is at Namur, and is called St. Loup; you should go and see that when you are married, for it is worth the journey. Mademoiselle, I am entirely of your opinion; I wish girls to marry, for they are made for it. There is a certain Sainte Catharine whom I would always like to see with hair disordered. To remain a maid is fine, but it is cold. Multiply, says the Bible. To save the people a Joan of Arc is wanted; but to make a people we want Mother Gigogne. So marry, my darlings; I really do not see the use of remaining a maid. I know very well that they have a separate chapel in church, and join the confraternity of the Virgin; but, sapristi! a good-looking young husband, and at the end of a year a plump bantling, who sucks at you bravely, and who has rolls of fat on his thighs, and who clutches your bosom with his pink little paws, are a good deal better than holding a candle at vespers and singing *Turris Eburnea*."

The grandfather pirouetted on his nonagenarian heels, and began speaking again, like a spring which had been wound up : —

> " Ainsi, bornant le cours de tes rêvasseries,
>   Alcippe, il est donc vrai, dans peu tu te maries."

"By the bye?"

"What, father?"

"Had you not an intimate friend?"

"Yes, Courfeyrac."

"What has become of him?"

"He is dead."

"That is well."

He sat down by their side, made Cosette take a chair, and took their four hands in his old wrinkled hands.

"This darling is exquisite! This Cosette is a masterpiece! She is a very little girl and a very great lady. She will be only a baroness, and that is a derogation, for she is born to be a marchioness. What eyelashes she has! My children, drive it well into your pates that you are on the right road. Love one another ; be foolish over it, for love is the stupidity of men and the cleverness of God. So adore one another. Still," he added, suddenly growing sad, "what a misfortune! More than half I possess is sunk in annuities ; so long as I live it will be all right, but when I am dead, twenty years hence, ah! my poor children, you will not have a farthing! Your pretty white hands, Madame la Baronne, will be wrinkled by work."

Here a serious and calm voice was heard saying :

"Mademoiselle Euphrasie Fauchelevent has six hundred thousand francs."

It was Jean Valjean's voice. He had not yet uttered a syllable; no one seemed to remember that he was present, and he stood motionless behind all these happy people.

"Who is the Mademoiselle Euphrasie in question?" the startled grandfather asked.

"Myself," said Cosette.

"Six hundred thousand francs!" M. Gillenormand repeated.

"Less fourteen or fifteen thousand, perhaps," Jean Valjean said.

And he laid on the table the parcel which Aunt Gillenormand had taken for a book. Jean Valjean himself opened the packet; it was a bundle of bank-notes. They were turned over and counted; there were five hundred bank-notes for a thousand francs, and one hundred and sixty-eight for five hundred, forming a total of five hundred and eighty-four thousand francs.

"That's a famous book," said M. Gillenormand.

"Five hundred and eighty-four thousand francs!" the aunt murmured.

"That arranges a good many things, does it not, Mademoiselle Gillenormand the elder?" the grandfather continued. "That devil of a Marius has found a millionnaire grisette upon the tree of dreams! Now trust to the amourettes of young people! Students find studentesses with six hundred thousand francs. Cherubin works better than Rothschild."

"Five hundred and eighty-four thousand francs!"

Mademoiselle Gillenormand repeated; "five hundred and eighty-four thousand francs! We may as well say six hundred thousand."

As for Marius and Cosette, they were looking at each other during this period. and hardly paid any attention to this detail.

CHAPTER V.

DEPOSIT YOUR MONEY IN A FOREST RATHER THAN WITH A NOTARY.

OF course our readers have understood, and no lengthened explanation will be required, that Jean Valjean after the Champmathieu affair was enabled by his escape for a few days to come to Paris, and withdraw in time from Laffitte's the sum he had gained under the name of M. Madeleine at M.-sur-M. ; and that, afraid of being recaptured, which in fact happened to him shortly after, he buried this sum in the forest of Montfermeil, at the spot called the Blaru bottom. This sum, six hundred and thirty thousand francs, all in bank-notes, occupied but little space, and was contained in a box ; but in order to protect the box from damp he placed it in an oak coffer filled with chips of chestnut-wood. In the same coffer he placed his other treasure, the Bishop's candlesticks. It will be remembered that he carried off these candlesticks in his escape from M.-sur-M. The man seen on one previous evening by Boulatruelle was Jean Valjean, and afterwards, whenever Jean Valjean required money, he fetched it from the Blaru clearing, and hence his absences to which we have referred. He had a pick concealed somewhere in the shrubs, in a hiding-place known to

himself alone. When he found Marius to be convalescent, feeling that the hour was at hand when this
money might be useful, he went to fetch it; and it
was also he whom Boulatruelle saw in the wood, but
this time in the morning, and not at night. Boulatruelle inherited the pick.

The real sum was five hundred and eighty-four
thousand five hundred francs, but Jean Valjean kept
back the five hundred francs for himself. "We will
see afterwards," he thought. The difference between
this sum and the six hundred and thirty thousand
francs withdrawn from Laffitte's represented the expenditure of ten years from 1823 to 1833. The five
years' residence in the convent had cost only five
thousand francs. Jean Valjean placed the two
silver candlesticks on the mantel-piece, where they
glistened, to the great admiration of Toussaint.
Moreover, Jean Valjean knew himself freed from
Javert; it had been stated in his presence, and he
verified the fact in the *Moniteur* which had published it, that an Inspector of Police of the name of
Javert had been found drowned under a washer-
woman's boat between the Pont-au-change and the
Pont-Neuf, and that a letter left by this man, hitherto
irreproachable and highly esteemed by his chiefs, led
to the belief in an attack of dementia and suicide.
"In truth," thought Jean Valjean, " since he let me
go when he had hold of me, he must have been mad
at that time."

CHAPTER VI.

ALL preparations were made for the marriage,
and the physician, on being consulted, declared that
it might take place in February. It was now December, and a few ravishing weeks of perfect happiness slipped away. The least happy man was not
the grandfather: he sat for a whole quarter of an
hour contemplating Cosette.

"The admirably pretty girl!" he would exclaim,
"and she has so soft and kind an air! She is the
most charming creature I have ever seen in my life.
Presently she will have virtues with a violet scent.
She is one of the Graces, on my faith! A man can
only live nobly with such a creature. Marius, my
lad, you are a baron, you are rich; so do not be
a pettifogger, I implore you."

Cosette and Marius had suddenly passed from the
sepulchre into paradise : the transition had not been
prepared, and they would have been stunned if they
had not been dazzled.

"Do you understand anything of all this?" Marius
would say to Cosette.

"No," Cosette answered ; "but it seems to me
as if the good God were looking at us."

Jean Valjean did everything, smoothed everything, conciliated everything, and rendered everything easy. He hurried toward Cosette's happiness with as much eagerness and apparently with as much joy as Cosette herself. As he had been Mayor, he was called to solve a delicate problem, the secret of which he alone possessed, — the civil status of Cosette. To tell her origin openly might have prevented the marriage ; but he got Cosette out of all the difficulties. He arranged for her a family of dead people, a sure method of not incurring any inquiry. Cosette was the only one left of an extinct family. Cosette was not his daughter, but the daughter of another Fauchelevent. Two brothers Fauchelevent had been gardeners at the convent of the Little Picpus. They proceeded to this convent ; the best testimonials and most satisfactory character were given ; for the good nuns, little suited and but little inclined to solve questions of paternity, had never known exactly of which of the two Fauchelevents Cosette was the daughter. They said what was wanted, and said it zealously. An instrument was drawn up by a notary and Cosette became by law Mademoiselle Euphrasie Fauchelevent, and was declared an orphan both on the father's and mother's side. Jean Valjean managed so as to be designated, under the name of Fauchelevent, as guardian of Cosette, with M. Gillenormand as supervising guardian. As for the five hundred and eighty-four thousand francs, they were a legacy left to Cosette by a dead person who wished to remain unknown. The original legacy had been five hundred and ninety-four thousand francs,

but ten thousand had been spent in the education
of Mademoiselle Euphrasie, five thousand of which
had been paid to the convent. This legacy, deposited
in the hands of a third party, was to be handed over
to Cosette upon her majority, or at the period of
her marriage. All this was highly acceptable, as
we see, especially when backed up by more than
half a million francs. There were certainly a few
singular points here and there, but they were not
seen, for one of the persons interested had his eyes
bandaged by love, and the others by the six hundred
thousand francs.

Cosette learned that she was not the daughter
of the old man whom she had so long called father ;
he was only a relation, and another Fauchelevent
was her real father. At another moment this would
have grieved her, but in the ineffable hour she had
now reached it was only a slight shadow, a passing
cloud ; and she had so much joy that this cloud
lasted but a short time. She had Marius. The young
man came ; the old man disappeared : life is so.
And then, Cosette had been accustomed for many
long years to see enigmas around her ; every being
who has had a mysterious childhood is ever ready
for certain renunciations. Still she continued to call
Jean Valjean " father." Cosette, who was among the
angels, was enthusiastic about Father Gillenormand ;
it is true that he overwhelmed her with madrigals
and presents. While Jean Valjean was constructing
for Cosette an unassailable position in society, M.
Gillenormand attended to the wedding trousseau.
Nothing amused him so much as to be magnificent ;

and he had given Cosette a gown of Binche guipure, which he inherited from his own grandmother. "These fashions spring up again," he said; "antiquities are the great demand, and the young ladies of my old days dress themselves like the old ladies of my youth." He plundered his respectable round-bellied commodes of Coromandel lacquer, which had not been opened for years. "Let us shrive these dowagers," he said, "and see what they have in their paunch." He noisily violated drawers full of the dresses of all his wives, all his mistresses, and all his female ancestry. He lavished on Cosette Chinese satins, damasks, lampas, painted moires, gros de Naples dresses, Indian handkerchiefs embroidered with gold that can be washed, Genoa and Alençon point lace, sets of old jewelry, ivory bonbon boxes adorned with microscopic battles, laces, and ribbons. Cosette, astounded, wild with love for Marius and with gratitude to M. Gillenormand, dreamed of an unbounded happiness, dressed in satin and velvet. Her wedding-basket seemed to her supported by seraphim, and her soul floated in ether with wings of Mechlin lace. The intoxication of the lovers was only equalled, as we stated, by the ecstasy of the grandfather, and there was something like a flourish of trumpets in the Rue des Filles du Calvaire. Each morning there was a new offering of *bric-à-brac* from the grandfather to Cosette, and all sorts of ornaments were spread out splendidly around her. One day Marius, who not unfrequently talked gravely through his happiness, said, with reference to some incident which I have forgotten,—

"The men of the revolution are so great that they already possess the prestige of centuries, like Cato and like Phocion, and each of them seems a mémoire antique."

"Moire antique!" exclaimed the old gentleman; "thank you, Marius, that is the very idea which I was seeking for."

And on the morrow a splendid tea-colored moire antique dress was added to Cosette's outfit. The grandfather extracted a wisdom from this frippery: —

"Love is all very well, but this is required with it. Something useless is required in happiness; happiness is only what is absolutely necessary, but season it, say I, with an enormous amount of superfluity. A palace and her heart; her heart and the Louvre. Give me my shepherdess, and try that she be a duchess. Bring me Phillis crowned with cornflowers, and add to her one thousand francs a year. Open for me an endless Bucolic under a marble colonnade. I consent to the Bucolic and also to the fairy scene in marble and gold. Dry happiness resembles dry bread; you eat it, but you do not dine. I wish for superfluity, for the useless, for extravagance, for that which is of no use. I remember to to have seen in Strasburg Cathedral a clock as tall as a three-storied house, which marked the hour, which had the kindness to mark the hour, but did not look as if it was made for the purpose; and which, after striking midday or midnight, — midday, the hour of the sun, and midnight, the hour of love, or any other hour you please, — gave you the moon and the stars, earth and sea, birds and fishes, Phœbus

and Phœbe, and a heap of things that came out of a
corner, and the twelve apostles, and the Emperor
Charles V., and Éponine and Sabinus, and a number
of little gilt men who played the trumpet into the
bargain, without counting the ravishing chimes which
it scattered in the air on every possible occasion,
without your knowing why. Is a wretched, naked
clock, which only marks the hours, worth that? I
am of the opinion of the great clock of Strasburg,
and prefer it to the Black Forest cuckoo clock."

M. Gillenormand talked all sorts of nonsense about
the marriage, and all the ideas of the eighteenth century passed pell-mell into his dithyrambs.

"You are ignorant of the art of festivals, and do
not know how to get up a day's pleasure in these
times," he exclaimed. "Your nineteenth century is
soft, and is deficient in excess: it is ignorant of what
is rich and noble. In everything it is close-shorn.
Your third estate is insipid and has no color, smell,
or shape. The dream of your bourgeoises, who es-
tablish themselves, as they call it, is a pretty bou-
doir freshly decorated with mahogany and calico.
Make way, there! The Sieur Grigou marries the
Demoiselle Grippesou. Sumptuousness and splendor. A louis d'or has been stuck to a wax candle.
Such is the age. I insist on flying beyond the Sarma-
tians. Ah, so far back as 1787 I predicted that all
was lost on the day when I saw the Duc de Rohan,
Prince de Léon, Duc de Chabot, Duc de Montbazon,
Marquis de Soubise, Vicomte de Thouars, Peer of
France, go to Longchamps in a *tapecul:* that bore
its fruits. In this century men have a business,

gamble on the Stock Exchange, win money, and are mean. They take care of and varnish their surface : they are carefully dressed, washed, soaped, shaved, combed, rubbed, brushed, and cleaned externally, irreproachable, as polished as a pebble, discreet, trim, and at the same time, — virtue of my soul ! — they have at the bottom of their conscience dungheaps and cess-pools, at which a milkmaid who blows her nose with her fingers would recoil. I grant the present age this motto, — dirty cleanliness. Marius, do not be annoyed ; grant me the permission to speak, for I have been saying no harm of the people, you see. I have my mouth full of your people, but do let me give the bourgeoisie a pill. I tell you point-blank that at the present day people marry, but no longer know how to marry. Ah, it is true, I regret the gentility of the old manners ; I regret it all, — that elegance, that chivalry, that courteous and dainty manner, that rejoicing luxury which every one pos-sessed, the music forming part of the wedding, sym-phony above and drums beating below stairs, the joyous faces seated at table, the spicy madrigals, the songs, the fireworks, the hearty laugh, the devil and his train, and the large ribbon bows. I regret the bride's garter, for it is first cousin of the girdle of Venus. On what does the siege of Troy turn ? Par-bleu ! on Helen's garter. Why do men fight ? Why does the divine Diomedes smash on the head of Merioneus that grand brass helmet with the ten points ? Why do Achilles and Hector tickle each other with lances ? Because Helen let Paris take her garter. With Cosette's garter Homer would write the Iliad; he would place in his poem an old chatterer like myself, and call him Nestor. My friends, in former times, in those amiable former times, people married learnedly: they made a good contract and then a good merry-making. So soon as Cujas had gone out, Gamacho came in. Hang it all! the stomach is an agreeable beast, that demands its due, and wishes to hold its wedding too. We supped well, and had at table a pretty neighbor without a neckerchief, who only concealed her throat moderately. Oh, the wide laughing mouths, and how gay people were in those days! Youth was a bouquet, every young man finished with a branch of lilac or a posy of roses; if he were a warrior, he was a shepherd, and if by chance he were a captain of dragoons, he managed to call himself Florian. All were anxious to be pretty fellows, and they wore embroidery and rouge. A bourgeois looked like a flower, and a marquis like a precious stone. They did not wear straps, they did not wear boots; they were flashing, lustrous, gilt, light, dainty, and coquettish, but it did not prevent them wearing a sword by their side; they were humming-birds with beak and nails. It was the time of the *Indes galantes*. One of the sides of that age was delicate, the other magnificent; and, by the vertu-choux! people amused themselves. At the present day they are serious; the bourgeois is miserly, the bourgeoise prudish, — your age is out of shape. The Graces would be expelled because their dresses were cut too low in the neck. Alas! beauty is concealed as an ugliness. Since the revolution all wear trousers, even the ballet girls; a ballet

girl must be serious, and your rigadoons are doctri-
naire. A man must be majestic, and would feel very
much annoyed at not having his chin in his cravat.
The idea of a scamp of twenty, who is about to marry,
is to resemble Monsieur Royer-Collard. And do you
know what people reach by this majesty? They are
little. Learn this fact: joy is not merely joyous, it
is grand. Be gayly in love; though, hang it all!
marry, when you do marry, with fever and amazement and tumult, and a hurly-burly of happiness.
Gravity at church, if you will; but so soon as the
mass is ended, sarpejeu! you ought to make a dream
whirl round your wife. A marriage ought to be
royal and chimerical, and parade its ceremony from
the Cathedral of Rheims to the Pagoda of Chante-
loup. I have a horror of a scrubby marriage. Ventre-
goulette! Be in Olympus at least upon that day.
Be gods. Ah, people might be sylphs, jests and
smiles, Argyraspides, but they are scrubs! My
friends, every newly-married man ought to be Prince
Aldobrandini. Take advantage of this unique moment of life to fly into the Empyrean with the swans
and the eagles, even if you fall back to-morrow into
the bourgeoisie of frogs. Do not save upon the
hymeneal rites; do not nibble at this splendor, nor
split farthings on the day when you are radiant. A
wedding is not housekeeping. Oh, if I had my way
it should be a gallant affair, and violins should be
heard in the trees. Here is my programme: sky-
blue and silver. I would mingle in the fête the
rustic divinities, and convene the Dryads and the
Nereids. The wedding of Amphitrite, a pink cloud,

nymphs with their hair carefully dressed and quite nude, an academician offering quatrains to the Deess, a car drawn by marine monsters.

> ' Triton trottait devant, et tirait de sa conque,
> Des sons si ravissants qu'il ravissait quiconque ! '

There is a programme for a fête, or I'm no judge, sac à papier ! "

While the grandfather, in the heat of his lyric effusion, was listening to himself, Cosette and Marius were intoxicating themselves by looking freely at each other. Aunt Gillenormand regarded all this with her imperturbable placidity ; she had, during the last five or six months, a certain amount of emotions ; Marius returned, Marius brought back bleeding, Marius brought from a barricade, Marius dead, then living, Marius reconciled, Marius affianced, Marius marrying a poor girl, Marius marrying a millionnaire. The six hundred thousand francs had been her last surprise, and then the indifference of a leading communicant returned to her. She went regularly to her mass, told her beads, read her euchology, whispered in one corner of the house her *Aves*, while " I love you " was being whispered in another, and saw Marius and Cosette vaguely like two shadows. The shadow was herself. There is a certain state of inert asceticism in which the mind, neutralized by torpor, and a stranger to what might be called the business of living, does not perceive, with the exception of earthquakes and catastrophes, any human impressions, either pleasant or painful. " This devotion," Father Gillenormand would say to his daughter, " resembles a cold in the head ; you smell nothing of life, neither a good odor nor a bad one." However, the six hundred thousand francs had settled the old maid's indecision. Her father was accustomed to take her so little into account that he had not consulted her as to the consent to Marius's marriage. He had acted impetuously, according to his wont, having, as a despot who had become a slave, but one thought, that of satisfying Marius. As for the aunt, he had scarce remembered that the aunt existed, and that she might have an opinion of her own, and, sheep though she was, this had offended her. Somewhat roused internally, but externally impassive, she said to herself, "My father settles the marriage question without me, and I will settle the question of the inheritance without him." She was rich, in fact, and her father was not so, and it is probable that if the marriage had been poor she would have left it poor. "All the worse for my nephew ! If he chose to marry a beggar, he may be a beggar too." But Cosette's half a million of francs pleased the aunt and changed her feelings with respect to the loving couple ; consideration is due to six hundred thousand francs, and it was evident that she could not do otherwise than leave her fortune to these young people, because they no longer required it.

It was arranged that the couple should reside at M. Gillenormand's, and the grandfather insisted on giving them his bed-room, the finest room in the house. "It will make me younger," he declared. "It is an old place. I always had the idea that the wedding should take place in my room." He furnished this room with a heap of old articles of gallantry ; he had it hung with an extraordinary fabric which he had in the piece, and believed to be Utrecht, a gold satin ground with velvet auriculas. "It was with that stuff," he said, "that the bed of the Duchess d'Anville à la Rocheguyon was hung." He placed on the mantel-piece a figure in Saxon porcelain carrying a muff on its naked stomach. M. Gillenormand's library became the office which Marius required; for an office, it will be borne in mind, is insisted upon by the council of the order.

CHAPTER VII.

THE EFFECTS OF DREAMING BLENDED WITH HAPPINESS.

THE lovers saw each other daily, and Cosette came with M. Fauchelevent. "It is turning things topsy-turvy," said Mademoiselle Gillenormand, "that the lady should come to the gentleman's house to have court paid to her in that way." But Marius's convalescence had caused the adoption of the habit, and the easy-chairs of the Rue des Filles du Calvaire, more convenient for a *tête-à-tête* than the straw-bottomed chairs of the Rue de l'Homme Armé, had decided it. Marius and M. Fauchelevent saw each other, but did not speak, and this seemed to be agreed on. Every girl needs a chaperon, and Cosette could not have come without M. Fauchelevent; and for Marius, M. Fauchelevent was the condition of Cosette, and he accepted him. In discussing vaguely, and without any precision, political matters as connected with the improvement of all, they managed to say a little more than Yes and No. Once, on the subject of instruction, which Marius wished to be gratuitous and obligatory, multiplied in every form, lavished upon all like light and air, and, in a word, respirable by the entire people, they were agreed, and almost talked. Marius remarked on this occasion

that M. Fauchelevent spoke well, and even with a
certain elevation of language, though something was
wanting. M. Fauchelevent had something less than
a man of the world, and something more. Marius,
in his innermost thoughts, surrounded with all sorts
of questions this M. Fauchelevent, who was to him
simple, well-wishing, and cold. At times doubts occurred to him as to his own recollections ; he had a
hole in his memory, a black spot, an abyss dug by
four months of agony. Many things were lost in it,
and he was beginning to ask himself whether it was
the fact that he had seen M. Fauchelevent, a man so
serious and so calm, at the barricade.

This was, however, not the sole stupor which the
appearances and disappearances of the past had left
in his mind. We must not believe that he was
delivered from all those promptings of memory
which compel us, even when happy and satisfied,
to take a melancholy backward glance. The head
which does not turn to effaced horizons contains
neither thought nor love. At moments Marius
buried his face in his hands, and the tumultuous
and vague past traversed the fog which he had in
his brain. He saw Mabœuf fall again, he heard
Gavroche singing under the grape-shot, and he felt
on his lips the coldness of Éponine's forehead ;
Enjolras, Courfeyrac, Jean Prouvaire, Combeferre,
Bossuet, Grantaire, all his friends rose before him,
and then disappeared. Were they all dreams, these
dear, sorrowful, valiant, charming, and tragic beings ?
Had they really existed ? The riot had robed everything in its smoke, and these great fevers have great

dreams. He questioned himself, he felt himself, and
had a dizziness from all these vanished realities.
Where were they all, then? Was it really true that
everything was dead? A fall into the darkness had
carried away everything except himself; all this
had disappeared as it were behind the curtain of
a theatre. There are such curtains which drop on
life, and God passes on to the next act. In himself was he really the same man? He, poor, was
rich; he, the abandoned man, had a family; he,
the desperate man, was going to marry Cosette.
He seemed to have passed through a tomb, and to
have gone in black and come out white. And in
this tomb the others had remained. At certain times
all these beings of the past, returning and present,
formed a circle round him, and rendered him gloomy.
Then he thought of Cosette, and became serene
again, but it required no less than this felicity to
efface this catastrophe. M. Fauchelevent had almost
a place among these vanished beings. Marius hesitated to believe that the Fauchelevent of the barricade was the same as that Fauchelevent in flesh
and bone so gravely seated by the side of Cosette.
The first was probably one of those nightmares
brought to him and carried away by his hours of
delirium. However, as their two natures were so
far apart, it was impossible for Marius to ask any
question of M. Fauchelevent. The idea had not
even occurred to him; we have already indicated this
characteristic detail. Two men who have a common
secret, and who, by a sort of tacit agreement, do
not exchange a syllable on the subject, are not so

rare as may be supposed. Once, however, Marius made an effort; he turned the conversation on the Rue de la Chanvrerie, and turning to M. Fauchelevent, he said to him, —

"Do you know that street well?"

"What street?"

"The Rue de la Chanvrerie."

"I have never heard the name of that street," M. Fauchelevent said, in the most natural tone in the world.

The answer, which related to the name of the street, and not to the street itself, seemed to Marius more conclusive than it really was.

"Decidedly," he thought, "I must have been dreaming. I had an hallucination. It was some one that resembled him, and M. Fauchelevent was not there."

CHAPTER VIII.

TWO MEN IMPOSSIBLE TO FIND.

THE enchantment, great though it was, did not efface other thoughts from Marius's mind. While the marriage arrangements were being made, and the fixed period was waited for, he made some troublesome and scrupulous retrospective researches. He owed gratitude in several quarters; he owed it for his father, and he owed it for himself. There was Thénardier, and there was the stranger who had brought him back to M. Gillenormand's. Marius was anxious to find these two men again, as he did not wish to marry, be happy, and forget them, and feared lest these unpaid debts of honor might cast a shadow over his life, which would henceforth be so luminous. It was impossible for him to leave all these arrears suffering behind him, and he wished, ere he entered joyously into the future, to obtain a receipt from the past. That Thénardier was a villain took nothing from the fact that he had saved Colonel Pontmercy. Thénardier was a bandit for all the world excepting for Marius. And Marius, ignorant of the real scene on the battle-field of Waterloo, did not know this peculiarity, that his father stood to Thénardier in the strange situation of owing him life without owing him gratitude. Not one

of the agents whom Marius employed could find
Thénardier's trail, and the disappearance seemed
complete on that side. Mother Thénardier had died
in prison before trial, and Thénardier and his daughter Azelma, the only two left of this lamentable
group, had plunged again into the shadow. The
gulf of the social unknown had silently closed again
upon these beings. No longer could be seen on the
surface that quivering, that tremor, and those obscure concentric circles which announce that something has fallen there, and that a grappling-iron may
be thrown in.

Mother Thénardier being dead, Boulatruelle being
out of the question, Claquesous having disappeared,
and the principal accused having escaped from prison,
the trial for the trap in the Gorbeau attic had pretty
nearly failed. The affair had remained rather dark,
and the assize court had been compelled to satisfy itself with two subalterns, Panchaud, *alias*
Printanier, *alias* Bigrenaille, and Demi-Liard, *alias*
Deux Milliards, who had been condemned, after
hearing both parties, to ten years at the galleys.
Penal servitude for life was passed against their
accomplices who had escaped ; Thénardier, as chief
and promoter, was condemned to death, also in de-
fault. This condemnation was the only thing that
remained of Thénardier, casting on this buried name
its sinister gleam, like a candle by the side of a coffin.
However, this condemnation, by thrusting Thénardier
back into the lowest depths through the fear of being
recaptured, added to the dense gloom which covered
this man.

As for the other, the unknown man who had saved Marius, the researches had at first some result, and then stopped short. They succeeded in finding again the hackney coach which had brought Marius to the Rue des Filles du Calvaire on the night of June 6. The driver declared that on the 6th of June, by the order of a police agent, he had stopped from three P. M. till nightfall on the quay of the Champs Élysées, above the opening of the Great Sewer; that at about nine in the evening the gate of the sewer which looks upon the river-bank opened; that a man came out, bearing on his shoulders another man, who appeared to be dead; that the agent, who was watching at this point, had arrested the living man and seized the dead man; that he, the coachman, had taken "all these people" into his hackney coach; that they drove first to the Rue des Filles du Calvaire and deposited the dead man there; that the dead man was M. Marius, and that he, the coachman, recognized him thoroughly, though he was alive this time; that afterwards they got into his coach again, and a few yards from the gate of the Archives he was ordered to stop; that he was paid in the street and discharged, and the agent took away the other man; that he knew nothing more, and that the night was very dark. Marius, as we said, remembered nothing. He merely remembered that he had been seized from behind by a powerful hand at the moment when he fell backwards from the barricade, and then all was effaced for him. He had only regained his senses when he was at M. Gillenormand's.

He lost himself in conjectures; he could not doubt

as to his own identity, but how was it that he, who had fallen in the Rue de la Chanvrerie, had been picked up by the police agent on the bank of the Seine, near the bridge of the Invalides? Some one had brought him from the market district to the Champs Élysées, and how, — by the sewer? Extraordinary devotion! Some one? Who? It was the man whom Marius was seeking. Of this man, who was his saviour, he could find nothing, not a trace, not the slightest sign. Marius, though compelled on this side to exercise a great reserve, pushed on his inquiries as far as the Préfecture of Police, but there the information which he obtained led to no better result than elsewhere. The Préfecture knew less about the matter than the driver of the hackney coach; they had no knowledge of any arrest having taken place at the outlet of the great drain on June 6; they had received no report from the agent about this fact which, at the Préfecture, was regarded as a fable. The invention of this fable was attributed to the driver; for a driver anxious for drink-money is capable of anything, even imagination. The fact, however, was certain, and Marius could not doubt it, unless he doubted his own identity, as we have just said. Everything in this strange enigma was inexplicable; this man, this mysterious man, whom the driver had seen come out of the grating of the great drain, bearing the fainting Marius on his back, and whom the police agent caught in the act of saving an insurgent, — what had become of him? What had become of the agent himself? Why had this agent kept silence? Had the man succeeded in escaping?

Had he corrupted the agent? Why did this man
give no sign of life to Marius, who owed everything to
him? The disinterestedness was no less prodigious
than the devotion. Why did this man not reappear?
Perhaps he was above reward, but no man is above
gratitude. Was he dead? Who was the man? What
was he like? No one was able to say: the driver
replied, "The night was very dark." Basque and
Nicollette in their start had only looked at their
young master, who was all bloody. The porter,
whose candle had lit up Marius's tragic arrival, had
alone remarked the man in question, and this was
the description he gave of him: "The man was
frightful."

In the hope of deriving some advantage from them
for his researches, Marius kept his blood-stained
clothes which he wore when he was brought to his
grandfather's. On examining the coat it was noticed
that the skirt was strangely torn, and a piece was
missing. One evening Marius was speaking in the
presence of Cosette and Jean Valjean about all this
singular adventure, the countless inquiries he had
made, and the inutility of his efforts; Monsieur
Fauchelevent's cold face offended him, and he exclaimed with a vivacity which had almost the vibration of anger, —

"Yes, that man, whoever he may be, was sublime. Do you know what he did, sir? He inter-
vened like an archangel. He was obliged to throw
himself into the midst of the contest, carry me away,
open the sewer, drag me off, and carry me. He must
have gone more than a league and a half through

frightful subterranean galleries, bent and bowed in the darkness, in the sewer, for more than half a league, sir, with a corpse on his back! And for what object? For the sole object of saving that corpse; and that corpse was myself. He said to himself, 'There is, perhaps, a gleam of life left here, and I will risk my existence for this wretched spark!' and he did not risk his existence once, but twenty times! And each step was a danger, and the proof is, that on leaving the sewer he was arrested. Do you know, sir, that this man did all that? And he had no reward to expect. What was I? An insurgent. What was I? A conquered man. Oh! if Cosette's six hundred thousand francs were mine—"

"They are yours," Jean Valjean interrupted.

"Well, then," Marius continued, "I would give them to find that man again."

Jean Valjean was silent.

BOOK VI.

THE SLEEPLESS NIGHT.

CHAPTER I.

FEBRUARY 16, 1833.

THE night of February 16 was a blessed night,
for it had above its shadow the open sky. It was
the wedding-night of Marius and Cosette.

The day had been adorable; it was not the blue
festival dreamed of by the grandfather, a fairy scene,
with a confusion of cherubim and cupids above the
head of the married couple, a marriage worthy of
being represented over a door, but it had been sweet
and smiling. The fashion of marrying in 1833 was
not at all as it is now. France had not yet borrowed
from England that supreme delicacy of carrying
off a wife, of flying on leaving the church, hiding
one's self as if ashamed of one's happiness, and
combining the manœuvres of a bankrupt with the
ravishment of the Song of Songs. We had not yet
understood how chaste, exquisite, and decent it is
to jolt one's paradise in a postchaise; to vary the
mystery with click-clacks of the whip; to select an
inn bed as the nuptial couch, and to leave behind

one, at the conventional alcove at so much per night, the most sacred recollection of life, jumbled with the *tête-à-têtes* of the guard of the diligence and the chamber-maid. In the second half of the nineteenth century, in which we now are, the mayor and his scarf, the priest and his chasuble, the law and God, are no longer sufficient ; they must be complemented by the postilion of Lonjumeau ; blue jacket with red facings and bell buttons, a leather-bound plate, green leather breeches, oaths to the Norman horses with their knotted tails, imitation gold lace, oil-skin hat, heavy, dusty horses, an enormous whip, and strong boots. France does not carry the elegance to such an extent as to shower on the postchaise, as the English nobility do, old shoes and battered slippers, in memory of Churchill, afterwards Marlborough or Malbrouck, who was assailed on his wedding-day by the anger of an aunt which brought him good luck. Shoes and slippers do not yet form part of our nuptial celebrations ; but, patience, with the spread of good taste we shall yet come to it.

In 1833, — it is a century since then, — marriage was not performed at a smart trot ; people still supposed at that epoch, whimsically enough, that a marriage is a private and social festival, that a patriarchal banquet does not spoil a domestic solemnity ; that gayety, even if it be excessive, so long as it is decent, does no harm to happiness ; and finally, that it is venerable and good for the fusion of these two destinies from which a family will issue, to begin in the house, and that the household may have in future the nuptial chamber as a witness ;

and people were so immodest as to marry at home. The wedding took place, then, according to this fashion which is now antiquated, at M. Gillenormand's; and though this affair of marrying is so simple and natural, the publication of the banns, drawing up the deeds, the mayoralty, and the church always cause some complication, and they could not be ready before February 16. Now — we note this detail for the pure satisfaction of being exact — it happened that the 16th was Mardi Gras. There were hesitations and scruples, especially on the part of Aunt Gillenormand.

"A Mardi Gras!" the grandfather exclaimed; "all the better. There is a proverb that, —

> ' Mariage un Mardi gras
> N'aura point d'enfants ingrats.'

All right. Done for the 16th. Do you wish to put it off, Marius?"

"Certainly not," said the amorous youth.

"We 'll marry then," said the grandfather.

The marriage, therefore, took place on the 16th, in spite of the public gayety. It rained on that day, but there is always in the sky a little blue patch at the service of happiness, which lovers see, even when the rest of creation are under their umbrellas. On the previous day Jean Valjean had handed to Marius, in the presence of M. Gillenormand, the five hundred and eighty-four thousand francs. As the marriage took place in the ordinary way, the deeds were very simple. Toussaint was henceforth useless to Jean Valjean, so Cosette inherited her, and promoted her to the rank of lady's-maid. As for Jean Valjean, a nice room was furnished expressly for him at M. Gillenormand's, and Cosette had said to him so irresistibly, " Father, I implore you," that she had almost made him promise that he would come and occupy it. A few days before that fixed for the marriage an accident happened to Jean Valjean ; he slightly injured the thumb of his right hand. It was not serious, and he had not allowed any one to poultice it, or even see it, not even Cosette. Still, it compelled him to wrap up his hand in a bandage and wear his arm in a sling, and this, of course, prevented him from signing anything. M. Gillenormand, as supervising guardian to Cosette, took his place. We will not take the reader either to the mayoralty or to church. Two lovers are not usually followed so far, and we are wont to turn our back on the drama so soon as it puts a bridegroom's bouquet in its button-hole. We will restrict ourselves to noting an incident which, though unnoticed by the bridal party, marked the drive from the Rue des Filles du Calvaire to St. Paul's Church.

The Rue St. Louis was being repaired at the time, and it was blocked from the Rue du Parc Royal, hence it was impossible for the carriage to go direct to St. Paul's. As they were obliged to change their course, the most simple plan was to turn into the boulevard. One of the guests drew attention to the fact that, as it was Mardi Gras, there would be a block of vehicles. " Why so ? " M. Gillenormand asked. " On account of the masks." " Famous," said the grandfather ; " we will go that way. These young people are going to marry and see the serious side of life, and seeing the masquerade will be a slight preparation for it." They turned into the boulevard: the first of the wedding carriages contained Cosette and Aunt Gillenormand, M. Gillenormand, and Jean Valjean. Marius, still separated from his bride, according to custom, was in the second. The nuptial procession, on turning out of the Rue des Filles du Calvaire, joined the long file of vehicles making an endless chain from the Madeleine to the Bastille, and from the Bastille to the Madeleine. Masks were abundant on the boulevard: and though it rained every now and then, Paillasse, Pantalon, and Gille were obstinate. In the good humor of that winter of 1833 Paris had disguised itself as Venus. We do not see a Mardi Gras like this now-a-days, for as everything existing is a wide-spread carnival, there is no carnival left. The sidewalks were thronged with pedestrians, and the windows with gazers; and the terraces crowning the peristyles of the theatres were covered with spectators. In addition to the masks, they look at the file — peculiar to Mardi Gras as to Longchamp — of vehicles of every description, citadines, carts, curricles, and cabs, marching in order rigorously riveted to each other by police regulations, and, as it were, running on rails. Any one who happens to be in one of these vehicles is at once spectator and spectacle. Policemen standing by the side of the boulevard kept in place these two interminable files moving in a contrary direction, and watched that nothing should impede the double current of these two streams, one running up, the other down, one

towards the Chaussée d'Antin, the other towards the
Faubourg St. Antoine. The escutcheoned carriages
of the Peers of France and Ambassadors held the
crown of the causeway, coming and going freely; and
certain magnificent and gorgeous processions, notably
the Bœuf Gras, had the same privilege. In this
Parisian gayety England clacked his whip, for the
post-chaise of Lord Seymour, at which a popular
sobriquet was hurled, passed with a great noise.

In the double file, along which Municipal Guards
galloped like watch-dogs, honest family arks, crowded
with great-aunts and grandmothers, displayed at windows healthy groups of disguised children, Pierrots
of seven and Pierrettes of six, ravishing little creatures, feeling that they officially formed part of the
public merriment, penetrated with the dignity of their
Harlequinade, and displaying the gravity of function-
aries. From time to time a block occurred somewhere in the procession of vehicles; one or other of
the two side files stopped until the knot was untied,
one impeded vehicle sufficing to block the whole
line. Then they started again. The wedding carriages were in the file, going towards the Bastille on
the right-hand side of the boulevard. Opposite the
Rue du Pont-aux-Choux there was a stoppage, and
almost at the same moment the file on the other side
proceeding towards the Madeleine stopped too. At
this point of the procession there was a carriage of
masks. These carriages, or, to speak more correctly,
these cartloads of masks, are well known to the
Parisians; if they failed on Mardi Gras or at mid-
Lent, people would say, "There's something behind

it. Probably we are going to have a change of Ministry." A heap of Harlequins, Columbines, and Pantaloons jolted above the heads of the passers-by, — all possible grotesques, from the Turk to the savage. Hercules supporting Marquises, fish-fags who would make Rabelais stop his ears, as well as Mænads who would make Aristophanes look down, tow perukes, pink fleshings, three-cornered hats, pantaloons, spectacles, cries given to the pedestrians, hands on hips, bold postures, naked shoulders, masked faces, and unmuzzled immodesty; a chaos of effronteries driven by a coachman in a head-dress of flowers, — such is this institution. Greece felt the want of Thespis' cart, and France needs Vadé's fiacre. All may be parodied, even parody. The Saturnalia, that grimace of antique beauty, by swelling and swelling becomes the Mardi Gras: and the Bacchanal, formerly crowned with vine-leaves, inundated by sunshine, and displaying marble breasts in a divine semi-nudity, is now flabby under the drenched rags of the North, has ended by being called a chie-en-lit.

The tradition of the coaches of masks dates back to the oldest times of the Monarchy. The accounts of Louis XI. allow the Palace steward " twenty sous tournois for three coaches of masquerades." In our time these noisy piles of creatures generally ride in some old coucou the roof of which they encumber, or cover with their tumultuous group a landau the hood of which is thrown back. There are twenty in a carriage intended for six. You see them on the seat, on the front stool, on the springs of the hood, and on the pole, and they even straddle across the lamps. They are standing, lying down, or seated, cross-legged, or with pendent legs. The women occupy the knees of the men, and this wild pyramid is seen for a long distance over the heads of the crowd. These vehicles form mountains of merriment in the midst of the mob, and Collé, Panard, and Piron flow from them enriched with slang, and the fish-fag's catechism is expectorated from above upon the people. This fiacre, which has grown enormous through its burden, has an air of conquest; Hubbub is in front and Hurly-burly behind. People shout in it, sing in it, yell in it, and writhe with happiness in it; gayety roars there, sarcasm flashes, and joviality is displayed like a purple robe; two jades drag in it farce expanded into an apotheosis, and it is the triumphal car of laughter, — a laughter, though, too cynical to be frank, and in truth this laughter is suspicious. It has a mission, — that of verifying the carnival to the Parisians. These fish-fag vehicles, in which some strange darkness is perceptible, cause the philosopher to reflect; there is something of the government in them, and you lay your finger there on a curious affinity between public men and public women. It is certainly a sorry thought, that heaped-up turpitudes give a sum-total of gayety; that a people can be amused by building up ignominy on opprobrium; that spying, acting as a caryatid to prostitution, amuses the mob while affronting it; that the crowd is pleased to see pass on four wheels this monstrous living pile of beings, spangled rags, one half ordure, one half light, who bark and sing; that they should clap their hands at all this shame, and that no festival

is possible for the multitude unless the police prome-
nade in its midst these twenty-headed hydras of joy.
Most sad this certainly is, but what is to be done?
These tumbrels of beribboned and flowered filth are
insulted and pardoned by the public laughter, and
the laughter of all is the accomplice of the universal
degradation. Certain unhealthy festivals disintegrate
the people and convert them into populace; but a
populace, like tyrants, requires buffoons. The king
has Roquelaure, and the people has Paillasse. Paris
is the great mad city wherever it is not the great
sublime city, and the carnival there is political. Paris,
let us confess it, willingly allows infamy to play a
farce for its amusement, and only asks of its masters
— when it has masters — one thing, " paint the mud
for me." Rome was of the same humor; she loved
Nero, and Nero was a Titanic débardeur.

Accident willed it, as we have just said, that one
of the shapeless groups of masked men and women
collected in a vast barouche stopped on the left of
the boulevard while the wedding party stopped on
the right. The carriage in which the masks were,
noticed opposite to it the carriage in which was
the bride.

" Hilloh ! " said a mask, " a wedding."

" A false wedding," another retorted, " we are the
true one."

And, as they were too far off to address the wedding party, and as they also feared the interference
of the police, the two masks looked elsewhere. The
whole vehicle-load of masquers had plenty of work
a moment after, for the mob began hissing it, which

is the caress given by the mob to masquerades, and
the two masks who had just spoken were obliged
to face the crowd with their comrades, and found
all the missiles of the market repertory scarce sufficient to reply to the atrocious jaw-lashing from
the people. A frightful exchange of metaphors took
place between the masks and the crowd. In the
mean while two other masks in the same carriage,
a Spaniard with an exaggerated nose, an oldish look,
and enormous black moustaches, and a thin and very
youthful fish-girl, wearing a half-mask, had noticed
the wedding also, and while their companions and
the spectators were insulting each other, held a conversation in a low voice. Their aside was covered
by the tumult and was lost in it. The showers had
drenched the open carriage ; the February wind is
not warm, and so the fish-girl while answering the
Spaniard shivered, laughed, and coughed. This was
the dialogue, which we translate from the original
slang : —

" Look here."

" What is it, pa ? "

" Do you see that old man ? "

" What old man ? "

" There, in the wedding coach, with his arm in
a sling."

" Yes. Well ? "

" I feel sure that I know him."

" Ah ! "

" May my neck be cut, and I never said you, thou,
or I, in my life, if I do not know that Parisian."

" To-day Paris is Pantin."

" Can you see the bride by stooping ? "

" No."

" And the bridegroom ? "

" There is no bridegroom in that coach."

" Nonsense."

" Unless it be the other old man."

" Come, try and get a look at the bride by stooping."

" I can't."

" No matter, that old fellow who has something the matter with his paw, I feel certain I know him."

" And what good will it do you, your knowing him ? "

" I don't know. Sometimes ! "

" I don't care a curse for old fellows."

" I know him."

" Know him as much as you like."

" How the deuce is he at the wedding ? "

" Why, we are there too."

" Where does the wedding come from ? "

" How do I know ? "

" Listen."

" Well, what is it ? "

" You must do something."

" What is it ? "

" Get out of our trap and follow that wedding."

" What to do ? "

" To know where it goes and what it is. Make haste and get down ; run, my daughter, for you are young."

" I can't leave the carriage."

" Why not ? "

" I am hired."

" Oh, the devil ! "

" I owe the Préfecture my day's work."

" That's true."

" If I leave the carriage, the first inspector who sees me will arrest me. You know that."

" Yes, I know it."

" To-day I am bought by Pharos" (the government).

" No matter, that old fellow bothers me."

" All old men bother you, and yet you ain't a chicken yourself."

" He is in the first carriage."

" Well, what then ? "

" In the bride's carriage."

" What next ? "

" So he is the father."

" How does that concern me ? "

" I tell you he is the father."

" You do nothing but talk about that father."

" Listen."

" Well, what ? "

" I can only go away masked, for I am hidden here, and no one knows I am here. But to-morrow there will be no masks, for it is Ash Wednesday, and I run a risk of being nailed. I shall be obliged to go back to my hole, but you are free."

" Not quite."

" Well, more so than I am."

" Well, what then ? "

" You must try to find out where that wedding party is going to."

" Going to ? "

" Yes."

" Oh, I know."

" Where to, then ? "

" To the Cadran Bleu."

" But that is not the direction."

" Well, then ! to La Rapée."

" Or elsewhere."

" They can do as they like, for weddings are free."

" That is not the thing. I tell you that you must try to find out for me what that wedding is, and where it comes from."

" Of course ! that would be funny. It's so jolly easy to find out a week after where a wedding party has gone to that passed during the Mardi Gras. A pin in a bundle of hay. Is it possible ? "

" No matter, you must try. Do you hear, Azelma ? "

The two files recommenced their opposite movement on the boulevard, and the carriage of masks lost out of sight that which contained the bride.

CHAPTER II.

To realize one's dream — to whom is this granted? There must be elections for this in heaven; we are the unconscious candidates, and the angels vote. Cosette and Marius had been elected. Cosette, both at the mayoralty and at church, was brilliant and touching. Toussaint, helped by Nicolette, had dressed her. Cosette wore over a skirt of white taffetas her dress of Binche lace, a veil of English point, a necklace of fine pearls, and a crown of orange-flowers; all this was white, and in this whiteness she was radiant. It was an exquisite candor expanding and becoming transfigured in light; she looked like a virgin on the point of becoming a goddess. Marius's fine hair was shining and perfumed, and here and there a glimpse could be caught, under the thick curls, of pale lines, which were the scars of the barricade. The grandfather, superb, with head erect, amalgamating in his toilette and manners all the elegances of the time of Barras, gave his arm to Cosette. He took the place of Jean Valjean, who, owing to his wound, could not give his hand to the bride. Jean Valjean, dressed all in black, followed and smiled.

"Monsieur Fauchelevent," the grandfather said to him, "this is a glorious day, and I vote the end of afflictions and cares. Henceforth there must be no sorrow anywhere. By Heaven! I decree joy! misfortune has no right to exist, and it is a disgrace for the azure of heaven that there are unfortunate men. Evil does not come from man, who, at the bottom, is good; but all human miseries have their capital and central government in hell, otherwise called the Tuileries of the devil. There, I am making demagogic remarks at present! For my part I have no political opinions left; and all I stick to is that men should be rich, that is to say, joyous."

When, at the end of all the ceremonies, — after pronouncing before the mayor and before the priest every yes that is possible, after signing the register at the municipality and in the sacristy, after exchanging rings, after kneeling side by side under the canopy of white moire in the smoke of the censer, — they arrived holding each other by the hand, admired and envied by all. Marius in black, she in white, preceded by the beadle in the colonel's epaulettes, striking the flag-stones with his halbert, between two rows of dazzled spectators, at the church doors which were thrown wide open, ready to get into their carriage, — and then all was over. Cosette could not yet believe it. She looked at Marius, she looked at the crowd, she looked at heaven; it seemed as if she were afraid of awaking. Her astonished and anxious air imparted something strangely enchanting to her. In returning they both rode in the same carriage, Marius seated by Cosette's side, and M. Gillenormand and Jean Valjean forming their vis-à-vis. Aunt Gillenormand had fallen back a step and was in the second carriage. "My children," the grand-father said, "you are now M. le Baron and Madame la Baronne with thirty thousand francs a year." And Cosette, nuzzling against Marius, caressed his ear with the angelic whisper, "It is true, then, my name is Marius and I am Madame Thou." These two beings were resplendent; they had reached the irrevocable and irrecoverable moment, the dazzling point of in-tersection of all youth and all joy. They realized Jean Prouvaire's line; together they did not num-ber forty years. It was marriage sublimated, and these two children were two lilies. They did not see each other, but contemplated each other. Cosette perceived Marius in a glory, and Marius perceived Cosette upon an altar. And upon this altar, and in this glory, the two apotheoses blending behind a cloud for Cosette and a flashing for Marius, there was the ideal thing, the real thing, the meeting-place of kisses and of sleep, the nuptial pillow.

All the torments they had gone through returned to them in intoxication; it appeared to them as if the griefs, the sleeplessness, the tears, the anguish, the terrors, and the despair, by being converted into caresses and sunbeams, rendered more charming still the charming hour which was approaching; and that their sorrows were so many handmaidens who per-formed the toilette of joy. How good it is to have suffered! Their misfortunes made a halo for their happiness, and the long agony of their love ended in an ascension. There was in these two souls the same enchantment, tinged with voluptuousness in Marius and with modesty in Cosette. They said to each other in a whisper, " We will go and see again our little garden in the Rue Plumet." The folds of Cosette's dress were upon Marius. Such a day is an ineffable blending of dream and certainty: you possess and you suppose, and you still have time before you to divine. It is an indescribable emotion on that day to be at midday and think of midnight. The delight of these two hearts overflowed upon the crowd, and imparted merriment to the passers-by. People stopped in the Rue St. Antoine, in front of St. Paul's, to look through the carriage-window, — the orange flowers trembling on Cosette's head. Then they returned to the Rue des Filles du Calvaire, — home. Marius, side by side with Cosette, ascended, triumphantly and radiantly, that staircase up which he had been dragged in a dying state. The beggars, collected before the gate and dividing the contents of their purses, blessed them. There were flowers everywhere, and the house was no less fragrant than the church: after the incense the rose. They fancied they could hear voices singing in infinitude; they had God in their hearts; destiny appeared to them like a ceiling of stars ; they saw above their heads the flashing of the rising sun. Marius gazed at Cosette's charming bare arm and the pink things which could be vaguely seen through the lace of the stomacher, and Cosette, catching Marius's glance, blushed to the white of her eyes. A good many old friends of the Gillenormand family had been invited, and they thronged round Cosette, outvying one another in calling her Madame la Baronne. The officer, Théodule Gillenormand, now captain, had come from Chartres, where he was stationed, to be present at his cousin's marriage : Cosette did not recognize him. He, on his side, accustomed to be thought a pretty fellow by the women, remembered Cosette no more than any other.

" How right I was in not believing that story of the lancer !" Father Gillenormand said to himself aside.

Cosette had never been more affectionate to Jean Valjean, and she was in unison with Father Gillenormand ; while he built up joy in aphorisms and maxims, she exhaled love and beauty like a perfume. Happiness wishes everybody to be happy. She found again in speaking to Jean Valjean inflections of her voice of the time when she was a little girl, and caressed him with a smile. A banquet had been prepared in the dining-room ; an illumination *à giorno* is the necessary seasoning of a great joy, and mist and darkness are not accepted by the happy. They do not consent to be black : night, yes ; darkness, no ; and if there be no sun, one must be made. The dining-room was a furnace of gay things ; in the centre, above the white glistening tables, hung a Venetian chandelier, with all sorts of colored birds, blue, violet, red, and green, perched among the candles ; round the chandelier were girandoles, and on the walls were mirrors with three and four branches ; glasses, crystal, plate, china, crockery, gold, and silver, all flashed and rejoiced. The spaces between the candelebra were filled up with bouquets, so that where

there was not a light there was a flower.   In the ante-
room three violins and a flute played some of Haydn's
quartettes.   Jean Valjean had seated himself on a
chair in the drawing-room, behind the door, which,
being thrown back, almost concealed him.   A few
minutes before they sat down to table Cosette gave
him a deep courtesy, while spreading out her
wedding-dress with both hands, and with a tenderly
mocking look asked him, —

" Father, are you satisfied ? "

" Yes," said Jean Valjean, " I am satisfied."

" Well, then, laugh."

Jean Valjean began laughing.   A few minutes
later Basque came in to announce that dinner was
on the table.   The guests, preceded by M. Gillenormand, who gave his arm to Cosette, entered the
dining-room, and collected round the table in the
prescribed order.   There was a large easy-chair on
either side of the bride, one for M. Gillenormand, the
other for Jean Valjean.   M. Gillenormand seated
himself, but the other chair remained empty.   All
looked round for Monsieur Fauchelevent, but he was
no longer there, and M. Gillenormand hailed Basque :

" Do you know where M. Fauchelevent is ? "

" Yes, sir, I do," Basque replied.   " Monsieur
Fauchelevent requested me to tell you, sir, that his
hand pained him, and that he could not dine with
M. le Baron and Madame la Baronne.   He therefore
begged to be excused, but would call to-morrow.
He has just left."

This empty chair momentarily chilled the effusion
of the wedding feast ; but though M. Fauchelevent

was absent M. Gillenormand was there, and the grandfather shone for two. He declared that M. Fauchelevent acted rightly in going to bed early if he were in pain, but that it was only a small hurt. This declaration was sufficient; besides, what is a dark corner in such a submersion of joy? Cosette and Marius were in one of those egotistic and blessed moments when people possess no other faculty than that of perceiving joy; and then M. Gillenormand had an idea, " By Jupiter! this chair is empty ; come hither, Marius ; your aunt, though she has a right to it, will permit you ; this chair is for you ; it is legal, and it is pretty, — Fortunatus by the side of Fortunata." The whole of the guests applauded. Marius took Jean Valjean's place by Cosette's side, and things were so arranged that Cosette, who had at first been saddened by the absence of Jean Valjean, ended by being pleased at it. From the moment when Marius was the substitute, Cosette would not have regretted God. She placed her little white-satin-slippered foot upon Marius's foot. When the easy-chair was occupied, M. Fauchelevent was effaced, and nothing was wanting. Five minutes later all the guests were laughing from one end of the table to the other, with all the forgetfulness of humor. At dessert M. Gillenormand rose, with a glass of champagne in his hand, only half full, so that the trembling of ninety-two years might not upset it, and proposed the health of the new-married couple.

" You will not escape from two sermons," he exclaimed: " this morning you had the curé's, and this evening you will have grandpapa's. Listen to me, for

I am going to give you some advice : Adore each
other. I do not beat round the bush, but go straight
to the point; be happy. There are no other sages
in creation but the turtle-doves. Philosophers say,
Moderate your joys ; but I say, Throw the bridle on
the neck of your joys. Love like fiends, be furious.
The philosophers babble, and I should like to thrust
their philosophy down their throats for them. Can
we have too many perfumes, too many open rose-
buds, too many singing nightingales, too many green
leaves, and too much dawn in life ? Can we love too
much ? Can we please one another too much ? Take
care, Estelle, you are too pretty ! Take care, Némorin,
you are too handsome ! What jolly nonsense ! Can
people enchant each other, tease each other, and
charm each other too much ? Can they be too loving ? Can they be too happy ? Moderate your joys,
— oh, stuff ! Down with the philosophers, for wisdom is jubilation. Do you jubilate ? Let us jubilate ;
are we happy because we are good, or are we good
because we are happy ? Is the Sancy diamond called
the Sancy because it belonged to Harlay de Sancy,
or because it weighs one hundred and six carats ? I
do not know ; and life is full of such problems : the
important thing is to have the Sancy and happiness.
Let us be happy without quibbling. Let us blindly
obey the sun. What is the sun ? It is love ; and
when I say love, I mean woman. Ah, ah ! woman
is an omnipotence. Ask that demagogue, Marius,
if he is not the slave of that little she-tyrant,
Cosette, and willingly so, the coward ? Woman !
There is not a Robespierre who can stand ; but

woman reigns. I am now only a royalist of that royalty. What is Adam? The royalty of Eve. There is no '89 for Eve. There was the royal sceptre surmounted by the fleur-de-lys, there was the imperial sceptre surmounted by a globe, there was Charlemagne's sceptre of iron, and the sceptre of Louis the Great, which was of gold. The Revolution twisted them between its thumb and forefinger like straws. It is finished, it is broken, it lies on the ground, — there is no sceptre left. But just make a revolution against that little embroidered handkerchief which smells of patchouli! I should like to see you at it. Try it. Why is it solid? Because it is a rag. Ah! you are the nineteenth century. Well, what then? We were the eighteenth, and were as foolish as you. Do not suppose that you have made any tremendous change in the world because your gallant-trusser is called cholera-morbus, and your bourrée the cachucha. After all, woman must always be loved, and I defy you to get out of that. These she-devils are our angels. Yes, love, woman, and a kiss form a circle from which I defy you to issue, and for my own part I should be very glad to enter it again. Who among you has seen the star Venus, the great coquette of the abyss, the Celimène of ocean, rise in infinite space, appeasing everything below her, and looking at the waves like a woman? The ocean is a rude Alcestis; and yet, however much he may growl, when Venus appears he is forced to smile. That brute-beast submits, and we are all thus. Anger, tempest, thunder-bolts, foam up to the ceiling. A woman comes upon the stage, a star rises, and you crawl in the dust. Marius was fighting six months ago, and is marrying to-day, and that is well done. Yes, Marius, yes, Cosette, you are right. Exist bravely one for the other, make us burst with rage because we cannot do the same, and idolize each other. Take in both your beaks the little straws of felicity which lie on the ground, and make of them a nest for life. By Jove! to love, to be loved, — what a great miracle when a man is young! Do not suppose that you invented it. I too have dreamed, and thought, and sighed. I too have had a moonlit soul. Love is a child six thousand years of age, and has a right to a long white beard. Methuselah is a baby by the side of Cupid. Sixty centuries back man and woman got out of the scrape by loving. The devil, who is cunning, took to hating man; but man, who is more cunning still, took to loving woman. In this way he did himself more good than the devil did him harm. That trick was discovered simultaneously with the terrestrial paradise. My friends, the invention is old, but it is brand new. Take advantage of it; be Daphnis and Chloe while waiting till you are Baucis and Philemon. Manage so that when you are together you may want for nothing, and that Cosette may be the sun for Marius, and Marius the universe for Cosette. Cosette, let your fine weather be your husband's smiles. Marius, let your wife's tears be the rain, and mind that it never does rain in your household. You have drawn the good number in the lottery, love in the sacrament. You have the prize number, so keep it carefully under lock and key. Do not

squander it. Adore each other, and a fig for the
rest. Believe what I tell you, then, for it is good
sense, and good sense cannot deceive. Be to one
another a religion, for each man has his own way of
adoring God. Saperlotte! the best way of adoring
God is to love one's wife. I love you! that is my
catechism; and whoever loves is orthodox. The
oath of Henri IV. places sanctity between guttling
and intoxication. *Ventre Saint Gris!* I do not
belong to the religion of that oath, for woman is
forgotten in it, and that surprises me on the part of
Henri IV.'s oath. My friends, long live woman! I
am old, so people say; but it is amazing how dis-
posed I feel to be young. I should like to go and
listen to the bagpipes in the woods. These children,
who succeed in being beautiful and satisfied, intoxicate me. I am quite willing to marry if anybody
will have me. It is impossible to imagine that God
has made us for anything else than this, — to idolize,
to purr, to strut, to be a pigeon, to be a cock, to
caress our lovers from morning till night, to admire
ourselves in our little wife, to be proud, to be triumphant, and to swell. Such is the object of life.
That, without offence, is what we thought in our
time, when we were young men. Ah! vertu-bam-
boche! what charming women there were in those
days! what ducks! I made my ravages among them.
Then love each other. If men and women did not
love, I really do not see what use there would be in
having a spring. And for my part, I would pray the
good God to lock up all the fine things he shows
us and take them back from us, and to return to his

box the flowers, the birds, and the pretty girls. My
children, receive an old man's blessing."

The evening was lively, gay, and pleasant; the
sovereign good-humor of the grandfather gave the
tone to the whole festivity, and each was regulated
by this almost centenary heartiness.   There was a
little dancing and a good deal of laughter; it was
a merry wedding, to which that worthy old fellow
"Once on a time" might have been invited; however, he was present in the person of Father Gillenormand.   There was a tumult and then a silence;
the married couple disappeared.   A little after midnight the Gillenormand mansion became a temple.
Here we stop, for an angel stands on the threshold
of wedding-nights, smiling, and with finger on lip;
the mind becomes contemplative before this sanctuary in which the celebration of love is held.   There
must be rays of light above such houses, and the
joy which they contain must pass through the walls
in brilliancy, and vaguely irradiate the darkness.   It
is impossible for this sacred and fatal festival not to
send a celestial radiance to infinitude.   Love is the
sublime crucible in which the fusion of man and
woman takes place; the one being, the triple being,
the final being, the human trinity issue from it.
This birth of two souls in one must have emotion
for the shadows.   The lover is the priest, and the
transported virgin feels an awe.   A portion of this
joy ascends to God.   When there is really marriage,
that is to say, when there is love, the ideal is mingled
with it, and a nuptial couch forms in the darkness a
corner of the dawn.   If it was given to the mental

eye to perceive the formidable and charming visions of higher life, it is probable that it would see the forms of night, the unknown winged beings, the blue wayfarers of the invisible, bending down round the luminous house, satisfied and blessing, pointing out to each other the virgin bride, who is gently startled, and having the reflection of human felicity on their divine countenances. If, at this supreme hour, the pair, dazzled with pleasure, and who believe themselves alone, were to listen, they would hear in their chamber a confused rustling of wings, for perfect happiness implies the guarantee of angels. This little obscure alcove has an entire heaven for its ceiling. When two mouths, which have become sacred by love, approach each other in order to create, it is impossible but that there is a tremor in the immense mystery of the stars above this ineffable kiss. These felicities are the real ones, there is no joy beyond their joys; love is the sole ecstasy, and all the rest weeps. To love or to have loved is sufficient; ask nothing more after that. There is no other pearl to be found in the dark folds of life, for love is a consummation.

CHAPTER III.

THE INSEPARABLE.

WHAT had become of Jean Valjean? Directly after he had laughed in accordance with Cosette's request, as no one was paying any attention to him, Jean Valjean rose, and unnoticed reached the ante-room. It was the same room which he had entered eight months previously, black with mud and blood and gunpowder, bringing back the grandson to the grandfather. The old panelling was garlanded with flowers and leaves, the musicians were seated on the sofa upon which Marius had been deposited. Basque, in black coat, knee-breeches, white cravat, and white gloves, was placing wreaths of roses round each of the dishes which was going to be served up. Jean Valjean showed him his arm in the sling, requested him to explain his absence, and quitted the house. The windows of the dining-room looked out on the street, and Valjean stood for some minutes motion-less in the obscurity of those radiant windows. He listened, and the confused sound of the banquet reached his ears; he heard the grandfather's loud and dictatorial voice, the violins, the rattling of plates and glasses, the bursts of laughter, and amid all these gay sounds he distinguished Cosette's soft, happy voice. He left the Rue des Filles du Calvaire and returned to the Rue de l'Homme Armé. In going home he went along the Rue St. Louis, the Rue Culture-Sainte-Catherine, and the Blancs Manteaux ; it was a little longer, but it was the road by which he had been accustomed to come with Cosette during the last three months, in order to avoid the crowd and mud of the Rue Vieille du Temple. This road, which Cosette had passed along, excluded the idea of any other itinerary for him. Jean Valjean returned home, lit his candle, and went upstairs. The apartments were empty ; not even Toussaint was in there now. Jean Valjean's footsteps made more noise in the rooms than usual. All the wardrobes were open ; he entered Cosette's room, and there were no sheets on the bed. The pillow, without a case or lace, was laid on the blankets folded at the foot of the bed, in which no one was going to sleep again. All the small feminine articles to which Cosette clung had been removed ; only the heavy furniture and the four walls remained. Toussaint's bed was also unmade, and the only one made which seemed to be expecting somebody was Jean Valjean's. Jean Valjean looked at the walls, closed some of the wardrobe drawers, and walked in and out of the rooms. Then he returned to his own room and placed his candle on the table ; he had taken his arm out of the sling, and used it as if he were suffering no pain in it. He went up to his bed and his eyes fell — was it by accident or was it purposely ? — on the *inseparable* of which Cosette had been jealous, the little valise which never left him.

On June 4, when he arrived at the Rue de l'Homme
Armé, he laid it on a table; he now walked up to
this table with some eagerness, took the key out of
his pocket, and opened the portmanteau. He slowly
drew out the clothes in which, ten years previously,
Cosette had left Montfermeil; first, the little black
dress, then the black handkerchief, then the stout
shoes, which Cosette could almost have worn still,
so small was her foot; next the petticoat, then the
apron, and lastly, the woollen stockings. These
stockings, in which the shape of a little leg was
gracefully marked, were no longer than Jean Valjean's hand. All these articles were black, and it
was he who took them for her to Montfermeil. He
laid each article on the bed as he took it out, and he
thought and remembered. It was in winter, a very
cold December; she was shivering under her rags,
and her poor feet were quite red in her wooden shoes.
He, Jean Valjean, had made her take off these rags
and put on this mourning garb; the mother must
have been pleased in her tomb to see her daughter
wearing mourning for her, and above all, to see that
she was well clothed and was warm. He thought
of that forest of Montfermeil, he thought what
the weather was, of the trees without leaves, of the
wood without birds and the sky without sun; but
no matter, it was charming. He arranged the little
clothes on the bed, the handkerchief near the petticoat, the stockings along with the shoes, the apron
by the side of the dress, and he looked at them one
after the other. She was not much taller than that,
she had her large doll in her arms, she had put her

louis d'or in the pocket of this apron, she laughed, they walked along holding each other's hand, and she had no one but him in the world.

Then his venerable white head fell on the bed, his old stoical heart broke, his face was buried in Cosette's clothes, and had any one passed upstairs at that moment he would have heard frightful sobs.

CHAPTER IV.

IMMORTALE JECUR.

THE old formidable struggle, of which we have already seen several phases, began again. Jacob only wrestled with the angel for one night. Alas! how many times have we seen Jean Valjean caught round the waist in the darkness by his conscience, and struggling frantically against it. An extraordinary struggle! At certain moments the foot slips, at others the ground gives way. How many times had that conscience, clinging to the right, strangled and crushed him! How many times had inexorable truth set its foot on his chest! How many times had he, felled by the light, cried for mercy! How many times had that implacable light, illumined within and over him by the Bishop, dazzled him when he wished to be blinded! How many times had he risen again in the contest, clung to the rock, supported himself by sophistry, and been dragged through the dust, at one moment throwing his conscience under him, at another thrown by it! How many times, after an equivocation, after the treacherous and specious reasoning of egotism, had he heard his irritated conscience cry in his ears, " Trickster! wretch!" How many times had his refractory thoughts groaned con-

vulsively under the evidence of duty! What secret
wounds he had, which he alone felt bleeding! What
excoriations there were in his lamentable existence!
How many times had he risen, bleeding, mutilated,
crushed, enlightened, with despair in his heart and
serenity in his soul! And though vanquished, he felt
himself the victor, and after having dislocated, tor-
tured, and broken him, his conscience, erect before
him, luminous and tranquil, would say to him, —
"Now go in peace!" What a mournful peace, alas!
after issuing from such a contest.

This night, however, Jean Valjean felt that he was
fighting his last battle. A crushing question presented itself; predestinations are not all straight;
they do not develop themselves in a rectilinear avenue before the predestined man; they have blind
alleys, zigzags, awkward corners, and perplexing
cross-roads. Jean Valjean was halting at this moment at the most dangerous of these cross-roads. He
had reached the supreme crossing of good and evil,
and had that gloomy intersection before his eyes.
This time again, as had already happened in other
painful interludes, two roads presented themselves
before him, one tempting, the other terrifying; which
should he take? The one which frightened him was
counselled by the mysterious pointing hand which
we all perceive every time that we fix our eyes upon
the darkness. Jean Valjean had once again a choice
between the terrible haven and the smiling snare.
Is it true, then? The soul may be cured, but not
destiny. What a frightful thing, — an incurable destiny! The question which presented itself was this:

In what way was Jean Valjean going to behave
to the happiness of Cosette and Marius? That happiness he had willed, he had made; and at this hour,
in gazing upon it, he could have the species of satisfaction which a cutler would have who recognized
his trade-mark upon a knife when he drew it all
smoking from his chest. Cosette had Marius, Marius
possessed Cosette; they possessed everything, even
wealth, and it was his doing. But now that this
happiness existed and was there, how was he, Jean
Valjean, to treat it? Should he force himself upon
it and treat it as if belonging to himself? Doubtless
Cosette was another man's; but should he, Jean
Valjean, retain of Cosette all that he could retain?
Should he remain the sort of father, scarce seen
but respected, which he had hitherto been? Should
he introduce himself quietly into Cosette's house?
Should he carry his past to this future without saying a word? Should he present himself there as one
having a right, and should he sit down, veiled, at
this luminous hearth? Should he smilingly take the
hands of these two innocent creatures in his tragic
hands? Should he place on the andirons of the
Gillenormand drawing-room his feet, which dragged
after them the degrading shadow of the law? Should
he render the obscurity on his brow and the cloud
on theirs denser? Should he join his catastrophe to
their two felicities? Should he continue to be silent?
In a word, should he be the sinister dumb man of
destiny by the side of these two happy beings? We
must be accustomed to fatality and to meeting it, to
raise our eyes when certain questions appear to us in

their terrible nudity. Good and evil are behind this stern note of interrogation. What are you going to do? the Sphinx asks. This habit of trial Jean Valjean had, and he looked at the Sphinx fixedly, and examined the pitiless problem from all sides. Cosette, that charming existence, was the raft of this shipwrecked man; what should he do, cling to it, or let it go? If he clung to it, he issued from disaster, he remounted to the sunshine, he let the bitter water drip off his clothes and hair, he was saved and lived. Suppose he let it go? Then there was an abyss. He thus dolorously held counsel with his thoughts, or, to speak more correctly, he combated; he rushed furiously within himself, at one moment against his will, at another against his convictions. It was fortunate for Jean Valjean that he had been able to weep, for that enlightened him, perhaps. Still, the beginning was stern; a tempest, more furious than that which had formerly forced him to Arras, was let loose within him. The past returned to him in the face of the present; he compared and sobbed. Once the sluice of tears was opened, the despairing man writhed. He felt himself arrested, alas! in the deadly fight between one egotism and one duty. When we thus recoil inch by inch before our ideal, wildly, obstinately, exasperated at yielding, disputing the ground, hoping for a possible flight, and seeking an issue, what a sudden and sinister resistance behind us is the foot of the wall! To feel the holy shadow standing in the way! The inexorable, invisible, — what a pressure!

Hence we have never finished with our conscience.

Make up your mind, Brutus; make up your mind,
Cato. It is bottomless, for it is God. You cast into
this pit the labor of your whole life, — your fortune,
your wealth, your success, your liberty, or your country, your comfort, your repose, your joy. More, more,
more ! Empty the vase, tread over the urn, you must
end by throwing in your heart. There is a barrel
like this somewhere in the Hades of old. Is it not
pardonable to refuse at last ? Can that which is inexhaustible have any claim ? Are not endless chains
beyond human strength ? Who then would blame
Sisyphus and Jean Valjean for saying, It is enough !
The obedience of matter is limited by friction : is
there not a limit to the obedience of the soul ? If
perpetual motion be impossible, why is perpetual devotion demanded ? The first step is nothing, it is the
last that is difficult. What was the Champmathieu
affair by the side of Cosette's marriage ? What did
it bring with it ? What is returning to the hulks by
the side of entering nothingness ? Oh, first step to
descend, how gloomy thou art ! oh, second step, how
black thou art ! How could he help turning his head
away this time ? Martyrdom is a sublimation, a cor-
rosive sublimation, it is a torture which consecrates.
A man may consent to it for the first hour; he sits
on the throne of red-hot iron, the crown of red-hot
iron is placed on his head, — he accepts the red-hot
globe, he takes the red-hot sceptre, but he still has
to don the mantle of flame, and is there not a moment
when the miserable flesh revolts and he flies from the
punishment ? At length Jean Valjean entered the
calmness of prostration; he wished, thought over, and

considered the alternations, the mysterious balance of light and shadow. Should he force his galleys on these two dazzling children, or consummate his own irremediable destruction? On one side was the sacrifice of Cosette, on the other his own.

On which solution did he decide? What determination did he form? What was in his inner self the definitive reply to the incorruptible interrogatory of fatality? What door did he resolve on opening? Which side of his life did he make up his mind to close and condemn? Amid all those unfathomable precipices that surrounded him, which was his choice? What extremity did he accept? To which of these gulfs did he nod his head? His confusing reverie lasted all night; he remained till daybreak in the same position, leaning over the bed, prostrate beneath the enormity of fate, perhaps crushed, alas! with hands convulsed, and arms extended at a right angle like an unnailed crucified man thrown with his face on the ground. He remained thus for twelve hours, — the twelve hours of a long winter's night, frozen, without raising his head or uttering a syllable. He was motionless as a corpse, while his thoughts rolled on the ground or fled away; sometimes like a hydra, sometimes like the eagle. To see him thus you would have thought him a dead man; but all at once he started convulsively, and his mouth pressed to Cosette's clothes, kissed them; then one saw that he was alive.

What One, since Jean Valjean was alone and nobody was there?

The One who is in the darkness.

BOOK VII.

THE LAST DROP IN THE BITTER CUP.

CHAPTER I.

THE SEVENTH CIRCLE AND THE EIGHTH HEAVEN.

THE day after a wedding is solitary, for people respect the retirement of the happy, and to some extent their lengthened slumbers. The confusion of visits and congratulations does not begin again till a later date. On the morning of Feb. 17 it was a little past midday when Basque, with napkin and feather-brush under his arm, dusting the anteroom, heard a low tap at the door. There had not been a ring, which is discreet on such a day. Basque opened and saw M. Fauchelevent; he conducted him to the drawing-room, which was still topsy-turvy, and looked like the battle-field of the previous day's joys.

" Really, sir," observed Basque, " we woke late."

" Is your master up ? " Jean Valjean asked.

" How is your hand, sir ? " Basque replied.

" Better. Is your master up ? "

" Which one, the old or the new ? "

" Monsieur Pontmercy."

" Monsieur le Baron ! " said Basque, drawing himself up.

A baron is before all a baron to his servants; a portion of it comes to them, and they have what a philosopher would call the spray of the title, and that flatters them. Marius, we may mention in passing, a militant republican as he had proved, was now a baron in spite of himself. A little revolution had taken place in the family with reference to this title it was M. Gillenormand who was attached to it, and Marius who had fallen away from it. But Colonel Pontmercy had written, " My son will bear my title," and Marius obeyed. And then Cosette, in whom the woman was beginning to germinate, was delighted at being a baroness.

" Monsieur le Baron ? " repeated Basque; " I will go and see. I will tell him that Monsieur Fauchelevent is here."

" No, do not tell him it is I. Tell him that some one wishes to speak to him privately, and do not mention my name."

" Ah ! " said Basque.

" I wish to surprise him."

" Ah ! " Basque repeated, giving himself his second " Ah ! " as an explanation of the first.

And he left the room, and Jean Valjean remained alone. The drawing-room, as we said, was all in disorder, and it seemed as if you could still hear the vague sounds of the wedding. On the floor were all sorts of flowers, which had fallen from garlands and head-dresses, and the candles burned down to the socket added wax stalactites to the

crystal of the lustres. Not an article of furniture
was in its place; in the corner three or four easy-
chairs, drawn close together, and forming a circle,
looked as if they were continuing a conversation.
The *ensemble* was laughing, for there is a certain
grace left in a dead festival, for it has been happy.
Upon those disarranged chairs, amid those fading
flowers and under those extinguished lamps, persons
have thought of joy. The sun succeeded the chandelier, and gayly entered the drawing-room. A few
moments passed, during which Jean Valjean remained
motionless at the spot where Basque left him. His
eyes were hollow, and so sunk in their sockets by
sleeplessness that they almost disappeared. His black
coat displayed the fatigued creases of a coat which
has been up all night, and the elbows were white
with that down which friction with linen leaves on
cloth. Jean Valjean looked at the window designed
on the floor at his feet by the sun. There was a
noise at the door, and he raised his eyes. Marius
came in with head erect, laughing mouth, a peculiar
light over his face, a smooth forehead, and a flashing
eye. He, too, had not slept.

"It is you, father!" he exclaimed, on perceiving
Jean Valjean; "why, that ass Basque affected the
mysterious. But you have come too early; it is
only half-past twelve, and Cosette is asleep."

That word, father, addressed to M. Fauchelevent
by Marius, signified supreme felicity. There had
always been, as we know, a cliff, a coldness and
constraint between them; ice to melt or break.
Marius was so intoxicated that the cliff sank, the

ice dissolved, and M. Fauchelevent was for him, as for Cosette, a father. He continued, the words overflowed with him, which is peculiar to these divine paroxysms of joy, —

"How delighted I am to see you! If you only knew how we missed you yesterday! Good-day, father. How is your hand? Better, is it not?"

And, satisfied with the favorable answer which he gave himself, he went on, —

"We both spoke about you, for Cosette loves you so dearly. You will not forget that you have a room here, for we will not hear a word about the Rue de l'Homme Armé. I do not know how you were able to live in that street, which is sick, and mean, and poor, which has a barrier at one end, where you feel cold, and which no one can enter! You will come and install yourself here, and from to-day, or else you will have to settle with Cosette. She intends to lead us both by the nose, I warn you. You have seen your room; it is close to ours, and looks out on the gardens. We have had the lock mended; the bed is made; it is all ready, and you have only to move in. Cosette has placed close to your bed a large old easy-chair, of Utrecht velvet, to which she said, 'Hold out your arms to him!' Every spring a nightingale comes to the clump of acacias which faces your windows, and you will have it in two months. You will have its nest on your left, and ours on your right; at night it will sing, and by day Cosette will talk. Your room faces due south; Cosette will arrange your books in it; the Travels of Captain Cook, and the other, Vancouver's

Travels, and all your matters. There is, I believe,
a valise to which you are attached, and I have
arranged a corner of honor for it. You have won
my grandfather, for you suit him. We will live
together. Do you know whist? You will over-
whelm my grandfather if you are acquainted with
whist. You will take Cosette for a walk on the
day when I go to the Courts; you will give her
your arm, as you used to do, you remember, formerly
at the Luxembourg. We are absolutely determined
to be very happy, and you will share in our happiness,
do you hear, father? By the bye, you will breakfast
with us this morning?"

"Sir!" said Jean Valjean, "I have one thing to
say to you. I am an ex-convict."

The limit of the perceptible acute sounds may
be as well exceeded for the mind as for the ear.
These words, "I am an ex-convict," coming from
M. Fauchelevent's mouth and entering Marius's ear
went beyond possibility. Marius did not hear. It
seemed to him as if something had been just said
to him, but he knew not what. He stood with
gaping mouth. Jean Valjean unfastened the black
handkerchief that supported his right arm, undid
the linen rolled round his hand, bared his thumb,
and showed it to Marius.

"I have nothing the matter with my hand," he said.

Marius looked at the thumb.

"There was never anything the matter with it,"
Jean Valjean added.

There was, in fact, no sign of a wound. Jean
Valjean continued, —

"It was proper that I should be absent from your marriage, and I was so as far as I could be. I feigned this wound in order not to commit a forgery, and render the marriage-deeds null and void."

Marius stammered, —

"What does this mean?"

"It means," Jean Valjean replied, "that I have been to the galleys."

"You are driving me mad!" said the horrified Marius.

"Monsieur Pontmercy," said Jean Valjean, "I was nineteen years at the galleys for robbery. Then I was sentenced to them for life, for robbery and a second offence. At the present moment I am an escaped convict."

Although Marius recoiled before the reality, refused the facts, and resisted the evidence, he was obliged to yield to it. He was beginning to understand, and as always happens in such a case, he understood too much. He had the shudder of a hideous internal flash, and an idea that made him shudder crossed his mind. He foresaw a frightful destiny for himself in the future.

"Say all, say all," he exclaimed; "you are Cosette's father!"

And he fell back two steps, with a movement of indescribable horror. Jean Valjean threw up his head with such a majestic attitude that he seemed to rise to the ceiling.

"It is necessary that you should believe me here, sir, although the oath of men like us is not taken in a court of justice —"

Here there was a silence, and then with a sort of sovereign and sepulchral authority he added, speaking slowly and laying a stress on the syllables, —

"You will believe me. I, Cosette's father! Before Heaven, no, Monsieur le Baron Pontmercy. I am a peasant of Faverolles, and earned my livelihood by pruning trees. My name is not Fauchelevent, but Jean Valjean. I am nothing to Cosette, so reassure yourself."

Marius stammered, —

"Who proves it to me?"

"I do, since I say it."

Marius looked at this man: he was mournful and calm, and no falsehood could issue from such calmness. What is frozen is sincere, and the truth could be felt in this coldness of the tomb.

"I do believe you," said Marius.

Jean Valjean bowed his head, as if to note the fact, and continued, —

"What am I to Cosette? A passer-by. Ten years ago I did not know that she existed. I love her, it is true, for men love a child which they have seen little when old themselves; when a man is old he feels like a grandfather to all little children. You can, I suppose, imagine that I have something which resembles a heart. She was an orphan, without father or mother, and needed me, and that is why I came to love her. Children are so weak that the first comer, even a man like myself, may be their protector. I performed this duty to Cosette. I cannot suppose that so small a thing can be called a good action: but if it be one, well, assume that I did it. Record that extenuating fact. To-day Cosette leaves my life, and our two roads separate. Henceforth I can do no more for her; she is Madame Pontmercy; her providence has changed, and she has gained by the change, so all is well. As for the six hundred thousand francs, you say nothing of them, but I will meet your thought half-way: they are a deposit. How was it placed in my hands? No matter. I give up the deposit, and there is nothing more to ask of me. I complete the restitution by stating my real name, and this too concerns myself, for I am anxious that you should know who I am."

And Jean Valjean looked Marius in the face. All that Marius experienced was tumultuous and incoherent, for certain blasts of the wind of destiny produce such waves in our soul. We have all had such moments of trouble in which everything is dispersed within us: we say the first things that occur to us, which are not always precisely those which we ought to say. There are sudden revelations which we cannot bear, and which intoxicate like a potent wine. Marius was stupefied by the new situation which appeared to him, and spoke to this man almost as if he were angry at the avowal.

"But why," he exclaimed, "do you tell me all this? Who forces you to do so? You might have kept your secret to yourself. You are neither denounced, nor pursued, nor tracked. You have a motive for making the revelation so voluntarily. Continue; there is something else: for what purpose do you make this confession? For what motive?"

"For what motive?" Jean Valjean answered in a

voice so low and dull that it seemed as if he were
speaking to himself rather than Marius. "For what
motive, in truth, does this convict come here to say,
' I am a convict'? Well, yes, the motive is a strange
one : it is through honesty. The misfortune is that
I have a thread in my heart which holds me fast,
and it is especially when a man is old that these
threads are most solid. The whole of life is undone
around, but they resist. Had I been enabled to tear
away that thread, break it, unfasten or cut the knot,
and go a long way off, I would be saved and needed
only to start. There are diligences in the Rue du
Bouloy; you are happy, and I am off. I tried to
break that thread. I pulled at it, it held out, it did
not break, and I pulled out my heart with it. Then
I said, I cannot live anywhere else, and must remain.
Well, yes, but you are right. I am a fool ; why not
remain simply? You offer me a bed-room in the
house. Madame Pontmercy loves me dearly, she
said to that fauteuil, ' Hold out your arms to him ;'
your grandfather asks nothing better than to have me.
I suit him, we will live all together, have our meals in
common, I will give my arm to Cosette,— to Madame
Pontmercy, forgive me, but it is habit,— we will have
only one roof, one table, one fire, the same chimney-
corner in winter, the same walk in summer : that is
joy, that is happiness, that is everything. We will
live in one family."

At this word Jean Valjean became fierce. He
folded his arms, looked at the board at his feet, as if
he wished to dig a pit in it, and his voice suddenly
became loud.

"In one family? No. I belong to no family; I do not belong to yours, I do not even belong to the human family. In houses where people are together I am in the way. There are families, but none for me; I am the unhappy man, I am outside. Had I a father and mother? I almost doubt it. On the day when I gave you that child in marriage, it was all ended; I saw her happy, and that she was with the man she loved, that there is a kind old gentleman here, a household of two angels, and every joy in this house, and I said to myself, Do not enter. I could lie, it is true, deceive you all, and remain Monsieur Fauchelevent; so long as it was for her, I was able to lie, but now that it would be for myself I ought not to do so. I only required to be silent, it is true, and all would have gone on. You ask me what compels me to speak? A strange sort of thing, my conscience. It would have been very easy, however, to hold my tongue; I spent the night in trying to persuade myself into it. You are shriving me, and what I have just told you is so extraordinary that you have the right to do so. Well, yes, I spent the night in giving myself reasons. I gave myself excellent reasons, I did what I could. But there are two things in which I could not succeed; I could neither break the string which holds me by the heart, fixed, sealed, and riveted here, nor silence some one who speaks to me in a low voice when I am alone. That is why I have come to confess all to you this morning, — all, or nearly all, for it is useless to tell what only concerns myself, and that I keep to myself. You know the essential thing. I took my mystery,

then, and brought it to you, and ripped it up before
your eyes. It was not an easy resolution to form,
and I debated the point the whole night. Ah! you
may fancy that I did not say to myself that this was
not the Champmathieu affair, that in hiding my
name I did no one any harm, that the name of
Fauchelevent was given me by Fauchelevent himself
in gratitude for a service rendered, and that I might
fairly keep it, and that I should be happy in this
room which you offer me, that I should not be at all
in the way, that I should be in my little corner, and
that while you had Cosette I should have the idea of
being in the same house with her; each would have
his proportioned happiness. Continuing to be Monsieur Fauchelevent arranged everything. Yes, except my soul; there would be joy all over me, but
the bottom of my soul would remain black. Thus
I should have remained Monsieur Fauchelevent. I
should have hidden my real face in the presence of
your happiness; I should have had an enigma, and
in the midst of your broad sunshine I should have
had darkness; thus, without crying 'Look out,' I
should have introduced the hulks to your hearth,
I should have sat down at your table with the thought
that if you knew who I was you would expel me,
and let myself be served by the servants who, had
they known, would have said, 'What a horror!' I
should have touched you with my elbow, which you
have a right to feel offended at, and swindled you
out of shakes of the hand. There would have been
in your house a divided respect between venerable
gray hairs and branded gray hairs; in your most

intimate hours, when all hearts formed themselves to each other, when we were all four together, the grandfather, you two, and I, there would have been a stranger there. Hence I, a dead man, would have imposed myself on you who are living, and I should have sentenced her for life. You, Cosette, and I would have been three heads in the green cap! Do you not shudder? I am only the most crushed of men, but I should have been the most monstrous. And this crime I should have committed every day, and this falsehood I should have told every day, and this face of night I should have worn every day, and to you I should have given a portion of my stain every day,—to you, my beloved, to you, my children, to you, my innocents! Holding one's tongue is nothing? Keeping silence is simple? No, it is not simple, for there is a silence which lies; and my falsehood, and my fraud, and my indignity, and my cowardice, and my treachery, and my crime I should have drunk drop by drop; I should have spat it out, and then drunk it again; I should have ended at midnight and begun again at midday, and my good day would have lied, and my good night would have lied, and I should have slept upon it, and eaten it with my bread; and I should have looked at Cosette, and responded to the smile of the angel with the smile of the condemned man; and I should have been an abominable scoundrel, and for what purpose? To be happy. I, happy! Have I the right to be happy? I am out of life, sir."

Jean Valjean stopped, and Marius listened, for such enchainments of ideas and agonies cannot be interrupted. Jean Valjean lowered his voice again, yet it was no longer the dull voice, but the sinister voice.

"You ask why I speak? I am neither denounced, nor pursued, nor tracked, you say. Yes, I am denounced! Yes, I am pursued! Yes, I am tracked! By whom? By myself. It is I who bar my own passage, and I drag myself along, and I push myself, and I arrest myself, and execute myself, and when a man holds himself he is securely held."

And, seizing his own collar, and dragging it toward Marius, he continued, —

"Look at this fist. Do you not think that it holds this collar so as not to let it go? Well, conscience is a very different hand! If you wish to be happy, sir, you must never understand duty; for so soon as you have understood it, it is implacable. People may say that it punishes you for understanding it; but no, it rewards you for it, for it places you in a hell where you feel God by your side. A man has no sooner torn his entrails than he is at peace with himself."

And with an indescribable accent he added, —

"Monsieur Pontmercy, that has no common-sense. I am an honest man. It is by degrading myself in your eyes that I raise myself in my own. This has happened to me once before, but it was less painful ; it was nothing. Yes, an honest man. I should not be one if you had, through my fault, continued to esteem me ; but now that you despise me I am so. I have this fatality upon me, that as I am never able to have any but stolen consideration, this consideration humiliates and crushes me internally, and in order that I may respect myself people must despise me. Then I draw myself up. I am a galley-slave who obeys his conscience. I know very well that this is not likely; but what would you have me do? It is so. I have made engagements with myself and keep them. There are meetings which bind us; there are accidents which drag us into duty. Look you, Monsieur Pontmercy, things have happened to me in my life."

Jean Valjean made another pause, swallowing his saliva with an effort, as if his words had a bitter after-taste, and he continued, —

"When a man has such a horror upon him; he has no right to make others share it unconsciously; he has no right to communicate his plague to them; he has no right to make them slip over his precipice without their perceiving it; he has no right to drag his red cap over them, and no right craftily to encumber the happiness of another man with his misery. To approach those who are healthy and touch them in the darkness with his invisible ulcer is hideous. Fauchelevent may have lent me his name, but I have no right to use it: he may have given it to me, but I was unable to take it. A name is a self. Look you, sir, I have thought a little and read a little, though I am a peasant, and you see that I express myself properly. I explain things to myself, and have carried out my own education. Well, yes; to abstract a name and place one's self under it is dishonest. The letters of the alphabet may be filched like a purse or a watch. To be a false signature in flesh and blood, to be a living false key, to enter among honest folk by picking their lock, never to look, but always to squint, to be internally infamous, — no! no! no! no! It is better to suffer, bleed, weep, tear one's flesh with one's nails, pass the nights writhing in agony, and gnaw one's stomach and soul. That is why I have come to tell you all this, — voluntarily, as you remarked."

He breathed painfully, and uttered this last remark, —

"Formerly I stole a loaf in order to live; to-day I will not steal a name in order to live."

"To live!" Marius interrupted; "you do not require that name to live."

"Ah! I understand myself," Jean Valjean replied, raising and drooping his head several times in succession. There was a stillness; both remained silent, sunk as they were in a gulf of thought. Marius was sitting near a table, and supporting the corner of his mouth on one of his fingers. Jean Valjean walked backwards and forwards; he stopped before a glass and remained motionless. Then, as if answering some internal reasoning, he said, as he looked in this glass, in which he did not see himself, —

"While at present I am relieved."

He began walking again, and went to the other end of the room. At the moment when he turned he perceived that Marius was watching his walk, and he said to him, with an indescribable accent, —

"I drag my leg a little. You understand why, now."

Then he turned round full to Marius.

" And now, sir, imagine this. I have said nothing. I have remained Monsieur Fauchelevent. I have taken my place in your house. I am one of your family. I am in my room. I come down to break-fast in my slippers; at night we go to the play, all three. I accompany Madame Pontmercy to the Tuileries and to the Place Royale ; we are together, and you believe me your equal. One fine day I am here, you are there. We are talking and laughing, and you hear a voice cry this name, — Jean Valjean ! and then that fearful hand, the police, issues from the shadow and suddenly tears off my mask ! "

He was silent again. Marius had risen with a shudder and Jean Valjean continued, —

" What do you say to that ? "

Marius's silence replied, and Jean Valjean con-tinued : —

" You see very well that I did right in not hold-ing my tongue. Be happy, be in heaven, be the angel of an angel, be in the sunshine and content yourself with it, and do not trouble yourself as to the way in which a poor condemned man opens his heart and does his duty; you have a wretched man before you, sir."

Marius slowly crossed the room, and when he was by Jean Valjean's side offered him his hand. But Marius was compelled to take this hand which did not offer itself. Jean Valjean let him do so, and it seemed to Marius that he was pressing a hand of marble.

" My grandfather has friends " said Marius. " I will obtain your pardon."

"It is useless," Jean Valjean replied; "I am supposed to be dead, and that is sufficient. The dead are not subjected to surveillance, and are supposed to rot quietly. Death is the same thing as pardon."

And liberating the hand which Marius held, he added with a sort of inexorable dignity, —

"Moreover, duty, my duty, is the friend to whom I have recourse; and I only need one pardon, that of my conscience."

At this moment the door opened gently at the other end of the drawing-room, and Cosette's head appeared in the crevice. Only her sweet face was visible. Her hair was in admirable confusion, and her eyelids were still swollen with sleep. She made the movement of a bird thrusting its head out of the nest, looked first at her husband, then at Jean Valjean, and cried to them laughingly, — it looked like a smile issuing from a rose, —

"I will bet that you are talking politics. How stupid that is, instead of being with me!"

Jean Valjean started.

"Cosette," Marius stammered, and he stopped. They looked like two culprits; Cosette, radiant, continued to look at them both, and there were in her eyes gleams of Paradise.

"I have caught you in the act," Cosette said; "I just heard through this, Father Fauchelevent saying, 'Conscience, doing one's duty.' That is politics, and I will have none of it. People must not talk politics on the very next day; it is not right."

"You are mistaken, Cosette;" Marius replied, "we

are talking of business. We are talking about the best way of investing your six hundred thousand francs."

"I am coming," Cosette interrupted. "Do you want me here?"

And resolutely passing through the door, she entered the drawing-room. She was dressed in a large combing gown with a thousand folds and large sleeves, which descended from her neck to her feet. There are in the golden skies of old Gothic paintings, these charming bags to place an angel in. She contemplated herself from head to foot in a large mirror, and then exclaimed with an ineffable outburst of ecstasy, —

"There was once upon a time a king and queen. Oh, how delighted I am!"

This said, she courtesied to Marius and Jean Valjean.

"Then," she said, "I am going to install myself near you in an easy-chair; we shall breakfast in half an hour. You will say all you like, for I know very well that gentlemen must talk, and I will be very good."

Marius took her by the arm and said to her lovingly, —

"We are talking about business."

"By the way," Cosette answered, "I have opened my window, and a number of sparrows [pierrots] have just entered the garden. Birds, not masks. To-day is Ash Wednesday, but not for the birds."

"I tell you that we are talking of business, so go, my little Cosette; leave us for a moment. We are talking figures, and they would only annoy you."

"You have put on a charming cravat this morning, Marius. You are very coquettish, Monseigneur. No, they will not annoy me."

"I assure you that they will."

"No, since it is you, I shall not understand you, but I shall hear you. When a woman hears voices she loves, she does not require to understand the words they say. To be together is all I want, and I shall stay with you, — there!"

"You are my beloved Cosette! Impossible."

"Impossible?"

"Yes."

"Very good," Cosette remarked; "I should have told you some news. I should have told you that grandpapa is still asleep, that your aunt is at Mass, that the chimney of my papa Fauchelevent's room smokes, that Nicolette has sent for the chimney-sweep, that Nicolette and Toussaint have already quarrelled, and that Nicolette ridicules Toussaint's stammering. Well, you shall know nothing. Ah, it is impossible? You shall see, sir, that in my turn I shall say, 'It is impossible.' Who will be caught then? I implore you, my little Marius, to let me stay with you two."

"I assure you that we must be alone."

"Well, am I anybody?"

Jean Valjean did not utter a word, and Cosette turned to him.

"In the first place, father, I insist on your coming and kissing me. What do you mean by saying nothing, instead of taking my part? Did one ever see a father like that? That will show you how unhappy my marriage is, for my husband beats me. Come and kiss me at once."

Jean Valjean approached her, and Cosette turned to Marius.

" I make a face at you."

Then she offered her forehead to Jean Valjean, who moved a step towards her. All at once Cosette recoiled.

" Father, you are pale ; does your arm pain you ? "

" It is cured," said Jean Valjean.

" Have you slept badly ? "

" No."

" Are you sad ? "

" No."

" Kiss me. If you are well, if you sleep soundly, if you are happy, I will not scold you."

And she again offered him her forehead, and Jean Valjean set a kiss on this forehead, upon which there was a heavenly reflection.

" Smile."

Jean Valjean obeyed, but it was the smile of a ghost.

" Now, defend me against my husband."

" Cosette — " said Marius.

" Be angry, father, and tell him I am to remain. You can talk before me. You must think me very foolish. What you are saying is very astonishing, then ! Business, — placing money in a bank, — that is a great thing. Men make mysteries of nothing. I mean to say I am very pretty this morning. Marius, look at me."

And with an adorable shrug of the shoulders and

an exquisite pout she looked at Marius. Something like a flash passed between these two beings, and they cared little about a third party being present.

"I love you," said Marius.

"I adore you," said Cosette.

And they irresistibly fell into each other's arms.

"And now," Cosette continued, as she smoothed a crease in her dressing-gown, with a little triumphant pout, "I remain."

"No," Marius replied imploringly, "we have something to finish."

"Again, no?"

Marius assumed a serious tone.

"I assure you, Cosette, that it is impossible."

"Ah, you are putting on your man's voice, sir; very good, I will go. You did not support me, father; and so you, my hard husband, and you, my dear papa, are tyrants. I shall go and tell grandpapa. If you believe that I intend to return and talk platitudes to you, you are mistaken. I am proud, and I intend to wait for you at present. You will see how wearisome it will be without me. I am going, very good."

And she left the room, but two seconds after the door opened again, her fresh, rosy face passed once again between the two folding-doors, and she cried to them, —

"I am very angry."

The door closed again, and darkness returned. It was like a straggling sunbeam, which, without suspecting it, had suddenly traversed the night. Marius assured himself that the door was really closed.

" Poor Cosette !" he muttered, "when she learns —"

At these words Jean Valjean trembled all over, and he fixed his haggard eyes on Marius.

" Cosette! Oh, yes, it is true. You will tell Cosette about it. It is fair. — Stay, I did not think of that. A man has strength for one thing, but not for another. I implore you, sir, I conjure you, sir, give me your most sacred word, — do not tell her. Is it not sufficient for you to know it? I was able to tell it of my own accord, without being compelled. I would have told it to the universe, to the whole world, and I should not have cared; but she, — she does not know what it is, and it would horrify her. A convict. What! You would be obliged to explain to her, tell her it is a man who has been to the galleys. She saw the chain-gang once. Oh, my God!"

He sank into a chair and buried his face in his hands; it could not be heard, but from the heaving of his shoulders it could be seen that he was weeping. They were silent tears, terrible tears. There is a choking in a sob; a species of convulsion seized on him, he threw himself back in the chair, letting his arms hang, and displaying to Marius his face bathed in tears, and Marius heard him mutter so low that his voice seemed to come from a bottomless abyss, " Oh! I would like to die!"

"Be at your ease," Marius said; "I will keep your secret to myself."

And, less affected than perhaps he ought to have been, but compelled for more than an hour to listen to unexpected horrors, gradually seeing a convict taking M. Fauchelevent's place, gradually overcome by this mournful reality, and led by the natural state of the situation to notice the gap which had formed between himself and this man, Marius added, —

"It is impossible for me not to say a word about the trust money which you have so faithfully and honestly given up. That is an act of probity, and it is but fair that a reward should be given you; fix the sum yourself, and it shall be paid you. Do not fear to fix it very high."

"I thank you, sir," Jean Valjean replied gently.

He remained pensive for a moment, mechanically passing the end of his forefinger over his thumb-nail, and then raised his voice, —

"All is nearly finished; there is only one thing left me."

"What is it?"

Jean Valjean had a species of supreme agitation, and voicelessly, almost breathlessly, he stammered, rather than said, —

"Now that you know, do you, sir, who are the master, believe that I ought not to see Cosette again?"

"I believe that it would be better," Marius replied coldly.

"I will not see her again," Jean Valjean murmured. He walked toward the door; he placed his hand upon the handle, the door opened, Jean Valjean was going to pass out, when he suddenly closed it again, then opened the door again and returned to Marius. He was no longer pale, but livid, and in his eyes was a sort of tragic flame instead of tears. His voice had grown strangely calm again.

"Stay, sir," he said ; "if you are willing, I will come to see her, for I assure you that I desire it greatly. If I had not longed to see Cosette I should not have made you the confession I have done, but have gone away ; but wishing to remain at the spot where Cosette is, and continue to see her, I was obliged to tell you everything honestly. You follow my reasoning, do you not ? It is a thing easy to understand. Look you, I have had her with me for nine years : we lived at first in that hovel on the boulevard, then in the convent, and then near the Luxembourg. It was there that you saw her for the first time, and you remember her blue plush bonnet. Next we went to the district of the Invalides, where there were a railway and a garden, the Rue Plumet. I lived in a little back yard where I could hear her pianoforte. Such was my life, and we never separated. That lasted nine years and seven months; I was like her father, and she was my child. I do not know whether you understand me, M. Pontmercy, but it would be difficult to go away now, see her no more, speak to her no more, and have nothing left. If you have no objection, I will come and see Cosette every now and then, but not too often, and I will not remain long. You can tell them to show me into the little room on the ground-floor ; I would certainly come in by the back door, which is used by the servants, but that might cause surprise, so it is better, I think, for me to come by the front door. Really, sir, I should like to see Cosette a little, but as rarely as you please. Put yourself in my place. I have only that left. And then, again, we must be careful, and if I did not come at all it would have a bad effect, and appear singular. For instance, what I can do is to come in the evening, when it is beginning to grow dark."

"You can come every evening," said Marius, "and Cosette will expect you."

"You are kind, sir," said Jean Valjean.

Marius bowed to Jean Valjean, happiness accompanied despair to the door, and these two men parted.

CHAPTER II.

THE OBSCURITY WHICH A REVELATION MAY CONTAIN.

MARIUS was overwhelmed; the sort of estrangement which he had ever felt for the man with whom he saw Cosette was henceforth explained. There was in this person something enigmatic, against which his instinct warned him. This enigma was the most hideous of shames, the galleys. This M. Fauchelevent was Jean Valjean the convict. To find suddenly such a secret in the midst of his happiness is like discovering a scorpion in a turtle-dove's nest. Was the happiness of Marius and Cosette in future condensed to this proximity? Was it an accomplished fact? Did the acceptance of this man form part of the consummated marriage? Could nothing else be done? Had Marius also married the convict? Although a man may be crowned with light and joy, though he be enjoying the grand hour of life's purple, happy love, such shocks would compel even the archangel in his ecstasy, even the demigod in his glory, to shudder.

As ever happens in sudden transformation-scenes of this nature, Marius asked himself whether he ought not to reproach himself? Had he failed in divination? Had he been deficient in prudence?

Had he voluntarily been headstrong? Slightly so, perhaps. Had he entered upon this love-adventure, which resulted in his marriage with Cosette, without taking sufficient precaution to throw light upon the surroundings? He verified, — it is thus, by a series of verifications of ourselves on ourselves, that life is gradually corrected, — he verified, we say, the visionary and chimerical side of his nature, a sort of internal cloud peculiar to many organizations, and which in the paroxysms of passion and grief expands, as the temperature of the soul changes, and invades the entire man to such an extent that he merely becomes a conscience enveloped in a fog. We have more than once indicated this characteristic element in Marius's individuality. He remembered that during the intoxication of his love in the Rue Plumet, during those six or seven ecstatic weeks, he had not even spoken to Cosette about the drama in the Gorbeau hovel, during which the victim was so strangely silent both in the struggle and eventual escape. How was it that he had not spoken to Cosette about it, and yet it was so close and so frightful? How was it that he had not even mentioned the Thénardiers, and especially on the day when he met Éponine? He found almost a difficulty in explaining to himself now his silence at that period, but he was able to account for it. He remembered his confusion, his intoxication for Cosette, his love absorbing everything, the carrying off of one by the other into the ideal world, and perhaps, too, as the imperceptible amount of reason mingled with that violent and charming state of the mind, a vague and dull instinct to hide and efface from his memory that formidable adventure with which he feared contact, in which he wished to play no part, from which he stood aloof, and of which he could not be narrator or witness without being an accuser. Moreover, these few weeks had been a lightning flash; he had not had time for anything except to love. In short, when all was revolved, and everything examined, supposing that he had described the Gorbeau trap to Cosette, had mentioned the Thénardiers to her, what would have been the consequence, even if he had discovered that Jean Valjean was a convict; would that have changed him, Marius, or his Cosette? Would he have drawn back? Would he have loved her less? Would he have refused to marry her? No. Would it have made any change in what had happened? No. There was nothing, therefore, to regret, nothing to reproach, and all was well. There is a God for those drunkards who are called lovers, and Marius had blindly followed the road which he had selected with his eyes open. Love had bandaged his eyes to lead him whither? To paradise.

But this paradise was henceforth complicated by an infernal proximity, and the old estrangement of Marius for this man, for this Fauchelevent who had become Jean Valjean, was at present mingled with horror; but in this horror, let us say it, there was some pity, and even a certain degree of surprise. This robber, this relapsed robber, had given up a deposit, and what deposit? Six hundred thousand francs. He alone held the secret of that deposit, he could have kept it all, but he gave it all up. Moreover, he had revealed his situation of his own accord, nothing compelled him to do so; and if he, Marius, knew who he was it was through himself. There was in this confession more than the acceptance of humiliation; there was the acceptance of peril. For a condemned man a mask is not a mask but a shelter, and he had renounced that shelter. A false name is a security, and he had thrown away that false name. He, the galley-slave, could conceal himself forever in an honest family, and he had resisted that temptation, and for what motive? Through scruples of conscience. He had explained himself with the irresistible accent of truth. In short, whoever this Jean Valjean might be, his was incontestably an awakened conscience. Some mysterious rehabilitation had been begun, and according to all appearances scruples had been master of this man for a long time past. Such attacks of justice and honesty are not peculiar to vulgar natures, and an awakening of the conscience is greatness of soul. Jean Valjean was sincere; and this sincerity, visible, palpable, irrefragable, and evident in the grief which it caused him, rendered his statements valuable, and gave authority to all that this man said. Here, for Marius, was a strange inversion of situations. What issued from M. Fauchelevent? Distrust. What was disengaged from Jean Valjean? Confidence. In the mysterious balance-sheet of this Jean Valjean which Marius mentally drew up, he verified the credit, he verified the debit, and tried to arrive at a balance. But all this was as in a storm, Marius striving to form a distinct idea of this man, and pursuing Jean Valjean, so to speak, to the bottom of his thoughts, lost him, and found him again in a fatal mist.

The honest restoration of the trust-money and the probity of the confession were good, and formed as it were a break in the cloud; but then the cloud became black again. However confused Marius's reminiscences might be, some shadows still returned to him. What, after all, was that adventure in the Jondrette garret? Why, on the arrival of the police, did that man, instead of complaining, escape? Here Marius found the answer, — because this man was a convict who had broken his ban. Another question, Why did this man come to the barricade? For at present Marius distinctly saw again that recollection, which reappeared in his emotions like sympathetic ink before the fire. This man was at the barricade and did not fight; what did he want there? Before this question a spectre rose and gave the answer, — Javert. Marius perfectly remembered now the mournful vision of Jean Valjean dragging the bound Javert out of the barricade, and heard again behind the angle of the little Mondétour Lane the frightful pistol-shot. There was probably a hatred between this spy and this galley-slave, and one annoyed the other. Jean Valjean went to the barricade to revenge himself; he arrived late, and was probably aware that Javert was a prisoner there. Corsican Vendetta has penetrated certain lower strata of society, and is the law with them; it is so simple that it does not astonish minds which have half returned to virtue, and their hearts are so constituted that a criminal, when on the path of repentance, may be scrupulous as to

a robbery and not so as to a vengeance. Jean Valjean had killed Javert, or at least that seemed evident. The last question of all admitted of no reply,
and this question Marius felt like a pair of pincers.
How was it that the existence of Jean Valjean had
so long brushed against that of Cosette? What was
this gloomy sport of Providence which had brought
this man and this child in contact? Are there chains
for two forged in heaven, and does God take pleasure
in coupling the angel with the demon? A crime and
an innocence can, then, be chamber companions in
the mysterious hulks of misery? In that defile of
condemned men which is called human destiny, two
foreheads may pass along side by side, one simple,
the other formidable, — one all bathed in the divine
whiteness of dawn, the other eternally branded?
Who can have determined this inexplicable approximation? In what way, in consequence of what prodigy, could a community of life have been established
between this celestial child and this condemned old
man? Who could have attached the lamb to the
wolf, and even more incomprehensible still, the wolf
to the lamb? For the wolf loved the lamb, the ferocious being adored the weak being, and for nine
years the angel had leaned on the monster for support.
The childhood and maidenhood of Cosette and her
virgin growth toward life and light had been protected by this deformed devotion. Here questions
exfoliated themselves, if we may employ the expression, into countless enigmas; abysses opened at the
bottom of abysses, and Marius could no longer bend
over Jean Valjean without feeling a dizziness: what

could this man-precipice be? The old genesiacal
symbols are eternal: in human society, such as it
now exists until a greater light shall change it, there
are ever two men, — one superior, the other subterranean; the one who holds to good is Abel, the one
who holds to bad is Cain. What was this tender
Cain? What was this bandit religiously absorbed in
the adoration of a virgin, watching over her, bringing
her up, guarding her, dignifying her, and though
himself impure, surrounding her with purity? What
was this cloaca which had venerated this innocence
so greatly as not to leave a spot upon it? What
was this Valjean carrying on the education of Cosette? What was this figure of darkness, whose sole
care it was to preserve from every shadow and every
cloud the rising of a star?

That was Jean Valjean's secret; that was also
God's secret, and Marius recoiled before this double
secret. The one, to some extent, reassured him about
the other, for God was as visible in this adventure
as was Jean Valjean. God has his instruments, and
employs whom he likes as tool, and is not responsi-
ble to him. Do we know how God sets to work?
Jean Valjean had labored on Cosette, and had to
some extent formed her mind; that was incontestable. Well, what then? The workman was horrible,
but the work was admirable, and God produces his
miracles as he thinks proper. He had constructed
that charming Cosette, and employed Jean Valjean
on the job, and it had pleased him to choose this
strange assistant. What explanation have we to ask
of him? Is it the first time that manure has helped

spring to produce the rose? Marius gave himself
these answers, and declared to himself that they were
good. On all the points which we have indicated
he had not dared to press Jean Valjean, though he
did not confess to himself that he dared not. He
adored Cosette, he possessed Cosette; Cosette was
splendidly pure, and that was sufficient for him.
What enlightenment did he require when Cosette
was a light? Does light need illumination? He had
everything; what more could he desire? Is not
everything enough? Jean Valjean's personal affairs
in no way concerned him, and in bending down over
the fatal shadow of this wretched man he clung to
his solemn declaration, "I am nothing to Cosette;
ten years ago I did not know that she existed." Jean
Valjean was a passer-by; he had said so himself.
Well, then, he passed, and whoever he might be, his
part was played out. Henceforth Marius would
have to perform the functions of Providence toward
Cosette; she had found again in ether her equal,
her lover, her husband, her celestial male. In flying
away, Cosette, winged and transfigured, left behind
her on earth her empty and hideous chrysalis, Jean
Valjean. In whatever circle of ideas Marius might
turn, he always came back to a certain horror of
Jean Valjean; a sacred horror, perhaps, for, as we
have stated, he felt a *quid divinum* in this man.
But though it was so, and whatever extenuating
circumstances he might seek, he was always compelled to fall back on this: he was a convict, that
is to say, a being who has not even a place on the
social ladder, being beneath the lowest rung. After

the last of men comes the convict, who is no longer, so to speak, in the likeness of his fellow-men. The law has deprived him of the entire amount of humanity which it can strip off a man. Marius, in penal matters, democrat though he was, was still of the inexorable system, and he entertained all the ideas of the law about those whom the law strikes. He had not yet made every progress, we are forced to say; he had not yet learned to distinguish between what is written by man and what is written by God, — between the law and the right. He had examined and weighed the claim which man sets up to dispose of the irrevocable, the irreparable, and the word *vindicta* was not repulsive to him. He considered it simple that certain breaches of the written law should be followed by eternal penalties, and he accepted social condemnation as a civilizing process. He was still at this point, though infallibly certain to advance at a later date, for his nature was good, and entirely composed of latent progress.

In this medium of ideas Jean Valjean appeared to him deformed and repelling, for he was the punished man, the convict. This word was to him like the sound of the trumpet of the last Judgment, and after regarding Jean Valjean for a long time his last gesture was to turn away his head — *vade retro*. Marius, — we must recognize the fact and lay a stress on it, — while questioning Jean Valjean to such an extent that Jean Valjean himself said, " You are shriving me," had not, however, asked him two or three important questions. It was not that they had not presented themselves to his mind, but he

had been afraid of them. The Jondrette garret?
The barricade? Javert? Who knew where the revelations might have stopped? Jean Valjean did not
seem the man to recoil, and who knows whether
Marius, after urging him on, might not have wished
to check him? In certain supreme conjunctures has
it not happened to all of us that after asking a
question we have stopped our ears in order not to
hear the answer? A man is specially guilty of such
an act of cowardice when he is in love. It is not
wise to drive sinister situations into a corner, especially
when the indissoluble side of our own life is fatally
mixed up with them. What a frightful light might
issue from Jean Valjean's desperate explanations,
and who knows whether that hideous brightness
might not have been reflected on Cosette? Who
knows whether a sort of infernal gleam might not
have remained on that angel's brow? Fatality knows
such complications, in which innocence itself is branded
with crime by the fatal law of coloring reflections,
and the purest faces may retain forever the impression of a horrible vicinity. Whether rightly or
wrongly, Marius was terrified, for he already knew
too much, and he tried rather to deafen than to enlighten himself. He wildly bore off Cosette in his
arms, closing his eyes upon Jean Valjean. This man
belonged to the night, the living and terrible night;
how could he dare to seek its foundation? It is
a horrible thing to question the shadow, for who
knows what it will answer? The dawn might be
eternally blackened by it. In this state of mind
it was a crushing perplexity for Marius to think that

henceforth this man would have any contact with Cosette; and he now almost reproached himself for not having asked these formidable questions before which he had recoiled, and from which an implacable and definitive decision might have issued. He considered himself too kind, too gentle, and, let us say it, too weak; and the weakness had led him to make a fatal concession. He had allowed himself to be affected, and had done wrong. He ought simply and purely to have rejected Jean Valjean. Jean Valjean was an incendiary, and he ought to have freed his house from the presence of this man. He was angry with himself; he was angry with that whirlwind of emotions which had deafened, blinded, and carried him away. He was dissatisfied with himself.

What was he to do now? The visits of Jean Valjean were most deeply repulsive to him. Of what use was it that this man should come to his house? What did he want here? Here he refused to investigate the matter; he refused to study, and he was unwilling to probe his own heart. He had promised; he had allowed himself to be drawn into a promise. Jean Valjean held that promise, and he must keep his word even with a convict, — above all with a convict. Still, his first duty was toward Cosette. On the whole, a repulsion, which overcame everything else, caused him a loathing. Marius confusedly revolved all these ideas in his mind, passing from one to the other, and shaken by all. Hence arose a deep trouble which it was not easy to conceal from Cosette; but love is a talent, and

Marius succeeded in doing it. However, he asked, without any apparent motive, some questions of Cosette, who was as candid as a dove is white, and suspected nothing. He spoke to her of her childhood and her youth, and he convinced himself more and more that this convict had been to Cosette as good, paternal, and respectful as a man can be. Everything which Marius had imagined and supposed, he found to be real: this sinister nettle had loved and protected this lily.

BOOK VIII.

TWILIGHT DECLINES.

CHAPTER I.

THE GROUND-FLOOR ROOM.

ON the morrow, at nightfall, Jean Valjean tapped at the gateway of the Gillenormand mansion, and it was Basque who received him. Basque was in the yard at the appointed time, as if he had had his orders. It sometimes happens that people say to a servant, "You will watch for Mr. So-and-so's arrival." Basque, without waiting for Jean Valjean to come up to him, said, —

"Monsieur le Baron has instructed me to ask you, sir, whether you wish to go upstairs or stay down here?"

"Stay down here," Jean Valjean replied.

Basque, who, however, was perfectly respectful in his manner, opened the door of the ground-floor room, and said, "I will go and inform her ladyship." The room which Jean Valjean entered was a damp, arched, basement room, employed as a cellar at times, looking out on the street, with a flooring of red tiles, and badly lighted by an iron-barred window. This room was not one of those which are harassed by the broom and mop, and the dust was quiet there. No persecution of the spiders had been organized; and a fine web, extensively drawn out, quite black, and adorned with dead flies, formed a wheel on one of the window-panes. The room, which was small and low-ceiled, was furnished with a pile of empty bottles collected in a corner. The wall, covered with a yellow-ochre wash, crumbled off in large patches; at the end was a mantel-piece of panelled black wood, with a narrow shelf, and a fire was lighted in it, which indicated that Jean Valjean's reply, "Stay down here," had been calculated on. Two chairs were placed, one in each chimney-corner, and between the chairs was spread, in guise of carpet, an old bed-room rug, which displayed more cord than wool. The room was illumined by the flickering of the fire, and the twilight through the window. Jean Valjean was fatigued; for several days he had not eaten or slept, and he fell into one of the arm-chairs. Basque returned, placed a lighted candle on the mantel-piece, and withdrew. Jean Valjean, who was sitting with hanging head, did not notice either Basque or the candle, till all at once he started up, for Cosette was behind him: he had not seen her come in, but he felt that she was doing so. He turned round and con-templated her; she was adorably lovely. But what he gazed at with this profound glance was not the beauty, but the soul.

"Well, father," Cosette exclaimed, "I knew that you were singular, but I could never have expected this. What an idea! Marius told me that it was your wish to see me here."

" Yes, it is."

" I expected that answer, and I warn you that I am going to have a scene with you. Let us begin with the beginning : kiss me, father."

And she offered her cheek, but Jean Valjean remained motionless.

" You do not stir : I mark the fact ! It is the attitude of a culprit. But I do not care, I forgive you. Christ said, ' Offer the other cheek ; ' here it is."

And she offered the other cheek, but Jean Valjean did not stir ; it seemed as if his feet were riveted to the floor.

" Things are growing serious," said Cosette. " What have I done to you ? I am offended, and you must make it up with me ; you will dine with us ? "

" I have dined."

" That is not true, and I will have you scolded by M. Gillenormand. Grandfathers are made to lay down the law to fathers. Come, go with me to the drawing-room. At once."

" Impossible ! "

Cosette here lost a little ground ; she ceased to order and began questioning.

" But why ? And you choose the ugliest room in the house to see me in. It is horrible here."

" You know — "

Jean Valjean broke off —

" You know, Madame, that I am peculiar, and have my fancies."

" Madame — *you* know — more novelties ; what does this all mean ? "

Jean Valjean gave her that heart-broken smile to which he sometimes had recourse.

"You wished to be Madame. You are."

"Not for you, father."

"Do not call me father."

"What?"

"Call me Monsieur Jean, or Jean, if you like."

"You are no longer father? I am no longer Cosette? Monsieur Jean? Why, what does it mean? These are revolutions. What has happened? Look me in the face, if you can. And you will not live with us! And you will not accept our bed-room! What have I done to offend you? Oh, what have I done? There must be something."

"Nothing."

"In that case, then?"

"All is as usual."

"Why do you change your name?"

"You have changed yours."

He smiled the same smile again, and added, —

"Since you are Madame Pontmercy, I may fairly be Monsieur Jean."

"I do not understand anything, and all this is idiotic. I will ask my husband's leave for you to be Monsieur Jean, and I hope that he will not consent. You cause me great sorrow; and though you may have whims, you have no right to make your little Cosette grieve. That is wrong, and you have no right to be naughty, for you are so good."

As he made no reply, she seized both his hands eagerly, and with an irresistible movement raising them to her face she pressed them against her neck under her chin, which is a profound sign of affection.

"Oh," she said, "be kind to me!" And she continued : "This is what I call being kind, — to behave yourself, come and live here, for there are birds here as in the Rue Plumet; to live with us, leave that hole in the Rue de l'Homme Armé, give us no more riddles to guess ; to be like everybody else, dine with us, breakfast with us, and be my father."

He removed her hands, —

"You no longer want a father, as you have a husband."

Cosette broke out, —

"I no longer want a father! Things like that have no common sense, and I really do not know what to say."

"If Toussaint were here," Jean Valjean continued, like a man seeking authorities and who clings to every branch, "she would be the first to allow that I have always had strange ways of my own. There is nothing new in it, for I always loved my dark corner."

"But it is cold here, and we cannot see distinctly; and it is abominable to wish to be Monsieur Jean; and I shall not allow you to call me Madame."

"As I was coming along just now," Jean Valjean replied, "I saw a very pretty piece of furniture at a cabinet-maker's in the Rue St. Louis. If I were a pretty woman, I should treat myself to it. It is a very nice toilette table in the present fashion, made of rosewood, I think you call it, and inlaid. There is a rather large glass with drawers, and it is very nice."

"Hou! the ugly bear!" Cosette replied. And clenching her teeth, and parting her lips in the most graceful way possible, she blew at Jean Valjean; it was a grace imitating a cat.

"I am furious," she went on, "and since yesterday you have all put me in a passion. I do not understand it at all; you do not defend me against Marius, Marius does not take my part against you, and I am all alone. I have a nice room prepared, and if I could have put my dear father in it, I would have done so; but my room is left on my hands and my lodger fails me. I order Nicolette to prepare a nice little dinner, and — they will not touch your dinner, Madame. And my father Fauchelevent wishes me to call him Monsieur Jean, and that I should receive him in a frightful old, ugly, mildewed cellar, in which the walls wear a beard, and empty bottles represent the looking-glasses, and spiders' webs the curtains. I allow that you are a singular man, it is your way; but a truce is accorded to newly-married folk, and you ought not to have begun to be singular again so soon. You are going to be very satisfied, then, in your Rue de l'Homme Armé; well, I was very wretched there. What have I done to offend you? You cause me great sorrow. Fie!"

And suddenly growing serious, she looked intently at Jean Valjean and added, —

"You are angry with me for being happy; is that it?"

Simplicity sometimes penetrates unconsciously very deep, and this question, simple for Cosette, was profound for Jean Valjean. Cosette wished to scratch, but she tore. Jean Valjean turned pale, he remained for a moment without answering, and then murmured with an indescribable accent, and speaking to himself, —

"Her happiness was the object of my life, and at present God may order my departure. Cosette, thou art happy, and my course is run."

"Ah! you said *thou* to me," Cosette exclaimed, and leaped on his neck.

Jean Valjean wildly strained her to his heart, for he felt as if he were almost taking her back again.

"Thank you, father," Cosette said to him.

The excitement was getting too painful for Jean Valjean; he gently withdrew himself from Cosette's arms, and took up his hat.

"Well?" said Cosette.

Jean Valjean replied, —

"I am going to leave you, Madame, as you will be missed."

And on the threshold he added, —

"I said *thou* to you; tell your husband that it shall not happen again. Forgive me."

Jean Valjean left Cosette stupefied by this enigmatical leave-taking.

CHAPTER II.

OTHER BACKWARD STEPS.

THE next day Jean Valjean came at the same hour, and Cosette asked him no questions, was no longer astonished, no longer exclaimed that it was cold, no longer alluded to the drawing-room; she avoided saying either father or Monsieur Jean. She allowed herself to be called Madame; there was only a diminution of her delight perceptible, and she would have been sad, had sorrow been possible. It is probable that she had held with Marius one of those conversations in which the beloved man says what he wishes, explains nothing, and satisfies the beloved woman; for the curiosity of lovers does not extend far beyond their love. The basement room had been furbished up a little; Basque had suppressed the bottles, and Nicolette the spiders. Every following day brought Jean Valjean back at the same hour; he came daily, as he had not the strength to take Marius's permission otherwise than literally. Marius arranged so as to be absent at the hour when Jean Valjean came, and the house grew accustomed to M. Fauchelevent's new mode of behaving. Toussaint helped in it; "My master was always so," she repeated. The grandfather issued this decree, " He is an original," and everything was said. Moreover, at the age of ninety no connection is possible ; everything is juxtaposition, and a new-comer is in the way ; there is no place for him, for habits are unalterably formed. M. Fauchelevent, M. Tranchelevent, — Father Gillenormand desired nothing better than to get rid of " that gentleman," and added, " Nothing is more common than such originals. They do all sorts of strange things without any motive. The Marquis de Canoples did worse, for he bought a palace in order to live in the garret."

No one caught a glimpse of the sinister reality, and in fact who could have divined such a thing ? There are marshes like this in India: the water seems extraordinary, inexplicable, rippling when there is no breeze, and agitated when it ought to be calm. People look at the surface of this ebullition which has no cause, and do not suspect the hydra dragging itself along at the bottom. Many men have in this way a secret monster, an evil which they nourish, a dragon that gnaws them, a despair that dwells in their night. Such a man resembles others, comes and goes, and no one knows that he has within him a frightful parasitic pain with a thousand teeth, which dwells in the wretch and kills him. They do not know that this man is a gulf; he is stagnant but deep. From time to time a trouble which no one understands is produced on his surface; a mysterious ripple forms, then fades away, then reappears ; a bubble rises and bursts. It is a slight thing, but it is terrible, for it is the respiration of the unknown beast. Certain strange habits, such as arriving at

the hour when others go away, hiding one's self when
others show themselves, wearing on all occasions
what may be called the wall-colored cloak, seeking
the solitary walk, preferring the deserted street, not
mixing in conversation, avoiding crowds and festivi-
ties, appearing to be comfortably off and living poorly,
having, rich though one is, one's key in one's pocket
and one's candle in the porter's lodge, entering by the
small door and going up the back stairs, — all these
insignificant singularities, ripples, air-bubbles, and
fugitive marks on the surface, frequently come from a
formidable depth.

Several weeks passed thus; a new life gradually
seized on Cosette, — the relations which marriage
creates, visits, the management of the houshold, and
pleasures, that great business.   The pleasures of
Cosette were not costly; they consisted in only one,
being with Marius.   To go out with him, remain at
home with him, was the great occupation of her life.
It was for them an ever novel joy to go out arm in
arm, in the sunshine, in the open streets, without hiding themselves, in the face of everybody, both alone.
Cosette had one vexation : Toussaint could not agree
with Nicolette (for the welding of the two old maids
was impossible), and left.   The grandfather was
quite well; Marius had a few briefs now and then ;
Aunt Gillenormand peacefully lived with the married
pair that lateral life which sufficed her, and Jean Valjean came daily.   The Madame and the Monsieur
Jean, however, made him different to Cosette, and the
care he had himself taken to detach himself from her
succeeded.   She was more and more gay, and less

and less affectionate; and yet she loved him dearly still, and he felt it. One day she suddenly said to him, "You were my father, you are no longer my father; you were my uncle, you are no longer my uncle; you were Monsieur Fauchelevent, and are now Jean. Who are you, then? I do not like all this. If I did not know you to be so good, I should be afraid of you." He still lived in the Rue de l'Homme Armé, as he could not resolve to remove from the quarter in which Cosette lived. At first he stayed only a few minutes with Cosette, and then went away; but by degrees he grew into the habit of making his visits longer. It might be said that he took advantage of the lengthening days; he arrived sooner and went away later. One day the word "father" slipped over Cosette's lips, and a gleam of joy lit up Jean Valjean's old solemn face, but he chided her: "Say Jean."

"Ah, that is true," she replied, with a burst of laughter, "Monsieur Jean."

"That is right," he said; and he turned away that she might not see the tears in his eyes.

CHAPTER III.

THEY REMEMBER THE GARDEN IN THE RUE PLUMET.

THIS was the last occasion, and after this last flare total extinction took place. There was no more familiarity, no more good-day with a kiss, and never again that so deeply tender word "father;" he had been, at his own request and with his own complicity, expelled from all those joys in succession, and he underwent this misery, — that, after losing Cosette entirely on one day, he was then obliged to lose her again bit by bit. The eye eventually grows accustomed to cellar light, and he found it enough to have an apparition of Cosette daily. His whole life was concentrated in that hour; he sat down by her side, looked at her in silence, or else talked to her about former years, her childhood, the convent, and her little friends of those days. One afternoon — it was an early day in April, already warm but still fresh, the moment of the sun's great gayety; the gardens that surrounded Marius's and Cosette's windows were rousing from their slumber, the hawthorn was about to bourgeon, a jewelry of wallflowers was displayed on the old wall, there was on the grass a fairy carpet of daisies and buttercups, the white butterflies were springing forth, and the wind, that minstrel of the eternal wedding, was trying in the trees the first notes of that great auroral symphony which the old poets called the renewal — Marius said to Cosette, "We said that we would go and see our garden in the Rue Plumet again. Co..ne, we must not be ungrateful." And they flew off like two swallows toward the spring. This garden in the Rue Plumet produced on them the effect of a dawn, for they already had behind them in life something that resembled the springtime of their love. The house in the Rue Plumet, being taken on lease, still belonged to Cosette; they went to this garden and house, found themselves again, and forgot themselves there. In the evening Jean Valjean went to the Rue des Filles du Calvaire at the usual hour. "My lady went out with the Baron," said Basque, "and has not returned yet." He sat down silently and waited an hour, but Cosette did not come in; he hung his head and went away. Cosette was so intoxicated by the walk in "their garden," and so pleased at having "lived a whole day in her past," that she spoke of nothing else the next day. She did not remark that she had not seen Jean Valjean.

"How did you go there?" Jean Valjean asked her.

"On foot."

"And how did you return?"

"On foot too."

For some time Jean Valjean had noticed the close life which the young couple led, and was annoyed at it. Marius's economy was severe, and that word had its full meaning for Jean Valjean; he hazarded a question.

"Why do you not keep a carriage? A little coupé would not cost you more than five hundred francs a month, and you are rich."

"I do not know," Cosette answered.

"It is the same with Toussaint," Jean Valjean continued; "she has left, and you have engaged no one in her place. Why not?"

"Nicolette is sufficient."

"But you must want a lady's maid?"

"Have I not Marius?"

"You ought to have a house of your own, servants of your own, a carriage, and a box at the opera. Nothing is too good for you. Then why not take advantage of the fact of your being rich? Wealth adds to happiness."

Cosette made no reply. Jean Valjean's visits did not grow shorter, but the contrary; for when it is the heart that is slipping, a man does not stop on the incline. When Jean Valjean wished to prolong his visit and make the hour be forgotten, he sung the praises of Marius; he found him handsome, noble, brave, witty, eloquent, and good. Cosette added to the praise, and Jean Valjean began again. It was an inexhaustible subject, and there were volumes in the six letters composing Marius's name. In this way Jean Valjean managed to stop for a long time, for it was so sweet to see Cosette and forget by her side. It was a dressing for his wound. It frequently happened that Basque would come and say twice, "M. Gillenormand has sent me to remind Madame la Baronne that dinner is waiting." On those days Jean Valjean would return home very thoughtful. Was there any truth in that comparison of the chrysalis which had occurred to Marius's mind? Was Jean Valjean really an obstinate chrysalis, constantly paying visits to his butterfly? One day he remained longer than usual, and the next noticed there was no fire in the grate. "Stay," he though, "no fire?" And he gave himself this explanation: "It is very simple; we are in April, and the cold weather has passed."

"Good gracious! How cold it is here!" Cosette exclaimed as she came in.

"Oh no," said Jean Valjean.

"Then it was you who told Basque not to light a fire?"

"Yes; we shall have May here directly."

"But fires keep on till June; in this cellar there ought to be one all the year round."

"I thought it was unnecessary."

"That is just like one of your ideas," Cosette remarked.

The next day there was a fire, but the two chairs were placed at the other end of the room, near the door. "What is the meaning of that?" Jean Valjean thought; he fetched the chairs and placed them in their usual place near the chimney. This rekindled fire, however, encouraged him, and he made the conversation last even longer than usual. As he rose to leave, Cosette remarked to him, —

"My husband said a funny thing to me yesterday."

"What was it?"

"He said to me, 'Cosette, we have thirty thousand francs a year, — twenty-seven of yours, and

three that my grandfather allows me.' I replied,
' That makes thirty ; ' and he continued, ' Would you
have the courage to live on the three thousand ? ' I
answered, ' Yes, on nothing, provided that it be with
you ; ' and then I asked him, ' Why did you say that
to me ? ' He replied, ' I merely wished to know.' "

Jean Valjean had not a word to say. Cosette
probably expected some explanation from him, but
he listened to her in a sullen silence. He went back
to the Rue de l'Homme Armé, and was so pro-
foundly abstracted that, instead of entering his own
house, he went into the next one. It was not till
he had gone up nearly two flights of stairs that he
noticed his mistake, and came down again. His
mind was crammed with conjectures : it was evident
that Marius entertained doubts as to the origin of
the six hundred thousand francs, that he feared some
impure source ; he might even — who knew ? — have
discovered that this money came from him, Jean
Valjean ; that he hesitated to touch this suspicious
fortune, and was repugnant to use it as his own,
preferring that Cosette and he should remain poor
rather than be rich with dubious wealth. Moreover,
Jean Valjean was beginning to feel himself shown
to the door. On the following day he had a species of shock on entering the basement room ; the
fauteuils had disappeared, and there was not even
a seat of any sort.

" Dear me, no chairs ! " Cosette exclaimed on entering ; " where are they ? "

" They are no longer here," Jean Valjean replied.

" That is rather too much."

Jean Valjean stammered, —

"I told Basque to remove them."

"For what reason?"

"I shall only remain a few minutes to-day."

"Few or many, that is no reason for standing."

"I believe that Basque required the chairs for the drawing-room."

"Why?"

"You have probably company this evening."

"Not a soul."

Jean Valjean had not another word to say, and Cosette shrugged her shoulders.

"Have the chairs removed! The other day you ordered the fire to be left off! How singular you are!"

"Good-by," Jean Valjean murmured.

He did not say "Good-by, Cosette," and he had not the strength to say "Good-by, Madame."

He went away crushed, for this time he had comprehended. The next day he did not come, and Cosette did not remark this till the evening.

"Dear me," she said, "Monsieur Jean did not come to-day."

She felt a slight pang at the heart, but she scarce noticed it, as she was at once distracted by a kiss from Marius. The next day he did not come either. Cosette paid no attention to this, spent the evening, and slept at night as usual, and only thought of it when she woke; she was so happy! She very soon sent Nicolette to Monsieur Jean's to see whether he were ill, and why he had not come to see her on the previous day, and Nicolette brought back Monsieur

Jean's answer. "He was not ill, but was busy, and would come soon, — as soon as he could. But he was going to make a little journey, and Madame would remember that he was accustomed to do so every now and then. She need not feel at all alarmed or trouble herself about him." Nicolette, on entering Monsieur Jean's room, had repeated to him her mistress's exact words, — " That Madame sent to know ' why Monsieur Jean had not called on the previous day ? ' "

"I have not called for two days," Jean Valjean said quietly ; but the observation escaped Nicolette's notice, and she did not repeat it to Cosette.

CHAPTER IV.

ATTRACTION AND EXTINCTION.

DURING the last months of spring and the early months of summer, 1833, the scanty passers-by in the Marais, the shop-keepers, and the idlers in the door-ways, noticed an old gentleman, decently dressed in black, who every day, at nearly the same hour in the evening, left the Rue de l'Homme Armé, in the direction of the Rue Sainte Croix de la Bretonnerie, passed in front of the Blancs Manteaux, reached the Rue Culture Sainte Catharine, and on coming to the Rue de l'Écharpe, turned to his left and entered the Rue St. Louis. There he walked slowly, with head stretched forward, seeing nothing, hearing nothing, with his eye incessantly fixed on a spot which always seemed his magnet, and which was nought else than the corner of the Rue des Filles du Calvaire. The nearer he came to this corner the more brightly his eye flashed; a sort of joy illumined his eyeballs, like an internal dawn; he had a fascinated and affectionate air, his lips made obscure movements as if speaking to some one whom he could not see, he smiled vaguely, and he advanced as slowly as he could. It seemed as if, while wishing to arrive, he was afraid of the moment when he came quite close.

When he had only a few houses between himself and the street which appeared to attract him, his step became so slow that at moments he seemed not to be moving at all. The vacillation of his head and the fixedness of his eye suggested the needle seeking the pole. However he might delay his arrival, he must arrive in the end; when he reached the corner of the Rue des Filles du Calvaire, he trembled, thrust his head with a species of gloomy timidity beyond the corner of the last house, and looked into this street, and there was in this glance something that resembled the bedazzlement of the impossible and the reflection of a closed paradise. Then a tear, which had been gradually collecting in the corner of his eyelashes, having grown large enough to fall, glided down his cheeks, and sometimes stopped at his mouth. The old man tasted its bitter flavor. He stood thus for some minutes as if he were of stone; then returned by the same road, at the same pace, and the farther he got away the more lustreless his eye became.

By degrees this old man ceased going as far as the corner of the Rue des Filles du Calvaire; he stopped half-way in the Rue St. Louis: at times a little farther off, at times a little nearer. One day he stopped at the corner of the Rue Culture Sainte Catharine and gazed at the Rue des Filles du Calvaire from a distance; then he silently shook his head from right to left, as if refusing himself something, and turned back. Ere long he did not reach even the Rue St. Louis; he arrived at the Rue Pavie, shook his head, and turned back; then he did not go beyond the

Rue des Trois Pavillons; and then he did not pass the Blancs Manteaux. He seemed like a clock which was not wound up, and whose oscillations grow shorter and shorter till they stop. Every day he left his house at the same hour, undertook the same walk but did not finish it, and incessantly shortened it, though probably unconscious of the fact. His whole countenance expressed this sole idea, Of what good is it? His eyes were lustreless, and there was no radiance in them. The tears were also dried up; they no longer collected in the corner of his eye-lashes, and this pensive eye was dry. The old man's head was still thrust forward; the chin moved at times, and the creases in his thin neck were painful to look on. At times, when the weather was bad, he had an umbrella under his arm, which he never opened. The good women of the district said, "He is an innocent," and the children followed him with shouts of laughter.

BOOK IX.

SUPREME DARKNESS, SUPREME DAWN.

CHAPTER I.

PITY THE UNHAPPY, BUT BE INDULGENT TO THE HAPPY.

It is a terrible thing to be happy! How satisfied people are! How sufficient they find it! How, when possessed of the false object of life, happiness, they forget the true one, duty! We are bound to say, however, that it would be unjust to accuse Marius. Marius, as we have explained, before his marriage asked no questions of M. Fauchelevent, and since had been afraid to ask any of Jean Valjean. He had regretted the promise which he had allowed to be drawn from him, and had repeatedly said to himself that he had done wrong in making this concession to despair. He had restricted himself to gradually turning Jean Valjean out of his house, and effacing him as far as possible in Cosette's mind. He had to some extent constantly stationed himself between Cosette and Jean Valjean, feeling certain that in this way she would not perceive it or think of it. It was more than an effacement, — it was an eclipse. Marius did what he considered necessary and just; he believed that he had serious reasons, some of which we have seen, and some we have yet to see, for getting rid of Jean Valjean, without harshness, but without weakness. Chance having made him acquainted, in a trial in which he was retained, with an ex-clerk of Laffitte's bank, he had obtained, without seeking it, mysterious information, which, in truth, he had not been able to examine, through respect for the secret he had promised to keep, and through regard for Jean Valjean's perilous situation. He believed, at this very moment, that he had a serious duty to perform, — the restitution of the six hundred thousand francs to some one whom he was seeking as discreetly as he could. In the mean while he abstained from touching that money.

As for Cosette, she was not acquainted with any of these secrets, but it would be harsh to condemn her either. Between Marius and her was an omnipotent magnetism, which made her do instinctively and almost mechanically whatever Marius wished. She felt a wish of Marius in the matter of Monsieur Jean, and she conformed to it. Her husband had said nothing to her, but she suffered the vague but clear pressure of his tacit intentions, and blindly obeyed. Her obedience in this case consisted in not remembering what Marius forgot; and she had no effort to make in doing so. Without knowing why herself, and without there being anything to blame her for, her mind had so thoroughly become that of her husband, that whatever covered itself with a shadow in Marius's thoughts was obscured in hers. Let us not go too far, however; as regards

Jean Valjean, this effacement and this forgetfulness were only superficial, and she was thoughtless rather than forgetful. In her heart she truly loved the man whom she had so long called father; but she loved her husband more, and this had slightly falsified the balance of this heart, which weighed down on one side only. It happened at times that Cosette would speak of Jean Valjean and express her surprise, and then Marius would calm her. "He is away, I believe; did he not say that he was going on a journey?" "That is true," Cosette thought, "he used to disappear like that, but not for so long a time." Twice or thrice she sent Nicolette to inquire in the Rue de l'Homme Armé whether Monsieur Jean had returned from his tour, and Jean Valjean sent answer in the negative. Cosette asked no more, as she had on earth but one want, — Marius. Let us also say that Marius and Cosette had been absent too. They went to Vernon, and Marius took Cosette to his father's tomb. Marius had gradually abstracted Cosette from Jean Valjean, and Cosette had allowed it. However, what is called much too harshly in certain cases the ingratitude of children is not always so reprehensible a thing as may be believed. It is the ingratitude of nature; for nature, as we have said elsewhere, "looks before her," and divides living beings into arrivals and departures. The departures are turned to the darkness, and the arrivals toward light. Hence a divergence, which on the part of the old is fatal, on the part of the young is involuntary; and this divergence, at first insensible, increases slowly, like every separation of branches, and the twigs separate without detaching themselves from the parent stem. It is not their fault, for youth goes where there is joy, to festivals, to bright light, and to love, while old age proceeds toward the end. They do not lose each other out of sight, but there is no longer a connecting link: the young people feel the chill of life, and the old that of the tomb. Let us not accuse these poor children.

CHAPTER II.

THE LAST FLUTTERINGS OF THE LAMP WITHOUT OIL.

ONE day Jean Valjean went down his staircase, took three steps in the street, sat down upon a post, the same one on which Gavroche had found him sitting in thought on the night of June 5; he stayed there a few minutes, and then went up again. This was the last oscillation of the pendulum; the next day he did not leave his room; the next to that he did not leave his bed. The porter's wife, who prepared his poor meals for him, some cabbage or a few potatoes and a little bacon, looked at the brown earthenware plate and exclaimed, —

"Why, poor dear man, you ate nothing yesterday!"

"Yes, I did," Jean Valjean answered.

"The plate is quite full."

"Look at the water-jug: it is empty."

"That proves you have drunk, but does not prove that you have eaten."

"Well," said Jean Valjean, "suppose that I only felt hungry for water?"

"That is called thirst, and if a man does not eat at the same time it is called fever."

"I will eat to-morrow."

"Or on Trinity Sunday. Why not to-day? Whoever thought of saying, I will eat to-morrow? To leave my plate without touching it; my rashers were so good."

Jean Valjean took the old woman's hand.

" I promise you to eat them," he said, in his gentle voice.

" I am not pleased with you," the woman replied.

Jean Valjean never saw any other human creature but this good woman: there are in Paris streets through which people never pass, and houses which people never enter, and he lived in one of those streets and one of those houses. During the time when he still went out he had bought at a brazier's for a few sous a small copper crucifix, which he suspended from a nail opposite his bed; that gibbet is ever good to look on. A week passed thus, and Jean Valjean still remained in bed. The porter's wife said to her husband, " The old gentleman up-stairs does not get up; he does not eat, and he will not last long. He has a sorrow, and no one will get it out of my head but that his daughter has made a bad match."

The porter replied, with the accent of marital sovereignty, —

" If he is rich, he can have a doctor; if he is not rich, he can't. If he has no doctor, he will die."

" And if he has one?"

" He will die," said the porter.

The porter's wife began digging up with an old knife the grass between what she called her pave-ment, and while doing so grumbled, —

"It's a pity — an old man who is so tidy. He is as white as a pullet."

She saw a doctor belonging to the quarter passing along the bottom of the street, and took upon herself to ask him to go up.

"It's on the second floor," she said; "you will only have to go in, for, as the old gentleman no longer leaves his bed, the key is always in the door."

The physician saw Jean Valjean and spoke to him: when he came down again the porter's wife was waiting for him.

"Well, doctor?"

"He is very ill."

"What is the matter with him?"

"Everything and nothing. He is a man who, from all appearances, has lost a beloved person. People die of that."

"What did he say to you?"

"He told me that he was quite well."

"Will you call again, doctor?"

"Yes," the physician replied, "but some one beside me ought to come too."

CHAPTER III.

A PEN IS TOO HEAVY FOR THE MAN WHO LIFTED FAUCHELEVENT'S CART.

ONE evening Jean Valjean had a difficulty in rising on his elbow; he took hold of his wrist and could not find his pulse; his breathing was short, and stopped every now and then, and he perceived that he was weaker than he had ever yet been. Then, doubtless, under the pressure of some supreme preoccupation, he made an effort, sat up, and dressed himself. He put on his old workman's clothes; for, as he no longer went out, he had returned to them and preferred them. He was compelled to pause several times while dressing himself; and the perspiration poured off his forehead, merely through the effort of putting on his jacket. Ever since he had been alone he had placed his bed in the anteroom, so as to occupy as little as possible of the deserted apartments. He opened the valise and took out Cosette's clothing, which he spread on his bed. The Bishop's candlesticks were at their place on the mantel-piece; he took two wax candles out of a drawer and put them up, and then, though it was broad summer daylight, he lit them. We sometimes see candles lighted thus in open day in rooms where dead men are lying. Each step he took in going from one article of furniture to another exhausted him, and he was obliged to sit down. It was not ordinary fatigue, which expends the strength in order to renew it ; it was the remnant of possible motion ; it was exhausted life falling drop by drop in crushing efforts which will not be made again.

One of the chairs on which he sank was placed near the mirror, so fatal for him, so providential for Marius, in which he had read Cosette's reversed writing on the blotting-book. He saw himself in this mirror, and could not recognize himself. He was eighty years of age ; before Marius's marriage he had looked scarce fifty, but the last year had reckoned as thirty. What he had on his forehead was no longer the wrinkle of age, but the mysterious mark of death, and the laceration of the pitiless nail could be traced on it. His cheeks were flaccid ; the skin of his face had that color which makes one think that the earth is already over it ; the two corners of his mouth drooped as in that mask which the ancients sculptured on the tomb. He looked at space reproachfully, and he resembled one of those tragic beings who have cause to complain of some one. He had reached that stage, the last phase of dejection, in which grief no longer flows ; it is, so to speak, coagulated, and there is on the soul something like a clot of despair. Night had set in, and he with difficulty dragged a table and the old easy-chair to the chimney, and laid on the table, pen, ink, and paper. This done he fainted away, and when he regained his senses he was thirsty. As he could not lift the water-jar, he bent down with an effort and drank a mouthful. Then he turned to the bed, and, still seated, for he was unable to stand, he gazed at the little black dress and all those dear objects. Such contemplations last hours which appear minutes. All at once he shuddered, and felt that the cold had struck him. He leaned his elbows on the table which the Bishop's candlesticks illumined, and took up the pen. As neither the pen nor the ink had been used for a long time, the nibs of the pen were bent, the ink was dried up, and he was therefore obliged to put a few drops of water in the ink, which he could not do without stopping and sitting down twice or thrice, and was forced to write with the back of the pen. He wiped his forehead from time to time, and his hand trembled as he wrote the few following lines : —

" Cosette, — I bless you. I am about to explain to you. Your husband did right in making me understand that I ought to go away ; still, he was slightly in error as to what he believed, but he acted rightly. He is a worthy man, and love him dearly when I am gone from you. Monsieur Pontmercy, always love my beloved child. Cosette, this paper will be found : this is what I wish to say to you ; you shall see the figures if I have the strength to remember them ; but listen to me, the money is really yours. This is the whole affair. White jet comes from Norway, black jet comes from England, and black beads come from Germany. Jet is lighter, more valuable, and dearer ; but imitations can be made in France as well as in Germany. You must have a small anvil two inches square, and a spirit lamp to soften the wax. The wax used to be made with resin and smoke-black, and costs four francs the pound; but I hit on the idea of making it of gum-lac and turpentine. It only costs thirty sous, and is much better. The rings are made of violet glass, fastened by means of the wax on a small black iron wire. The glass must be violet for iron ornaments, and black for gilt ornaments. Spain buys large quantities; it is the country of jet—"

Here he stopped, the pen slipped from his fingers, he burst into one of those despairing sobs which rose at times from the depths of his being. The poor man took his head between his hands and thought.

"Oh!" he exclaimed internally (lamentable cries heard by God alone), "it is all over. I shall never see her again; it is a smile which flashed across me, and I am going to enter night without even seeing her. Oh! for one moment, for one instant to hear her voice, to touch her, to look at her,—her, the angel, and then die! Death is nothing, but the frightful thing is to die without seeing her! She would smile on me, say a word to me, and would that do any one harm? No, it is all over forever. I am now all alone. My God! my God! I shall see her no more."

At this moment there was a knock at his door.

CHAPTER IV.

A BOTTLE OF INK WHICH ONLY WHITENS.

THAT same day, or, to speak more correctly, that same evening, as Marius was leaving the dinner-table to withdraw to his study, as he had a brief to get up, Basque handed him a letter, saying, "The person who wrote the letter is in the anteroom." Cosette had seized her grandfather's arm, and was taking a turn round the garden. A letter may have an ugly appearance, like a man, and the mere sight of coarse paper and clumsy folding is displeasing. The letter which Basque brought was of that description. Marius took it, and it smelt of tobacco. Nothing arouses a recollection so much as a smell, and Marius recognized the tobacco. He looked at the address, "To Monsieur le Baron Pommerci, At his house." The recognized tobacco made him recognize the handwriting. It might be said that astonishment has its flashes of lightning, and Marius was, as it were, illumined by one of these flashes. The odor, that mysterious aid to memory, had recalled to him a world: it was really the paper, the mode of folding, the pale ink; it was really the well-known handwriting; and, above all, it was the tobacco. The Jondrette garret rose again before him. Hence — strange blow of accident! — one of the two trails which he had so long sought, the one for which he had latterly made so many efforts and believed lost forever, came to offer itself voluntarily to him. He eagerly opened the letter and read: —

" MONSIEUR LE BARON, — If the Supreme Being had endowed me with talents, I might have been Baron Thénard, member of the Institute (academy of ciences), but I am not so. I merely bear the same name with him, and shall be happy if this reminisence recommends me to the excellense of your kindness. The benefits with which you may honor me will be reciprocal, for I am in possession of a secret conserning an individual. This individual conserns you. I hold the secret at your disposal, as I desire to have the honor of being uceful to you. I will give you the simple means for expeling from your honorable family this individual who has no right in it, Madam la Barronne being of high birth. The sanctuary of virtue could no longer coabit with crime without abdicating.

" I await in the anteroom the order of Monsieur le Baron.
" Respectfully."

The letter was signed " THÉNARD." This signature was not false, but only slightly abridged. However, the bombast and the orthography completed the revelation, the certificate of origin was perfect, and no doubt was possible. Marius's emotion was profound; and after the movement of surprise he had a movement of happiness. Let him now find the other man he sought, the man who had saved him, Marius, and he would have nothing more to desire. He opened a drawer in his bureau, took out several bank-notes, which he put in his pocket, closed the drawer again, and rang. Basque opened the door partly.

" Show the man in," said Marius.

Basque announced, —

" M. Thénard."

A man came in, and it was a fresh surprise for Marius, as the man he now saw was a perfect stranger to him. This man, who was old, by the way, had a large nose, his chin in his cravat, green spectacles, with a double shade of green silk over his eyes, and his hair smoothed down and flattened on his forehead over his eyebrows, like the wig of English coachmen of high life. His hair was gray. He was dressed in black from head to foot, — a very seedy but clean black, — and a bunch of seals, emerging from his fob, led to the supposition that he had a watch. He held an old hat in his hand, and walked bent, and the curve in his back augmented the depth of his bow. The thing which struck most at the first glance was that this person's coat, too large, though carefully buttoned, had not been made for him. A short digression is necessary here.

There was at that period in Paris, in an old house situated in the Rue Beautreillis near the arsenal, an old Jew whose trade it was to convert a rogue into an honest man, though not for too long a period, as it might have been troublesome to the rogue. The change was effected at sight, for one day or two, at the rate of thirty sous a day, by means of a costume resembling as closely as possible every-day honesty. This letter-out of suits was called the "exchange-broker." Parisian thieves had given him that name, and knew him by no other. He had a very complete wardrobe, and the clothes in which he invested people suited almost every condition. He had specialties and categories : from each nail of his store hung a social station, worn and threadbare ; here the magistrate's coat, there the curé's coat, and the banker's coat ; in one corner the coat of an officer on half pay, elsewhere the coat of a man of letters, and further on the statesman's coat. This creature was the costumer of the immense drama which roguery plays in Paris, and his den was the side-scene from which robbery went out or swindling re-entered. A ragged rogue arrived at this wardrobe, deposited thirty sous, and selected, according to the part which he wished to play on that day, the clothes which suited him ; and, on going down the stairs again, the rogue was somebody. The next day the clothes were faithfully brought back, and the "exchange-broker," who entirely trusted to the thieves, was never robbed. These garments had one inconvenience, — they did not fit ; not being made for the man who wore them, they were tight on one, loose on another, and fitted nobody. Any swindler who exceeded the average mean in height or shortness was uncomfortable in the "exchange-broker's" suits. A man must be neither too stout nor too thin, for the broker had only provided for ordinary mortals, and had taken the measure of the species in the person of the first thief who turned up, and is neither stout nor thin, nor tall nor short. Hence arose at times difficult adaptations, which the broker's customers got over as best they could. All the worse for the exceptions! The statesman's garments, for instance, black from head to foot, would have been too loose for Pitt and too tight for Castelcicala. The statesman's suit was thus described in the broker's catalogue, from which we copied it : " A black cloth coat, black moleskin trousers, a silk waistcoat, boots, and white shirt." There was on the margin " Ex-Ambassador," and a note which we also transcribe : " In a separate box a carefully-dressed peruke, green spectacles, bunch of seals, and two little quills an inch in length, wrapped in cotton." All this belonged to the statesman or ex-ambassador. The whole of this costume was, if we may say so, extenuated. The seams were white, and a small button-hole gaped at one of the elbows ; moreover, a button was missing off the front, but that is only a detail, for as the hand of the statesman must always be thrust into the coat, and upon the heart, it had the duty of hiding the absence of the button.

Had Marius been familiar with the occult institutions of Paris, he would at once have recognized in the back of the visitor whom Basque had just shown in, the coat of the statesman borrowed from the Unhook-me-that of the " exchange-broker." Marius's disappointment on seeing a different man from the one whom he expected to enter, turned into disgust with the new-comer. He examined him from head to foot, while the personage was giving him an ex-

aggerated bow, and asked him curtly, "What do
you want? "

The man replied with an amiable *rictus*, of which
the caressing smile of a crocodile would supply some
idea : —

"It appears to me impossible that I have not
already had the honor of seeing Monsieur le Baron in
society. I have a peculiar impression of having met
him a few years back at the Princess Bagration's,
and in the salons of his Excellency Vicomte Dambray,
Peer of France."

It is always good tactics in swindling to pretend
to recognize a person whom the swindler does not
know. Marius paid attention to the man's words,
he watched the action and movement, but his disappointment increased; it was a nasal pronunciation,
absolutely different from the sharp dry voice he expected. He was utterly routed.

" I do not know," he said, " either Madame
Bagration or Monsieur Dambray. I never set foot
in the house of either of them."

The answer was rough, but the personage continued with undiminished affability, —

"Then it must have been at Chateaubriand's that
I saw Monsieur ! I know Chateaubriand intimately,
and he is a most affable man. He says to me sometimes, Thénard, my good friend, will you not drink a
glass with me ? "

Marius's brow became sterner and sterner. " I
never had the honor of being received at M. de
Chateaubriand's house. Come to the point; what do
you want with me ? "

The man bowed lower still before this harsh voice.

"Monsieur le Baron, deign to listen to me. There is in America, in a country near Panama, a village called La Joya, and this village is composed of a single house. A large square house three stories high, built of bricks dried in the sun, each side of the square being five hundred feet long, and each story retiring from the one under it for a distance of twelve feet, so as to leave in front of it a terrace which runs all round the house. In the centre is an inner court, in which provisions and ammunition are stored; there are no windows, only loop-holes, no door, only ladders, — ladders to mount from the ground to the first terrace, and from the first to the second, and from the second to the third; ladders to descend into the inner court; no doors to the rooms, only traps; no staircases to the apartments, only ladders. At night the trap-doors are closed, the ladders are drawn up, and blunderbusses and carbines are placed in the loop-holes; there is no way of entering; it is a house by day, a citadel by night. Eight hundred inhabitants, — such is this village. Why such precautions? Because the country is dangerous, and full of man-eaters. Then, why do people go there? Because it is a marvellous country, and gold is found there."

"What are you driving at?" Marius, who had passed from disappointment to impatience, interrupted.

"To this, M. le Baron. I am a worn-out ex-diplomatist. I am sick of our old civilization, and wish to try the savages."

" What next ? "

" Monsieur le Baron, egotism is the law of the
world. The proletarian peasant-wench who works
by the day turns round when the diligence passes,
but the peasant-woman who is laboring on her own
field does not turn. The poor man's dog barks after
the rich, the rich man's dog barks after the poor;
each for himself, and self-interest is the object of
mankind. Gold is the magnet."

" What next?   Conclude."

" I should like to go and settle at La Joya.   There
are three of us.   I have my wife and my daughter, a
very lovely girl.   The voyage is long and expensive,
and I am short of funds."

" How does that concern me ? " Marius asked.

The stranger thrust his neck out of his cravat, with
a gesture peculiar to the vulture, and said, with a
more affable smile than before, —

" Monsieur le Baron cannot have read my letter ? "

That was almost true, and the fact is that the contents of the epistle had escaped Marius ; he had seen
the writing rather than read the letter, and he scarce
remembered it. A new hint had just been given
him, and he noticed the detail, " My wife and daughter." He fixed a penetrating glance on the stranger,
— a magistrate could not have done it better, — but
he confined himself to saying, —

" Be more precise."

The stranger thrust his hands in his trousers'
pockets, raised his head without straightening his
backbone, but on his side scrutinizing Marius through
his green spectacles.

"Very good, M. le Baron. I will be precise. I have a secret to sell you."

"Does it concern me?"

"Slightly."

"What is it?"

Marius more and more examined the man while listening.

"I will begin gratis," the stranger said; "you will soon see that it is interesting."

"Speak."

"Monsieur le Baron, you have in your house a robber and an assassin."

Marius gave a start.

"In my house? No," he said.

The stranger imperturbably brushed his hat with his arm, and went on.

"An assassin and a robber. Remark, M. le Baron, that I am not speaking here of old-forgotten facts, which might be effaced by prescription before the law — by repentance before God. I am speaking of recent facts, present facts, of facts still unknown to justice. I continue. This man has crept into your confidence, and almost into your family, under a false name. I am going to tell you his real name, and tell it you for nothing."

"I am listening."

"His name is Jean Valjean."

"I know it."

"I will tell, equally for nothing, who he is."

"Speak."

"He is an ex-convict."

"I know it."

"You have known it since I had the honor of telling you."

"No, I was aware of it before."

Marius's cold tone, this double reply, "I know it," and his stubborn shortness in the conversation aroused some latent anger in the stranger, and he gave Marius a furious side-glance, which was immediately extinguished. Rapid though it was, the glance was one of those which are recognized if they have once been seen, and it did not escape Marius. Certain flashes can only come from certain souls; the eyeball, that cellar-door of the soul, is lit up by them, and green spectacles conceal nothing; you might as well put up a glass window to hell. The stranger continued, smiling, —

"I will not venture to contradict M. le Baron, but in any case you will see that I am well informed. Now, what I have to tell you is known to myself alone, and it affects the fortune of Madame la Baronne. It is an extraordinary secret, and is for sale. I offer it you first. Cheap! twenty thousand francs."

"I know that secret as I know the other," said Marius.

The personage felt the necessity of lowering his price a little.

"Monsieur le Baron, let us say ten thousand francs, and I will speak."

"I repeat to you that you have nothing to tell me. I know what you want to say to me."

There was a fresh flash in the man's eye, as he continued, —

"Still, I must dine to-day. It is an extraordinary

secret, I tell you. Monsieur, I am going to speak. I am speaking. Give me twenty francs."

Marius looked at him fixedly.

" I know your extraordinary secret, just as I knew Jean Valjean's name, and as I know yours."

" My name ? "

" Yes."

" That is not difficult, M. le Baron, for I had the honor of writing it and mentioning it to you. Thénard— "

" —dier."

" What ? "

" Thénardier."

" What does this mean ? "

In danger the porcupine bristles, the beetle feigns death, the old guard forms a square. This man began laughing. Then he flipped a grain of dust off his coat-sleeve. Marius continued, —

" You are also the workman Jondrette, the actor Fabantou, the poet Genflot, the Spanish Don Alvares, and Madame Balizard."

" Madame who ? "

" And you once kept a pot-house at Montfermeil."

" A pot-house ! Never."

" And I tell you that you are Thénardier."

" I deny it."

" And that you are a scoundrel. Take that."

And Marius, taking a bank-note from his pocket, threw it in his face.

" Five hundred francs ! Monsieur le Baron ! "

And the man, overwhelmed and bowing, clutched the note and examined it.

"Five hundred francs!" he continued, quite dazzled. And he stammered half aloud, "No counterfeit;" then suddenly exclaimed, "Well, be it so. Let us be at our ease."

And with monkey-like dexterity, throwing back his hair, tearing off his spectacles, and removing the two quills to which we alluded just now, and which we have seen before in another part of this book, he took off his face as you or I take off our hat. His eye grew bright, the forehead — uneven, gullied, scarred, hideously wrinkled at top — became clear, the nose sharp as a beak, and the ferocious and shrewd profile of the man of prey reappeared.

"Monsieur le Baron is infallible," he said in a sharp voice, from which the nasal twang had entirely disappeared ; "I am Thénardier."

And he straightened his curved back.

Thénardier — for it was really he — was strangely surprised, and would have been troubled could he have been so. He had come to bring astonishment, and it was himself who was astonished. This humiliation was paid for with five hundred francs, and he accepted it ; but he was not the less stunned. He saw for the first time this Baron Pontmercy, and in spite of his disguise this Baron Pontmercy recognized him, and recognized him thoroughly ; and not alone was this Baron acquainted with Thénardier, but he also seemed acquainted with Jean Valjean. Who was this almost beardless young man, so cold and so generous ; who knew people's names, knew all their names, and opened his purse to them ; who bullied rogues like a judge, and paid them like a dupe? Thénardier, it will be remembered, though he had been Marius's neighbor, had never seen him, which is frequently the case in Paris. He had formerly vaguely heard his daughter speak- of a very poor young man of the name of Marius, who lived in the house, and he had written him, without knowing him, the letter we formerly read. No approximation between this Marius and M. le Baron Pontmercy was possible in his mind. With regard to the name of Pontmercy, we must recollect that on the battle-field of Waterloo he had heard only the last two syllables, for which he had always had the justifiable disdain which one is likely to have for what is merely thanks.

However, he had managed through his daughter Azelma, whom he put on the track of the married couple on February 16, and by his own researches, to learn a good many things, and in his dark den had succeeded in seizing more than one mysterious thread. He had by sheer industry discovered, or at least by the inductive process had divined, who the man was whom he had met on a certain day in the Great Sewer. From the man he had easily arrived at the name, and he knew that Madame la Baronne Pontmercy was Cosette. But on that point he intended to be discreet. Who Cosette was he did not know exactly himself. He certainly got a glimpse of some bastardism, and Fantine's story had always appeared to him doubtful. But what was the good of speaking, — to have his silence paid? He had, or fancied he had, something better to sell than that; and according to all expectation, to go and make to Baron Pontmercy, without further proof, the revelation, " Your wife is only a bastard," would only have succeeded in attracting the husband's boot to the broadest part of his person.

In Thénardier's thoughts the conversation with Marius had not yet begun; he had been obliged to fall back, modify his strategy, leave a position, and make a change of front; but nothing essential was as yet compromised, and he had five hundred francs in his pocket. Moreover, he had something decisive to tell, and he felt himself strong even against this Baron Pontmercy, who was so well-informed and so well-armed. For men of Thénardier's nature every dialogue is a combat, and what was his situation in the one which was about to begin? He did not know to whom he was speaking, but he knew of what he was speaking. He rapidly made this mental review of his forces, and after saying, " I am Thénardier," waited. Marius was in deep thought; he at length held Thénardier, and the man whom he had so eagerly desired to find again was before him. He would be able at last to honor Colonel Pontmercy's recommendation. It humiliated him that this hero owed anything to this bandit, and that the bill of exchange drawn by his father from the tomb upon him, Marius, had remained up to this day protested. It seemed to him, too, in the complex state of his mind as regarded Thénardier, that he was bound to avenge the Colonel for the misfortune of having been saved by such a villain. But, however this might be, he was satisfied; he was at length going to free the Colonel's shadow from this un-

worthy creditor, and felt as if he were releasing his
father's memory from a debtor's prison. By the side
of this duty he had another, clearing up if possible
the source of Cosette's fortune. The opportunity
appeared to present itself, for Thénardier probably
knew something, and it might be useful to see to the
bottom of this man; so he began with that. Thénardier put away the "no counterfeit" carefully
in his pocket, and looked at Marius with almost
tender gentleness. Marius was the first to break
the silence.

"Thénardier, I have told you your name, and
now do you wish me to tell you the secret which
you have come to impart to me? I have my information also, and you shall see that I know more
than you do. Jean Valjean, as you said, is an assassin and a robber. A robber, because he plundered
a rich manufacturer, M. Madeleine, whose ruin he
caused: an assassin, because he murdered Inspector
Javert."

"I do not understand you, M. le Baron," said
Thénardier.

"I will make you understand; listen. There was
in the Pas de Calais district, about the year 1822, a
man who had been in some trouble with the authorities, and who had rehabilitated and restored himself
under the name of Monsieur Madeleine. This man
had become, in the fullest extent of the term, a just
man, and he made the fortune of an entire town by a
trade, the manufacture of black beads. As for his pri-
-vate fortune, he had made that too, but secondarily,
and to some extent as occasion offered. He was the

foster-father of the poor, he founded hospitals, opened schools, visited the sick, dowered girls, supported widows, adopted orphans, and was, as it were, guardian of the town. He had refused the cross, and was appointed mayor. A liberated convict knew the secret of a penalty formerly incurred by this man; he denounced and had him arrested, and took advantage of the arrest to come to Paris and draw out of Laffitte's — I have the facts from the cashier himself — by means of a false signature, a sum of half a million and more, which belonged to M. Madeleine. The convict who robbed M. Madeleine was Jean Valjean; as for the other fact, you can tell me no more than I know either. Jean Valjean killed Inspector Javert with a pistol-shot, and I, who am speaking to you, was present."

Thénardier gave Marius the sovereign glance of a beaten man who sets his hand again on the victory, and has regained in a minute all the ground he had lost. But the smile at once returned, for the inferior, when in presence of his superior, must keep his triumph to himself, and Thénardier confined himself to saying to Marius, —

"Monsieur le Baron, we are on the wrong track."

And he underlined this sentence by giving his bunch of seals an expressive twirl.

"What!" Marius replied, "do you dispute it? They are facts."

"They are chimeras. The confidence with which Monsieur le Baron honors me makes it my duty to tell him so. Before all, truth and justice, and I do not like to see people accused wrongfully. Monsieur le Baron, Jean Valjean did not rob M. Madeleine, and Jean Valjean did not kill Javert."

"That is rather strong. Why not?"

"For two reasons."

"What are they? Speak."

"The first is this: he did not rob M. Madeleine, because Jean Valjean himself is M. Madeleine."

"What nonsense are you talking?"

"And this is the second: he did not assassinate Javert, because the man who killed Javert was Javert."

"What do you mean?"

"That Javert committed suicide."

"Prove it, prove it!" Marius cried wildly.

Thénardier repeated slowly, scanning his sentence after the fashion of an ancient Alexandrian, —

"Police-Agent-Javert-was-found-drowned-un-der-a boat-at-Pont-au-Change."

"But prove it, then."

Thénardier drew from his side-pocket a large gray paper parcel which seemed to contain folded papers of various sizes.

"I have my proofs," he said calmly, and he added: "Monsieur le Baron, I wished to know Jean Valjean thoroughly on your behalf. I say that Jean Valjean and Madeleine are the same, and I say that Javert had no other assassin but Javert; and when I say this, I have the proofs, not manuscript proofs, for writing is suspicious and complaisant, but printed proofs."

While speaking, Thénardier extracted from the parcel two newspapers, yellow, faded, and tremendously saturated with tobacco. One of these two papers, broken in all the folds, and falling in square rags, seemed much older than the other.

"Two facts, two proofs," said Thénardier, as he handed Marius the two open newspapers.

These two papers the reader knows; one, the older, a number of the *Drapeau Blanc,* for July 25, 1823, of which the exact text was given in the second volume of this work, established the identity of M. Madeleine and Jean Valjean. The other, a *Moniteur,* of June 15, 1832, announced the suicide of Javert, adding that it was found, from a verbal report made by Javert to the Préfet, that he had been made prisoner at the barricade of the Rue de la Chanvrerie, and owed his life to the magnanimity of an insurgent, who, when holding him under his pistol, instead of blowing out his brains, fired in the air. Marius read; there was evidence, a certain date, irrefragable proof, for these two papers had not been printed expressly to support Thénardier's statement, and the note published in the *Moniteur* was officially communicated by the Préfecture of Police. Marius could no longer doubt; the cashier's information was false, and he was himself mistaken. Jean Valjean, suddenly growing great, issued from the cloud, and Marius could not restrain a cry of joy.

"What, then, this poor fellow is an admirable man! All this fortune is really his! He is Madeleine, the providence of an entire town! He is Jean Valjean, the savior of Javert! He is a hero! He is a saint!"

"He is not a saint, and he is not a hero," said Thénadier; "he is an assassin and a robber." And he added with the accent of a man beginning to feel himself possessed of some authority, " Let us calm ourselves."

Robber, assassin, — those words which Marius believed had disappeared, and which had returned, fell upon him like a cold shower-bath. " Still — " he said.

" Still," said Thénardier, " Jean Valjean did not rob M. Madeleine, but he is a robber ; he did not assassinate Javert, but he is an assassin."

" Are you alluding," Marius continued, " to that wretched theft committed forty years back, and expiated, as is proved from those very papers, by a whole life of repentance, self-denial, and virtue ? "

" I say assassination and robbery, M. le Baron, and repeat that I am alluding to recent facts. What I have to reveal to you is perfectly unknown and unpublished, and you may perhaps find in it the source of the fortune cleverly offered by Jean Valjean to Madame la Baronne. I say cleverly, for it would not be a stupid act, by a donation of that nature, to step into an honorable house, whose comforts he would share, and at the same time hide the crime, enjoy his robbery, bury his name, and create a family."

" I could interrupt you here," Marius observed, " but go on."

" Monsieur le Baron, I will tell you all, leaving the reward to your generosity, for the secret is worth its weight in gold. You will say to me, ' Why not apply to Jean Valjean ? ' For a very simple reason. I know that he has given up all his property in your favor, and I consider the combination ingenious ; but he has not a halfpenny left ; he would show me his

empty hands, and as I want money for my voyage to
La Joya, I prefer you, who have everything, to him,
who has nothing. As I am rather fatigued, permit
me to take a chair."

Marius sat down, and made him a sign to do the
same. Thénardier installed himself in an easy-chair,
took up the newspapers, put them back in the parcel,
and muttered as he dug his nail into the *Drapeau
Blanc*, " It cost me a deal of trouble to procure this."
This done, he crossed his legs, threw himself in the
chair in the attitude of men who are certain of what
they are stating, and then began his narrative gravely,
and laying a stress on his words : —

" Monsieur le Baron, on June 6, 1832, about a
year ago, and on the day of the riots, a man was in
the Great Sewer of Paris, at the point where the
sewer falls into the Seine between the Pont des Invalides and the Pont de Jéna."

Marius hurriedly drew his chair closer to Thénardier's. Thénardier noticed this movement, and continued with the slowness of an orator who holds his
hearer, and feels his adversary quivering under his
words : —

" This man, forced to hide himself, for reasons,
however, unconnected with politics, had selected the
sewer as his domicile, and had the key of it. It was,
I repeat, June 6, and about eight in the evening the
man heard a noise in the sewer ; feeling greatly surprised, he concealed himself and watched. It was a
sound of footsteps ; some one was walking in the
darkness, and coming in his direction ; strange to say,
there was another man beside himself in the sewer.

As the outlet of the sewer was no great distance off, a little light which passed through enabled him to see the new-comer, and that he was carrying something on his back. He walked in a stooping posture; he was an ex-convict, and what he had on his shoulders was a corpse. A flagrant case of assassination, if there ever was one; as for the robbery, that is a matter of course, for no one kills a man gratis. This convict was going to throw the body into the river, and a fact worth notice is, that, before reaching the outlet, the convict, who had come a long way through the sewer, was obliged to pass a frightful hole, in which it seems as if he might have left the corpse; but the sewer-men who came to effect the repairs next day would have found the murdered man there, and that did not suit the assassin. Hence he preferred carrying the corpse across the slough, and his efforts must have been frightful; it was impossible to risk one's life more perfectly, and I do not understand how he got out of it alive."

Marius's chair came nearer, and Thénardier took advantage of it to draw a long breath; then he continued: —

"Monsieur le Baron, a sewer is not the Champ de Mars; everything is wanting there, even space, and when two men are in it together they must meet. This happened, and the domiciled man and the passer-by were compelled to bid each other good-evening, to their mutual regret. The passer-by said to the domiciled man, 'You see what I have on my back. I must go out; you have the key, so give it to me.' This convict was a man of terrible strength, and there was no chance of refusing him; still, the man who held the key parleyed, solely to gain time. He examined the dead man, but could see nothing, except that he was young, well dressed, had a rich look, and was quite disfigured with blood. While talking, he managed to tear off, without the murderer perceiving it, a piece of the skirt of the victim's coat, as a convincing proof, you understand, a means of getting on the track of the affair, and bringing the crime home to the criminal. He placed the piece of cloth in his pocket; after which he opened the grating, allowed the man with the load on his back to go out, locked the grating again, and ran away, not feeling at all desirous to be mixed up any further in the adventure, or to be present when the assassin threw the corpse into the river. You now understand: the man who carried the corpse was Jean Valjean; the one who had the key is speaking to you at this moment, and the piece of coat-skirt — "

Thénardier completed the sentence by drawing from his pocket and holding level with his eyes a ragged piece of black cloth all covered with dark spots. Marius had risen, pale, scarce breathing, with his eye fixed on the black patch, and, without uttering a syllable, or without taking his eyes off the rag, he fell back, and, with his right hand extended behind him, felt for the key of a wall-cupboard near the mantel-piece. He found this key, opened the cupboard, and thrust in his hand without looking or once taking his eyes off the rag which Thénardier displayed. In the mean while Thénardier continued, —

" Monsieur le Baron, I have the strongest grounds

for believing that the assassinated young man was a wealthy foreigner, drawn by Jean Valjean into a trap, and carrying an enormous sum about him."

"I was the young man, and here is the coat!" cried Marius, as he threw on the floor an old black coat all covered with blood. Then, taking the patch from Thénardier's hands, he bent over the coat and put it in its place in the skirt; the rent fitted exactly, and the fragment completed the coat. Thénardier was petrified, and thought, "I'm sold." Marius drew himself up, shuddering, desperate, and radiant; he felt in his pocket, and walking furiously towards Thénardier, thrusting almost into his face his hand full of five hundred and thousand franc notes, —

"You are an infamous wretch! You are a liar, a calumniator, and a villain! You came to accuse that man, and you have justified him; you came to ruin him, and have only succeeded in glorifying him. And it is you who are the robber! It is you who are an assassin! I saw you, Thénardier — Jondrette, at that den on the Boulevard de l'Hôpital. I know enough about you to send you to the galleys, and even farther if I liked. There are a thousand francs, ruffian that you are!"

And he threw a thousand-franc note at Thénardier.

"Ah! Jondrette — Thénardier, vile scoundrel, let this serve you as a lesson, you hawker of secrets, you dealer in mysteries, you searcher in the darkness, you villain, take these five hundred francs, and be off. Waterloo protects you."

"Waterloo!" Thénardier growled, as he pocketed the five hundred francs.

" Yes, assassin ! You saved there the life of a colonel."

" A general ! " Thénardier said, raising his head.

" A colonel!" Marius repeated furiously. " I would not give a farthing for a general. And you come here to commit an infamy ! I tell you that you have committed every crime ! Begone ! Disappear ! Be happy, that is all I desire. Ah, monster ! Here are three thousand francs more : take them. You will start to-morrow for America with your daughter, for your wife is dead, you abominable liar ! I will watch over your departure, bandit, and at the moment when you set sail, pay you twenty thousand francs. Go and get hanged elsewhere."

" Monsieur le Baron," Thérnardier answered, bowing to the ground, " accept my eternal gratitude."

And Thénardier left the room, understanding nothing of all this, but stupefied and ravished by this sweet crushing under bags of gold, and this lightning flashing over his head in the shape of banknotes. Let us finish at once with this man : two days after the events we have just recorded he started for America, under a false name, with his daughter Azelma, and provided with an order on a New York banker for twenty thousand francs. The moral destitution of Thénardier, the spoiled bourgeois, was irremediable, and he was in America what he had been in Europe. The contact with a wicked man is sometimes sufficient to rot a good action, and to make something bad issue from it : with Marius's money Thénardier turned slave dealer.

So soon as Thénardier had departed, Marius ran into the garden where Cosette was still walking.

"Cosette, Cosette!" he cried, "come, come quickly, let us be off! Basque, a hackney coach! Cosette, come! Oh, heavens! It was he who saved my life! Let us not lose a minute! Put on your shawl."

Cosette thought him mad, and obeyed. He could not breathe, and laid his hand on his heart to check its beating. He walked up and down with long strides, and embraced Cosette. "Oh, Cosette!" he said, "I am a wretch." Marius was amazed, for he was beginning to catch a glimpse of some strange, lofty, and sombre figure in this Jean Valjean. An extraordinary virtue appeared to him, supreme and gentle, and humble in its immensity, and the convict was transfigured into Christ. Marius was dazzled by this prodigy, and though he knew not exactly what he saw, it was grand. In an instant the hackney coach was at the gate. Marius helped Cosette in, and followed her.

"Driver," he cried, "No. 7, Rue de l'Homme Armé."

"Oh, how glad I am!" said Cosette. "Rue de l'Homme Armé; I did not dare speak to you about Monsieur Jean, but we are going to see him."

"Your father, Cosette! your father more than ever. Cosette, I see it all. You told me that you never received the letter I sent you by Gavroche. It must have fallen into his hands, Cosette, and he came to the barricade to save me. As it is his sole duty to be an angel, in passing he saved others: he saved Javert. He drew me out of that gulf to give me to you; he carried me on his back through that frightful sewer. Ah! I am a monstrous ingrate! Cosette, after having been your providence, he was mine. Just imagine that there was a horrible pit, in which a man could be drowned a hundred times, drowned in mud, Cosette; and he carried me through it. I had fainted; I saw nothing, I heard nothing, I could not know anything about my own adventures. We are going to bring him back with us, and whether he is willing or not he shall never leave us again. I only hope he is at home! I only hope we shall find him! I will spend the rest of my life in revering him. Yes, it must have been so, Cosette, and Gavroche must have given him my letter. That explains everything. You understand."

Cosette did not understand a word.

"You are right," she said to him.

In the mean while the hackney coach rolled along.

CHAPTER V.

A NIGHT BEHIND WHICH IS DAY.

At the knock he heard at his door Jean Valjean turned round.

"Come in," he said feebly.

The door opened, and Cosette and Marius appeared. Cosette rushed into the room. Marius remained on the threshold, leaning against the doorpost.

"Cosette!" said Jean Valjean, and he sat up in his chair, with his arms outstretched and opened, haggard, livid, and sinister, but with an immense joy in his eyes. Cosette, suffocated with emotion, fell on Jean Valjean's breast.

"Father!" she said.

Jean Valjean, utterly overcome, stammered, "Cosette! She — you — Madame! It is thou! Oh, my God!"

And clasped in Cosette's arms, he exclaimed, —

"It is you! You are here; you forgive me, then!"

Marius, drooping his eyelids to keep his tears from flowing, advanced a step, and muttered between his lips, which were convulsively clenched to stop his sobs, —

" Father ! "

" And you too, you forgive me ! " said Jean Valjean.

Marius could not find a word to say, and Jean Valjean added, " Thank you." Cosette took off her shawl, and threw her bonnet on the bed.

" It is in my way," she said.

And sitting down on the old man's knees, she parted his gray hair with an adorable movement, and kissed his forehead. Jean Valjean, who was wandering, let her do so. Cosette, who only comprehended very vaguely, redoubled her caresses, as if she wished to pay Marius's debt, and Jean Valjean stammered, —

" How foolish a man can be ! I fancied that I should not see her again. Just imagine, Monsieur Pontmercy, that at the very moment when you came in I was saying, ' It is all over.' There is her little dress. ' I am a wretched man, I shall not see Cosette again,' I was saying at the very moment when you were coming up the stairs. What an idiot I was ! A man can be as idiotic as that ! But people count without the good God, who says, ' You imagine that you are going to be abandoned ; no, things will not happen like that. Down below there is a poor old fellow who has need of an angel.' And the angel comes, and he sees Cosette again, and he sees his little Cosette again. Oh, I was very unhappy ! "

For a moment he was unable to speak ; then he went on, —

" I really wanted to see Cosette for a little while every now and then, for a heart requires a bone to gnaw. Still, I knew well that I was in the way. I said to myself, 'They do not want you, so stop in your corner; a man has no right to pay everlasting visits.' Ah, blessed be God! I see her again. Do you know, Cosette, that your husband is very handsome? What a pretty embroidered collar you are wearing; I like that pattern. Your husband chose it, did he not? And then, you will need cashmere shawls. Monsieur Pontmercy, let me call her Cosette, it will not be for long."

And Cosette replied, —

"How unkind to have left us like that! Where have you been to? Why were you away so long? Formerly your absences did not last over three or four days. I sent Nicolette, and the answer always was, 'He has not returned.' When did you get back? Why did you not let us know? Are you aware that you are greatly changed? Oh, naughty papa, he has been ill, and we did not know it. Here, Marius, feel how cold his hand is!"

"So you are here! So you forgive me, Monsieur Pontmercy?" Jean Valjean repeated.

At this remark, all that was swelling in Marius's heart found a vent, and he burst forth, —

"Do you hear, Cosette? He asks my pardon. And do you know what he did for me, Cosette? He saved my life; he did more, he gave you to me, and, after saving me, and after giving you to me, Cosette, what did he do for himself? He sacrificed himself. That is the man. And to me, who am so ungrateful, so pitiless, so forgetful, and so guilty, he says, 'Thank you!' Cosette, my whole life spent at this man's feet would be too little. That barricade, that sewer, that furnace, that pit, — he went through them all for me and for you, Cosette! He carried me through every form of death, which he held at bay from me and accepted for himself. This man possesses every courage, every virtue, every heroism, and every holiness, and he is an angel, Cosette!"

"Stop, stop!" Jean Valjean said in a whisper; "why talk in that way?"

"But why did you not tell me of it?" exclaimed Marius, with a passion in which was veneration; "it is your fault also. You save people's lives, and conceal the fact from them! You do more; under the pretext of unmasking yourself, you calumniate yourself. It is frightful!"

"I told the truth," Jean Valjean replied.

"No!" Marius retorted, "the truth is the whole truth, and you did not tell that. You were Monsieur Madeleine; why not tell me so? You saved Javert; why not tell me so? I owed you my life; why not tell me so?"

"Because I thought like you, and found that you were right. It was necessary that I should leave you. Had you known of the sewer, you would have compelled me to remain with you, and hence I held my tongue. Had I spoken, I should have been in the way."

"Been in the way of whom, — of what?" Marius broke out. "Do you fancy that you are going to remain here? We mean to take you back with us. Oh, good heaven! when I think that I only learned all this by accident! We shall take you away with

us, for you form a part of ourselves. You are her
father and mine. You shall not spend another day
in this frightful house, so do not fancy you will be
here to-morrow."

"To-morrow," said Jean Valjean, "I shall be no
longer here; but I shall not be at your house."

"What do you mean?" Marius asked. "Oh,
no! we shall not let you travel any more. You
shall not leave us again, for you belong to us, and
we will not let you go."

"This time it is for good," Cosette added. "We
have a carriage below, and I mean to carry you off;
if necessary, I shall employ force."

And laughing, she feigned to raise the old man
in her arms.

"Your room is still all ready in our house," she
went on. "If you only knew how pretty the garden
is just at present! The azaleas are getting on splendidly; the walks are covered with river sand, and
there are little violet shells. You shall eat my strawberries, for it is I who water them. And no more
Madame and no more Monsieur Jean, for we live
in a republic, do we not, Marius? The programme
is changed. If you only knew, father, what a sorrow
I had; a redbreast had made its nest in a hole in
the wall, and a horrible cat killed it for me. My
poor, pretty little redbreast, that used to thrust its
head out of its window and look at me! I cried
at it, and could have killed the cat! But now,
nobody weeps, everybody laughs, everybody is happy.
You will come with us; how pleased grandfather
will be! You will have your bed in the garden,

you will cultivate it, and we will see whether your strawberries are as fine as mine. And then, I will do all you wish, and you will obey me."

Jean Valjean listened without hearing; he heard the music of her voice rather than the meaning of her words, and one of those heavy tears, which are the black pearls of the soul, slowly collected in his eye. He murmured, —

"The proof that God is good is that she is here."

"My father!" said Cosette.

Jean Valjean continued, —

"It is true it would be charming to live together. They have their trees full of birds, and I should walk about with Cosette. It is sweet to be with persons who live, who say to each other good-morning, and call each other in the garden. We should each cultivate a little bed; she would give me her strawberries to eat, and I would let her pick my roses. It would be delicious, but — "

He broke off, and said gently, "It is a pity!"

The tear did not fall, it was recalled, and Jean Valjean substituted a smile for it. Cosette took both the old man's hands in hers.

"Good Heaven!" she said, "your hands have grown colder. Can you be ill? Are you suffering?"

"I — no," Jean Valjean replied, "I am quite well. It is only — " He stopped.

"Only what?"

"I am going to die directly."

Marius and Cosette shuddered.

"Die!" Marius exclaimed.

"Yes; but that is nothing," said Jean Valjean.

He breathed, smiled, and added, —

"Cosette, you were talking to me; go on, speak again. Your redbreast is dead, then? Speak, that I may hear your voice."

Marius, who was petrified, looked at the old man, and Cosette uttered a piercing shriek.

"Father, father, you will live! You are going to live. I insist on your living, do you hear?"

Jean Valjean raised his head to her with adoration.

"Oh, yes, forbid me dying. Who knows? Perhaps I shall obey. I was on the road to death when you arrived, but that stopped me. I fancied I was coming to life again."

"You are full of strength and life," Marius exclaimed; "can you suppose that a man dies like that? You have known grief, but you shall know no more. It is I who ask pardon of you, and on my knees! You are going to live, and live with us, and live a long time. We will take you with us, and shall have henceforth but one thought, your happiness!"

"You hear," said Cosette, who was all in tears. "Marius says that you will not die."

Jean Valjean continued to smile.

"Even if you were to take me home with you, Monsieur Pontmercy, would that prevent me being what I am? No. God has thought the same as you and I, and he does not alter his opinion. It is better for me to be gone. Death is an excellent arrangement, and God knows better than we do what we want. I am certain that it is right, that you should be happy, that Monsieur Pontmercy should have

Cosette, that youth should espouse the dawn, that there should be around you, my children, lilacs and nightingales, that your life should be a lawn bathed in sunlight, that all the enchantments of Heaven should fill your souls, and that I who am good for nothing should now die. Come, be reasonable ; nothing is possible now, and I fully feel that all is over. An hour ago I had a fainting-fit, and last night I drank the whole of that jug of water. How kind your husband is, Cosette ! You are much better with him than with me ! "

. There was a noise at the door ; it was the physician come to pay his visit.

" Good-day, and good-by, doctor," said Jean Valjean ; " here are my poor children."

Marius went up to the physician, and addressed but one word to him, " Sir ? " — but in the manner of pronouncing it there was a whole question. The physician answered the question by an expressive glance.

" Because things are unpleasant," said Jean Valjean, " that is no reason to be unjust to God."

There was a silence, and every breast was oppressed. Jean Valjean turned to Cosette, and began contemplating her, as if he wished to take the glance with him into eternity. In the deep shadow into which he had already sunk ecstasy was still possible for him in gazing at Cosette. The reflection of her sweet countenance illumined his pale face, for the sepulchre may have its brilliancy. The physician felt his pulse.

" Ah, it was you that he wanted," he said, looking at Marius and Cosette.

And bending down to Marius's ear, he whispered, "Too late!"

Jean Valjean, almost without ceasing to regard Cosette, looked at Marius and the physician with serenity, and the scarcely articulated words could be heard passing his lips.

"It is nothing to die, but it is frightful not to live."

All at once he rose ; such return of strength is at times a sequel of the death-agony. He walked with a firm step to the wall, thrust aside Marius and the doctor, who wished to help him, detached from the wall the small copper crucifix hanging on it, returned to his seat with all the vigor of full health, and said, as he laid the crucifix on the table, —

"There is the great Martyr."

Then his chest sank in, his head vacillated, as if the intoxication of the tomb were seizing on him, and his hands, lying on his knees, began pulling at the cloth of his trousers. Cosette supported his shoulders, and sobbed, and tried to speak to him, but was unable to do so. Through the words mingled with that lugubrious saliva which accompanies tears, such sentences as this could be distinguished : "Father, do not leave us. Is it possible that we have only found you again to lose you ? " It might be said that the death-agony moves like a serpent ; it comes, goes, advances toward the grave, and then turns back toward life ; there is groping in the action of death. Jean Valjean, after this partial syncope, rallied, shook his forehead as if to make the darkness fall off it, and became again almost lucid. He caught hold of Cosette's sleeve and kissed it.

"He is recovering, doctor, he is recovering," Marius cried.

"You are both good," said Jean Valjean, "and I am going to tell you what causes me sorrow. It causes me sorrow, Monsieur Pontmercy, that you have refused to touch that money; but it is really your wife's. I will explain to you, my children, and that is why I am so glad to see you. Black jet comes from England, and white jet from Norway; it is all in that paper there, which you will read. I invented the substitution of rolled-up snaps for welded snaps in bracelets; they are prettier, better, and not so dear. You can understand what money can be earned by it; so Cosette's fortune is really hers. I give you these details that your mind may be at rest!"

The porter's wife had come up, and was peeping through the open door; the physician sent her off, but could not prevent the zealous old woman shouting to the dying man before she went,—

"Will you have a priest?"

"I have one," Jean Valjean answered.

And he seemed to point with his finger to a spot over his head, where it seemed as if he saw some one; it is probable, in truth, that the Bishop was present at this death-scene. Cosette gently placed a pillow behind Jean Valjean's loins, and he continued, —

"Monsieur Pontmercy, have no fears, I conjure you. The six hundred thousand francs are really Cosette's! I should have thrown away my life if you did not enjoy them! We had succeeded in making those beads famously, and we competed with what

is called Berlin jewelry. For instance, the black
beads of Germany cannot be equalled; for a gross,
which contains twelve hundred well-cut beads, only
costs three francs."

When a being who is dear to us is about to die,
we regard him with a gaze which grapples him, and
would like to retain him. Cosette and Marius stood
before him hand in hand, dumb through agony, not
knowing what to say to death, despairing and trembling. With each moment Jean Valjean declined
and approached nearer to the dark horizon. His
breathing had become intermittent, and a slight rattle impeded it. He had a difficulty in moving his
fore-arm, his feet had lost all movement, and at the
same time, as the helplessness of the limbs and the
exhaustion of the body increased, all the majesty of
the soul ascended and was displayed on his forehead.
The light of the unknown world was already visible
in his eyeballs. His face grew livid and at the same
time smiling; life was no longer there, but there was
something else. His breath stopped, but his glance
expanded; he was a corpse on whom wings could
be seen. He made Cosette a sign to approach, and
then Marius; it was evidently the last minute of the
last hour, and he began speaking to them in so faint
a voice that it seemed to come from a distance, and it
was as if there were a wall between them and him.

"Come hither, both of you; I love you dearly.
Oh, how pleasant it is to die like this! You too
love me, my Cosette; I felt certain that you had
always a fondness for the poor old man. How kind

it was of you to place that pillow under my loins !
You will weep for me a little, will you not? But not
too much, for I do not wish you to feel real sorrow.
You must amuse yourselves a great deal, my children. I forgot to tell you that more profit was
made on the buckles without tongues than on all
the rest; the gross cost two francs to produce, and
sold for sixty. It was really a good trade, so you
must not feel surprised at the six hundred thousand
francs, Monsieur Pontmercy. It is honest money.
You can be rich without any fear. You must have
a carriage, now and then a box at the opera, handsome ball-dresses, my Cosette, and give good dinners
to your friends, and be very happy. I was writing
just now to Cosette. She will find my letter. To
her I leave the two candlesticks on the mantel-piece.
They are silver, but to me they are made of gold, of
diamonds; they change the candles placed in them
into consecrated tapers. I know not whether the
man who gave them to me is satisfied with me above,
but I have done what I could. My children, you
will not forget that I am a poor man, you will have
me buried in some corner with a stone to mark the
spot. That is my wish. No name on the stone. If
Cosette comes to see it now and then, it will cause
me pleasure. And you, too, Monsieur Pontmercy.
I must confess to you that I did not always like you,
and I ask your forgiveness. Now, she and you are
only one for me. I am very grateful to you, for I
feel that you render Cosette happy. If you only
knew, Monsieur Pontmercy; her pretty pink cheeks
were my joy, and when I saw her at all pale, I was

miserable. There is in the chest of drawers a five-hundred-franc note. I have not touched it; it is for the poor, Cosette. Do you see your little dress there on the bed? Do you recognize it? And yet it was only ten years ago! How time passes! We have been very happy, and it is all over. Do not weep, my children; I am not going very far, and I shall see you from there. You will only have to look when it is dark, and you will see me smile. Cosette, do you remember Montfermeil? You were in the wood and very frightened: do you remember when I took the bucket-handle? It was the first time I touched your pretty little hand. It was so cold. Ah, you had red hands in those days, Miss, but now they are very white. And the large doll? Do you remember? You christened it Catherine, and were sorry that you did not take it with you to the convent. How many times you have made me laugh, my sweet angel! When it had rained, you used to set straws floating in the gutter, and watched them go. One day I gave you a wicker battledore and a shuttlecock with yellow, blue, and green feathers. You have forgotten it. You were so merry when a little girl. You used to play. You would put cherries in your ears. All these are things of the past. The forests through which one has passed with one's child, the trees under which we have walked, the convent in which we hid, the sports, the hearty laughter of childhood, are shadows. I imagined that all this belonged to me, and that was my stupidity. Those Thénardiers were very wicked, but we must forgive them. Cosette, the moment has arrived to tell you your mother's name. It was Fantine. Remember this name, — Fantine. Fall on your knees every time that you pronounce it. She suffered terribly. She loved you dearly. She knew as much misery as you have known happiness. Such are the distributions of God. He is above. He sees us all, and he knows all that he does, amid his great stars. I am going away, my children. Love each other dearly and always. There is no other thing in the world but that : love one another. You will sometimes think of the poor old man who died here. Ah, my Cosette, it is not my fault that I did not see you every day, for it broke my heart. I went as far as the corner of the street, and must have produced a funny effect on the people who saw me pass, for I was like a madman, and even went out without my hat. My children, I can no longer see very clearly. I had several things to say to you, but no matter. Think of me a little. You are blessed beings. I know not what is the matter with me, but I see light. Come hither. I die happy. Let me lay my hands on your beloved heads."

Cosette and Marius fell on their knees, heartbroken and choked with sobs, each under one of Jean Valjean's hands. These august hands did not move again. He had fallen back, and the light from the two candles illumined him : his white face looked up to heaven, and he let Cosette and Marius cover his hands with kisses.

He was dead.

The night was starless and intensely dark ; doubtless some immense angel was standing in the gloom, with outstretched wings, waiting for the soul.

CHAPTER VI.

THE GRASS HIDES, AND THE RAIN EFFACES.

THERE is at the cemetery of Père-Lachaise, in the vicinity of the poor side, far from the elegant quarter of this city of sepulchres, far from those fantastic tombs which display in the presence of eternity the hideous fashions of death, in a deserted corner near an old wall, under a yew up which bind-weed climbs, and amid couch-grass and moss, a tombstone. This stone is no more exempt than the others from the results of time, from mildew, lichen, and the deposits of birds. Water turns it green and the atmosphere blackens it. It is not in the vicinity of any path, and people do not care to visit that part because the grass is tall and they get their feet wet. When there is a little sunshine the lizards disport on it; there is all around a rustling of wild oats, and in spring linnets sing on the trees.

This tombstone is quite bare. In cutting it, only the necessities of the tomb were taken into consideration; no further care was taken than to make the stone long enough and narrow enough to cover a man.

No name can be read on it.

Many, many years ago, however, a hand wrote on

it in pencil these lines, which became almost illegible through rain and dust, and which are probably effaced at the present day : —

> " Il dort. Quoique le sort fût pour lui bien étrange,
> Il vivait. Il mourut quand il n'eut pas son ange;
> La chose simplement d'elle-même arriva,
> Comme la nuit se fait lorsque le jour s'en va."

THE END.